Praise for Jo Watson's charming rom-coms!

'A complete joy: funny, charming, heartwarming and insightful'
PAIGE TOON

'This sizzling, steamy enemies to lovers romance will keep you
hooked throughout – and have you laughing out loud, too!'
BETH REEKLES

'A total joy to read. Witty, romantic and laced with *chef's kiss*
sexual tension, it's the perfect slice of summer escapism'
CATHERINE WALSH

'Sizzling, sexy and great fun – the perfect holiday read'
SOPHIE COUSENS

'Delicious rom-com and a genre I personally call autistic-uplit meet
in a perfect match. I LOVED this book'
GAIL SCHIMMEL

'Sparkling and sincere, *Love at First Flight* perfectly encapsulates
what romance readers love most about the genre: that everyone
deserves the joy and beauty of falling in love. What a gem!'
THERESE BEHARRIE

Jo Watson is the bestselling author of the Destination Love series, *Love to Hate You* which has sold over 140,000 copies, *Love You, Love You Not, You, Me, Forever, Truly, Madly, Like Me* and *Just The Way I Am.* She's a two-time Watty Award winner with over 50 million reads on Wattpad and 85,000 followers. Jo is an Adidas addict and a Depeche Mode devotee. She lives in South Africa with her family.

For more information, visit her website **www.jowatsonwrites.co.uk**, follow her on X and Instagram **@JoWatsonWrites** and find her on Facebook at **/jowatsonwrites.**

THE EX EFFECT

JO WATSON

HEADLINE
ETERNAL

First published in Great Britain in 2025 by Headline Eternal
An imprint of Headline Publishing Group Limited

3

Cataloguing in Publication Data is available from the British Library

ISBN 978 1 0354 0049 2

Typeset in 11/14pt Granjon LT Std by Jouve (UK), Milton Keynes

Printed and bound in Great Britain by Clays Ltd, Elcograf S.p.A.

Headline's policy is to use papers that are natural, renewable and recyclable products
and made from wood grown in well-managed forests and other controlled sources.
The logging and manufacturing processes are expected to conform to
the environmental regulations of the country of origin.

Headline Publishing Group Limited
An Hachette UK Company
Carmelite House
50 Victoria Embankment
London EC4Y 0DZ

The authorised representative in the EEA is Hachette Ireland, 8 Castlecourt Centre,
Dublin 15, D15 XTP3, Ireland (email: info@hbgi.ie)

www.headline.co.uk
www.hachette.co.uk
www.headlineeternal.com

THE EX
EFFECT

CHAPTER 1

Ash

Can you be sexually cursed?

And I don't mean that in a cute "magical hex" kind of way. The old *"Oh shame, she has such bad luck"* kind of way. I mean in the most serious way possible. In the *"Oh fuck, her eyes are rolling back in her head—she's projectile vomiting green stuff"* kind of way. Because that's me. Seriously, sexually cursed. If there was an exorcist for the kind of curse that I've been living under, I would call them. But I don't think the Catholic Church has a branch that deals with sexual curses. In fact, it would be easier if I was possessed by Satan himself, then I could call someone who would arrive with a rosary and holy water, and chant incantations at me.

I've even thought of going to a sangoma, a traditional healer who would throw the bones and give me a concoction of herbs and ground-up dried chicken foot in an attempt to break this evil curse. I haven't yet, but after last night's Datr date, I think that powdered animal hoof and dried tree bark would be preferable to what I'd had to endure and was currently enduring.

"And you injured yourself how?" the physiotherapist asked in a thoughtful manner as he laid his fingers round my neck.

"Yoga," I said, wincing as he attempted to push my neck forward.

"You really shouldn't push yourself too hard," he said, taking my chin between his hands and moving my head from side to side. "One really needs to listen to one's body."

"I'll remember that for next time," I mumbled sarcastically, because I knew there would absolutely *not* be a next time. Last night was the first time, the last time and the only time all rolled into one. Datr date Brad—*35, Adventurer, Dreamer, Explorer*—was not going to be exploring another centimeter of my body if I had anything to say about it. Last night he'd been such an eager beaver explorer that he'd dropped me on my head while trying to dangle me over a chair so he could take me from behind, evidently. But, as the stupid adventurer had removed his foot from the chair to undo his zipper, the entire chair fell over. I'd fallen flat on my head, hence the need to be at my physio's office at the crack of dawn before a very busy workday, for which I was now definitely running late and which would have severe knock-on consequences for hours to follow.

"It's very tight," the physio said, pulling my neck as far back as he could so I was now looking at the celling.

"Mmm," I managed, and then tasted something sour in the back of my throat. Because the last time someone had used the word "tight" in relation to me, I'd almost vomited. Call me a prude, but when someone, a man—Simon, *32, looking for someone to keep up with my witty banter*—had whispered in my ear while watching the Barbie movie, that he hoped I would be wet and tight for him, I'd put the popcorn down at my feet and walked out. Not before turning to him and telling him I did not think his style of witty banter was for me, or any other women on the planet, for that matter.

"I think you're going to have to come in again this week so I can continue manipulating it."

"Sure," I said, now looking at the left wall of his office where a large medical diagram of the human musculature hung. I zoned in on the thing dangling between the legs of the male medical drawing. *Yup!* That, right there, was the problem. It could all be blamed on *that*, that appendage. That was the cause of it all. The cause of my neck injury, the cause of the terrible yeast infection that took weeks to get over, the cause of one of my broken crowns—and do you have any idea how much a dentist charges to fix one of those things? I almost considered taking out a second mortgage on my apartment—one trip to the emergency room, for him, not me, when Charles, *40, young at heart*, had a mini heart attack while humping me. Doing chest compression while waiting for an ambulance to come is a serious mood killer. Not that the mood had been that good to begin with, him banging away on top of me had not actually been that enjoyable. So call me a bad person, but when he'd fallen backwards off the bed and started grabbing at his chest in what looked like pure panicked agony, a part of me was actually relieved.

That appendage over there, which nestled so perfectly between the abductor muscles, had also been the cause of another emergency-room visit, for me, not him. Who knew one could be allergic to tingling and warming condoms? And who knew your labia majora could grow to such a majora size? That appendage had been the cause of many, many, many fake orgasms over the years, copious amounts of pretend moans and a lot of pornographic lip biting. I've discovered that biting your lip seems to drive them wild, making them reach orgasm far quicker, thank God! That appendage had done nothing but cause heartbreak—so much heartbreak—and pain over the years, and none more so than a very unlucky number thirteen years ago . . .

THIRTEEN YEARS AGO

"I can't believe you guys are finally going to do it tonight," my best friend Sarah said, sitting on the closed toilet while I sat in the bath and shaved my legs to within an inch of their life. I wanted everything to be perfect, and having one hair left on my leg was not in line with the vision of perfection I had for myself.

"It's going to be amazing," I said, taking the razor to my big toe as well.

"You guys have waited so long," Sarah added, fiddling with my various bottles of nail polish, trying the different shades on.

"I know. We just wanted it to be special. We didn't want to rush into it, even though it's been really hard not to at times."

"It's going to be so worth it," Sarah replied. "I wish Brad and I had waited a while."

"Why?" I asked as I focused carefully on my knee now.

"I think we rushed it. I mean I liked him when we had sex, but I wasn't in love. Not like you and Logan."

I felt a hot swell in my belly. "I am so completely in love with him. And that's why everything needs to be perfect tonight!"

"Speaking of, this is the *perfect* nail polish—it'll match the lingerie you bought."

She held up the soft pink polish that did indeed match the corset-style bra, matching G-string panties and a suspender belt and stockings I'd bought for tonight.

I slid down further into the warm, lavender-scented bath water. Tonight was going to be perfect. *Magical*. Logan and I had been dating for two years and tonight, the night of our farewell ball, the end of our school careers, we were *finally* going to have sex. This was it—the perfect time we had been waiting for. We were going into a new phase of our lives: adulthood, university, the next chapter. And I wanted to start that next chapter of my life the right way, with him. All of him. I was so glad we'd waited, because this was going to be a moment that we would remember forever, because we intended on spending forever together. And this was the start of that.

～

"Like this?" Logan asked.

"I mean, sort of . . . maybe . . . I don't know."

"This?"

"Nooo, not like that."

"Let me try again."

"Maybe try a different angle . . . ?"

"I could go a little left?"

"Yes, left. Good idea. Left."

"Like this?"

"Mmmm, maybe that's a little too far left? . . . NO, too far right now!"

"Okay, I think I almost have it."

"Nope, still wrong direction—maybe a little bit up . . ."

"Up, okay, up."

"A little too far up, definitely down a little."

"Down."

"Yup, keep going down . . ."

"Okay."

"And push a little more."

"Pushing."

". . . TOO FAR DOWN! TOO FAR DOWN! STOP PUSHING!"

"I'm just going to the uh . . ." I jumped off the bed, not bothering to finish that sentence, and ran for the bathroom leaving Logan sitting on the bed. As soon as I was inside, I looked around. I climbed into the shower and closed the door, hoping that would muffle the sounds of the talking I was about to do as I dialed Sara's number.

She answered on the first ring. "Hey, how's it going?"

"Oh my God, it's a disaster."

"Have you guys had sex yet?"

I put my hand over the phone receiver and lowered my voice even more. "We tried. It didn't work."

"Why are you whispering? Wait, where are you? Is he there?"

"I'm in the shower in the bathroom. He's in the bedroom." I raised my voice slightly so she could hear.

"What do you mean it didn't work?"

"It just . . ." I held my head. "Didn't go where it was supposed to go."

"Okay, what does that mean?"

I took a deep breath. "It means that it didn't go in the right place, okay?"

"What place did it go?"

"The *other* place."

"OH MY GOD."

I pulled the phone away from my ear at the loud sound. "Shhhh, don't shout."

"Okay, I won't." Sarah was whispering again. "But let me get this straight. Are you saying what I think you're saying?"

"Yes, it was terrible. I thought sex was meant to be good! Especially when you're so in love, but it's been a disaster since it started."

"Tell me exactly what happened."

"Okay, so you know we've done almost everything, right?"

"Except you haven't gone down on each other, and, like, actual sex."

"Right, so he tried to go down on me, and it, *God this is so embarrassing*, it didn't . . . He'd didn't . . . He licked the wrong place, okay!"

"NO, not that place???"

"NO! God no, but he was nowhere near where he should have been. I kept trying to move him there, but that just made him more confused or something, because then he started to blow on me."

"Blow? As in, with air?"

"Yes!"

"This makes no sense. You've got to be joking, right?"

"I'm not. And it still gets worse, because when he went back to licking, I could feel him licking out the A, B, C. I could even hear him whispering the letters out loud. He went all the way to Q when I faked an orgasm just to get him to stop!"

"Oh God, Ash, this is . . . This is . . ." It was clear she didn't have the words. I didn't blame her either. Neither did I.

"And I wanted it to be amazing!"

"The first time is never amazing."

"Your first time wasn't like this!"

"No."

Suddenly I heard a knock on the door and quickly cut the call off.

"You okay in there?" Logan asked through the door.

"Fine! Fine!"

"I thought I heard you speaking to someone?"

I panicked and threw myself out of the shower and looked around. "Uh, no. I was watching something on . . . Just, I'm coming. Soon."

"You sure you're okay?" he asked again, sounding worried.

"Fine. Give me five," I shouted back, and waited until I heard him leave.

I went back to my phone, this time messaging Sarah.

Ash: He heard me talking. Let's message. What if we're just not sexually compatible?

Sarah: But you've been sexually compatible so far.

Ash: But what if we're not sexually compatible at actual sex.

Sarah: Is that a thing?

Ash: What if we're no good at sex?

Sarah: Okay, don't panic. This is your first attempt. Just take a deep breath.

Ash: I'm trying.

Ash: Crap, and now my phone battery is also low. I'm going to have to go soon. What should I do?

Sarah: You guys have waited so long you're probably both just freaking out.

Sarah: Try again. But be more chilled. Take the pressure off. Have a glass of champagne or something. It's probably just nerves.

Ash: You're right—it's probably nerves.

Sarah: Totally!

Ash: Okay! I'll try again.

Ash: I just wanted tonight to be perfect.

Sarah: I'm sure it'll be perfect when it happens.

Ash: You think?

Sarah: I know.

Ash: You're right. I mean it's impossible to love someone so much and hate having sex with them, right? When you're in love, sex is meant to be amazing. It's not meant to be this terrible, right?

Sarah: Exactly!

Sarah: Go make it happen!

Ash: Okay. I will.

Sarah: It'll be amazing.

Ash: I know it will.

I HOUR LATER

Ash: Can you come and fetch me please?

Sarah: Did you guys have sex?

Ash: Well, he got it inside the right place this time.

Sarah: That's great.

Ash: But only for five seconds . . .

Sarah: Oh, that happens. They finish really fast the first time.

Ash: That's not what happened.

Sarah: ?

Ash: I don't think Logan should drink champagne again. Ever.

Sarah: Did he pass out?

Ash: Yes . . . but not before vomiting all over my naked body . . .

Little did I know that would be the last time I saw him. And little did I know how badly it would cause my heart to shatter into a million microscopic pieces that took me years to retrieve and painstakingly put back together until it was whole again—well, *almost* whole.

Because sometimes I feel like there's still a tiny part that I'm yet to retrieve, a part that is still missing. I guess that's what happens when you lose the love of your life.

CHAPTER 2

Ash

"*H*e did what?" Sarah asked while I waited at the red traffic light that I'd been caught behind for more than ten minutes. Going to the physiotherapist before work had now made me late, and being late in my line of work meant the entire day would probably fall down like a set of dominoes. I'd be playing catch-up until well past 5 p.m.

"He dropped me on my head," I said, cranking up the AC. The heat was stifling today. Cape Town was in the grip of a heatwave—in fact, the whole of Southern Africa was.

"Okay . . ." She sounded thoughtful. "I'm trying to picture this, but you're going to have to give me more details."

"I was bent over the chair, he had his leg up on it, which I guess was acting as a counterweight. I'm not a physicist, but I think that's how it works. The laws of motion, or whatever it's called. Then he took his fucking leg off the chair to take his dick out of his pants, and bam!"

"Christ!"

"I know."

"On your head?"

"On my head," I repeated.

Sarah was silent for a while, and I took the opportunity to honk my horn at the woman in front of me who clearly didn't understand the phrase "early morning rush" but instead was leisurely filming herself in the traffic. She was probably a wannabee influencer. There were so many around here that whenever you were out in public you were constantly dodging being in the background of someone's shot.

"I don't know what to say," Sarah finally said, breaking the silence.

"Me neither."

"The laws of motion are clearly against you. If you're not being dropped on your head, you're breaking your finger by being crushed under the gravitational pull of a hotel bed to the floor."

"That thing was rickety from the start, and it wasn't even vigorous sex! We hadn't even technically started *having* sex."

"He was a little larger than your usual dates," Sarah offered.

"I guess that's what you get from trying to have sex with a bodybuilder from the gym. I've had to cancel my membership."

"Obviously," Sarah replied.

"I've even been forced to change my grocery store, since it's right next to the gym and he shops there. I've had to relearn the entire layout of a new store. Do you know how traumatic it is when you can't find the cheese and you're having a cheese emergency?"

"Sorry, Ash. I could try and say something comforting if you want me to?"

"You don't have to say anything," I replied, finally making it through the demonic red light. Because she didn't. We'd had this exact conversation, or a variation thereof, so many times it was boring and quite frankly totally shitty. In fact, my sex life was the only shitty thing in my otherwise amazing life. Everything else in my life was great!

I had a job I absolutely loved and I was really good at it: I was the director of cinematography at one of the best production companies in South Africa, working with arguably the most talented director. I had a big circle of friends who had become like family to me, which I desperately needed after my family fell apart following my sister's death twenty-three years ago.

Twenty-three years . . . It sounds like a long time. Sounds like everyone should have gotten over it by now, but it's impossible to get over what was such a shocking, unexpected tragedy. I know I'm still not over it. It's shaped me in so many ways.

I was financially stable. I owned my own top-floor apartment with an incredible view over Camps Bay in Cape Town, voted most beautiful city in the world. I'd just bought myself a new car, a zooty little red Mini Cooper Sport convertible, which I'd wanted ever since I'd seen an old photo of my mom from the sixties standing next to her Mini. She'd looked so happy in that photo, and I wanted to remember her like that, before it had all gone so wrong. I'd just adopted a rescue kitten, Petal, who I loved more than I ever thought was possible to love an animal. I had awesome neighbors with whom I'd become friends. I was attractive, healthy and had heard myself described as someone with a sparkling personality to boot. There was only one thing that was not going right for me, that had never gone right.

It had been just over thirteen years since the sex curse had been placed on me, and since then, despite a lot of effort and trying, I was yet to break it. I've slept with a variety of people too, in an attempt to put an end to it. Initially, I'd thought the curse might be confined to a specific type of person, so I'd ventured out of my comfort zone a few times. From creative artists with twirly moustaches, to beefy bodybuilders, my local barista, to an anesthetist named Sibu who looked like a younger Denzel Washington and had been so, so sexy and the chemistry had been so, so off the hook that I was sure he was going to be the one to finally break it. But when he'd cried during sex and then apologized to me and said he still wasn't over his divorce, I realized the curse was still firmly in place. Perhaps even more so.

There had been a gorgeous Greek man named Stavros who'd tried to eat an olive out of my belly button as foreplay, an American who'd wanted me to call him Daddy, which I'd refused to do, and of course the many, many Datr fails. It sounds as if I have a sky-high body count, but that's not actually true. My conversion rate from dating to sex was actually incredibly low. As with my latest chair crasher, Barbie movie man, and the bodybuilder, none of those dates had actually turned into sex. In fact, my sex curse was so bad that even before we'd attempted sex it was already horrific. My sex curse is so strong that the only orgasms I've ever had have been at the hands of a toy named Roger.

"I'm almost at work," I said, turning left towards my office.

"I have to start drafting a long and very boring contract myself. I'm tempted to order up a margarita just to make it a little bit more exciting."

"I could do with a margarita." I put my indicator on for the parking lot.

"Shall we round up the gang and do dinner on Friday night?" she asked.

"Please. But you do the rounding—I'm going to have so much work to catch up on."

"Perfect."

"Okay, bye," I said, finally pulling into the office parking lot.

"Byyyeeee," Sarah replied, hanging up as I pulled up to the security boom and scanned my finger.

"Hi, Ed," I said, waving over at the building security guard. The poor guy looked boiling in this heat and I made a note to bring him down a cold Coke at lunchtime.

"Hi, Leigh," he replied, fanning himself. Leigh was my work name. When I'd had to register with the Cinematographers Association of South Africa, there was already an Ashley Smith, so I'd gone with Leigh. It was rather strange at first having different people call me by different names, but I was used to it now.

CHAPTER 3

Max

I climbed off my bed and pulled on my pants. It was midnight and Jenny, Jolie . . . Jane? Christ, I don't know, was still sprawled out naked on the bed, snoring. I'd tried to wake her up several times and suggested as politely as possible that it was time to go home—I never let women sleep over—but she was too spent to go anywhere. I'd even offered to call her an Uber so she didn't have to drive home, a hint I was sure she was going to get, but she'd just rolled over and started snoring in a different position this time.

I walked over to the other end of the room where my T-shirt was lying on the floor and pulled it on. I was struggling to fall asleep next to Julie—*Jessica, Jemma?* It wasn't about her—I struggled to fall asleep next to women full stop. I found the act of sleeping with someone way too intimate. And I didn't mean "intimacy" as in the naked gymnastics we'd just been doing for the last two hours. Sex, fucking, wasn't intimate. But being unconscious next to someone in a bed, totally exposed and vulnerable, that to me was the ultimate act of intimacy. And I hadn't done that with a woman for so many years now that it might as well be never.

I padded quietly to my study at the end of the passage on my side of the house. The other side of the house was reserved for my mother and the nursing staff who took care of her. She'd been diagnosed with dementia almost a year ago, which had caused me to move back home to South Africa from Greece, where I'd been living and running my own successful location agency for twelve years. It was late, I needed sleep, and I contemplated crashing on the couch in my office, but there was something on my mind—well, *someone* to be more specific.

I sat at my desk, opened my laptop, and started trying to type a professional, yet slightly witty and flirty email to the cinematographer, Leigh, that I'd been chatting to for the last three weeks. Her production company was searching for various locations to shoot a very large, high-profile international commercial and they'd employed my agency to provide locations, as well as scout for locations and then organize bookings and management. Our regular correspondence had become something I looked forward to, the highlight of my day actually—God, what did that say about my days, that emails to someone I didn't even know had become the best part of them? But she made me laugh and emailing her was fun.

And I hated to admit it, but I spent far too long writing and rewriting my emails to her because I was conscious of how I sounded and how I wanted to sound. And I wanted to sound cool, yet casual. Not too casual that I was unprofessional. Smart-casual. Wait, that's a dress code. Point was that, for some reason, I seemed to care a lot about how this stranger perceived me. And I didn't even know what she looked like. I'd gone onto the company's website and clicked on the staff profiles, hoping for a photo of her. But all the staff pics were cartoony avatars. I'd googled her name too, obviously, and found two photos featuring her from industry-award ceremonies. In one of the photos, she was standing behind her director Sebastian and all you could see of her was her arm holding the trophy. She had the most beautiful floral tattoo on her arm, bright, yellow sunflowers. And in the other photo she had her back to the camera. I'd then tried to find her social-media pages, but after an exhaustive search, came up empty handed. It was strange for someone not to have any social media in this day and age, but the truth was I didn't have any either. Some of us have a good reason to stay offline, like I do. Maybe she had one too? This just piqued my curiosity about her even more.

But despite not knowing what she looked like, despite never hearing her voice or knowing anything personal about her, I liked her. She was so easy to communicate with, and not just professionally. Over the last week or so, our emails had become more and more personal, friendly even. There was just something about her—it was hard to describe or pinpoint. I smiled to myself. Perhaps it also had something to do with the fact that she seemed to like cheese as much as I did. Massive bonus. I think liking cheese says a lot about the caliber of a person.

My love affair with cheese had started after school when I'd gone off to backpack around Europe. I'd soon learned that it was almost compulsory to eat cheese there, especially in France and Italy. And my love of cheese was only further cemented when I decided to settle in Greece and call it home. I looked at the photo on my desk of my old home at sunset right on the Ionian Sea. I'd fallen in love with that spot from the second I'd laid eyes on it.

Staying overseas for so long and only returning home twelve years later had never been the intention. Going traveling had been a knee-jerk reaction to a situation that I'd desperately needed to distance myself from. I'd needed to think, clear my head, figure some stuff out. But I'd landed up putting so much distance between myself and home that returning to South Africa at the beginning of the year had felt like returning to a foreign country. Truthfully, it had not been easy coming back. I'd left friends and familiarity behind to find a mother who barely knew who I was, and a place that no longer felt anything like home.

Maybe that's why I was enjoying emailing Leigh so much. She was a reprieve from all that, a momentary escape. The feeling I got when talking to her reminded me somewhat of another feeling I'd once had, many, many years ago, for someone else.

I quickly shook my head. I was not going to think about that now.

So I started typing up a first-draft email to send to her in the morning. I was sure that by the time I did actually send it to her, it would probably be on draft ten.

CHAPTER 4

Ash

Dear Leigh,

Hope you're having a good day so far. Personally, I'm really looking forward to the weekend, weather report also says that the temperature should drop by a few degrees, so that's a bonus. I took your advice and have actually invested in a handheld fan, which I'm carrying around with me everywhere.

I have enclosed the links to two more possible shoot locations. They are not on my books personally, but I have already contacted both of them and started a discussion. Both are open to the idea of film-shoot rental. One is a camp in Botswana, surrounded by the Makgadikgadi Pans National Park. I think you'll like it and I think it works perfectly for the brief. It's a luxury tented camp reminiscent of a traditional East African safari camp. The second one is on the beaches of Lake Malawi. Again, I think it's just what you're looking for. It has that rustic feel your director was talking about, without looking

like—how did he put it so eloquently?—"a fuck-
ing dump."

I chuckled to myself. Our director, Sebastian, was not known for mincing his words. In fact, he'd offended most of the people we'd ever worked with, and our producer did less producing work than she should, and more smoothing over and relationship repair. Sebastian was one of those eccentric and very often misunderstood geniuses, but I'd always worked really well with him. It was my job to take his vision and translate that using camera angles, lenses, and lighting to create the mood and feel of the film. In fact, our working relationship was so good that we, and everyone else, referred to us as work husband and wife.

Let me know if you and your director like any
of these locations. If they're not suitable,
please let me know so I can get on to others.
I have already booked Wellington's Bar, the
Chobe houseboat and the second villa we looked
at in Matobo Hills. We do need to hurry with
the others, though.

So, I took more of your great advice the
other night and tried the Manchego cheese. I
paired it with the Spanish green olives and
caramelized onions like you suggested. My
guests went wild for it. In fact, I think it
was the highlight of the dinner party. I would
like to think my sparkling personality and
generous hosting ability might also have con-
tributed to the praise lavished upon me, but
I think it was the cheese that stole the show.
I've been outdone by a chunk of Manchego!

I'm showing an overseas production company
around a villa in Camps Bay on Saturday night,

and I want to schmooze them—would love some more suggestions for a cheesy charcuterie board. I'm thinking French champagne and charcuterie. What do you think?

Looking forward to chatting soon and to hearing your next cheese suggestion,

Maximillian Adam
CEO
The Film Place
5 Longstreet Lofts
Cape Town

———

Dear Maximillian,

I feel you—the weekend could not come sooner for me. But only a few degrees?! I need the temp to drop by at least ten degrees. A friend of mine has taken to putting her clothes in the fridge in the morning before she changes. I'm thinking of trying that—the fan is not cutting it anymore.

I'll have a look at these locations and show them to Sebastian. A tented safari camp is exactly what he'd put into his treatment, so I'm glad you've finally found one. If he likes it, hopefully budget allows.

I'm so glad the Manchego was a hit. Don't feel too bad about not being the highlight of the evening. With a cheese like that, everything pales in comparison, so don't take it personally. In terms of your charcuterie board, I have a lot of suggestions, but it also depends

on how much you want to schmooze the respect-
ive clients?

Regards,
Leigh Smith
Director of cinematography, DP
Moving Pixel Films
Kalk Bay
Cape Town

P.S. Are you not concerned that you're taking
suggestions from a total stranger? You seem
to be putting a great deal of faith in this
stranger's suggestions?

———

Dear Leigh,

Clothes in the fridge . . . genius. I'm going to
try it.
   I want to schmooze them so hard they will
pay me $12,000 a day for a feature-film shoot!

P.S. Once two people have discussed their
mutual love of cheese so extensively, they can
no longer be considered strangers.

———

Dear Maximillian,

Well, in that case, there are only three
cheeses you will need. Pule—it is made from
the milk of a Balkan donkey. It has a tangy,
slightly sour taste and pairs really well with
something sweet like fresh dates and figs.

Another great choice is Comte, a French cheese that goes particularly well with champagne, and lastly, and still a firm favorite, a good quality baked Brie topped with toasted walnuts and fresh caramelized pear served with freshly baked French baguette. If you served me that, I would spend $12,000 a day for a location. In fact, I'd probably do anything to the person who served me that.

Regards,
Leigh Smith
Director of cinematography, DP
Moving Pixel Films
Kalk Bay
Cape Town

———

Dear Leigh,

I'll keep that in mind for the future! ☺

Winky face? Winky face? Was that, was he . . . *flirting with me?* I took a long, slow sip of my Coke as I stared at the screen. We'd been chatting for almost a month already, but I'd noticed that in the last two weeks Maximillian and I had started talking more about non-shoot-related things. The emails had become much more casual and friendly, and I'd certainly noticed that when I was refreshing my emails I always looked for one from him. Perhaps more eagerly than I should.

I shook my head. *Nope!* Not happening. The last thing I needed right now was to be email flirting with some location-agency guy. Flirting always ended badly for me. Besides, I needed to get through this shoot, which was proving to be a nightmare, not to mention work on about a million treatments in the next week. Today alone I had two studio-lighting tests and a gear check, followed by a very long meeting with very difficult clients. God, I did need that margarita. I picked up my phone and dropped Sarah a quick message.

Ash: Hope you're herding for Friday night? I'm in serious need of that drink. And sushi. Can we also have sushi please?
Sarah: Anything else your highness would like to request? What about foot massages while you eat the sushi?
Ash: That actually sounds great!
Sarah: K, see you tomorrow.

CHAPTER 5

Ash

I couldn't get home soon enough that night if I tried. It was 7 p.m. when I'd finally finished work. I arrived back at my apartment building and, instead of going to my place, knocked on my neighbor's door. Anushka opened for me.

"Long day?" she asked, and I nodded.

"Come in. Ayaan is about to dish up dinner, if you want some. Nothing fancy."

"Oooh, would love some," I said quickly, knowing that "nothing fancy" actually meant "really fancy," since they were both such foodies. I walked in and Petal came running up to me meowing, rubbing up against my legs. I bent down and picked her up.

"Baby girl, how was your day?" I asked rhetorically as I gave her some head kisses.

I was so grateful that Anushka and Ayaan loved Petal as much as I did and allowed her in their home. Well, they didn't have a choice in the matter, really. Very early on, Petal had figured out how to move from my balcony to theirs and back again. I'd found Petal on the side of the road and had brought her home. I'd taken her to the vet and told myself I would hand her over to the SPCA when she was well enough. With my lifestyle, out all day, often away on shoots, it would be cruel to keep a cat. But when I mentioned I was handing Petal over to the SPCA, Ayaan and Anushka were having none of it. Petal had already wormed her way into their hearts, and that's how she had become a kind of sharing cat between neighbors. They had her during the day and during my shoots, and I got to cuddle with her at night. Everyone won. Especially Petal, who got more love from more people than any animal I know.

I sat down at their dining-room table and Petal jumped onto my lap to cuddle.

"How was your guys' day?" I asked. Anushka and Ayaan both worked from home running a growing online jewelry company. They had met in college where they'd both studied jewelry design.

"Cool! We have to show you what this client wants us to make as an engagement ring." Anushka jumped up and raced into their home workshop, emerging moments later with a printed drawing. I took it from her and then turned it this way and that until I figured out what I was looking at.

"Wait, is that Darth Vader?"

"Made of black diamonds."

"A black diamond Darth Vader," I mused.

"They love Star Wars. Apparently, they met at a Star Wars convention." Ayaan walked up to the table and began laying bowls out.

"That's really cute," I said, feeling a little twinge of jealousy. I'd grown up being the biggest romantic. I'd had these huge romantic plans and notions for my future and since the age of ten knew exactly what I wanted my wedding to look like. Sometimes, I think that my younger self's expectations had been set way too high. Teenage me had been naïve, way too idealistic when it came to matters of the heart, not to mention matters of that organ somewhat south of the heart. But, despite all the bad sex and bad dates, I still wanted that. I wanted someone to get down on one knee and present me with a black diamond Darth Vader ring because they were so in love with me and knew me so, so well that they knew that giving me a Darth Vader ring would be an absolute dream come true and that I would look down at that ring every single day and know how loved and special I was. Well, I wanted *my* version of a Darth Vader ring anyway, which in my case would probably be a block of yellow diamond cheese.

"Do you get yellow diamonds?" I heard myself asking out loud as I imagined this block of shiny cheese on my finger.

"You do, but they are very, very rare," Ayaan said.

"Huh," I said thoughtfully, imagining how awful a cheese ring would look, but simultaneously feeling that the sentiment would be so incredibly sweet. I sighed and popped a piece of salmon into my mouth.

"Mmmm, this is amazing," I moaned.

"I added ponzu sauce in today," Ayaan said.

"Oh my God, ponzu sauce for the win," I said, and then passed Petal a little bit of salmon.

"And you? What's new this week?" Anushka asked.

"Same-same, really. A lot happening at work and I had the most awful date last night, so nothing new."

"Have you ever thought of going on a dating detox?" Anushka asked. "A friend of mine who's also been having the worst time dating, going from one crappy relationship that lasted five minutes to another one, decided to actively *not* date for an entire year. No dating, no flirting, no sex, nothing. She went totally cold turkey."

"And?" I asked, somewhat intrigued by the suggestion.

"Well, I guess it worked, because she's now happily engaged."

"Really?" I leaned over the table.

"Yeah, she said it was really good for her. She needed to break the destructive cycle she was in. She did a lot of work on herself too, read self-help books, went to a therapist, took herself out on dates and took up hobbies, like pottery." Anushka pointed at a large and strange-looking vase behind her. "I didn't say she was good at pottery," she quickly said when she caught me smiling. "And she also did a lot of yoga to quell her sexual frustration so at the end of the year she also looked amazing. And supple. Seriously, she can put her leg behind her head." Anushka raised her brows up and down at me, in case I didn't know what she was getting at.

"Huh." I mused on this notion for a while. Maybe it wasn't a bad idea. Maybe a detox was just what I needed to reset everything. I'd never really tried one, not properly anyway. I'd sworn many times over the years that I was giving up on dating and men, but that had never really stuck. I'd never consciously tried to be single for a while. I was always actively dating or looking for a date—trying to break the damn curse—even if I was just sitting on my couch swiping left and right.

"I'll definitely think about that," I said thoughtfully, wondering if my pottery would look better than hers and what kind of dates I could take myself on. The yoga I wouldn't need—I had Roger for that.

CHAPTER 6

Ash

Friday night was finally here and I couldn't wait to see my friends. Sarah had chosen the restaurant, a new Afro-sushi bar that apparently, according to Yelp, served some of the best sushi in town and really good cocktails. I hadn't been sure what was going to be "Afro" about the sushi, but after a quick Google search, I soon discovered.

"Geisha: Japanese sushi with an African twist." The menu featured things like springbok carpaccio, to replace some of the fish, chakalaka dipping sauce and biltong sushi. Personally, I thought the normal old-school Japanese sushi was perfect just the way it was, but I wasn't against the idea of trying something new, especially if that something new came with cool cocktails and my friends.

The Uber driver turned into Long Street where the restaurant was located. Long Street was packed with clubs, restaurants, and bars located inside old historic Victorian-style buildings with wrought-iron balconies. It gave the place a bit of a New Orleans feel, as if you were walking through the French quarter. The road was a fusion of old and new too, though, with some modern office buildings having sprung up here and there. The inhabitants of these workspaces usually ran cool companies. I knew some advertising agencies and film companies here, and also a few galleries.

"Waaaiit," I said out loud as I read the sign hanging from the building when the driver stopped.

"Is something the matter?" he asked.

"No, not at all." Something about this place was very familiar, but I knew I hadn't been here before. I climbed out and looked up at the building above the restaurant.

Longstreet Lofts . . . why the hell was that so familiar? I walked over to the placards on the wall and started reading them, and finally it clicked. This was where Maximillian Adam worked. There it was—first floor: The Film Place. I had a desire to suddenly take a photo of it and email it to him, but didn't. That would be stupid! And weird, right?

"Ash!" I heard my name being shouted from the big table on the pavement. I waved and walked over. They all stood up and our hugging session began. We were big huggers. We'd been friends since university, where most of us had studied something to do with film, the only exception being Sarah, who'd studied law, but she'd been with me since high school and quickly became friends with my film-school friends once I'd dumped accounting. I'd accidentally walked into a film lecture while looking for an advisor's office and been so captivated that I'd decided right there and then that this was what I wanted to do.

I flopped down in the chair next to Melusi, one of the best production designers around. I worked with him as much as I could, and this upcoming job was no exception—he'd already been booked for it.

"So, how's everyone?" I asked, but they were all smiling at me. "Oh, I see. Sarah's already told you about my latest sexcapade?" I shot her a look.

"I thought I would save you the trouble of having to repeat yourself." She raised a blue cocktail to her lips and sipped out of the tiniest straw I'd ever seen.

"The physiotherapist says I have a mildly strained tendon." At that, the entire table burst out laughing and then all proceeded to apologize profusely for the laughter.

"I'm glad my sex life is so amusing to you all." I reached for

Yolandi's drink as she was opposite me, pulled it across the table and sipped it.

"Hey," she protested with a smile.

"I need it more than you do," I said, sucking it down. Yolandi, Yo for short, worked as a sound mixer at one of the biggest and best post-production facilities we always used. She also played guitar in a band. They had a slightly underground cult following, thanks to their eclectic mix of Tibetan singing bowls, EDM and jazzy guitar riffs. The fact that Yo even worked was something we were all in awe of, because she was actually in possession of an eye-wateringly huge trust fund she'd inherited from her grandfather, who'd been some billionaire mining magnate. She also lived in a really humble, but nice, house. Not the kind of house someone with hundreds of millions tucked away in a trust fund might buy. She always gave the best, most extravagant birthday and Christmas presents, though. Last year, she'd bought me this insanely expensive drone, and she often sneakily paid our bill.

"Mmm, what is this?" I finished her cocktail and passed back the empty glass.

"It's called 'Santa's Little Helper.'"

"'Gin infused with a ginger, orange and star-anise syrup.'" Frank rolled his eyes as he said it. We were always poking fun at these ridiculous names that places were constantly coming up with in a bid to be more original than the next.

"Work injury?" I looked down at the fresh-looking plasters on Frank's hand.

"I was attacked by a tripod followed by a set of tracks and then a camera stand," he said, wiggling his fingers at me. Frank worked as a grip, mainly for international feature films that were shot in South Africa. In fact, he was currently lined up for a movie that—rumor had it—Zendaya was set to star in. He'd promised he would smuggle all of us onto set if she did sign on for the film.

"Where's Charlie?" I asked.

"Late," everyone echoed in unison. Charlie was always late. She probably had the most stressful job out of all of us. As a talent manager, she managed actors and voice-over artists, so she basically managed a bunch of people with rather large egos who regularly threw dramatic tantrums that she was forced to fix.

"Where's hubby tonight?" I asked Sarah.

"Editing—he said he'd be here soon."

We'd all been so excited when Russ and Sarah had gotten together. I mean, what's better than two of your closest friends falling in love and getting married? We'd all agreed that their wedding had been one of the happiest days of our collective lives. And we were now all eagerly awaiting a marriage between Melusi and Marcel, the French fashion designer he'd been long-distance relationshipping for several years. Although we have all made it quite clear that for any blessings of ours to be given, Marcel would have to agree to move here, because we needed Melusi far too much, and France was very far away. They were apparently still talking about where to live, a conversation they'd been having for probably two years now. Yo was the only other one of us in a serious relationship; she'd been in her polyamorous throuple for a couple of years already. Yo was just as generous with her heart as she was with her wallet, and much like money, had more than enough love to go around.

"So I have an announcement to make," I said, and everyone turned and looked at me. "I'm thinking of going on a dating detox." The entire table burst out laughing again and I glared at them.

"No, seriously, it would be good for me to give up men for a while. To break this bad cycle I'm in. I could date myself instead and take up hobbies like knitting and start swimming and cold dipping and listen to motivational podcasts and—"

The table's laughter escalated, and I stopped talking and folded my arms, feeling suddenly angry, although I wasn't totally sure why. My friends sensed this shift in mood and stopped laughing.

"What's wrong?" Sarah was the first to ask. I looked at her and shrugged and then felt a lump in my throat very suddenly and unexpectedly. I tried to swallow it away.

"Oh my God." Yo reached across the table and put a hand on mine. "What's up? Tell us."

"I don't think I can do it anymore, guys. All the crappy dates, even crappier sex, or almost sex. Maybe I'm just one of those people who's not cut out for romance. Maybe I'm one of those people who's meant to be alone. Not everyone finds their soul mate and gets to have an amazing love story."

"NO! Stop it," the entire table shouted at once.

"The right guy is out there—you just haven't met him yet," Melusi said.

I raised my brows at him. "I've met and tried to date half of Cape Town. If the right guy was here, I'm sure I would have found him by now."

"Maybe he's not in Cape Town yet," Sarah offered.

"Exactly," Melusi and Frank piped up together.

"Maybe he's from abroad," Melusi elaborated.

"Guys, I'm nearly thirty-two, my last serious relationship was over thirteen years ago, and we all know how that ended. I've gone on more dates than I can count, and not one guy has made it past the sixth date, except one, but then he cried during sex, which is a real confidence booster, I might add. I think I need a break from all that."

Everyone at the table went silent and looked at me sympathetically.

"As long as it's not permanent. I don't want you closing yourself off to anything. Your luck is going to change—I'm sure of it. Hang in there a bit longer," Sarah said.

"I'm not sure how much hanging I can carry on doing—the last hanging sprained my tendon." I rubbed my neck as I said it. "And the previous hanging also ended in disaster, if you remember . . . the infamous sex-swing incident?"

"Oh God," Melusi gasped. "That was bad."

"It's all bad," I said, pulling a drink from him this time. "It's all very, very bad and that's the problem." I sucked on Melusi's drink, grimaced, and shook my head as a loud, familiar voice put a halt to the conversation. We all turned to watch Charlie weave her way through the tables, talking loudly on her phone as she went.

"No, I told you. She is *not* shooting it unless you fly her hair stylist and make-up artist down too." She looked at us all and mouthed the word "sorry" as she flung her bag down on the floor and pulled out a chair with one of her red-heeled shoes—she was a multitasker.

"Yes, I know the production has its own hair stylist and make-up artist, but she will only work with her own team. We told you that right at the beginning of the contract negotiation . . ." She shook her head at us all and rolled her eyes dramatically. "Well, it's not my fault if you didn't clear it with your producer and you don't have the budget for it. She is *not* shooting unless she has her own people there." Charlie did what I had and grabbed the closest drink she could and started sipping on it. "I don't know, cut down on coffee, or snacks, lose one of the extras, or fuck knows what else. . ." She grimaced at the taste of the cocktail and mouthed a very clear "disgusting" at us. "I am well aware the shoot is on Monday. I drafted and read the contract, if you'll remember, unlike some other people who didn't read the section in which I laid out very clearly what my artist's requests and non-negotiables were." She tapped her fingers on the table, clearly irritated. We were always so in awe of how hardcore Charlie was, but she needed to be, in her line of work. "Well, then, you go back to your client and tell them the *only* actress that they wanted in their washing-powder commercial will no longer be in their commercial." That seemed to be the phrase that got the person on the phone to change their tune. "Yes, I think that's a very good idea. Producers are magic like that—they always seem to find more money in the budget when they have to." And just like that she hung up.

"For fuck's sake, it's a bloody washing-powder commercial. For washing your clothes. With powder. You would think we're shooting an Oscar contender here. How's everyone? I need a drink." Charlie waved her hand in the air and summoned the waitress while we all listened to her work stories and consoled her, telling her she was the best talent agent any of us knew.

"What have I missed?" she asked.

"I'm thinking of going on a dating detox," I said quickly.

Charlie eyed me while nodding her head, she had this habit of nodding while she thought. I loved it.

"This guy from work has decided to be single for a while and now he's doing transcendental meditation and running all these marathons—so good for him."

"God, that sounds fucking awful," Frank groaned.

"He seems happy," Charlie shot back.

"Anyone who's running a marathon and doing transcendental meditation as a substitute for not having sex is *not* happy," Frank fired back and soon he and Charlie were having one of their very frequent debates. They had always done this with each other, like some kind of sibling bickering, but they always made up in the end.

I sat back and watched them all. God, I loved my friends. If it wasn't for them, I don't think I would have made it this far. They'd become my family over the years, which I was grateful for, since I was seriously lacking in the family department.

"I'm going for a quick stress vape round back," Charlie announced, and stood up. Whenever she was stressed, she vaped, which was basically all the time. "And don't you all look at me like that. I said I'll give it up, just not now!" She raced off, not waiting to hear more of our objections.

"Maximillian Adam."

I swung round at the sound of the familiar name. It was being spoken from a table in the corner, where two of the most gorgeous women I'd ever seen were sitting. My curiosity was definitely piqued. I leaned back in my chair to listen and then gave my friends the "I'm eavesdropping" gesture we'd come up with years ago. They all nodded and lowered the volume of their conversations with each other. Frank, who was sitting next to me, was the only one who leaned along with me.

"Who we listening to?" he whispered.

"Gorgeous probably models in the corner."

He nodded and adjusted his chair, casually creeping closer to them.

"Apparently he made Star come ten times!"

Frank and I clocked each other with wide eyes and I had to stifle a gasp. We both leaned back even more.

"Seriously?" the hot one with the amazing breasts said.

"She even said she squirted. She's never squirted. Can you believe that?"

Frank turned and mouthed "Oh my God" to me.

"You know he also went out on a date with Bianca, right?" one of them said.

"Oh my God, what did Bianca say?"

"You can't tell anyone this—she told me in confidence."

"Of course I won't."

Frank and I rolled our eyes at each other knowingly. "Bianca said he made her pass out. Literally. She fell over and lost consciousness from all the orgasms, and then she had to beg him to stop!"

"Fuuuck!" the other one said.

"She said it was the best sex she's ever had in her entire life, and we all know how much Bianca gets around. If anyone knows what good sex is, it's her." The girls at the table laughed cattily.

"I heard a rumor he was a tantric sex practitioner, or something like that."

"Like Sting?" the one with the amazing breasts asked. "Doesn't Sting do tantra? I think I read an article about that somewhere. It doesn't surprise me, though. Star said he lasted hours, literal hours. She had a limp the next day on the catwalk."

"Holy crap!"

"And he's so hot. Have you seen him?"

"No, hang on. Let me Google him." She started digging in her bag.

Frank pulled out his phone and looked at me. "Who we Googling?" he whispered.

"Maximillian Adam," I whispered back.

"You won't find him online," the other model said. "The guy's a ghost. He doesn't even have social media. Apparently, he lives in an off-grid house in Noordhoek. He even owns llamas or something ridiculous like that."

"No wonder he's so good at sex. I would be too if I didn't have the internet." They both laughed and that seemed to signal the end of the conversation.

Frank and I looked at each other. "Who were they talking about?"

"He's this guy I'm working with. He owns a location agency."

"Why don't I know his name? I thought I knew everyone in the industry."

"He's been living abroad for the last twelve years or so. Came out here at the beginning of the year and started his company. He has the best locations."

"Apparently he has the best dick in town too."

I laughed. "Well, the best dick in town actually works in this building." I pointed up.

"Oh my God, you won't believe the story I just heard out back while smoking with the kitchen staff," Charlie said, lowering herself into the chair, smelling of something vaguely watermelon-y. We all leaned in.

"Apparently, the other night, all the staff heard this hectic screaming. So the manager called the cops, because they thought someone was getting attacked, right?" She laughed. "When the police arrived, turns out it was this girl in the office above the restaurant. She was screaming her head off while having sex with the guy whose office it is."

Frank and I both lurched forward and spoke at the same time. "Maximillian Adam?"

Charlie looked at us oddly. "Yes, how did you know?"

"Are you going to tell them, or should I?" Frank asked.

"You do it. You're better at telling these kinds of stories than I am," I said, and Frank launched into it.

CHAPTER 7

Ash

I got home that night and started my bedtime routine, only to find our group WhatsApp chat had gone wild. I started reading through the messages and almost choked on my toothpaste when I did. I typed back quickly.

Ash: NO! I am not having sex with this Maximillian Adam.

Yo: But maybe Maximillian Adam is finally the guy to break the curse and give you orgasms.

Charlie: Screaming-so-loudly-they-called-the-cops orgasms!

Sarah: Ten orgasms!

Yo: Lose-consciousness orgasms.

Melusi: Not to mention the squirting ones.

Ash: OMG! Stop saying orgasm.

Yo: We're not joking.

Ash: I know you're not! And, believe me, I'm deeply disturbed.

Melusi: We've all taken a vote, and we all agree that you need to have sex with this guy.

Russ: Even I think you should have sex with him.

Ash: Guys! I am not having sex with him.

Melusi: Marcel agrees!

Ash: Of course you've told Marcel already!

Melusi: I think it's a sign from the universe or something like that.

Ash: What is?

Melusi: Think about it. What are the chances of hearing two stories about him while sitting at a restaurant under his office?

Yo: Not to mention he's from abroad. Like we were saying earlier!

Ash: Nope! I'm turning my phone off now. I have an early morning meeting and I need to sleep off Santa's Little Helper. Love you all, but NO. I am not having sex with this mysterious man who may or may not own llamas!

Yo: I think it's hot he owns llamas.

Ash: We don't even know if he owns llamas.

Charlie: They make excellent watchdogs, like geese.

Sarah: Don't they spit at you?

Frank: That's right! They do. They fucking spit.

Melusi: Hahah!

Russ: Lol

Charlie: Beware! The guard dog—it spits.

I laughed, despite myself. But I was glad the conversation had moved on from squirting to spitting. I rubbed Petal's head and she purred next to me.

Sarah: But seriously, have sex with him.

Ash: Guys, those stories are ridiculous. Rumors! Do you really believe them? It's not possible to come ten times and no one screams that loudly during sex unless they are in a porno.

Frank: Okay, you do have a point there.

Charlie: And I did read an article about squirting actually just being peeing.

Frank: NOOO.

Yo: I need to read that!

Melusi: Stop. Please.

Sarah: I think the most far-fetched thing about the story is the llamas, personally. Apparently, you can do all sorts of things if you practice tantra.

Ash: I'm going, guys. I need my rest. I have Sebastian first thing in the morning, and you know what he's like before his micro-dosed mushrooms have kicked in.

Russ: You deserve a medal for working with him. The other day he told me to "make the match cuts match like a motherfucker and not feel like jump cuts."

Ash: Hey, don't trash talk my work hubby.

Russ: Hahah! Sorry.

Sarah: You know, if he wasn't really married, maybe you two could actually be husband and wife.

Ash: Oh God NO! I would hate to be married to him. He would drive me insane. Working with him is fine, thanks. Got to go. Bye, guys.

I plugged my phone in to charge and walked onto my small balcony, Petal close behind me. The wind wasn't howling, which was a miracle for Cape Town, especially perched up here on the mountain. I had the best view. In front of me were the bent-over trees that had been disfigured like little old men leaning over walking sticks from the years of gale-force winds. Beyond that, further down the hill, was the sea, its horizon dotted with the lights from cargo ships, and to my right, a perfect view of Lion's Head mountain.

But tonight, I wasn't able to appreciate my views like I normally did. Tonight my thoughts were very much elsewhere. Even though I wouldn't admit it to my friends, I *was* thinking about Maximillian Adam. More specifically, whether or not all those rumors were true. No one could be *that* good at sex, could they? But I was intrigued.

I suppose there was something about him that had had me intrigued long before tonight's very revealing eavesdropping. Plus he

also liked cheese, and in my book, that always said a lot about a
person. I had to admit it—there was just something about Maximillian Adam, and I had a sudden urge to email him, not that he would
respond at this hour. I paused for a while and thought about it, but
before my brain had even made the decision, my fingers were already
tapping away on the screen.

Dear Maximillian,

Just come back from eating springbok sushi and
drinking Santa's Little Helpers—sound familiar?

I almost jumped when a response came back immediately.

Dear Leigh,

You should have come upstairs and said "hi."
I'm still here.

A bolt of something deliciously warm shot through me. The idea
that he'd been right there was weirdly thrilling.

Dear Maximillian,

Late night at the office? I hope it's not our
job that's keeping you up?

Dear Leigh,

Not at all. I didn't feel like commuting home
in the busy traffic to Noordhoek, so stayed to
work a little longer, but then I got very distracted with something that came up.

Came up? My thoughts immediately plunged into the gutter. Very distracted? Another gutter thought. But he had confirmed part of the rumor to be true. Perfect opportunity to pry further.

Noordhoek? That's a long drive home.

I'd dropped the formal *Dear Maximillian* now. So had he.

I've been thinking of moving my office there actually.

————

Well, it would make sense with the long commute.

————

And also the people in this office park can be a little intrusive, to be honest.

Intrusive? My thoughts plummeted right back to that now well-visited gutter. *Intrusive, as in calling the police because you were making a woman scream so loudly during sex that you had people concerned.* Perhaps there was some truth to these rumors after all? I continued to test the waters.

So Noordhoek—are you a horse rider?

It was a perfectly good question: everyone in Noordhoek owned horses. It was the kind of place that instead of normal traffic signs it had horse signs in the road to remind you that you may just bump into one in the traffic.

Never been a horse rider! But I do keep chick-ens, which I suppose makes me a total Noordhoek cliché.

This was it, my in.

Hahah! Total cliché. And I never took you as someone who conformed. You're going to have to break out of it. I suggest owning something more unexpected, like, I don't know, an ostrich, kangaroo, or even a llama.

Or I could get a Balkan donkey and invite you over to make cheese?

I nearly fell off my chair as my heart—be still, beating heart, be still—jumped into my throat. Was he flirting with me? This felt like flirting. Yes! This absolutely, one hundred per cent felt like hardcore flirting!

I leaned forward in my chair and stared at my phone. Petal seemed to have sensed something was up, as she looked at me with big, wide, expectant eyes.

"Should I flirt back?" I asked her and she immediately turned her back on me and started walking away.

I nodded to myself. "I know. You're right." I put the phone down on the coffee table next to me. The answer was no, I should not be flirting back. Flirting never ended well. Besides, *detox*!

But this wasn't just any guy. This was Maximillian Adam. A man who may or may not be an utter sex god. A guy who may or may not own llamas. Who talked cheese to me like no one had ever talked cheese to me before. Funny, intelligent, successful, so nice to talk to . . .

"Oh, fuck it," I said out loud, and grabbed my phone off the coffee table, typing:

I'm not sure I'd enjoy donkey milking. How about you make the cheese and I'll eat it?

———

I'm sure that can be arranged.

There was a moment of silence between us. I sensed a mutual holding back. We were poised at a moment where certain things could be said. Certain things that once said could not be unsaid and would cross a line. I held back. He held back. He finally broke the holding pattern.

> I should drive home at some stage tonight, so I better get off my email. Really nice chatting to you, though. I always enjoy it. Have a great night, Leigh, and hopefully we'll speak soon.

His sudden sweetness made my heart actually feel as if it was fluttering.

> Yes, I always enjoy our chats too. Drive safely, Max.

———

> Night, Leigh.

———

> Night, Max.

I put my phone down and couldn't help but notice how warm and tingly my body felt. God, maybe this Maximillian could be the one to break the curse after all, even if that's not what the psychic had said . . .

Five years ago, we'd thrown an engagement party for Sarah and Russ, and because they'd said no strippers, we'd thought up some other creative entertainment for the night. This had resulted in us hiring an Elvis impersonator, an "illusionist"—whose only illusion was calling himself an illusionist—and the worst-rated tarot-card reader in Cape Town.

The evening was a total hoot, the illusionist had tried to make the Elvis impersonator disappear, which had not worked, and the Elvis impersonator had been so fun that he managed to turn the party into a massive sing-a-long.

Then there was the Tarot reader who'd told Sarah she would probably only get married much later on in life, if ever. Who'd told Melusi that the right *woman* would come along for him, and told Russ that the right *man* would come along for him. And then she'd come to me . . .

She'd shuffled the cards intently, eyes closed, humming to herself. I'll give her this: the whole thing looked very authentic, right down to the Bohemian-style scarf she'd tied round her head, and the long necklaces with crystals and what looked like sharks' teeth.

"I'm going to do the Celtic spread with you. It tells us so much more, and you are a more complicated case," she'd said in this strange, mystical-sounding accent.

"Oh, am I?" I'd winked at my friends, waiting for her to tell me what this "complication" was.

She started putting the cards down dramatically and we all stifled giggles.

"I can see that you have been living under a great curse, and you have not been able to break it," she'd said.

I'd felt hot and cold all at once.

"What do you mean?" I asked for clarification.

"Mmmm, yes, a very, very strong curse that can't easily be broken," she'd said.

"It can't?" I'd repeated slowly. By this stage, I was hanging on her words, and so were my friends.

"Mmmmmm, I see now," she'd said, waving her hands around the cards as if they had now transformed into a crystal ball.

"What do you see? What do you see?" I jumped in. My friends had moved closer too. It was clear we were all thinking the exact same thing.

"Mmmm, this curse has cost you great pain over the years."

"Tell us more," Melusi half shouted, waving at the cards.

"But you are trying to lift the curse in the wrong way."

"What should I do?" I sounded quite frantic now. I was fully invested in this woman's words, despite her numerous one-star ratings.

"You have to go back to the beginning, to where the curse was cast. You can only undo the curse at the source."

"At the . . . What does that mean?" Yo asked. She looked as if she was the most taken in by all of this.

"Whoever, or whatever circumstance caused the curse, you must go back and redo what wrong was done in order to undo it."

I widened my eyes and looked at my friends. Their eyes were as wide as mine.

"That means . . ." Russ started.

"Logan M. McAdam Junior," Sarah concluded.

That had been the second time only that I'd actually searched for him. I wasn't sure I believed in going back to the source to break the curse, but of course, after receiving information like that, one couldn't help one's curiosity.

I hadn't found him. I'd searched on social media, even called some old school friends. But nothing. It was as if he'd dropped off the face of the planet. There would be no going back to the source, even if I'd wanted to. Ever.

CHAPTER 8

Ash

Dear Max,

I showed the locations to Sebastian and he absolutely loves them. (Well done to you—do you have any idea how rare that is?) He wants you to book them for the shoot, and also arrange with them for me to scout the locations and conduct sun surveys.

Curious to know how the client schmoozing went. Was the cheese worth $12,000 a day?

Leigh

———

Dear Leigh,

Glad to know Sebastian is happy with the locations. I was starting to think we weren't going to get them right. Are the shoot dates still the same? Just want to confirm before I book. I'll speak to them about you scouting the locations. Are there any dates that do not suit you, travel wise?

The cheese went down really well. So well, in fact, that I think I might have to give you a commission. Will 10% suffice?

Dear Max,

The sooner I can conduct the surveys, the better. Some of the shots are very complicated, so the more prep work I can do, the better. Am okay to travel anytime.

10% seems a bit too generous. I don't think three cheese suggestions warrants that much compensation.

Dear Leigh,

I think you underestimate the brilliance of your suggestions. I'll get on to those bookings now and come back to you as soon as I have dates for the survey. Will one full day at each location suffice, or will you need more?

Max

Dear Max,

We'd better make it two days.

I'm flattered by your compliment. I've always considered myself to be an excellent fromager.

Dear Leigh,

I couldn't agree more with that assessment of yourself. I'll get back to you soonest. As always, it was a pleasure chatting to you.

Max

——

Dear Max,

You too! Have to run. I have to go to a pitch now at one of my "favorite" places.

——

Dear Leigh,

Okay, you cannot leave me hanging with inverted commas like that. Now I have to know what your "favorite" place is.

——

Dear Max,

I'll tell you, but only if you swear yourself to secrecy!

——

Dear Leigh,

Cross my heart, hope to die, stick a needle in my eye.

——

Dear Max,

Hahah! I have not heard that in years! I'm off to VGC Advertising agency to sit around with too many creative directors who think they *actually know how to shoot. If I have another creative director tell me that he wants everything to have a real cinematic look to it and tell me how I should light the actor's face, I think I might toss a C-stand at them.*

Dear Leigh,

I would probably pay to see that. I've been on a couple of sets where I've had the pleasure of seeing a few of those kinds of creative directors in action.

Dear Max,

I didn't think your job would put you on set that often?

Dear Leigh,

I pride myself on providing a very hands-on, premium offering. I like to make sure that both the production and the location are happy, and no one steps on each other's toes. After a few issues where production tried to shoot in areas of the location that were not agreed upon, and disrupted the location's daily operations, and the location didn't allow the production enough time in one area, when previously they'd agreed on a set amount of time, I decided it was in everyone's best interest that I be there. Especially when it's a big shoot like this. I don't stress as much when it's not such a high-stakes job. But I've never worked with your production company before, or with any of these locations, so I like to be there to make sure everything runs smoothly.

———

Dear Max,

Wow! That is a premium service indeed.

———

Dear Leigh,

It doesn't come cheaply, though, obviously!

———

Dear Max,

I would never dream of assuming you are not well compensated. I've seen where your office is located, remember. And I do know where you live.

———

Dear Leigh,

It sounds like you're stalking me.

———

Dear Max,

Only outside of work hours!

———

Dear Leigh,

Hahah! Is it weird to say I think I'm flattered?

———

Dear Max,

You should be.

———

Dear Leigh,

Well in that case, I'm very flattered.

———

Dear Max,

Then I guess I'm flattered that you're flattered.

There was a long pause in the conversation again. *Holding back . . . holding back.* Were we going to cross the line?

Dear Max,

As much as I would like to continue discussing your obvious flattery, I really do need to get to that meeting.

———

Dear Leigh,

Pity, this conversation was just getting interesting . . .

———

Dear Max,

Perhaps we can pick it up later?

———

Dear Leigh,

I would like that. A lot.

We seemed to have dipped our toes over the line slightly, but not so much that the line could not be redrawn if necessary. I smiled to myself as the warm feeling filled my chest once more, but then I very deliberately stopped myself from smiling. Wait, what the hell was I doing, *again*? Dating detox. I sighed out loud, but semi-flirting with Maximillian felt so good. I closed my laptop angrily, cursing myself and Maximillian's obviously irresistibly charming and flirty nature. I would need to be stronger. I needed to recommit myself to this detox. Surely I had more will power than this! It felt as if I'd gone on a diet on the first of January, only to be smashing an entire soft, silky Brie topped with candied walnuts and soft poached pear on the second.

Well, Maximillian was not a cheese and I was not going to eat him. No matter how delicious he seemed to be turning out to be.

CHAPTER 9

Ash

I was trying not to roll my eyes as I sat there giving my presentation, only to hear the scrawny creative director with the big black-framed glasses tell me, "You know what would look good?" I hadn't replied, but of course he'd continued. "If we punch in on the actor's face as he smiles!" I'd nodded vaguely and told him I would consider it, but was incredibly happy when Sebastian announced I was the only cinematographer he would work with because I was brilliant, and they should stay in their lanes, because nothing they could suggest would ever be better than what I would come up with. I tried to stifle my smile. I zoned out for the rest of the presentation as Melusi in the art department presented, then wardrobe and make-up and lastly the editor. My part was over. But my ears certainly pricked up when the words "location" and "the Film Place" started being thrown around. Melusi and I clocked each other across the boardroom table.

"The Film Place?" I asked.

"You know them?" the agency producer replied. "They're kind of new."

"I'm actually working with them on this job. They've been great, really went above and beyond." The least I could do was get Max some more work, especially since he was new in town, and that would also give me another (real) reason to email him.

"The guy who runs it is Maximillian Adam," I added quickly.

A terrible noise followed and we all turned, only to find the junior copywriter in the corner choking and coughing. She had sprayed a mouthful of coffee across the desk.

"Sorry, sorry." She frantically wiped the table, but her face was the shade of a beetroot, and it didn't look like it was from choking. In fact, I think I knew what it was from. Melusi and I gave each other one more knowing look, and then I fixed my eyes on her as I spoke again.

"Yes, I was saying *Maximillian Adam* is the name of the guy who runs the company."

I scrutinized her. Her hands began to tremble, her eyes widened until they looked like they might explode from her head. She cleared her throat and then rubbed her collarbones nervously.

Holy shit! She knew him! Either very, very well, or she knew *of* him. When the meeting was over, my curiosity was too piqued to ignore, besides Melusi was now nudging me to go and investigate further. I would usually never do something like this, but I was driven by something far greater than professional etiquette right now.

"Hey, Lauren. Sorry, was it Lauren?" The very pretty copywriter turned and looked at me. She seemed young, no older than twenty-one, and Max didn't come across as someone in his early twenties—he'd been overseas for twelve years. I hoped a possibly thirty-year-old was not sleeping with this girl who looked as if she was right out of high school.

"Yes, Lauren."

"So . . . I'm sorry if this comes across as totally weird, but I kind of noticed you had a strong reaction when I said *Maximillian Adam*, and I was just wondering if—"

She stepped forward and whispered, "You've heard the stories too?"

"Yes, I have," I said solemnly.

"Oh my God. I would never have believed it, but this friend of mine, who has a friend, who has a sister, went on a date with him and . . ." She paused and flushed again. She was young, and you could tell not very experienced in that department.

"She said the guy literally gave her an orgasm just by looking at her."

I burst out laughing. "That's impossible."

"I thought so too, but then I heard from someone else, who knows this girl who works as a vet in Noordhoek—"

"Noordhoek?" I interrupted her.

"*Ja*, I know, random, but whatever."

No, it wasn't random. This one could actually be true.

"I don't know—he has some weird pet, like one of those things from Mexico . . . What are they called?"

"A llama?" I asked.

"Yes, that's it, a llama. So, apparently, she went to check on it at his house—he lives in this mansion, by the way—and they landed up hooking up in his pool, and he got her into this position she didn't even know existed, and then she had the most intense orgasm of her life and fainted afterwards."

"Fainted in the pool?"

"I mean, she didn't drown or anything—he was holding her up."

"Obviously."

"She woke up like an hour later in his bed and they had sex again, and she was screaming so loudly the entire time that the next day she actually lost her voice."

"Seriously?"

"She had to take the day off work because she couldn't talk."

"Riiight," I said, and eyed this copywriter up and down.

"What have you heard?" she asked, her eyes lighting up, and for some reason, I actually didn't want to tell her.

"I also heard he owns llamas," I said, and then turned and walked out the office, feeling something I couldn't quite name.

CHAPTER 10

Ash

"No one comes from someone just looking at them," I said as Sarah, Yo and I sat on my balcony enjoying the sunset while Petal rubbed herself against our legs. "No one's eyes have orgasmic fucking laser beams embedded in them. That's just ridiculous."

"Not according to Google." Sarah's smile could only be described as a wicked smirk. The kind of smirk she only ever gives me when she's up to no good. Like when she smuggled a bottle of alcohol into Tom Swanson's party, or she copied Jenna Higgins's answers in a test, or when she talked a bouncer into letting us into the club without IDs. Despite lawyerly appearances, Sarah has a very naughty streak.

"Fine, I'll bite. Tell me," I said.

"I'm dying to hear this too," Yo said, stretching her legs out into the last of the sunbeams.

"According to several Reddit users on a very long and fascinating thread, they too have orgasmed without any physical touch."

"Since when did Reddit users' posts become gospel?"

"Since I wanted them to," Sarah said defiantly.

"Hey, I'm starved. I'm ordering Uber Eats. Who wants what?" Russ stuck his head round the corner and we all immediately threw orders at him. Pizza for Sarah, vegan burger for Yo and a three-cheese pasta for me, obviously. His head disappeared round the corner once more.

"Let's get back to the sex," Yo said quickly.

"Yes!" I agreed. "And no one faints after it either, for the record," I countered.

"Not according to Google, again." Sarah's smile had grown once more.

"You mean Reddit?" I said sarcastically.

"Nope, this time I mean a scientific journal I read that said it was very possible, and also quite common, to faint after orgasm due to hyperventilating."

"That actually makes sense," Yo said.

"So you honestly believe there is a guy out there called Maximillian Adam who lives in an off-grid mansion in Noordhoek, who keeps llamas, and who is basically God's sexual gift to women on earth, who can conjure up a fainting, screaming orgasm just by breathing on them?"

"I'm more inclined to believe that than him actually owning llamas," Sarah replied.

I shook my head. "What's with you and these llamas?"

"*Alleged* llamas," she quickly added. "But given all this information— or 'discovery', to use a more legal term—I think if anyone can break your sex curse and get you out of the rut, it's Maximillian Adam."

"Not according to the psychic," Yo jumped in quickly. She was a big believer in the curse as an actual supernatural thing. And sometimes we spoke about "The Curse" like that, as if it was some powerful, supernatural thing that had been invisibly placed on me against my will. But most of us also didn't quite believe that either. When it really came down to it, we didn't really believe in the supernatural world of sex hexes . . . did we?

"Do we really all believe it's a curse? An actual magic-wand kind of curse?" I asked.

"I do!" Yo said quickly.

"I mean, normally, I don't believe in things like that, but . . ." Sarah started, and then stopped. "It *is* really weird, though. And you can't be that unlucky, can you? And the psychic did say—"

"That psychic was terrible, though," I said.

"But she got it *all* right," Yo replied. "Okay, so not with everyone, but with you it was spot on. Face it, you were cursed. And you've been trying to break it for the last thirteen years. But instead of a wand a dick was used!"

We all burst out laughing.

"What's got you all cackling like witches?" Russ stuck his head around the door again.

"Magical cocks!" Yo said quickly, and Russ looked somewhat perplexed. Or was that repulsed?

"I think I'll stay out of this one." His head disappeared round the corner again.

I stopped laughing and thought about it. If I hadn't been cursed, then what was the cause of my disastrous sex life? The answer to that question was of course that the problem actually lay with me . . . *didn't it?*

"Well, it's not like going back to the source is ever going to happen," I said. "No one has seen or heard from Logan in forever." I hated saying his name out loud. It always had a physical effect on me. Even now.

"Nope. Casper the ghost," Sarah agreed.

"Last bloody thing I ever heard was that he was on holiday with his uncle in Scotland and then disappeared into Europe, never to be seen or heard from again," I said. There was still some anger and bitterness in my tone, despite the time that had lapsed.

"No, I think Maximillian's your guy," Yo reiterated.

"And how do you propose I have sex with him? Drop him an email and say, 'Hi, how are you? Want to have sex with me?'"

"Personally, I'd take a more subtle approach, but I guess your way would probably work too," Yo replied, sounding amused.

My phone lit up on the table next to me and Petal looked at it in horror.

"Oh my God, look at that! She's doing that thing where she puffs up. I have to film it." I grabbed my phone quickly, in hopes of catching this cuteness, but as soon as I saw the notification across my screen, I forgot all about my cute cat.

"It's him!" I held my screen up for Sarah and Yo to see.

They both leaned in excitedly. "Well, read it. Read it," they chorused together.

"Weird, it's on WhatsApp and we only ever email." I unlocked my screen with a swipe.

"Ooooh, WhatsApp, so much more personal. Quick, start flirting with him, even if he does own llamas," Sarah said.

"Your obsession with the llamas is starting to worry me."

Max: Hi Leigh, this is me picking it up later.

Leigh: How did you get my number? Are YOU stalking ME now?

Max: Well, it is in your email signature . . .

Leigh: Fair enough. So what are we picking up?

Max: There are a few work things we need to iron out first, and then we can circle back to our mutual feelings of flattery.

I felt my cheeks go warm and, God help me, a soft giggle escaped my lips. Yo and Sarah both noticed this and leaned in. I angled myself away from their prying eyes a little.

Leigh: Well, what can I help you with?

Max: I chatted to the locations—all of them can do the recce this week. So leaving this Wednesday and coming back next Wednesday? Does that work for you?

Leigh: That should be good, I just need to find a cat sitter.

Max: You have a cat?

Leigh: Her name is Petal.

Max: Are you one of those cat owners that bombards their friends with cat videos all day?

I laughed out loud. It was weird how many times he'd made me laugh and we didn't even know each other.

Leigh: Guilty as charged.

"What's he saying? What's so funny?" Sarah asked.

"We're just discussing dates for the location scouting."

"Now segue into discussing the potential of having sex with him," Yo said.

I lowered my phone and gave Yo a look. "And how should I go about that?"

"Dear Max, the dates for the locations are great, but you know what would also be great? Sex."

We all laughed but stopped when another message came through.

Max: The bar had to redo their plumbing this week, something about someone blocking the toilet (I don't want to even imagine) so we can only see that next week. That okay?

Leigh: We?

Max: Oh, yes, I hope you don't mind if I tag along. I want to see these locations myself and meet with the owners and managers. They've all expressed an interest in signing with my agency. I'm still building up my books here, and this would be a good opportunity to sign on some more clients.

"Oh my God, he wants to come with me," I screeched at my friends, and Petal puffed up again.

"That's it. You are *so* having sex with him," Yo said. "Cursebreaker loading."

"But I don't even know what he looks like," I argued back.

"Well, apparently he's hot," Sarah said, scratching Petal who depuffed at the head scratch.

"Hot is subjective," I said quickly.

"If a gorgeous model with what I might just add are incredibly perky breasts thinks he's hot, then he's also probably hot by our, less perky-boobed, standard," Sarah said.

"Hey, speak for yourself. My boobs are still very perky!" Yo said, pushing out her chest.

"Mine too." I looked down at my chest. "Well, they're too small for gravity to have any effect on them."

Sarah sighed. "When I bend down to pick stuff up, they hit my chin."

"Seriously."

I burst out laughing and then patted Sarah's shoulder in mock sympathy as Yo leaned forward to inspect her chest. We were a boundary-less group for sure.

My phone beeped again.

Max: Sorry, are you uncomfortable with that?

I lowered my phone and looked at my friends.

"He wants to know if I'm uncomfortable with him coming along?"

"Why would you be? That's kind of a normal work thing," Yo said.

"I suppose . . ."

"Sebastian often tags along on recces and surveys, not to mention other crew members and agency people, who you haven't met. Unless . . . you're uncomfortable for another reason." She winked at me.

"It's not like we'll be sharing a room. And I'll be working the entire time, and he will too, so we probably won't even see each other."

Yo shrugged, but also gave me another mischievous smile. I looked over at Sarah, wanting her take on the situation, but she also reciprocated with a grin.

"You guys are loving this way too much. It makes me wonder about your sex lives."

"Russ and I have amazing sex, I'll have you know," Sarah replied quickly.

"I can second that." Russ popped his head round the corner again. Clearly he *had* been listening.

We all turned and looked at Yo, who gave a very conspiratorial look. "A lady never kisses and tells."

"But this is about *your* sex life." Sarah pointed at me. "Not ours."

I looked at them for a while, weighing it up in my head, and then quickly put my fingers down to my screen.

Leigh: Yeah. Totally fine with that. I'll be really busy though, but it will be nice meeting you in person.

Max: Yes, it will be really, really great meeting you in person too.

Two "really"s. I felt my cheeks go red and warm again. This man had the power to alter my body temperature through the phone. *Oh my God*, maybe he did make women come just by looking at them.

Max: And I promise I won't get in your way . . . unless you want me to?

My cheeks instantly flushed as I imagined all the ways that he could get in my way. He could get in my way a lot, but would I let him?

Max: Even though we'll both be busy, perhaps we can steal a moment to eat some cheese together?

My cheeks flushed even more.

"You're blushing." Sarah pointed at me.

"I think he's trying to use cheese to flirt with me."

"Oh my God, he's your perfect man," Sarah sighed.

"He's seducing me with cheese," I repeated.

"Who's seducing you with cheese?" Russ's head was back round the corner again.

"Llama-man," Sarah said.

"No. Absolutely not. You cannot make llama-man his moniker. It makes me think of something half man, half llama," Yo said firmly.

"And then that raises the question of which half is llama and which half is man," Russ added.

"Exactly." Yo visibly cringed and so did I.

I looked back down at my phone and typed a message back.

> **Leigh:** What cheese do you have in mind?
>
> **Max:** What cheese do you suggest for a professional semi-work-related date with a cheese connoisseur?

"He just used the word 'date.'" I looked up at everyone quickly.

"Ask him what kind of date?" Yo clicked her fingers at my phone. But I didn't have time to type back, as he sent a response through immediately.

> **Max:** Unless you don't like to mix business and pleasure?

I almost died. "And now he's using the word 'pleasure.'"

"Okay, perfect, now segue into the sex part. Type, 'What kind of pleasure did you have in mind?'" Sarah said.

"Babe! So forward," Russ scolded playfully.

"I agree. I'm not typing that. That's too much. That's crossing the line." I looked at Sarah and she raised her brows at me. I raised mine back and we held each other's gazes. We didn't need to talk to each other—we had known each other for so long, and been through so much, that our conversations often happened telepathically. Then I moved my eyes over to Yo who gave me a smile that I knew exactly how to interpret.

"You two are such bad influences," I said, shaking my head. "I'm supposed to be on a detox."

"Fuck detoxes," Sarah said. "They never work anyway; you just land up binge eating everything in sight afterwards."

"And anyone who says they actually like celery juice is lying," Yo added.

"Okay, fine! Fine!" I started typing . . . *Oh my God I was probably going to regret this.*

"I can't watch this," Russ declared, and disappeared again.

Leigh: That depends on what kind of pleasure we're talking about.

"Shit! I regret that," I said instantly. "I should delete it, quickly— nope, two blue ticks." I inhaled, holding my breath, knowing full well that I had just officially walked us both over the line.

Line Crossed ✔

Max: I've learned over the years that pleasure is very subjective.

"I'm sure he has," I scoffed out loud.

"Sure he has what?" Sarah asked, and I passed her the phone. She made a dramatic show of fanning her face while Yo leaned in to read as well.

"This guy is good!" Sarah said as another message came through and she passed the phone back to me. I looked down at the screen and must admit I was somewhat disappointed that he was back to being professional again.

Max: So I'll email you our full itinerary tomorrow.

Leigh: Thanks, that will be great.

Max: I'll make sure I get that to you first thing in the morning so you have plenty of time to prepare and pack.

Leigh: Looking forward to it, thanks.

Max: Perfect. Have a really good evening. And as always, I loved chatting to you, Leigh.

Leigh: You too, Max.

Oh my God, there was something so seductive and sexy about him typing my name. My name felt as if it held some kind of question and answer all at once.

"What the hell have I gotten myself into?" I asked Sarah and Yo when I'd put my phone down. It was a rhetorical question, though, because I knew exactly what I was getting myself into. "I guess I'm going on location with Maximillian Adam who may or may not own alleged llamas, who can apparently bring someone to orgasm just by looking at them, and makes women faint in the pool," I said, and we all burst out laughing just as my phone pinged again.

Max: Forgot to ask, can I have a copy of your ID to book flights?

Leigh: Sure, will send you one. I have a copy on my phone.

Leigh: Oh, and in case you start wondering whether I really am a stalker/psycho, my real name is Ashley Smith. I had to go with Leigh professionally.

I began searching my phone for my ID, all the while expecting some witty banter about my name to come back. But it never did. I found my ID and sent it.

Leigh: Here we go. And please don't judge the picture. I had allergies that day. I swear I don't look like that in real life.

I pressed send and waited for a response. It didn't come. Even after my message had gotten two blue ticks and a whole five minutes had passed. Perhaps he really was taken aback by my ID photo and had now regretted setting up a cheese date with me. Suddenly, it was very important that he didn't think I looked like my ID photo in real life.

CHAPTER 11

Max

$\mathcal{T}$he second I read that name, a tight feeling coiled round my stomach. It squeezed like a vice. Constricting until I had to sit. *That name.*

Ashley Smith.

What the hell were the chances? Zero? Less than zero? But still that name brought back memories that I'd been working so hard to forget for so many years. Unfortunately, since returning home, those memories were becoming harder and harder to suppress.

"*Ashley Smith. Ash.*" I said the name out loud and took notice of the way it rolled off my tongue, the way it felt in my mouth, the way my vocal cords formed so easily around it, as if it was a name I said daily. It wasn't. *Maybe it's been running through your head daily, though?* a part of my brain suggested, and I quickly shut it down. I had become good at shutting that part down. Practice makes perfect, after all. And I'd decided long ago to never listen to that part again. Because that part was home to all the memories and the images of her. Of us. I'd forced the door closed on that part of my mind years ago. Locked the door, nailed it shut, and walked away from it. But when I'd moved back to South Africa, the echo of that name had been everywhere, and it was becoming harder and harder to push it all away. In fact, that name had been on my mind so much lately that it made being physically confronted with it now even more unnerving. As if I'd manifested it in some way.

Which I hadn't. I didn't believe in such things, but still. It was weird.

The door in my mind cracked open a little more and now memories and images were flooding me. Happy memories, the best memories of my life, but, with those, also the worst memories of my life too.

I cursed out loud and walked to the other end of my room. "Shit." It always shocked me when I felt like this. I thought I had this under control. But the mere mention of that name clearly still had the power to rattle me. Maybe it was more than just hearing the name, though.

Leigh and I were definitely flirting. And I liked her, probably more than I'd liked anyone in a while, and I didn't even know her. Maybe that's why it suddenly felt as if the floor had shifted under my feet. Because these small, fledgling feelings I was having for Leigh were ever so slightly reminiscent of the feelings I'd had for Ashley . . .

My phone delivered another beep. The ID. I raced over to it, the photo that she'd sent was just waiting to be downloaded. All I had to do was tap the arrow on the screen and then, then . . . My finger hovered over the button. Why was I hesitating? A feeling, huge and vast and overwhelming, built inside me. A feeling that I hadn't felt in forever.

"Fuck it." I pressed the button and the image crystalized before my eyes, and as soon as it did, my phone slipped through my fingers as if it was suddenly made of melted butter. It fell to the floor, bounced once, twice, the torch turned on, and then it settled. I looked down at it, the light from the torch shinning up at me as if I was in some kind of interrogation room. It felt like I was. Because there were so many questions coming at me right now that I was trying desperately to answer. The first and biggest one being: *Had I really just seen that?*

Or had I imagined it because I'd wanted to see it? I didn't know which thought was most terrifying, and I didn't know why it now felt that picking up my phone and looking at the screen was the hardest task that had ever been laid out in front of me.

I bent down on my haunches and stared at my phone as if waiting for it to do something to me. But when it didn't, when it simply lay there motionless, I picked it up. I traced my finger over the screen, a large crack running the length of it now. I turned the torch off quickly and then looked at the screen.

"Fuuuck." The word escaped my dry mouth as I crossed my legs and sat flat on the floor, staring at the photo in front of me.

It was her.

Ash.

My Ash.

I clutched my head. It hurt from all the spinning it was doing and all the questions racing through it. I hadn't seen this face in thirteen years. I hadn't googled her once in all those years for fear that I'd feel exactly like this. I wasn't on social media either in case she Googled me and reached out. I had done everything possible to *never* see this face again, and yet here she was. The locked door at the back of my brain, keeping back all those memories, cracked open even more.

Those eyes. Big and round as ever.

Small, button nose that I used to touch with the tip of my finger. That I used to plant soft kisses on.

Lips. Small lips that almost disappeared when she smiled that megawatt smile. A smile that had the power to knock you off your feet and make time stop. When she smiled at you, everything in the world was perfect.

The fucking door was cracking open even more. I tried to mentally slam it shut, but it was no use. Everything rushed back now.

Kissing those lips, Jesus Christ. There was no better feeling in the entire world. Nothing beat sinking into those lips, into her mouth and tasting her.

"Shit!" I stood up abruptly and ran a hand across my forehead. It was damp with sweat. I had to stop thinking like this. I had to stop staring at her picture and remembering. But I couldn't.

Her hair was totally different now. It was short, hanging just below her ears. She'd always had this long hair that was always getting knotty, and that I was constantly helping her brush. Sitting behind her on the bed carefully trying to work out the knots that had gathered under her ponytail at the nape of her neck. Her hair was no longer blonde either. She'd clearly stopped bleaching it to within an inch of its life. It was dark and chocolaty brown, just like those manga-sized eyes of hers.

The shape of her face was also different, cheekbones and a sharper jawline had replaced youthful softness. She no longer looked like a girl, with those faint lines by her eyes and mouth, and her face seemed slimmer and longer, but . . .

She was still, without a doubt, the most gorgeous girl—woman now—that I'd ever laid eyes on.

When the initial shock had worn off, the full implications hit me. I had been unknowingly talking to the only woman I had ever loved for the last month. It all made sense now. I'd felt this inexplicable connection to her and I hadn't known why. Now I knew. This thought scared me so much that I reached for a glass of whiskey in hopes of taking the edge off the painful jagged feeling that was ripping me up inside.

What did this all mean?

"No!" I downed the glass. I was reading too deeply into this. It was thirteen years ago. I was over her. That's what the last thirteen years of my life had been all about. Getting over her.

Work. Traveling. Sex. Work. Traveling . . .

Sex.

So much meaningless sex.

I shook my head, turned my phone off and tossed it onto my bed. I walked straight into the bathroom and peeled off my clothes. I climbed into the shower and blasted myself with water. I needed to wash it away, these feelings, these thoughts, the sweat that had formed on my forehead and palms. I stood there and let the water rush over me, imagining it taking away all those feelings I didn't want to be having. I looked down and pictured them all falling into the drain and disappearing once again.

I was over her.

I had to be.

CHAPTER 12

Max

Dear Leigh (or should I call you Ashley, now that I know your real name?)...

———

Dear Max,

You can call me whatever you want—I've gotten used to both. Although it was a bit weird going by a different name professionally, but I chose something as close-sounding to my real name as I could. So call me whatever feels easier.

———

Dear Ash?

———

Dear Max,

That's what my friends call me.

———

Is it okay if I call you that then?

———

Sure, I actually prefer it.

———

Have we just become friends?

———

Aaah. Cute!

———

So cute.

I tapped my keypad nervously. I'd wrestled with whether to tell her who I was. But I figured it was something to tell her in person, not over email. It seemed wrong over email . . .

Bullshit. Who was I kidding? That was not the reason at all. The truth was that I was terrified that if she knew who I *really* was she wouldn't come on this trip with me. After all, the last thing she'd ever said to me was: "I hate you." Her last three words to me. I'd wanted to say my last three words back to her: "I love you." But didn't. I'd been such a coward. A stupid nineteen-year-old idiot who didn't know that he was in the process of making the single worst mistake of his life by running away from a difficult situation. I lowered my fingers and typed back. Knowing who I was talking to felt exhilarating and terrifying, *so terrifying*.

Well, on that note,

Dear Ash,

Hope you had a great weekend?
Everything is booked and confirmed. I have attached the weather reports for the locations, so you know what to pack for yourself. Our flight to Matobo Hills takes off at 9:30. The lodge is sending a driver to pick you up and take you to the airport where we'll depart in their own plane. Please send me your address so I can forward it on to the driver.

Max

P.S. Hope you found a cat sitter?

P.P.S. you didn't look as bad as you made out in your ID photo.

———

Dear Max,

Seriously, my nose is red and at least two times bigger than it usually is. It was allergy season. But thanks.

I smiled to myself. I remember how badly she used to get allergies. If an insect bit her, she'd come up with a giant red splotch. She'd brushed past a certain plant once and her entire body itched for an hour. I'd had to help her scratch it until it stopped. She also made the most adorable sneezing sounds during pollen season.

Fucking stop it, Max, I mentally scolded myself.

My address is 3 Whalesong, Seaview Road, Camps Bay. My neighbors are going to look after Petal. She's always at their place during the day anyway. They both work from home and she's found a way to slink from my balcony to theirs.

I appreciate you organizing this, Max!

———

Dear Ash,

It's my job, but it was also my pleasure to do it.

Glad you have such good neighbors. Do they also lend you cups of sugar? Or cheese?

———

Dear Max,

Haha! No cheese. But they have come to my rescue in some other kinds of "emergencies."

———

Dear Ash,

You have me intrigued once again with your use of inverted commas. May I ask what the nature of these "emergencies" was?

———

Dear Max,

I think if I told you it would probably be oversharing. We don't know each other well enough to be discussing those kinds of "emergencies." Especially not over email.

I pulled my phone towards me and started typing my message to her. I'd already changed her name in my contacts to Ash, and felt like a kid opening a Christmas present on Christmas morning as I'd deleted "Leigh" and typed in those three letters.

Max: Is Whatsapp better?
Ash: You really want to know?
Ash: It'll probably just be a boring story for you.
Max: I doubt anything you could say or do would be boring.

I paused, wondering if that gave too many of my feelings away. I was struggling to hold them back, though.

Ash: Fine. I'll tell you, but only if you tell me something personal too?

Max: Deal.

Ash: Okay then, let's just say it was an "emergency" of the personal nature.

Max: You're going to have to elaborate.

Ash: Put it this way, have you ever been on a date with someone and it was going so terribly that you had to send a secret message to your neighbors asking them to fabricate some kind of emergency to get said person out of your apartment?

My stomach dropped. Of course I knew she dated. But having her actually tell me made my forehead clammy and cold. I swallowed and tried to keep those feelings to myself.

Max: I've had a few dates over the years that I wished I could have put an end to, so I know the feeling.

Ash: Oh, I doubt you really know the feeling. Because trust me, I have a bit of a strange history of going on dates that usually end badly in some certain, special kind of way.

My forehead felt even clammier now. I wasn't exactly sure what she was alluding to, but I knew I didn't like it.

Max: Hopefully the cheese will save ours from that.

Ash: But this is not that kind of date, right? What did you call it, "professional semi-work-related"?

Butterflies—fucking pterodactyls—in my stomach.

Max: What if I was using the word "professional" in a very semi-loose manner?

Ash: Were you?

Max: There's a strong possibility I was . . .
Max: So with that in mind, should I still bring the cheese?

There was another long pause on the phone and I waited in anticipation for her reply.

Ash: Depends on what cheese you're talking about?
Max: Only the best kind.
Ash: Then there's also a strong semi-possibility I won't say no . . .
Max: Those are a lot of possibilities. And semis.
Ash: With a lot of possible outcomes.
Max: Indeed there are. I'm now very excited to see you.

I nearly typed "again"—thank God I didn't. There was another long pause on the phone. I was smiling, my face awash with color, and even though I couldn't see her, I could sense she probably looked exactly like I did now.

Ash: Me too.
Max: See you very soon, Ash.
Ash: See you soon, Max.

I put my phone down and stress-paced my room a few times. I was seeing her soon. I looked down at my watch, in twenty-three hours, soon. I had twenty-three hours to figure out exactly what I was going to say to her and how. I had a feeling, though, that no matter how it was said or explained, she would still be very pissed off.

A knock on the door made me turn.

"Mr. McAdamson," the nurse called. They still called me by my old surname.

"Coming." I walked over to my door and opened it. "What is it, Thuli?"

"I thought you'd want to know that your mom asked to go and see her animals."

I nodded. "Thanks, I'll be there soon."

I quickly changed into a pair of sneakers I didn't mind getting dirty. Taking my mom outside to see the animals was one of the few things we could still do together, and one of the only mother–son activities that actually made me happy. Because my main emotion when I was around her was sadness. When I'd moved back here, I'd chosen Noordhoek for its peaceful tranquility and country feeling. The properties and houses here were all huge, huge enough that I could have my mom stay with me, as well as around-the-clock nursing and care staff for her. I'd tailormade a wing of my house for her specifically. She had a sensory room, something that has yielded a lot of results in dementia patients. I'd also put together a small home gym for her to use with her physiotherapist to keep her muscles from deteriorating further. I'd tried to create a perfect little world for her here that she could enjoy for as long as she had left, and that included the animals.

When I'd brought her here for the first time, in one of her rare lucid moments, she'd looked at the huge garden and told me it reminded her of the family farm she'd grown up on. I'd made a joke about, "Well, it can't be a farm without any animals," to which she'd replied that she would love animals. When I'd asked what animals she'd wanted, I'd almost fallen over when she'd said llamas. She'd always wanted a llama, ever since she was a little girl and had seen their picture in a book. And so I'd fucking bought a llama! A llama! Of all the things she could have said.

She'd also asked for chickens and a parrot. The chickens had been easy. Everyone in this area had chickens and so I'd asked my neighbor if he had any he wouldn't mind parting with. The parrot I'd gotten from Parrot Rescue; I thought it was the right thing to do. The woman there had warned me that since the parrot had not been particularly well cared for, it would probably not be able to talk, and probably not be as social as one that had been hand reared. Oh, how wrong she was . . .

I walked out of my room and down the main staircase to the bottom level. This area was luckily very big, and my mom's section was at the furthest end of the house. I needed some space between my bedroom and her wing. Sometimes I would have guests over, and sometimes they'd get loud. I opened the door to her area and heard the very familiar, "Fuck you!"

"Shhhh!" My mom scolded the bird, who as it turned out was anything but quiet and unsocial.

"Who's a naughty girl?" the bird squawked at my mother and then ran across the series of perches until he was right next to my mother, who he was very fond of.

"Sexy girl, sexy girl, sexy girl!" the bird said as my mom ran a hand over his head.

Out of all the parrots in the world, we'd landed up with a potty-mouthed pervert parrot.

"Mom!" I said brightly as I walked in. On some days she recognized me and knew who I was, and on other days she didn't. But she was never afraid of me, like she was of other people. In fact, on the days she didn't know me, she always told me what a nice and polite young man I was. Something that I both loved and hated to hear. But whatever her mental state was that day, she always looked the same, and it always took my breath away.

Only a year ago she'd been on her feet, lucid and full of life. Now she was so thin that her skin hung off her bones and her body no longer looked as if it could support life. A lot of the time she used a wheelchair, but on other days she was able to stand and wanted to walk around.

"Who are you?" she asked.

"I'm a friend of yours," I said. "And someone told me you want to go and see Lucy and the chickens." She'd named her llama Lucy and always remembered her, even when she was far from lucid.

"I want to see Lucy," she agreed. "And I need to feed the chickens, or they won't give us eggs. Daddy says a happy chicken is a laying chicken."

"Your dad sounds very wise," I said, going along with whatever she said. She was clearly remembering her childhood today.

"Right then, let's go." I pushed her wheelchair towards the door. I'd had a wheelchair-friendly path built right across the garden, so she could still go outside whenever she wanted to. My mother had loved gardening, had loved being outside, and I wanted her to still be able to enjoy those things. I pushed her down the path. The weather was beautiful today mainly because there was a slight breeze cooling everything down. There was a clear view down to the sea and the mountains, and a flowery perfume hung in the air.

"Why are the gladioli not blooming? Has someone not been giving them water?" my mom asked.

"They're not blooming because it's summer. They only bloom in winter," I explained.

"Oh. Why did we become friends?"

"I think we became friends because we like the same things," I said.

"Like what?"

"We like watching the wildlife channel together, we like jelly and custard, and we like llamas," I said, listing the things we still did, or ate together. She barely ate, but I could always get her to eat jelly and custard.

"That's nice, dear," she said sweetly. She was in a good mood today, which I was relieved about. Because sometimes she spent all day in terror and panic, not knowing what was going on around her.

"Here we go." We reached the large enclosure that I'd built for Lucy and the chickens. Previously, I'd just let them wander around the garden, but I'd soon discovered that both Lucy, and the chickens, were very fond of sneaking inside the house. Lucy was particularly fond of eating whatever she found in the kitchen. On one specific occasion, she'd caused me to call an emergency vet over after she'd ingested my mom's entire birthday cake, and then proceeded to vomit all over the lounge and dining room.

Lucy and the chickens ran up to the fence as soon as they saw us.

I'd had no idea when getting a llama just how domestic and sociable they could be. They were like dogs sometimes. I pushed my mom up to the fence, passed her some chicken seed and celery sticks and then sat down in the chair I'd put there for myself and the nurses. My mom could simply sit and talk, or even sing to, Lucy and the chickens for hours. They really did bring her happiness, and I was more than happy to sit out here with her for as long as she wanted to be here. While my mom fed Lucy her favorite celery sticks and the chickens frantically pecked at the seed, I pulled my phone out and reread all the messages Ash and I'd exchanged so far. I'd done this a lot recently. She was still as funny as she used to be. No one had ever made me laugh like Ash.

"Where is that lovely fiancée of yours, son?" my mom suddenly asked me.

I smiled at her, so happy that she'd called me "son" that it dulled the pain of that now-familiar question just a little bit. "She'll be here just now."

"Good! Good!" she said, and then looked back at Lucy. Her memory was such that sometimes she seemed to remember the events of her life as they were, and sometimes she believed some alternate version of it. One of the ways that played out was with Ash. On some days, my mom knew Ash and I were not together, and on other days she imagined that I'd proposed to her that night with the ring I'd been saving up for, for a year.

I'd planned on asking Ash to marry me that night. We knew we wanted to be together, and had spoken about our future for hours and hours at a time, but in retrospect, at that age, maybe I'd taken it too far by buying a ring. It had definitely added to the overall stress of that disastrous evening. I was a nineteen-year-old kid with a ring burning a hole in my pocket, waiting for the perfect time to give it to the girl I wanted to spend the rest of my life with, while trying to have sex for the first time too.

We'd waited so long to have sex because we'd both had this notion that waiting for the "perfect" moment would make it even more special. We'd seen most of our friends have sex, and none of them had spoken about it the way that we imagined we wanted it to be. It was almost throwaway for them, we wanted it to be different. Special. Perfect. But it had been the opposite of that, because once we'd done all the things we'd already done, and began heading into uncharted sexual waters, I just panicked.

And the fact that my mother seemed to dwell on this exact moment of my failed proposal—and unbeknownst to her, something else that was also failed—so often was unimaginably cruel. Not that she was trying to be cruel—it was just what her mind went to. But still, it was the most painful moment of my life and whenever she mentioned it I was forced to relive that pain. A pain I had tried to ignore for so many years. And when she brought it up, I had to play along. Her psychiatrist had told me to go along with these fantasies, and so I did. Even if it was painful to imagine this alternative reality in which things hadn't gone so wrong with Ash. A reality where she had a ring on her finger, and we were happy. A house, a dog, kids even. Maybe a llama or two. I tried not to think about it. But it was very hard right now because after thirteen years of trying to push her away, she was fucking back in my life. The thoughts of what might have been with her were coming crashing back. And I was asking myself—was I ready for how it was going to feel to be in her presence again after all this time?

CHAPTER 13

Ash

"*I*s that the plane we're going in?" I pointed at the small propeller plane. It was a stupid question, though, and I knew it. The words painted across the side that read "Matobo Hills" were a dead giveaway. But I'd decided to err on the side of unrealistic hope.

"You can only access the lodge by plane—it's not accessible by car."

"Right." I looked at the plane again, but was not reassured. "And this is the plane we're going in? *This* one?"

The pilot nodded at me.

"And you're sure it's safe?"

"I've been flying this plane to and from Matobo Hills for ten years. Sure, the ride is a little bumpy at times, but there's nothing to worry about, I assure you."

I was not assured. "And what kind of plane is this again?"

"It's a Cessna Skyhawk."

"Indeed."

I walked around the plane. But the more I looked, the less reassured I was. When Max had said private plane, maybe stupidly I'd not imagined something so small. It had a propeller. It had little wheel legs that looked as if they could be snapped in a strong breeze.

"I don't think it's going to fit all my luggage and gear in," I said, changing my tune a little.

"You'll be surprised how much she can take." The pilot patted the plane affectionately and smiled at me. I did not smile back. I reached for the sunflower tattoo on my arm and rubbed it gently, trying to ease away the panic that was building inside me. I did this whenever I didn't feel safe. I hated feeling unsafe. *Hated it.* And I did everything possible to avoid any kind of potentially dangerous situation. No one likes feeling unsafe, but I disliked it more than most, because of what had happened to me and my family. Because I know that life can simply just end. In a sudden, unexpected split second. One moment a person is sitting next to you, breathing and laughing, and the next second that person is gone forever. I looked down at the tattoo and took a deep breath.

"Okay! Okay!" I said out loud, psyching myself up. At least I wasn't going to be alone on the plane. If I was going to die in this little flying tin box, then at least I would not be dying alone.

I heard a car and turned. Another transfer vehicle had arrived and this had to be Max. My stomach swelled in anticipation. I was dying to put a face to the man I'd been having some of the nicest conversations with, which had progressed into flagrant flirting with a possible cheese date to boot. The man that I'd decided to temporarily drop my detox for because I had this little voice in the back of my head whispering at me, and a flutter in my stomach that had been there for a while, every time I saw his name drop into my inbox.

The back door of the car opened, and he climbed out. First thing I noticed was his height—he was tall. Next was his physique. Broad shoulders, muscular-looking all over. He clearly worked out. It didn't surprise me. Everyone who lived in Cape Town worked out. It was a prerequisite for living here, almost a clause in some silent contract you signed when you moved to the Cape. His hair was longer than I'd expected, though. For some reason, I'd imagined a clean, short cut. But it wasn't. It was slightly shaggy and hung around his face. It was an ashy blond color and had the slightest wave to it. I'd also imagined him to be clean shaven, but he wasn't. He was bearded. It was *not* one of those huge hipster beads, but it also wasn't a five o'clock shadow—it was more a three-day shadow. He was still in profile, pulling his bag from the backseat, but then he turned. He was wearing dark glasses. Strands of hair fell into his face as he ran his hand through his hair, pushing it back with a smooth, self-assured sexiness that dripped off him like a wet sponge being squeezed between your hands.

Holy shit, he was hot!

His walk too. This was the walk of a man that knew where he was going—*straight to the bedroom, maybe?* He was wearing shorts, a T-shirt, Adidas sneakers, nothing like I'd imagined. For some reason in my befuddled mind, Maximillian Adam wore a suit and tie. He did not wear casual clothes that made him look as if he was walking down a beach on holiday and any second now about to peel his clothes off to dive into the sea . . . (*or into someone's bed*). He got closer to me, still closer, and then something peculiar happened. He pulled his sunglasses off and I saw his eyes.

My breath stuck in my throat. I forgot how to breathe entirely for a moment as I locked eyes with him.

I stumbled backwards. "What the—the . . . what?" I'd lost all words.

The hair was totally different! His physique was nothing vaguely like it had been! The face had become more masculine, beard hiding the lines and shapes of the jaw, but those eyes. Those icy blue eyes. I would recognize those eyes anywhere, because I had stared into those eyes for years and those were the eyes that had made regular, and I must say very unwanted, appearances in my dreams too. He was still walking towards me. The boy, now turned very much man, who had broken my heart and sent me into a cursed downward sexual spiral, was walking towards me with those unmistakable eyes. I had no idea what was going on, what to make of it all, and what I was supposed to do, and then he was standing right in front of me. And if there had been the slightest doubt in my mind, it was all gone.

It was him.

I managed a garbled, "What the . . . fuck? Fuck!" before the unimaginable happened. The unimaginable that sent me right back in time fifteen years ago. I stepped backwards, trying to move away from Logan, but the general shock of the moment had me shaking and my knee simply buckled under me. I felt myself falling backwards, and in that slow-motion fall, I imagined how painful it would be to hit my head on the tarmac. As I was contemplating this, something tightened round my wrist. As if a time-machine had been turned on, I was in the corridor at school all over again, the new boy catching me as I almost fell to the floor. The cute new boy grabbing me by the wrist, hoisting me up until we were face to face, eyes locked and falling in love at first sight as we disappeared into each other's gazes.

He pulled me up. The tarmac was getting further away, but he was getting closer. *No, this was not happening. I refused to let this happen.* Not this time.

I pulled my arm from his tight grip, yanking it free with such force that my whole body began to fall. And now it was my face that was rushing towards the tarmac.

This was really, *really* going to hurt. But then I felt two big hands round my waist and my whole body stopped falling. My heart was thrashing inside my chest, adrenalin pumping so hard that it took me a few seconds to realize that I was now suspended, in a dangling position. My fingertips were touching the tarmac—it was all very reminiscent of a few nights ago, when I'd found myself dangling from a chair.

"Shit," I hissed under my breath, and looked backwards over my shoulder. I knew exactly what kind of position I was in and what view I was currently presenting. It was all very doggy-style-esque, only this time the man whose groin was pressed into my ass was my ex-boyfriend. I stood up as fast as I could, my back smashing into what felt like a solid wall. It was his chest. I froze.

"You okay?" His mouth was so, so close to my ear. Too close. Our bodies were pressed up against each other in the most intimate way possible, his hands still on my waist. This was exactly what I'd been trying to avoid with all my stepping and pulling—and look where it had landed me. Right back to thirteen years ago.

Oh God, he smelled good.

"Ash, are you okay?" he asked again.

"L . . . L . . . Logan?" I heard myself say.

"Hello, Ash."

I looked down at my waist. His hands had grown. His fingers wrapped round me so completely and I . . . I . . .

"Get your hands off me!" I pushed myself away and then swung round to face him. And this time I found the words.

"What the fuck are you doing here?"

He smiled at me. And despite how much he'd changed in other ways, I recognized that smile. It was slightly obscured by the beard, but it was the same. That little lopsided smile I used to tease him playfully about. The one that gave him a deeper dimple in his left cheek than his right, which I'd thought was the cutest thing in the entire world. Those dimples had once made him cute and boyish, but now they were gone, covered by that beard and there was no longer anything cute and boyish about this man standing in front of me.

"What are you doing here?" I whipped my head around, frantically looking for Max. Where was he and why, *oh why the hell*, was my ex-boyfriend here?

"Are you looking for Max?" he asked, his voice familiar. Deeper now, but something about the rhythm and pacing of his words was the same.

"How do you know him?" I reached down and squeezed my waist. Hard. Hoping I would squeeze away the feeling of his hands there, which seemed to be lingering like an echo that would not stop repeating.

He looked down momentarily and his hair—fuck, he had great hair, the kind of hair a woman wants to grab hold of—tumbled into his face. And then he looked up again and locked eyes with me. "*Icy blue meeting warm chocolate*." Cheesy and nonsensical, but that's what we used to say. And now here he was, looking at me in the exact same way he'd looked at me when he'd first caught me at school all those years ago. But that was an entire lifetime ago.

"I'm Max," he said softly, his smile nowhere to be seen now.

"No. You're not. I've been speaking to Max for nearly a month now. Not you. What the hell is going on here? I don't understand."

"You've been speaking to me."

"No, I haven't. Your name is Logan M. McAdamson Junior. Not Maximillian Adam—" I stopped and blinked in confusion.

"I dropped the Mc and used my middle name, sort of."

"Your middle name is Maximus."

He smiled at me. "You remember how much I hated that, and how you teased me that it sounded like a pompous old guy's name."

I shook my head vigorously. "I still don't understand what's happening here, Logan."

"I'll explain it all to you, but we do have to go now." He pointed to the plane, and I'd almost forgotten that we were meant to be going anywhere.

Then something hit me as I eyed him up and down, looking so cool, calm and collected. "Why don't you look shocked to see me?" I paused and let the implications of that sink in. "Wait, you knew you were going to see me?"

He nodded.

"You knew who I was this entire time?"

"No, not this entire time, but when you told me your real name and sent me your ID."

"That was two whole days ago!" I stared at him in absolute shock.

"And trust me, two days ago I was just as shocked as you are."

"You've known for two days and you didn't tell me?"

"I'll explain it all to you when we're on the plane."

I shook my head. "No. Explain it to me now. I need to know what's going on here. I explained my name to you, so why are you no longer Logan Maximus McAdamson Junior?"

"Because I didn't want to be Logan Maximus McAdamson Junior anymore after my dad had an affair and left my mom and decided he no longer wanted his existing kids either. That's why I changed my name."

"Oh." I was totally taken aback by this response. It had not been at all what I was expecting. "Fine. Okay. Sorry. But still, you should have said something the second you knew it was me."

"I know I should have."

"So why didn't you?"

"Would we be standing on this runway right now if I'd told you? Things didn't exactly end well between us . . ."

I scoffed, shock beginning to give way to anger now. "End well? Are you serious? They didn't end at all—you just disappeared. I haven't seen or heard from you in thirteen years, and now here you are standing in front of me with a different name and . . . Oh God . . ." I put my hands over my eyes as if trying to make him disappear again. "We've been, you and I . . ." I couldn't get the words out they were so utterly horrifying.

"Flirting," he said matter-of-factly, and I took my hands off my eyes and looked at him again.

"Did you know it was me when you were being all flirty and suggesting semi-something-cheese dates?" I asked.

"You were flirty back."

"That's not the point. I didn't know who you were."

"I only found out who you were two days ago, I swear." He took a step, a stride, closer to me. He looked stern and serious and, damn, so damn sexy. "I honestly had no idea who you were until you sent me your ID. I'm not lying."

He wasn't lying, I knew what he looked like when he was lying and I kind of hated that. I hated that I knew this stranger standing in front of me so well that I could tell whether or not he was lying.

"God!" I exclaimed, and squeezed my waist again. Why did I still feel his hands there? I walked round in a small, tight circle, shaking my head, because I didn't know what else to do.

"Sorry, is there some kind of problem here?" the pilot asked. I swung round and glared at him too.

"You could say that," I said to the pilot, stopping my second circle.

"What's the problem?"

I looked around—why, I don't know. Maybe looking to pull some kind of sense of all this from the world around me. But the tarmac and the sky and the bird pecking on the grass were not going to give me any answers that would help my mind sort through this bizarre moment.

"We really need to get going," the pilot said.

I bit my lip and nodded once. Then nodded twice, three times. Each nod an attempt to spur me on.

"Ash, come on. We can talk about this all on the plane," said Logan. The way he said my name, Ash, was exactly like he used to say it and I did not know how to feel about it. No, actually I did. Angry. That's how I felt.

"Now you want to talk?" My voice came out loudly enough for the pilot to hear. I didn't care. "Last time I wanted to talk, you just vanished. And now, more than a decade later, you want to talk!"

"I'm not the same kid who didn't want to talk to you then."

"Clearly." I ran my eyes over him. He was no longer a kid. The man in front of me didn't have one vaguely kiddish thing about him. He was all man, and I was all anger.

The pilot cleared his throat in that uncomfortable way a person does when they know they shouldn't be listening to what's going on. "I hate to break up this . . . reunion, but we really do need to get going."

"Ash," he implored me in a soft, soothing voice and I rolled my eyes. I didn't want his soothing tones right now. They were having the opposite effect on me. I found everything about this situation, and about him, as soothing as an annual cervical smear test. I took a deep breath and closed my eyes. I must have looked a little deranged right now as I inhaled slowly, held for three counts, and then exhaled for six.

I was a professional. I had a job to do. A very important job. So clearly I was getting on a plane with whoever the hell this guy was. I opened my eyes and looked at the pilot, giving him a big smile.

"Lead the way," I said to the man and walked after him as confidently as I could, despite the very less than ideal situation.

CHAPTER 14

Max

"Is it normal for the plane to bounce like this?" Ash called over to the pilot.

"Perfectly normal," the pilot yelled back. The plane was so small inside that Ash and I were pressed up against each other. I didn't mind the close proximity. On the contrary, being this close to her felt right.

Ash, on the other hand, was a different story. It was clear she was trying to lean as far away from me as possible and every now and then she would swivel her head round, look me up and down, shoot me a very displeased grimace while shaking her head, and looking away again.

"I get the sense you want to say something to me," I said when she turned and glared at me for the fourth time.

"I just don't get it. Any of it. I don't understand."

"What do you want to know? Ask me. I'm an open book."

"Open boo—Oh please. There is nothing open about you or your book. You lied to me for two days, pretending to be someone you're not. What the hell was even real?"

"I wasn't pretending. Everything I said to you was real."

"And where the hell have you been?" An accumulation of years and years of frustration was plastered across her face. And I could also see hurt. I hated that I'd hurt her. "One minute you were there, and the next you were gone. Your mom said you just went to

Scotland to visit your uncle. And then you went to backpack around Europe. Europe is a big fucking place."

"I did go and spend some time with my uncle. You'll remember he had invited me on holiday, but I wasn't going to go because you and I were meant to go on holiday together."

"How can I forget?" She looked away from me, her shoulders drooping slightly. "We were meant to do that long road trip together. I'd spent weeks planning it all, and . . . and . . ." She shook her head. "I mean, you just . . . You were gone."

"I know." Shame and guilt and sadness and pain hit me in the chest. It was unbearable seeing her like this.

"Where have you been, seriously? I need to know." I thought I heard something in her voice crack, but she quickly cleared her throat, sat up straighter, and turned her gaze on me again. She wore a mask of bravado on her face, but I could see underneath it.

"I was with my uncle for a while, and then I backpacked around Europe for a year or so, and then landed up settling down in Greece. I've been there for the past eleven years."

"Settling down in Greece. What does that even mean?" She gasped and slapped her hands over her mouth. "*Settled down.* Do you have a wife? And kids?" She looked down at my hands, and I wiggled my ringless finger at her. "Please don't tell me you're a married man who's flirting with a work colleague, because that would make this even—"

"No. Not married. No kids," I cut her off quickly. "I just mean I lived there."

"So why are you not living there anymore?" she asked.

"My mom is sick. Dementia. I came back to look after her." As I said it, my stomach plunged. My stomach always plunges when I'm forced to say it out loud to someone. I could almost handle saying it in my head, but hearing the actual words spoken out loud made it worse somehow. I thought I saw her face soften for a second there.

"I'm sorry to hear that. I always liked your mom." For a few seconds, she looked at me the way she used to and another kind of feeling filled me. "Even so, what you did wasn't right! There's no excuse for it."

"I'm not using my mother's illness as an excuse."

"Then what the hell is your excuse for lying to me?"

"I didn't know how to tell you. After . . . what happened between us. I didn't know how you would react to seeing me after all these years, and with all the things hanging over us and . . . with how it ended."

"How it ended?" she scoffed loudly. "Well, that's the thing! It hasn't exactly ended for me. In fact, that night is still *veeery* much hanging over me today. But I'm glad it ended for you, though."

"What do you mean it hasn't ended?" I asked.

"Nothing, I mean nothing."

"Clearly you mean something."

She shook her head and for a second I saw sadness flash across her face and my chest tightened. In the last twenty minutes of being in this plane together, she had made me feel more than anyone had made me feel in the last thirteen years.

"Are you really sure it should be bouncing like this?" she called again over the noise of the plane, after a particularly large turbulent bump that even I had not enjoyed. To be honest, when the lodge had said it was sending its own plane, I had imagined something a little bigger. It was fine for me—I'd been in plenty of small planes over the years, flying to remote locations and islands to look at properties— but I knew Ash didn't like bouncing. It made her feel sick. Not to mention flying. In fact, she didn't like anything that made her feel out of control and unsafe. While we'd been together, we were never able to go on roller coasters, too high and too dangerous. I always had to drive at least ten kilometers under the speed limit. Heights were out. At school, she'd refused point blank to do the tall obstacle course. I suddenly remembered the time she'd clung to me for a full two hours on a flight. Face buried in my chest, me stroking her hair, assuring her we would not plummet from the sky, kissing the top of her head . . .

"Is there no way of making it bounce less?" she shouted again.

"Here," I said, passing her a pack of mint gum. She looked down at my hand with an expression that screamed "I'm not taking anything from you."

"I know that peppermint helps with your nausea," I said softly, hoping she would consider taking it now.

"You remember that?" she asked, taking the gum from my hand in an awkward movement, which I had to assume was an attempt *not* to touch me.

"I remember a lot of things," I replied. *Even though I've tried to forget them.*

I remembered how it felt to hold her. How it felt to kiss her. I remembered how beautiful she'd looked that night, and how incredible she'd smelled. She always wore the same perfume, but that night there had been something else on her skin. Something so intoxicating. I'd never quite figured out what that scent was. All I knew was that it was my favorite smell.

"Hhmmf." She ripped the gum open and popped one into her mouth, chewing frantically. Then she stopped chewing and looked down at it. "You don't like chewing gum. You used to say it hurt your jaw."

"Still don't like it." I knew where she was going with this, so decided to save her from having to ask. "But I thought you might need it. The mint and, also, you always said you liked chewing, that it distracted you. Especially when you were anxious."

Silence slipped its way in between us. By this stage, Ash was not looking good. Her face was devoid of any color; she was a strange ash-white hue.

I leaned forwards and looked at her. "You okay?"

She pursed her lips together and shook her head vigorously.

I looked at the seat pocket in front of me. I knew exactly what she needed. I'd seen that look on her face before. I found the sick bag and handed it to her. She looked panicked. Clammy and sick and desperate. Fuck, I didn't like that.

"What can I do?" I asked.

"You've done enough," she said through a clenched jaw.

"Looks like we're about to hit some turbulence, so tighten those seatbelts," the pilot said.

"WHAT?" Ash shouted. "But we *are* in turbulence."

"It won't be for too long—we're flying round a storm."

"A STORM!"

"Don't worry. It's perfectly normal."

"Normal?" Her eyes widened, and she looked out the window in horror at the darkening clouds. The pilot banked the plane to the left without much warning, sending the already shaken Ash into my lap.

"Get off me!" She pushed herself up, only to fall back down as the plane continued its angular bank.

"I'm not on you. You're on me!" I replied as she pushed herself up again.

"Well, I didn't do it deliberately!" she protested.

"Oh, trust me, I know that." I couldn't help smiling at this, which I knew was the wrong thing to do, because it immediately elicited a scowl from her. But the scowl was quickly replaced by a look of sheer, panicked sickness as the turbulence got rougher still.

"Shit, shit!" Ash gripped the seat and the color in her face went from ash-white to a strange shade of sickly green.

I quickly opened the sick bag in her hands and maneuvered it to her mouth just as she . . .

I wished I could have reached out and pushed her hair out of her face. Rubbed her back even. But I just waited for it to be over. And when it was, I pulled some tissues out of my bag and passed them over. She wiped the corners of her mouth and color started returning to her cheeks.

"Feeling better?" I asked softly.

"Feeling embarrassed," she whispered.

"Don't be. I sort of did that to you once, so I guess you could say we're even."

Her head whipped round and she glared at me. Any sign of previous sickness was gone.

"Too soon to be joking about that?" I asked.

"Way, way too soon. If you knew what I've had to endure the last thirteen years, you would know that there isn't a parallel universe out there where joking about that would ever be acceptable." She said this so emphatically that it took my breath away. I stared at her, trying to figure out what the hell that meant.

"Ash, what do you mean by that?" I asked tentatively, but she looked away. She gave me a shoulder shrug, followed by a "nothing" that I knew was actually a "something", but I didn't press. I left it there, even though I had so, so many questions.

CHAPTER 15

Ash

The lodge and its surrounds were so breathtakingly gorgeous that I momentarily forgot how awful it had been getting here and with whom I'd come here. This is exactly what Sebastian had pictured in his treatment. I'd never seen a landscape like this before, never seen so many massive boulders rising up out of the ground. Some balanced on each other in shapes that were hard to imagine had been created naturally. It looked as if giants had once roamed this land and made these enormous granite boulder sculptures themselves. And their colors! Rust-colored boulders stood vertically out of green foliage made even greener by the contrasting colors. And as for the light!

The natural light was magnificent, the way it caught the boulders, highlighting slivers of them, as if someone had run a bright orange highlighter over parts of them. These rocks looked as if they had been standing here, presiding over this land, since the very dawn of time itself.

I rushed over to my bag and pulled my camera out. I looked at my watch. The sun was lower in the sky and the light was changing from cool, to warm. It drenched the fluffy tops of the wild grasses in a golden glow, shining through the branches of the iconic acacias, casting puddles of bronze and orange on the floor. I fiddled with the settings on my camera and Max/Logan/whoever was forgotten as I became swept up in all the things I loved most: light, shadows, and the interplay between them. The way in which when light falls across an object, it totally transforms it. The way it enhances drama, creates a sense of mystery, and the way it decides to show us things, sometimes whole things, and sometimes only tiny parts of things. It reveals to us what it wants to show. It is the great conductor of all we see and don't see.

I took out my shot list and started working my way through it, taking notes as I went and filming the shots as I saw them playing out. Doing them from various angles and sides, trying to work out how best to tell this story using the light and camera moves. A lot of time must have passed while I'd been busy, because the light changed completely and soon it was twilight and I could no longer work. As I started walking back to the villa, reality crashed in again. I'd been able to keep it at bay with my work, but now it was back and I realized a few things: I was here in a remote place with my ex-boyfriend who had a different name and was rumored to be a sex god, and who had held a sick bag open for me—*mortifying*. I was desperate to tell my friends what had happened, but even more desperate to pee.

It felt as if the outside of the villa flowed effortlessly into the inside. Everything was a rich, rust color, like the boulders themselves. Natural woods and materials had been used in all the furnishings and decorating. Old tree branches were the banisters of the stairs and the chandeliers were made from untreated leather and grasses. In every corner, the outside had been brought in, feathers and small rocks in bowls on the table, interesting twigs in vases and woven baskets and rugs. The place was also huge and I realized I didn't know where to go.

"Hi," I said when I found someone.

"Welcome," the man replied. "I didn't introduce myself to you earlier—you looked busy. I'm William, I'll be your host and ranger while you're here. Anything you need, just ask."

"Thank you, that's very kind. Where's my room?"

"Let me show you where you'll be staying." William picked up my gear and walked towards one of the two staircases. "So this villa has four rooms, and you are definitely staying in the nicest one."

"Ooh, thanks. I'm excited."

"It's our pleasure to have you staying with us. We're very excited that an advert is being shot at our lodge."

I smiled at the man. If he knew how that process really worked, from pre-production to post, he would probably not think it was as exciting as he did.

"And this is your room." He opened the doors with the kind of flourish that the room deserved, because it was possibly the most incredible room I'd ever been in before. It wasn't the ridiculously comfortable fourposter bed made of tree branches, or the massive balcony with views for days, it wasn't even the fact that the couches were the kind you could sink into and live in for the rest of your life—it was all about the bath.

"Dinner will be at seven thirty," the man said somewhere behind me. I almost didn't hear him, as I stood and stared at the bath, imagining the imminent and very delicious full-body submersion. It was a freestanding copper bath, but that wasn't what made this maybe one of the best baths on the planet. What made it amazing, was the view from it. From inside the bath, you could see out across the national park, the rugged terrain of acacias and boulders all drenched in the orange of the setting sun. It was perched at the end of the room, and with the balcony doors open like this it seemed as if it was outside, floating on the edge of the world. I turned on the taps and headed to the toilet for the long put-off pee.

Ash: Hey guys, I'm safe and landed in Zimbabwe. I'm at the lodge. Omg it is gorgeous—we should definitely do a friend weekend here.

Before I could even start the message in which I explained to them what was going on, they started flooding me with requests for pictures and questions about the flight and weather. I didn't let that distract me as I focused on typing the message, while simultaneously having the longest pee of my life.

Ash: I don't even know how to start or what to say, because never in a million years did I think I would ever be writing this to anyone. So, I met Max at the airport, only it's not Max at all. In fact, Max is actually none other than the sex hex himself, Logan. He says he changed his name nine years ago when his parents got divorced, because his father was also Logan McAdamsom—which I believe. But the thing is, I have been speaking to Maximillian Adam for almost a month and this entire time it was Logan. This whole thing is so bizarre! I'm away with my ex-boyfriend who cursed me and then disappeared, but also away with some guy called Maximillian Adam who looks nothing like the boy I used to know, and is some wildly successful businessman who lived in Greece and now looks like a fucking Greek god himself and I actually hate that he is so good-looking. So there you have it. What do you have to say about that?

There was a moment of silence as they read the message. I took the opportunity to take in a long, slow, deep breath because I knew we were about to plunge into chaos. Sarah was of course the first one who replied.

Sarah: AND YOU GUYS WERE FLIRTING WITH EACH OTHER!!!
Ash: I KNOW!
Ash: I feel sick to my stomach.
Yo: Wait, back up, I'm confused. What exactly are you saying?
Charlie: What she's saying is that she has just been cast in her very own real, like, theatre of the fucking absurd.
Ash: Absurd is right!
Sarah: What the actual F!
Sarah: Max is actually Logan?
Sarah: And now you are away with him???

Sarah: This is insane.

Ash: I know.

Charlie: God, are you okay, Ash? I think I would be freaking out.

Melusi: Who's freaking out? What's going on?

Ash: Max is Logan. My ex-boyfriend. And I am away with him.

Melusi: I'm confused. Looks like I need to go back and read the whole conversation.

Ash: Honestly, I don't know how I feel. I don't know whether I'm more shocked, or angry.

Sarah: I would be so pissed that he lied to me this entire time.

Ash: He said he only found out two days ago when I sent my ID to him.

Sarah: Do you believe him?

Ash: I do actually.

Melusi: WHAT THE FUCK!

Yo: Welcome to the convo.

Melusi: This is crazy.

Melusi: What's he like now? What does he look like?

Ash: Oh my God, he is gorgeous. Which I obviously hate. He looks nothing like he used to. I only recognized him by his eyes. He's still as tall as he was, obviously, but he's filled out with muscles everywhere. His hair is longer, he has a beard, but a really sexy one, and he seems so confident and self-assured.

Melusi: God, don't you hate it when that happens. Your ex turns out hot!

Charlie: It's the worst. And so inconvenient, given the bizarre circumstances.

Yo: Wait . . . you guys are missing something here.

Yo: Something HUGE!

Yo: So all those stories we heard about Max, were actually about Logan?

Charlie: God. Yes. I didn't think of that.

Sarah: How could you have forgotten the squirting orgasms?

Ash: I find that so hard to believe, given my experience with him. Those stories could not be about him, could they?

Sarah: It's been thirteen years—if he's changed so much in other ways, maybe he's changed in the bedroom too!

Ash: This is the man who blew air on my vagina!

Russ: Whoa! I just joined this and the first word I see is vagina.

Melusi: I suggest going back to the beginning of this conversation! Trust me. You're going to need to.

Sarah: I can't believe it. We were just talking about him the other night. We never talk about him and now here he is!

Ash: It's so bizarre.

Yo: Or . . .

Ash: What? Why are there dots there?

I waited for a response that was not coming. I started to get a strange little feeling inside.

Ash: WHAT?

Yo: You remember what that psychic said. She said go back to the source to undo the curse.

Ash: Please don't say another word.

Yo: You're at the source! And how bizarre is it that we were all teasing you about having sex with Max to break the curse, and now Max turns out to be Logan and Logan is the source! It's like the entire universe is in retrograde or something. Because something very weird is going on.

Russ: WHAT THE HELL!

Charlie: Welcome to the convo.

Russ: This is insane!

Ash: But what's more insane is Yo thinking this actually all means something deep and spiritual.

Charlie: Maybe it does.

Ash: Not you too.

Melusi: I'm also leaning towards the universe here.

Yo: You need to have sex with him!

Ash: WHAT!

Ash: Stop it. Immediately.

Melusi: I'm leaning towards sex too.

Frank: Who's having sex?

Melusi: Go back and read the convo!!

Sarah: I'm kind of agreeing with everyone here.

Ash: Nope. No! And this is the last thing I want to say on this matter.

Ash: If Logan was the last man on this planet, I would not have sex with him. I am not having sex with Logan McAdamson! End of story!

Melusi: What about having sex with Maximillian Adam?

Ash: Same goes for him.

Ash: In fact, same goes for every man on the planet. Because I am on a dating detox! Which everyone seems to forget.

Yo: I thought you quit that.

Sarah: Me too?

Ash: That was before I found out Max was Logan. So as of now the detox is still very much detoxing! And now I am going to bath!

Frank: What the FUCK?

I tossed my phone on the bed, lay down and looked at the ceiling. I tried to relax, but the incessant beeping from the WhatsApp group was going insane. I decided to mute it for a few hours, but not before seeing one of the messages on the screen.

Melusi: Well, let's hope he realizes this time that it's suck, not blow.

They were clearly still discussing the prospect of me having sex with him, even in my absence. God, we shared everything. I'd once been to a therapist to try to deal with all the trauma from my childhood, and she'd asked me what support system I had now, and to describe it. After I had, she'd proceeded to tell me that it was clear we were all co-dependent and we needed to set more boundaries with each other, because it wasn't healthy and . . . I'd stopped going to her that day.

Sure, we were total oversharers, but when you study something so creative and personal together, like film, you develop very deep bonds. Trust me. Staying in a tiny caravan with five other students and having to all sleep together under one blanket to keep warm because you're shooting your extremely low-budget student film in the middle of winter in the middle of nowhere means that oversharing stops being a thing. But my friends were very wrong about one thing. I was not going to be having sex with Logan, Max, whatever he was. The detox was very firmly in place.

I needed this dating detox, *a serious one*. No men, no sex, nothing even vaguely flirty and romantic. It always ended badly: if it wasn't men saying crude things to me in cinemas, or ending dates before they'd even started, it was things like me being bitten on the hand by a troop of fire ants (because in college I'd thought it a good idea to have sex with this gorgeous entomology student that I'd fancied for a whole two semesters in their lab, and while up on the counter, my legs wrapped around him, raring to go, I'd accidentally put my hand into the ant enclosure). And maybe worst of all, worse than all those things, it was me flirting with a guy who I'd really felt a connection with only to find out that he was none other than my ex-boyfriend. The same person who'd shattered me as a human so badly that it had taken me forever to put myself back together again! And who may or may not have cast an actual sex curse on me. And who may or may not own bloody llamas.

CHAPTER 16

Max

I suspect the dinner turned out the way it did because when I'd seen the huge flat rock the manager had shown me, I'd told him how I could imagine this as a great setting for a romantic picnic, or engagement shoot. I'd then mentioned that I was actually just briefed by a client, a major international jewelry brand, to find the perfect location for an advert for their latest range of very high-end engagement rings and that this might be an option I could present to them. Perhaps that's why management had gone so overboard with the dinner set-up I was now faced with.

"What is this?" I turned to see Ash standing at the bottom of the boulder, looking up at me in horror. It was evening, but we were in the grip of a heatwave, and the external heat just contributed to the internal heat I felt looking at her.

"Dinner," I said.

"I can see that, but why is it here? Why are there hundreds of candles and fairy lights in the trees, and champagne, and picnic blankets, on a giant boulder in the middle of one of the most beautiful places on earth?"

I shrugged. "I think they're trying to show me the kinds of unique selling points this place has to offer."

"It's very . . ." Ash looked around nervously. I knew her facial expressions so well.

"Very what?" I pushed.

"Romantic," she said with such disdain in her voice that it bordered on disgust.

"I guess it is rather romantic."

"Oh, please, Logan, anyone can see this is romantic. You don't even need to have your eyes open to know this is romantic. Just listen to the bloody music they're playing in the background. Where is the speaker even? No one plays background music like this if they are not trying to set a romantic mood."

"I suppose they have gone to great lengths setting this up for us," I said, trying to downplay the romance of it all. I could see that the last thing on earth Ash wanted was to be sitting with me on a beautiful flat boulder under the African sky surrounded by candlelight.

"Someone has painstakingly twirled thousands of fairy lights through the branches of a giant thorn tree! Not to mention the fact that the candles are placed in a heart shape."

"Are they? I hadn't noticed," I said innocently, still trying, once again, to downplay the very obvious romance of it all.

"Yes, they very much are!" She put her left hand on her hip and I tried to stop a smile. She still did that. She'd always done that when she was being angry or bossy. I'd watched her do that all through high school and she was still doing it thirteen years later. Some things clearly didn't change.

"This is all too, too . . ." She waved her arm around and I could see her searching for the words. "Too much. I've had a long day, a fucking bizarre day and I'm exhausted and boiling hot and I can't get cool and you cannot be standing there with heart-shaped petals and that many candles. I'm not having it."

"Not having what?" I asked, feeling a little lost.

"We haven't seen each other in thirteen years and now what? We're supposed to sit here and enjoy what is clearly an overtly romantic dinner together after everything that happened between us? It's so bizarre. God, this might actually be the most bizarre day of my life."

"It is bizarre," I echoed. "But I do have really good cheese."

"Please don't tell me you planned this whole thing?"

"No, I didn't, but I did ask the lodge to get some cheese for us, as per our previous conversations. If you remember what we talked about . . ." I paused and watched her face carefully before I said the next thing. I wanted to gauge if there were going to be any . . . "*Possibilities*." The second the word left my mouth her entire face changed. She straightened up and when she spoke again, looked flustered.

"Well, there is now officially zero—*zero*—possibility of any possibilities. Ever."

"So there were possibilities before?" I asked quickly.

"Before I knew it was you, maybe," she said, shaking her head at me. "I still cannot believe you continued to flirt with me when you knew who I was and then had the audacity to *still* ask me on a, what did you call it, 'semi-professional work date'?" She used air quotes on the word I do admit to using rather loosely. "You couldn't have possibly been serious, Logan!"

I shrugged. "I mean . . . *maybe*."

"*Maybe*? Are you serious? After everything that happened between us and all the time that's passed, you seriously thought I would have a semi-professional cheese date with you when I found out who you were?"

"I was hoping the cheese might win you over.

She shook her head aggressively now. "I don't get it. Thirteen years ago you clearly wanted nothing to do with me to the point of disappearing. You disappeared off the face of the planet. And now you've suddenly reanimated out of thin air and you want a '*maybe*'?"

"Maybe I do."

"Stop saying maybe! You don't get to have 'maybes' or 'possibilities,' Log—" She stopped herself and ran her hand through her short hair.

"Max. Your name is Max. And that is so fucking weird too. It's all weird."

"I know. But we were getting on really well while emailing—you have to at least admit that."

"If I'd known who you were, I would never have let that conversation go the way it did."

"I think it went that way naturally," I pointed out, and I nearly said, "*And I thought that meant something*," but didn't.

I watched her for a while before speaking again. The warm light from the candles and fairy lights illuminated her face. God, she was still so sexy. Her dark hair brought out the color of her eyes, accentuated her features, and drew my eyes to that soft curve of her neck. The shape of her body was still the same, although she had filled out in places in the sexiest way possible. She'd had the body of a girl before. Now she was all woman.

"What?" she asked.

"You look . . ." I paused. Beautiful, perfect, amazing. I could travel the entire world twice looking for the most beautiful woman and it would be a total waste of time because she was standing right in front of me . . . "Different." I could have kicked myself at that, because her face scrunched up in clear confusion. Of all the things I could have said, that had not even been on the long list.

"That was a compliment, by the way, just in case you thought it wasn't," I quickly qualified.

"You look different too," she said. But hers did not sound like a compliment. She looked around at all the decorations. I could see she was frantically weighing something up in her mind. She was frantically fanning herself with her hand too. The weighing came to an end and she delivered her verdict. "I think I'll ask them to bring my dinner to my room. This is way too weirdly romantic and I have officially given up on romance, so this would be like a romance relapse." She began turning.

"What do you mean *a romance relapse*?" I asked, but before she could answer she walked straight into the manager holding two champagne glasses.

"Oh my God, sorry, I—" She fell backwards into a seated position on the smooth boulder and then began slipping gently down it as if on a slide. I tried not to laugh as I watched her head disappear. I walked to the edge of the boulder and looked down. The man with the champagne looked panic-stricken and was busy looking for a place to put the champagne. I jumped off the boulder and walked up to her. She was still in a seated position.

"Well, that was . . ." I started, unable to conceal my smile, but stopped immediately when she shot me a look over her shoulder. "Sorry, did it hurt?"

"Not physically." She stood up, sweeping the debris off the back of her shorts. I wish she hadn't done that, because now my eyes were fixated on a part of her that they really should not have been.

"I am so sorry about that," the manager said, running back over.

"Not a problem—that was me. I seem to be falling a lot lately." She looked over at me and I tried to quickly avert my gaze from her ass.

"Hey!" she scolded, clicking her fingers at me. "I know that look. Stop it, immediately. And now I'll definitely be taking my dinner in my room, thanks," she said.

"Are you not feeling well?" the manager asked.

"I'm fine, thank you," she said.

"Do you not like it out here? We could move it all inside if you like, or onto the balcony?"

I watched her tense shoulders slump and she shook her head. Ash was the kind of person who would never hurt someone's feelings. She was the kind of person who went out of her way to make sure everyone around her was okay, and she had this way of making everyone around her feel good. She would give someone the shirt off her back.

"No, please don't move anything. It's absolutely gorgeous. You guys have done a great job." She dazzled the man with a smile. She had the greatest smile. A smile you could disappear into for days. It had always been her best feature. I hadn't seen that smile in thirteen years, and I hadn't realized how much I'd missed it. But it wasn't for me this time.

The man smiled back at her and then went to fetch the champagne glasses he'd balanced on a tree stump.

Ash looked down at the champagne with suspicion, and then looked back at me. I knew what she was thinking—the champagne had been part of the problem last time.

"Maybe we could ask for wine?" I said, a small smile playing at the corner of my mouth.

"Stop joking about it." When she took the glasses from the manager, he excused himself, and I became acutely aware that the two of us were alone again. Ash took a sip of champagne and then turned round and glared at me.

"You were looking at my ass," she said after swallowing.

"Only to make sure it was okay," I replied quickly.

She looked at me oddly and ran her free hand through her hair again.

"It looks good," I added, and her eyes widened in shock. "Your hair! Your hair I mean, not your ass, which, uh also . . ." I closed my mouth before I finished that sentence. "It always knotted when it was long. I used to have to brush it for you."

"Did you? I don't remember that." She took another sip of her champagne and looked away from me quickly. Of course she remembered. She pressed the cool glass of champagne to her neck, then held it against her forehead.

"You know what . . ." I jumped into action. "I'm going to blow these candles out. And we don't need these petals either." I picked up the petal heart off the picnic rug and scattered them randomly on the rock, then I went to work on all the millions of candles. God, there were a lot, and halfway through I was starting to regret my decision, but I carried on until the giant heart-shaped ring of candle lights was gone. I finally stood up and looked at her. "I'm not going to take the fairy lights down if you don't mind, thorns and all, but there," I gestured to the rock, "it's less romantic now."

She eyed me incredulously.

"Look, you need food. I need food. There's food here. Not to mention an ice bucket full of cool, cool, frozen cubes of water."

She hesitated, her expression visibly scrunching into a very familiar look. I'd forgotten how expressive her face was. She always had these large and visceral reactions to things and was never able to hide what she was feeling and thinking . . . which had made that night thirteen years ago so, so, so much worse. *I'd known exactly what she'd been thinking.*

"There's a French Camembert in the basket too." I pointed at the picnic basket. Her hesitation looked as if it might waver, and I had yet another trick up my sleeve.

"It's from Normandy." She tried to hide the little light that had switched on in those huge eyes of hers, but I could see it.

"Camembert de Normandie?" she asked.

"Yup. Real Norman cows."

"When did you become such a cheese connoisseur?" she asked.

"I could ask you the same question," I replied.

"You tell me first." She took another sip of her champagne and her eyes met mine. A flipping sensation took place in my chest. I'd forgotten how I used to feel when she looked at me. I ran my hand through my hair quickly, nervously.

Not entirely true.

I hadn't really forgotten; I'd just tried really hard to forget.

"In Italy. My love of cheese. That's where it first started," I said quickly, trying to forget again.

"So you were in Italy, then?" Her tone was icy.

"And Germany, Holland and then Greece obviously."

"Sounds like you had quite a lot of fun." Her sharp words came at me like daggers.

"Not really," I said empathically, and we looked at each other for a while again. There was so much between us. Thirteen years of unspoken words piled between us like Everest. But tonight did not feel like the right time to try to summit that beast of a mountain. I could see she was tired—I was tired—and we both needed to eat.

"I'm starting to feel like I could eat my own arm," I said, trying to lighten the mood and steer the conversation back towards the more mundane.

She accepted the offering and nodded. "Me too."

"Let's just sit and eat," I appealed to her, and moved towards the picnic blanket. She let out a loud, resigned sigh. "Forget the fairy lights and the . . ." I craned to listen. "Are they playing Marvin Gaye?"

She nodded. "'Let's Get It On,' to be exact."

"They really are pushing the romance," I said, amused because that was probably the last song I would play if I was trying to conjure up romance.

"Fine, I'll sit, and I'll eat, but don't think this means I'm not still angry you concealed your identity from me. And for the record, just because there are candles and petals and Marvin Gaye, there is nothing, and I mean *nothing*, romantic about this. At all! Ever."

"I wouldn't dream of assuming that," I said with a smile, and then gestured for her to join me.

CHAPTER 17

Ash

I took another sip of champagne as I walked onto the boulder where Logan . . . Max, whoever was standing next to the picnic blankets that had been spread out over the rock. The blankets were scattered with large pillows. I lowered myself to the blanket, but didn't dare lean back on the pillows. I wasn't feeling that comfortable. Slouching on a picnic blanket with my ex-boyfriend felt too intimate and strange. I stuck my hand into the ice bucket and pulled out an ice cube. I put one against my neck, running it up and down and then moved it down my chest before it melted completely.

"It is beautiful here, though," I admitted, and looked up. The sky was so clear you could see the stars clumped together to form the giant arm of the Milky Way, which stretched from one side of the sky to the other like a rainbow.

"Very beautiful," he said, and something in his voice made something deep in my stomach stir. I didn't like it. I reached for another ice cube and ran it over my collarbone. He on the other hand, despite the unbearable heat and awkward situation, seemed to be as cool as a fucking cucumber, and it pissed me off.

"Do you not sweat or something?" I blurted, and he laughed.

"What do you mean?"

"Look at you." I gestured towards him. "You're sitting there looking all cool and chilled, as if none of this bothers you. The heat. And me. Us. This. How is it that you look so relaxed?"

"I guess I'm just enjoying seeing you again."

"You are?" My neck snapped, a cartoonish double take of sorts.

"I take it you're not?" He smiled at me. It seemed faint and forced.

"Honestly, I wouldn't call this the highlight of my life—that's for sure." I sipped my champagne again and watched him over the rim of my glass.

"Sorry. I wish it wasn't so tense," he said, and I couldn't quite believe my ears.

"I'm not sure how you thought us seeing each other for the first time after everything that happened would be anything other than tense."

"Didn't you ever imagine this? Us meeting again," he asked.

"Nope," I lied.

"Not once?"

"Never," I lied again.

"Well, just because you didn't doesn't mean we can't talk, right?"

"About what?" I asked.

"Well, what have you been up to the past thirteen years?" he asked casually. His strange cool casualness, his entire relaxed vibe from the first moment I'd seen him, was almost stranger than us sitting here. Since seeing him, he had shown not an ounce of shock, or reticence. He'd never looked awkward or unsettled. In fact, all I'd seen was a man who clearly exuded the kind of confidence that most people could only dream of having. I didn't know what to make of his attitude, so I stopped trying to figure it out.

"I became a cinematographer," I stated, taking another sip of the champagne. I could taste it was the good stuff, the stuff that actually came from that region of Norman cows and vineyards in the Champagne valleys. This was the epitome of romance, and I was supposed to be on a romance detox.

"I know that. But what else?"

I took another sip and scrutinized him. "Is this what we're doing? Chatting as if nothing ever happened? Old friends who've bumped into each other and now we're have a chinwag over cheese?"

"Why not?"

"Why not? I could give you fifty reasons why not . . ." I sighed. "I don't really have the energy for fifty reasons, to be honest. I'm way too hot and way too tired for this."

"Don't give me fifty reasons, then. We used to talk for hours. Do you remember that?"

"Not really." Another lie, because of course I remembered. It had been the thing I'd missed most when we'd broken up, or when he'd run away, because technically we hadn't officially broken up. We used to sit for hours, my head in his lap, him playing with my hair while I talked about absolutely nothing and everything all at once. Late-night calls tucked under our blankets, talking to each other until we began to fall asleep and then listening to each other breathe as we did. Being able to have entire silent conversations with each other in the classroom, just with our eyes and facial expressions. Telling each other our every desire, fear, and worry. Talking was the thing I'd missed most. Sure, I had Sarah and my friends, but Logan and I had talked in a different kind of way. A way that was totally unique to us and a way I had never experienced since then.

"Of course you do, Ash," he said.

"No, not really, Logan."

"I don't go by Logan anymore. It's Max," he said, through a very tensed jaw. Ha! Not so nonchalant now.

"Okay, sorry. I can try and do that, Max." The second I said it, his jaw unclenched and his shoulders relaxed.

"Thanks," he said weakly, and I could sense the genuine hurt inside. It was clear all his previous cool-calmness went away when we touched on this issue. His name, his father. I'd always been able to sense what he was feeling when we were together. I didn't like that I found myself still being able to sense it now. I shuffled around uncomfortably. There was nothing about any of this that I liked. I did not want to be sitting here and that must have shown on my face.

"You look like you're planning your escape," he said, forcing a faint smile.

"I am," I admitted.

"I'm not," he said in a voice that grabbed my attention in a way I wished it hadn't. "I'm happy to see you, Ash."

"Happy?" I scoffed. "Well, that makes one of us."

"I know. You're making that very clear."

"Well, how else do you want me to make it, Lo—Max—*God, this is so confusing*—Max! If you're happy after everything that happened, then clearly you've suffered zero consequences following our 'break-up,' unlike me. So no, I'm not happy."

"Well, I'm not taking it back. I am happy to see you and I am happy that you're also doing so well."

"Really?"

"And I'm seriously impressed too. One of South Africa's most sought-after cinematographers, multi-award-winning no less. I'm proud of you."

"I don't need you to be proud of me," I said quickly, irritated by his admission.

He smiled. "I know, but I am. I'm glad your life is going so well and—"

"You know nothing about my life," I snapped, cutting him off quickly. "You don't know me anymore and I certainly don't know you. God, I have no idea how to feel about all of this. It's so, so . . ." I searched for a better word, but all that came was . . . "Weird! It's weird that you're here, it's weird that you have another name, it's weird that you look like that"—*God, why do you have to look like that*—"and it's weird that none of this seems to be fazing you at all. In fact, it's almost like you're enjoying it." I felt compelled to stand up. "I can't do this, Lo . . . *Max!* Max. For heaven's sake." I took a deep breath to try to calm my nerves. "I can't sit here anymore. I'm going to my room!" I announced, and started walking off. But then, as if by some kind of magic, so quickly it was almost impossible, he was next to me. He reached out and his fingertips brushed my arm. I came to a complete stop and looked down at them. A feeling rose in me. A feeling I did not want rising. I shrugged my arm away and he stepped back.

"Sorry," he said, backing away. "I get it. I had two days to prepare myself to see you. You need some time."

"I think I need more than time." I started walking away again.

"What about the cheese?" he called after me. I stopped. I was embarrassed to admit that this did give me pause. In fact, it gave me more than pause.

I turned and ran back onto the boulder. Not daring to look at him, I grabbed the cheese and then made a dash for my room, almost tripping over my feet as I went.

CHAPTER 18

Max

$\mathscr{S}$he grabbed the cheese, tucked it under her arm defiantly, and then jumped off the rock before making her speedy escape. On her hurried way down the path, she pulled her shorts down a few times because they kept creeping up—something that definitely did not go unnoticed by me. She craned her neck round like an ostrich and glared at me.

"Shit," I mumbled, and then sat back down on the rock and poured myself a glass of champagne. I drank it as I stared at the villa, waiting and watching for her light to come on upstairs. When it did, I saw her silhouette for a few moments before she rushed up to the balcony, stuck her head through the door, glanced in my direction briefly and closed the curtains with a dramatic flourish. Her silhouette disappeared.

"*Shiiit!*" I moaned, and then lay back down and looked up at the stars. I was slipping into some serious trouble here. Maybe I'd already slipped and was firmly in the "serious trouble" already. I was shocked, but maybe not totally surprised, by how quickly the slipping had happened. From the moment I'd heard her name, the moment I'd seen her ID photo, to the moment I'd walked across the tarmac and stood in front of her. *Slipping, slipping, slipping . . . slipped!*

She had been back in my life for all of three days, but I could feel the resolve of the last thirteen years crumbling in front of me, and it felt as if I had zero control over the crumbling. Every second I spent in close proximity to her seemed to erase an entire year spent away from her, until it felt like I was almost right back at the very beginning. The more time I spent with her, the more I remembered why I'd been so in love with her in the first place. And when she'd run that ice cube up and down her neck and chest, I remembered why I still considered her the sexiest woman alive.

I'd tried so hard to extinguish my feelings for her by pouring all I could over the raging flames, but clearly there had been some unseen ember silently simmering away that had now set everything ablaze again. And I was sure the fire had only just began. Yup, I was slipping once again, like I'd slipped all those years ago. I still remembered the day we met with the kind of crystal-clear clarity that is only reserved for the most important moments of a person's life. The day had been cold, windy and drizzling, there was this loud, repetitive car alarm blaring in the distance and a smell of antiseptic floor wash hung in the air, not exactly designed for romance, but romance had definitely happened.

I'd just turned fifteen, tall and pimply, silver braces across my teeth, and I'd transferred in from another school. I was late for my first class and had my nose in a book where the lady from the office had quickly scribbled a map of the school, so when Ash came round the corner unexpectedly, I'd crashed into her. She'd wobbled and looked like she was about to topple over, so I reached out and grabbed her wrist. I'd stopped her from falling, but I'd started another kind of falling entirely.

The second my fingers had come into contact with her body, a feeling hit me from all sides, all at once. From the inside as well, as if the entire universe was made up of one thing and one thing alone, *the feeling*. It was all-consuming; it had a sound, a taste, a physical sensation to it. We didn't say a word to each other. Instead, we'd just stayed there like that, me holding on to her arm, just looking at each other, as if we were seeing for the first time ever. She was the most beautiful girl I had ever seen in my life and I had not been able to tear my eyes away from her. I don't know how long the moment had lasted, maybe only a second, but it had felt like decades. In that one moment, it felt as if I'd lived an entire lifetime with this person. We'd let go of each other eventually, but then struggled to walk away. And when we did, we'd kept glancing back at each other, and then she'd smiled at me and I knew that my life would never be the same again.

That small moment turned out to be the biggest of my life, perhaps it still was—well, apart from when it had ended four years after we'd met.

⌒

I was exhausted when I woke up the next day, I'd tossed and turned all night, thoughts of Ash running through my mind. Staring at the ceiling for hours, me mentally playing out every single "what if" scenario I could think of. *What if I hadn't left? What if I'd come back after six months? A year? What if I hadn't been that nervous boy who'd known nothing about his own body, let alone the body of a woman and fucked it all up like that? What if I hadn't plugged in her phone that night . . .*

I dragged myself out of bed and made the strongest cup of coffee I could before pulling my phone out and sending off a message to a close friend of mine, also a client. In fact, he'd been one of the first people to hire one of my locations for a very high-profile stills shoot, and had then encouraged me to begin my business. He'd supported me from day one. I'd kept him in the loop about Ash, since he'd also been there for me all those years ago when I'd been a broken-hearted boy.

Max: Hey.

Max: So things here, with her, are actually worse than I could have ever imagined.

Vincenzo: Sorry to hear it, my friend.

Max: She can barely look at me.

Vincenzo: Maybe she needs a bit of time. It's a shock.

Max: Maybe. I just wish there was something I could say or do to make it better between us.

Vincenzo: Have you spoken about everything that happened?

Max: Not yet. She can barely speak to me about normal things—not sure I can speak to her about that.

Vincenzo: I think if you two are going to have any kind of relationship, even if it's just a working one, you have to clear the air.

Max: You're right.

Vincenzo: And you should tell her your side of the story. The full story.

Vincenzo: Maybe she will understand what happened better then?

I put the phone down on my lap. Maybe it *was* time that Ash and I spoke about what had happened all those years ago—we never had. Maybe I needed to finally tell her the full story of what had happened, from my perspective anyway. Maybe then she wouldn't hate me so much for running away. Maybe . . .

I sipped my coffee and stared out the window. The sun had come up, the early morning rays illuminating the boulders beautifully. I would definitely sign this place on. I could see a lot of potential production companies wanting to shoot something here. Not to mention some of my other international clients wanting to holiday here too. Not only did I run a film-location agency, either showcasing some of my own properties that I had bought over the years, or listing other people's properties, like this, but I also organized travel for a very niche clientele. Most of them were celebrity clients in the entertainment industry or wealthy studio executives that I'd gotten to know through my location work. It wasn't advertised on my website, but I acted as a travel agent for them, finding them the best locations for memorable holidays, booking and handling everything. At the moment, I had a famous pop star wanting to escape some recent scandal that he'd gotten himself into, and this seemed like the perfect escape for him, definitely no paparazzi here. I dropped him a quick email and attached some of the casual photos I'd taken of the place. I finished my coffee and walked onto the balcony, and the first sight that greeted me, *was her.*

She was working in the distance. She worked with a hyperfocus that was almost intimidating to observe. Not that I knew much about cinematography, but I knew enough to appreciate how precise and thorough she was being. She was a pro. When I'd last seen her, she'd been going off to study accounting at university. She'd been good at math, but I'd always thought she would hate being an accountant. In fact, I'd even tried to talk her out of it once, so I was really happy to see her working in a field like this now. I'd been dying to ask her the story of how she'd gone from accountancy to this, but we weren't exactly on conversational terms yet.

Watching her, so absorbed and passionate about something, so caught up in her own world, gave me that flipping sensation in my chest again. I rubbed it as the flipping became a tightening. God, seeing her and being near her was actually giving me physical discomfort. It was making my heart stop one moment, and then beat fast the next. She was doing so many things to my heart that I felt as if I was on a roller coaster, but I wasn't prepared for what she did to my heart next, because suddenly she screamed in agony.

Without thinking, I raced down the stairs and rushed to her side. When I reached her, she was sitting on a boulder, one leg up on her opposite knee, wincing.

"What happened?" I asked.

She grimaced and pointed down at her foot where a long acacia thorn protruded from the sole of her shoe.

"Those things can be nasty," I said, bending down for a better look.

"It's all the way through my shoe." She continued to wince in pain.

"Let's get you inside so we can take a look at that and get it out."

She stood up on one leg and then started trying to hop.

"You're not seriously considering hopping all the way to the villa, over those rocks, and that uneven surface."

"If not hopping, how do you propose I get back to the villa?"

I turned my back to her and patted it, realizing for the first time, that I wasn't wearing a shirt. "Climb on."

"On your shirtless back? And why are you shirtless?"

"Sorry, I just woke up. I always sleep shirtless." I almost added, *"don't you remember?"* but didn't.

"No, thank you. I can hop." She started hopping. "If you'll remember I did gymnastics at school and my balance is excell—Oh my GOD!" She started falling forwards and I grabbed her by the back of the shirt and yanked her towards me.

"You were saying something about your balance? I didn't quite get it." I smiled at her, which, judging by the scowl she flashed me, had not been the best thing to do.

"I just need a stick, like a walking stick, and I'll be fine." She held on to one of the rocks and started looking around. I scanned the ground too, but couldn't see one. "I'll just use the rocks then." She started trying to hop from one rock to the other, grabbing hold of them as she went, but stopped when the gap to the next rock was far too wide.

"Please can I help you?" I felt desperate watching her struggle like this.

"I'm fine," she insisted.

"At least pass me your bag and camera." I held my hand out and she looked at it as if this was a massive decision to be made.

"Okay." She sounded so reluctant, as if I were forcing her to do something against her will. It did not feel good. She started hopping again, but with nothing to support her she only managed a few meters before she had to stop again, balancing precariously on one leg.

"Ash, we should really get that thing out of your foot—it could get seriously infected—and at this rate it's going to take ages to get to the villa," I said as blood started oozing out of the bottom of her sole, dripping onto the earth below.

"Birds stick dead animals on acacia thorns too," she said suddenly, and then turned and looked at me, a bolt of panic in her eyes, as if imagining the kinds of life-threatening infections she could get from the thorn. "Fine. But I'm not climbing on your shirtless back!"

"Then what?"

She gestured for me to come closer to her. I approached slowly.

"I'll put my arm around you and you can put yours . . . *uurgggh*." She delivered a loud, frustrated-sounding sigh and then looked at my body as if it might jump at her and maul her. I took a small step backwards, giving her the space she clearly needed. Perhaps I'd downplayed how bad this all was to Vincenzo. Because even when faced with a medical emergency, she still didn't want to have anything to do with me. Not even if a bird had hung a dead, decaying mouse on the thorn that was now in her foot and she was headed towards sepsis.

"Okay, fine, come back." She gestured to me again and I inched my way over. I waited for her to touch me first. She made a show of sighing and huffing as she draped her arm over my shoulder and then moved closer to me, until we were standing side by side. I waited for her to tell me what to do next.

"I suppose you should—*uurgggh*, I can't believe I am going to say this—just put your arm round my waist. Now! Do it!" she declared, sounding really put out, and I bit back a smile. I knew I shouldn't be finding this funny—she was bleeding and hobbling—but fuck she was cute. And I knew I shouldn't be finding her cute either, because that just seemed so patronizing in the worst way possible, but fuck it! *She was.*

I slid my arm round her slowly and rested my hand on her waist. The effect this physical contact had on me was immediate and dizzying. My head swam as my fingers wrapped round her soft hip. God, I'd forgotten how her body felt in my hands: warm and delicious. And this seemed like the most inappropriate time to remember that, but it was unavoidable. We started walking together, me lifting and supporting her with each step she took, trying to push all those thoughts aside as I focused on helping her.

"I can't believe this," she muttered as we walked together.

"It is making this easier for you," I offered as consolation.

She huffed in response, and I glanced down to look at the way my hand sat on her waist. It looked good there. It felt good there. And most of all, it felt right and familiar there.

I got her into the villa and placed her on the couch. By this stage her face was contorted in pain, which stirred something deep inside me: a primitive, caveman-like instinct to protect her. Once I'd found the first-aid kit, I sat cross-legged in front of her on the floor. I gestured for her to give me her foot and when she did, there was only one thing to be done.

"You know I'm going to have to pull that out. And we don't know how deeply it's gone in."

She nodded. "Make it quick."

"I will," I said, and then lowered my fingers to the thick white thorn. She winced immediately. "Sorry." I hated hurting her like this, although I'm sure the pain I was causing her now was nothing compared to the pain I'd caused all those years ago.

"Ready?"

She nodded and before she was able to finish the move, I pulled as fast as I could.

"Fuck it!" she yelped, and instinctively pulled her foot away.

"Sorry, let's get your shoe off." I pulled her foot back and started undoing her shoelaces. "While I have you like this, somewhat incapacitated and unable to run away, I want to take this moment to really, truly apologize to you. I should have told you who I was the second I saw your ID photo."

"I'd like to know why you didn't?"

I peered up from her foot and then gave her a look that I hoped portrayed the obviousness of the answer. But when she didn't acknowledge it, I knew it was time to address the pile of Everest-sized elephants in the room.

"Well, after what happened, you know, and then me leaving like I did, I . . ." As soon as the words were out of my mouth, I realized how lame and vague they sounded. "Sorry. This isn't easy to talk about," I admitted. "But I suppose we need to. It's time. Maybe that's the problem—we haven't actually talked about it."

"You never gave us the opportunity to talk about it," she said snappily.

She winced as I took her sock off, blood immediately dripping from the wound. I pulled some cotton-wool balls out of the first-aid bag and applied pressure to her injured heel.

"So should we have the conversation now?" I asked.

"No time like the present." She leaned back on the couch while I cradled her leg and foot, waiting for the bleeding to stop.

"Okay, then, I'll go first . . ." I took a deep breath and tried to start. "Funny, I've rehearsed this conversation in my head a million times over and now I don't know where to start."

"The beginning is always best."

"Fine." One more deep breath. "It was really bad, that night. The sex. It was a fucking disaster. And it has haunted me since it happened. I've had actual nightmares about it."

"Me too," she confessed, and I didn't doubt that at all.

"I think we'd put too much pressure on ourselves," I said.

"I agree. We'd waited so long and built it up so much in our heads," she replied. "Maybe we should have just done it like everyone else back then? Quickly. Ripped the bandage off."

"Our intentions for waiting were good, Ash. We'd wanted it to really mean something. But I think our expectations were totally unrealistic too. Our expectations were set way too high and, well, they were definitely not me."

"No, they weren't."

"And for the record, I wasn't actually trying to have ana—"

"WHOA! No. No. Nope. Don't say that. Don't you dare say what I think you're going to say. Ever!"

I couldn't help the chuckle that escaped, despite the serious subject matter.

"It wasn't funny!" she said quickly.

"Oh, trust me, I know it wasn't. It was a shock for me too—believe me. I had no intention of landing up . . . *there*."

"Okay, can we please stop talking about . . . *that* part of it?"

"Fine, but I just wanted to get it clarified."

"It's clarified! Totally clarified. Got it."

"Good. I'm glad," I said, and smiled at her, even though she was looking a little red in the cheeks. I'd always imagined this conversation as awkward and embarrassing, but for some reason, despite the subject matter, there was a certain freedom to finally being able to talk about it with her.

"You had this look on your face that night," I continued, "and I just knew . . . *it was so, so bad*. It felt like one of those pivotal make-or-break moments and that look in your eyes, combined with your message to Sarah, the whole situation seemed much more break, than make."

"What message to Sarah?"

I met her eyes. "Your phone was dying and I plugged it in for you, only to discover you'd been messaging Sarah in the bathroom." Her eyes widened at the memory, and then she lowered her head. "I only read the messages on the screen—I didn't scroll."

"Fuck."

"That's probably why I drank too much that night. I was trying to block it out while simultaneously trying to redeem myself. As you know, that didn't exactly work."

"You weren't meant to see that."

"Obviously not. '*How can I love someone so much but hate having sex with him?*'"

"Shit, I did say that, didn't I?"

"Not to mention, '*Maybe that means we're not sexually compatible. And if we're not sexually compatible, what does that mean? That we're not meant to be together?*'"

"And you can quote that verbatim after all these years."

"Good memory. It's a curse."

She bit her lip and looked away from me for a while. She looked as if she was wrestling back tears.

"I was so awkward and uncomfortable in my body back then. And my only idea of how to have actual sex came from my friends' locker room talk, and watching porn, which we all know is acting. Not exactly the most reliable sources. And I just wanted it to be so perfect for us that night, perfect for you. But the truth was, I just had no real idea of what I was doing. And the more it went wrong, the more panicked I got and then I read those messages and drank far too much and, you know how it ended."

"I am so, so sorry about those messages. What I said, it was, was—"

"True," I stated simply.

She nodded, still not looking my way.

"And that's what made it so much worse," I continued. "You were one hundred per cent right. In that moment, we were as far from sexually compatible as two people could ever be, and you were also right in saying that sex is really important in a relationship and without that spark it's probably not going to work long-term. It was all true what you said."

"We didn't have a spark that night." She finally turned back to look at me, eyes slightly shining. It broke my heart.

"Understatement," I said, and smiled up at her to try to infuse this situation with some lightness, even though it was far from it. She smiled back at me, a small feeble smile.

"I couldn't face you after that," I said.

"Neither could I."

"In the week that followed, I picked up the phone so many times to call you, but I couldn't."

"Me too," she admitted. "Not talking on the phone is one thing, though, but you just left. Forever. Without so much as a message even. *A message*."

"I was so emotionally immature at that age. I didn't fully understand what the long-term consequences of leaving would be. And I hadn't planned on leaving—it was only after I saw you again that I knew I *had* to go."

"What do you mean, saw me again?"

I sighed and for the first time since the conversation started I felt a tightening in my throat. This memory always gave me the same feeling. "At the mall. Seven days later, I saw you there. You were just sitting on the bench outside in the food court eating a bag of chips."

She looked confused. "What about me eating chips on a bench made you *have* to leave?"

"It wasn't about you *doing* something, it was about me being *incapable* of doing something, doing what needed to be done." I forced myself to look at her and hold her gaze, like I should have so many years ago. "I wanted so badly to go over to you. I *knew* I should go over to you. But it was as if I was physically paralyzed. My body refused to move. I just froze. No matter how much I told myself I *needed* to do it, I couldn't. And in that moment I realized that there was no way I was going to be able to stand in front of you, look you in the eye again, not at that stage anyway. And so I did the cowardly thing, but it was the only thing I could think of doing at that time— I left. It wasn't meant to be for so long either."

She broke eye contact with me and turned to look at the wall. I watched her closely, watched the emotions swimming over her features. She clenched her jaw, bit her bottom lip. This was still so real and raw for her, even after all these years. Just as it was for me too.

"I felt so shit about myself after that night. My stupid fragile teenage ego couldn't take it, and leaving felt like some kind of self-preservation. I went to my uncle in the UK first. I told myself I was only going to be away for a while. A couple of weeks. A holiday, just to clear my head, and then you started messaging me."

"Well, I didn't know where you were." She sounded defensive.

"I know. It wasn't the fact you were messaging me that upset me, it was what the messages made me realize." I paused and looked at her, waiting for her to drop her defensiveness so she could really hear what I was about to say next. "They made me realize how badly I'd hurt you by leaving. I know that should have been obvious—I should have known how badly you would be hurt—but I wasn't thinking clearly at the time. And the more hurt I could see you were, the worse I felt, and then of course your last message came in . . . That's when I decided staying away was for the best."

"What did I say?"

"In your last message to me, um . . ."

"I said I hated you," she said quietly.

I nodded at her and she looked away again. We fell into a silence that was so heavy and suffocating that it made me physically ache.

"I didn't," she finally said. "I never hated you. I just said that because I wanted to hurt you as much as you'd hurt me. I did . . ." She took a deep breath in. Her chest rose with the air filling it up, and she blew it out quickly, as if needing to get rid of it as quickly as possible. "I did . . . I—It was . . . I did love you."

My heart felt like it was shattering in my chest. "I loved you so much." The long-unspoken words left my mouth so quickly that I wasn't even really aware of them until they filled the room around us, and shifted the atmosphere.

I removed the cotton-wool from her foot. "It's stopped bleeding."

"Thanks," she said softly.

"I'm going to put some antiseptic on it. It might sting."

She looked down at her foot and nodded at me. I reached for the antiseptic and wet a cotton-wool ball with it, I pressed it onto the wound, and she winced in pain again.

"Sorry," I said. I cleaned the area thoroughly. "I'm sorry about everything, Ash. I'm sorry about how it went that night, and I'm especially sorry for how I acted afterwards. I was young and, honestly, a fucking idiot. I didn't fully understand what I was losing when I left that day. I should have done it all differently, but I didn't."

She sat back in the chair and rubbed her neck, as if that hurt too. "Seems we both should have done things differently. I shouldn't have messaged Sarah. I could have at least waited. It was wrong of me to do it there."

I smiled at her. "You would have messaged her the second you left anyway."

She smiled back. "This is true."

"You needed her support," I added quickly.

"Did you have any support?"

I nodded. "I didn't tell anyone this story for years, until I got drunk one night on grappa with my first client ever and it all came pouring out. He actually encouraged me to talk to you about this now."

"I'm not sure if I feel better or worse for this conversation," she said, and I knew exactly what she meant. Because I wasn't sure either. A part of me was glad to have had it, and another part of me just felt heartbroken when I looked back on the series of stupid decisions that I'd made that had led me to being so far away from the very thing that being close to now felt so right.

"Me neither," I said. I stuck the last of the plasters over the small piece of antiseptic-soaked cotton wool and put her foot back onto the floor gently. "There we go, finished."

I was finished with her foot, but after that conversation, it felt like I was nowhere near finished with her. Not in the slightest.

CHAPTER 19

Ash

I stood on the little dusty airstrip feeling two very different yet equally overwhelming emotions. One, I did not want to get on that plane again. It had made me feel so sick the last time, not to mention utterly terrified, that walking through thorns in this relentless heat and dodging hungry lions sounded more appealing than climbing back into that thing. I'd taken two anti-nausea tablets, which I knew would make me feel woozy. I knew this probably meant I wouldn't get nearly enough work done today. And two, I couldn't look at Max, not even vaguely. *I guess I now knew how he must have felt all those years ago.*

I fixed my eyes on the ground, where I watched a line of small ants carrying a dead fly on their backs. Max was on the opposite side of the airstrip and, truthfully, I had not been able to look at him since yesterday morning's discussion. What had made the whole thing worse was that while pouring his heart out, telling me how emasculated and terrible he'd felt about himself, he was carefully, painstakingly, cleaning and bandaging a bleeding wound on my foot.

After reading those messages I'd sent, which I now regretted more than I think I had ever regretted anything, he should not be down on the floor carefully removing a thorn from my foot. We'd ripped the bandage off that part of our history, while he was putting an actual bandage on my foot. I'm sure there was some deep kind of meaning in that, but I wasn't about to go looking for it now. I just knew that I felt horrible.

I'd managed to limp around a little more that day and had gotten all my work done. Then I'd quickly made the excuse of having to send all my pictures and film to Sebastian, and call him about it, to escape up to my bedroom and not have to see him again. I took dinner in my room too, even though the chef had invited me downstairs for a *casual* dinner on the balcony. He'd been very clear to use the word "casual" and I suspect Max would have asked him to, so I didn't think I was walking into something as ridiculously romantic as the night before. But I couldn't. I couldn't sit there and eat food with him. I think I was feeling exactly what he'd felt all those years ago. It felt impossible to face him again in the wake of all those revelations.

He'd read those messages . . . Shame and guilt and a devastation so large it filled me up inside until I felt like I might actually burst, gripped me. It had happened thirteen years ago, for heaven's sake. So why did I feel so bad about it? The sex had been terrible, and even if it hadn't been, even if it had been mind-blowing and had exceeded all the unrealistic expectations we'd set for ourselves, we probably still wouldn't be together today anyway.

We were teenagers. What did we know about love and commitment? We'd talked about forever, but at that age, what the hell do you know about tomorrow or next year, let alone forever? But still, something was niggling at me. Maybe even more than niggling. What would have happened if he hadn't read those messages? What if he hadn't drunk so much to block out what I'd said? What if we hadn't put so much goddamn pressure on ourselves? What would have happened if we'd tried again and it had been different? What if Max hadn't gone away? *What bloody if?*

I finally looked up from the ants maneuvering the fly into their hole when I heard the noise of an approaching plane. But the noise was totally different this time. It wasn't that loud, awful shaking sound that the flying tin can death trap had made two days earlier. In fact, this sound was smooth, like butter. It was silky and comforting and as it came closer I could see why. It didn't have a propeller. It didn't have skinny caterpillar legs with tiny wheels that looked as if they should be on a child's bike, not something that launches itself into the sky. It was sleek and gorgeous and glinted in the sun like a diamond tennis bracelet.

"A private jet?" I called over to Max, and he gave me the smallest lopsided smile. Granted, it was small, but it was a private jet.

"I wasn't fond of that other plane either, to be honest."

"So you booked this?"

He shrugged casually as if this was nothing, as if he did this all the time. He probably did.

"I'm going to have to explain this to the producer somehow, though," I said, looking at the thing that clearly cost more than the previous plane and that the producer had not okayed for this part of the job's budget.

"Your producer doesn't need to know," he shouted over to me. "I managed to squeeze it into my budget." He said it, but I didn't believe him. I could see he was lying; he'd never been a good liar.

"You hired it personally," I shouted back at him, making a statement of fact.

"Like I said, I also didn't like that small plane."

Another lie. He'd been perfectly fine in the small plane. In fact, when I'd looked up at him, he'd seemed totally relaxed. But I hadn't been okay in the small plane. And now he'd hired a different plane. The implications of this did not escape me. For a second, I thought of making a joke about him needing it more because he didn't want me to almost vomit on him again, but it did not seem appropriate. He'd hired it because I'd hated flying in the previous plane. This was possibly one of the nicest things anyone had ever done for me. But then it got even nicer.

"I have gum too, if you need," he said, holding a pack up in the air.

CHAPTER 20

Max

*I*t had been expensive, but seeing the look of relief on her face had been priceless. And seeing her with her head back, looking relaxed and at peace while sitting inside, even better. I watched her drift off to sleep. She still made the same little noises from time to time that she used to make. She was always so embarrassed when I told her about them, but honestly, I'd missed them. I watched her sleep for a while, hoping like hell she wasn't going to open her eyes and find me staring at her.

I finally pried my eyes from her sleeping face and turned my attention to the landscape. We were flying from Zimbabwe to Botswana, to the middle of nowhere once again. I was very much looking forward to seeing this place, a tented safari camp in the middle of the Makgadikgadi salt pans. A beautiful, almost desolate expanse of land. The Makgadikgadi pans looked almost otherworldly, flat and white, broken up with majestic baobab trees that looked as if they didn't belong in this time or place at all. But the area was also teaming with wildlife, and it was so remote and private that I could definitely see a celebrity couple coming here for the ultimate African safari experience. In fact, I'd asked the camp manager to take me out on one, so I could see what their offering was like. And, of course, if someone needed to shoot an advert to showcase some of the best of southern Africa, like this ad, the tented camp was the perfect backdrop.

When the pilot asked us to put on our seatbelts, I looked over at Ash and thought about waking her. She looked so peaceful, though, and probably needed all the rest she could get. One side of her seatbelt was lying across her lap; the other had fallen and was hanging from the chair. I reached across the aisle carefully and took the hanging part in my hand. Then my arm accidentally grazed her knees as I reached for the one in her lap and I froze, hoping she wouldn't wake up. When she didn't, I continued, but it was the noise of the buckle that finally made her stir.

"What the fuck?" She jumped in her seat and batted my hands away. "Why are you touching me? Get your hands out of my lap."

"My hands are not in your lap. I'm doing up your seatbelt."

"But why?" She smacked my hands away and I pulled them back and held them in the air in a "hands up" gesture.

"You should have woken me!" she stammered, pulling the seatbelt towards herself.

"Sorry, you looked so . . ." I wanted to say peaceful, angelic, beautiful, but didn't. "You seemed like you needed the rest, and we're only landing in twenty minutes. I thought you could do with the extra twenty."

Her face softened somewhat as she pulled the seatbelt tightly across her waist and clicked it closed. "I got a fright, that's all. I wasn't expecting to wake up with your hands in my lap."

I chuckled. "You're deliberately trying to make it sound like I was feeling you up while you were asleep."

"Were you?" she asked, and I shook my head.

"You know me—I would never do something like that." I held eye contact with her. It was almost painful to do so, because as each second passed I felt as if I was slipping further and further, deeper and deeper.

"I don't actually, not anymore." Ash broke eye contact abruptly and looked away.

"What do you want to know? Ask me anything."

"Okay." She turned in her seat and faced me. "Do you own llamas?"

I looked at her for a second before laughing. "Seriously? That's what you want to know—out of every single thing you could ask me in the world—do I own llamas?"

"Well, do you?" she asked, more emphatically this time.

I stopped laughing. "Where did you hear that?"

"From around and about. It was a rumor. There are a lot of rumors about you, actually."

"What kind of rumors?" I asked, and I could see her weighing something up. But then she shook her head.

"You know—some people talk."

"And some of those people say I own llamas."

"Yes. They do!"

I looked away and fiddled with my watch strap. She didn't know this was a loaded question, but it was. Not that I could tell her anything more personal at this stage, because I'd basically bared my soul to her yesterday. "My mom—I told you she has dementia—I bought one for her. Strange choice, but she said she wanted an animal and when I asked what kind, she said llama. Apparently, she'd always been fascinated with them, from the time she was a girl and saw a picture of them. It's one of the only things that still makes her happy, going outside and watching Lucy—that's what she called the llama."

There was silence in the plane, a silence so big and heavy it somehow swallowed up the noise of the engines.

"Do they spit?" she asked, which I wasn't expecting, but for which I was grateful and relieved.

"Lucy has never spat on us. She is smelly, though, and have you ever tried washing a llama? Not possible. And do you think any mobile pet groomers will wash one either?"

"No, I imagine that washing llamas is not their thing. How big is she?" she asked.

"She's not that big, shorter than me. She's actually kind of cute."

"Cute?"

"You want to see a picture of her?" I pulled my phone out and started flipping through my photos.

"You have a photo of your pet llama on your phone?"

I chuckled. "I suppose I do."

"Do you want to see my cat?" She didn't wait for my response and pulled her phone out too. Once we'd located the photos, we swapped phones.

"Oh my God, she *is* cute!" She laughed. God, I loved her laugh. "She has a snaggle tooth." She laughed even more. I'd missed that sound.

"Your cat is very cute too," I said, looking more at her than the cat. Ash was holding the cat up to her face and smiling one of her full-blown, dazzling smiles. The kind that had the ability to knock grown men off their feet.

"Thanks. She's the best, keeps me warm in—AAAAH! Sorry, I didn't mean to . . . oops." My phone went flying and when I picked it up from the floor, I could see why she'd dropped it.

I felt panicked. "It was on a beach. Everyone tans topless in Europe. It's not like I—"

"You don't have to explain it to me."

"I want to explain it to you, though. They're friends. We were on holiday. It's just a—"

"Seriously, you don't have to explain it to me. You are a grown man who happens to have a photo of two gorgeous, half-naked women on your phone. Really, it's all cool."

"They're not that gorgeous," I said.

"What?" She looked at me with a shocked expression. "Seriously? If you don't consider that gorgeous, then I don't know who you've been with since me. Because one looks like Cindy Crawford and the other looks like Claudia bloody Schiffer. It's like a nineties super-model revival. God, I would love to look like them. Not to mention those breasts. I'd take one third of them, please."

I almost opened my mouth and said that they didn't hold a candle to her, but didn't. She was still the most beautiful woman I'd ever seen. She was perfect, exactly how she was. She had this sense of comfort and confidence in her own skin that was ridiculously hot. The way she tied her hair back messily, didn't care that she had a smudge on her cheek and no make-up on. This grown-up version of her had settled into her own skin and owned it. *Fucking hell, it was hot.* So hot that if I carried on looking at her, I was going to have a problem here.

I quickly looked out the window again when I realized I'd been staring at her hands, watching her fingers tap away nervously on the armrest as the plane began a descent that was a little bumpy.

"So, is that all you wanted to know?" I said in an attempt to distract her. "Just if I owned a llama? Seems like a pretty random thing to ask after thirteen years." Ash was silent, then her fingers stopped their nervous tapping and she turned to face me.

"What happened with your dad, if you don't mind me asking?"

"Well, he decided he was sick of us, so took up with his dental hygienist—how's that for a cliché?—married her and has two more children now."

"What? He's remarried?"

"I know, crazy."

"And you have half-siblings?"

"Half-brothers, apparently. I've never met them. In fact, I haven't seen or spoken to my dad in nine years."

"Oh God, I'm so sorry. That's . . ." She paused for a while and then started nodding. "I get it. Why you changed your name. Does he still speak to Alissa?"

I shook my head sadly.

"But she was such a daddy's girl."

"He sent her a birthday card one year, and then never again."

"Shit! What an asshole!" She sounded truly angry and indignant, and for a moment, it felt just like old times—when I was angry at the people who made her angry and vice versa. This little team of two against the world.

"Alissa just got engaged. Can you believe my little sister is going to get married? And she's immigrated to Iceland of all places. Her fiancé is Icelandic."

"I can't believe that. In my mind she's still nine."

"Nope, twenty-two and doing a masters in geothermal engineering in Iceland! Who would have thought, right?"

"Twenty-two is quite young to get engaged."

I paused. Swallowed hard. "We spoke about getting engaged at nineteen."

Her face immediately reddened. "What did we know at nineteen?"

"Maybe it's considered young, but when you know, you know, right?" I held her gaze meaningfully and she reciprocated for a few moments, but then looked down and tapped her fingers on the arm rest again.

"I don't think anyone can ever *just know*. I suppose at the time we think we might *know*, but actually we don't. And then some time passes and you look back on it all and you wonder how you ever thought you *knew* in the first place."

I leaned across the space between us and spoke up as the engines grew louder during our descent. "I knew. And once upon a time, you knew too."

"But did we really *know*?" she asked, glancing up again. "We were so young."

"We clearly thought we did, enough to talk about our future life together. A house by the beach, one beagle and a pug. You joked about breeding puggles. And two kids, but only in our early thirties. Remember?" I said.

Her reaction to my words was instantaneous. She sat up straight and looked so uncomfortable like she was about to climb out of her skin.

"You and I, *together*, it feels like it belongs to a different universe. It was a lifetime ago and it feels as if it happened in a totally different reality to the one we're living in now."

But as she said it, and as I looked at her, I began to wonder if that was entirely true, for me anyway. If you'd asked me a month ago whether Ash and I lying in bed together, fingers woven into each other's, planning our life together was in a different universe, I would have said yes. But now it didn't feel as far away as it used to, or perhaps it should be.

CHAPTER 21

Ash

*A*s soon as we landed, I pulled my phone out and messaged everyone while we waited for the car to fetch us from the landing strip.

Ash: HE DOES OWN A FUCKING LLAMA!!!!!!!

Ash: AND HE HAD HALF-NAKED PHOTOS OF MODELS ON HIS PHONE!!!!!

Frank: Top half or bottom half?

Melusi: Only a straight male asks that question.

Frank: Hahah.

Ash: Top half.

Frank: And?

Ash: Great boobs.

Yo: Perky?

Ash: Why are we asking so many boob questions? The point is, there were boobs, in a photo. A photo he had after a photo of his pet llama named Lucy.

Russ: How many women were in this half-naked photo?

Ash: Two.

Ash: OMG, does that mean what I think it means?

Charlie: Threesome.

Ash: He said that it was just topless tanning, you know, very European.

Yo: That is true. Europeans all have their boobs on display when the sun comes out.

Charlie: I'm still going with threesome. The guy has a llama, so one part of the rumor confirmed.

Frank: 😊

Sarah: So hang on . . . are we now thinking all the other rumors are true then?

Charlie: We're thinking there could be more truth in them than we initially thought.

Melusi: We are talking about ourselves in the collective first person!

Frank: Hahaha!

Frank: Just sitting back and watching this unfold.

Charlie: Crap, an influencer is being paid 30K to tweet about a lipstick brand, and she just tweeted about their competitor's product. Idiot! I have to fix this, but I'm going to leave you with this . . .

Charlie: It's going to be two parts.

Charlie: 1 the psychic said to go back to the source to break the curse.

Melusi: 😊

Charlie: 2 and as it turns out, that source might actually be the best sex in the world.

Charlie: So in case curses and psychics are real, just do it. It could be a double curse break.

Charlie: BYE!

Frank: Actually, we do agree with that.

Yo: We do too.

Ash: No amount of you guys agreeing to anything will change the fact that I am not having sex with him. Besides, dating detox, remember?

Melusi: Have a cheat day. All diets allow for a cheat day.

Sarah: Exactly! You need a cheat day.

Ash: Guys, not happening. I need to go though. I do have actual real work to do.

A distant clap of thunder caught my attention as the car pulled up.

"A storm like this is very unusual for this time of year," I heard someone say, and I turned to see the lodge manager standing in front of me.

"We do need rain, though," the game ranger replied.

"Air-traffic control says it's a potential category-three storm," the pilot commented. "They said I might not be able to take off."

"Very unusual. We have electric storms here every now and again, but not this bad, and not at this time of the year," the manager reiterated. I was not going to be able to get much done in this light, so today seemed like a write-off.

"Sorry about this," said Max.

"About what?" I asked.

"About the storm—you not being able to do the work you need to do right now."

"You didn't bring the bad weather," I said to him, causing that little lopsided smile again. His facial hair was a little longer than it had been. I'd never really been into facial hair, but holy crap, he looked good with it. What did Melusi always say? "Beards are make-up for men." And he refused to date a man with a squeaky-clean face.

"How long have you had that?" I pointed to his face.

"You like it?"

"Maybe," I teased.

"On and off for about ten years now. I shave it off at least three times a year, though. Apparently, it's good to let the skin breath, or so I've heard."

"Huh." I didn't know if this was true, but it made sense. "It looks good," I admitted, and immediately regretted it, because that lopsided smile grew.

"Careful, I wouldn't dispense too many compliments."

"And why's that?" I asked.

"I might start getting the wrong idea." His smile tilted even more and I could almost see that dimple through his hair.

"What. Wrong. Idea?" I emphasized the words.

"That you might actually like me," he said.

I shook my head at him. "I wouldn't take it that far."

"So you do like me, then?"

"Put it this way, I don't totally and utterly dislike you," I teased.

He smiled the biggest smile I'd seen so far. "I'll take that." He started walking away, but walking backwards, hands in pockets, watching me as he went. He looked ridiculous.

"You're going to trip." I pointed at the ground behind him.

He turned round and started walking the correct way. "Your concern for my wellbeing is rather heartwarming, Ash."

"For the record, the only reason I didn't want you to trip was because then you would trip me too."

"Don't believe you." He shot me a look over his shoulder as he climbed into the vehicle. The drive was short and when we got to the camp, I couldn't quite believe my eyes.

"This is incredible," I whispered in utter awe as I stared at the bedouin-style tents in front of us. All the sides were open, and the ground was covered in large Persian rugs. Furnishings from the early 1900s made you feel as if you were stepping back in time, the intrepid explorer setting out to explore unknown lands.

"Amazing, eh?" Max said next to me.

"You could say that again. This is one of the most unique places I've ever been to. And it's going to require zero styling from the art department too."

I walked through the massive tent, running my hands over the swathes of fabric that hung from the roof, billowing in the growing wind. I dropped down on one of the plush velvet couches and threw my head back to look up at the tented ceiling where giant crystal chandeliers hung. This place was an eclectic mix of things: African artifacts, opulent crystal and velvet, and then worn rugs that gave you the feel of an opium den somewhere.

"Can I show you to your rooms?" the ranger came over and asked.

"Sure." I stood up and followed him out of the main tent. The wind had picked up even more and walking in it felt difficult. He led us down a wooden pathway with smaller freestanding tents off it.

"Dinner will be at seven in the main dining tent, just off the tent you were in. And if there's anything you need, feel free to call us." The ranger took my bags inside and then left me to step into my tent alone. The interior of the tent was just as spectacular as the main tent, the only difference was the size and the presence of a massive four-poster bed. I threw myself down on it and let out a very contented sigh. Max was right—I was exhausted. This job had taken it out of me and traveling always made me stressed and tired. I turned my head to the side and noted what was on the bedside table. The product that had caused all this stress. A bottle of African Dreams cream liqueur. The company launching it was putting a ridiculous amount of money behind the product. They were clearly very confident about it. I hadn't even tried it, so I didn't know whether it tasted good or not.

But that wasn't my job. My job was to make it look like it tasted good. To make it look as if sipping it was like drinking a little slice of opulent African luxury. My job was to sell a dream of the product, which in turn would sell the product. The ad agency had come up with what I considered to be a rather generic, slightly cheesy ad, but I also knew that this kind of ad sold alcohol, so it was perfect for the brand. And I wasn't going to complain: the budget was huge and I seldom got to work with such a large amount. In fact, thanks to African Dreams, I was basically living *my* African Dream right now on this comfortable bed.

I woke up to the sides of my tent flapping wildly in what felt like borderline gale force winds. I could see why the pilot had been told not to take off in this. I raced to the edge of the tent, and tried to wrangle the material down, but it was like wrestling with a giant anaconda, and the anaconda was definitely winning. A clap of thunder made me leap backwards and almost out of my skin.

"Let me help you," the ranger said, coming out of nowhere. I stepped back to let him tie everything down.

"We're going to drop the weather screens," he said, and I watched as large heavy canvas sheets fell to the ground and were fastened tightly. But despite them, the inside of the tent felt alive. Everything rattled and moved. The sides billowed in and out in the wind. The ceiling shook, the chandelier swung wildly and bolts of lightning lit up the room like a strobe light in a club.

"Is it safe here?" I asked the ranger, not hiding my concern at all.

He nodded, but told me that dinner in the main tent had been cancelled and it would be brought to our rooms instead—they didn't want guests walking around outside. That made me feel less safe than I had been feeling moments ago. I walked into the very middle of the room to the large center pole that held up the tent. I grabbed hold of it and then sat down on the floor, clutching it tightly.

CHAPTER 22

Max

I lay on my bed staring up at the flapping roof. Ash would be hating this. She'd never been one for feeling scared. She hated horror films, hated roller coasters, and anything else that made her anxious or fear for her safety. I knew this need to always feel safe came from her little sister's freak death when Ash was only thirteen. It had been a tragic choking accident, the kind no one could ever imagine happening. Ash had seen the whole thing happen, seen her mother trying to save her sister. It had affected her profoundly, devastated her, and since then, she didn't like feeling even vaguely unsafe or scared. And this wind, this howling storm that was shaking the tent, I knew it would be making her feel just that. The need to go over there and make sure she was okay had me on my feet, pacing the room. But I wasn't sure she would want me there . . .

"Fuck it!" I said, exiting my tent. Whether she liked it or not, I was going to make sure she was okay. She could kick me out if she wanted to, but I just needed to know she wasn't freaking out. It was hard to walk straight down the wooden path as the raging wind battled with me, knocking me sideways off my feet. I finally made it to her tent and tried to scream her name above the wind, but my voice was carried away. I squeezed my way through the heavy canvas weather sheets and then found a small slit in the tent that I climbed through. And there she was, sitting on the floor in the middle of the tent, holding on to the pole.

"You okay?" I had to stop myself from running up to her and scooping her into my arms.

"Yes! No! Sort of," she said. "I figured that the safest place to be when the roof and sides blew off would probably be here. So here I am."

"Can I join you?" I asked tentatively.

She shrugged. "Sure. Why not. At least I won't die alone."

"No one is dying tonight," I said with as much authority as I could.

I walked over to her and sat down, careful to keep my distance, but close enough so that if, God forbid, something did actually happen, I would be able to do something about it.

"You're not holding on to the pole," she pointed out.

"I'm confident we're not going anywhere."

We sat in silence for a while, her still clutching the pole while the wind outside raged. More claps of loud thunder and then the rain. It was as if the sky had ripped itself open.

"God, if we're not blown away, we'll drown in raging flood waters or be incinerated by lightning."

"You're going to be fine," I promised her.

"Sorry," she blurted. "I must look ridiculous, a grown woman clinging to a pole—"

"Never apologize!" I cut her off. "Cling to as many poles as you want."

She nodded slowly. Her shoulders relaxed a little and my heart felt as if it had just expanded tenfold and was about to rip out of my chest. We sat in silence for a while and I looked around her room. It was similar to mine, but bigger and nicer. I'd asked them to give her the better one, just as I had at the villa too.

"Oh, look, African Dreams." I got up and grabbed the bottle, turning it over in my hands. I'd seen the storyboard, read the advert, but had never actually seen the product in real life. "What does it taste like?"

"I have no idea," she replied.

"Wait, you're shooting an ad for a product you've never tasted?"

She rolled her eyes at me. "That's like asking a male cinematographer who is shooting a tampon commercial why he's never tried the product."

I laughed. "I can't argue with that logic, but I *am* going to taste it." I walked over to the bar fridge and pulled out the ice tray, then took out two tumblers.

"Want to experience some African Dreams?" I asked, waving the glass at her.

"Mmm, undecided. I've never been a fan of creamy liquor."

"You didn't like anything creamy. You hated ice cream and never drank milk."

"You remember that?" she asked, a small smile tugging on the corners of her lips.

"I remember a lot of things," I said, pouring myself a glass. "Do you?" I asked as casually as I could, but it was a loaded question.

"You hated runny eggs—you said the liquid gave you the creeps. You had the biggest sweet tooth and were always chewing on sweets or sucking on something. You hated fish! To eat and to look at. You could eat an entire box of cereal after dinner—you called it your 'second supper'—and thirteen years later I still haven't met anyone who eats as much as you did. And you loved sweet-and-sour pickles. See, I also remember a lot of things."

A loud clap of thunder put a punctuation mark at the end of her confession. It felt apt, almost as if it had been planned, purposefully and perfectly timed. Because the silence that followed was so loud and resounding, for a moment it seemed to drown out the entire storm. I stared at her, fighting an urge to walk across the floor, pull her into my arms, and tell her that I remembered everything too. But I didn't.

"I'm impressed," I said instead.

"Don't be. I think I remember some of those because I have some PTSD from you spilling an entire bowl of cereal on me in bed, and then you dropped that pickle on the floor once and I stood on it barefoot in the dark and got the fright of my life because I thought it was a slimy animal."

I burst out laughing. "I remember that. Sorry."

She smiled at me. It was the biggest smile she'd given me so far and I felt incredibly lucky.

"I'm pouring you a glass of African Dreams, by the way," I said. "I insist you at least taste it. Perhaps it will inspire a different way of *lighting it*."

"Oh God, please no. No more lighting talk." She let out a small laugh, her first one, and my heart did a backflip.

I walked the drinks back to her and sat down on the floor. I passed her the tumbler of thick, creamy liquid and she peered inside it, then grimaced. She raised the glass and swirled it around. The creamy liquid coated the glass in a way that was very off-putting.

"I think I'm going to hate this."

"Me too," I said. "Also not a big fan of creamy alcohol. On the count of three?" I raised my brows in question.

She nodded at me, now smiling very openly over the rim of the glass. I was glad she'd let go of the pole.

"One, two, three." We both sipped at the same time, holding eye contact, and then once the liquid had gone down, we continued to look at each other for a while.

"Huh! It's not as bad as I thought it would be," I finally said.

"I know. It's not that creamy. And not too sickly sweet like these liqueurs can be." She took another contemplative sip. "Would you judge me terribly if I said I actually liked it?"

I laughed and topped her glass up without asking. She took another sip and nodded at me. "Not bad! Not bad."

"Do you feel more inspired now for the shoot? Ideas that would make it more 'cinematic'?"

She laughed. God, it felt good to make her laugh again. "I wouldn't take it that far." She eyed my glass thoughtfully. "You never used to drink that much."

"Still don't. Only on special occasions."

"And this is a special occasion?"

"We're still alive, aren't we?"

She looked up at the tent roof and then at the walls. "For now."

"Don't be such a Negative Nelly," I said, and she laughed again.

"I haven't heard that in thirteen years." I laughed too and when it petered out, we were staring at each other again. "What are you doing here anyway?"

I shrugged, trying to make it seem casual, make it seem like I hadn't been overwhelmed by that caveman instinct to run through a storm to protect her.

"I knew you wouldn't like this."

"So you came to rescue me?" she asked. "Because I'm more than capable of handling myself, you know. I'm not the girl I used to be who always wanted you by her side because it felt better that way. You haven't been around for a long time—not many people have, apart from my friends. I take care of myself now. I've had to."

I sensed big emotions swelling in her. "Your parents?" I asked softly.

"My parents," she stated coldly.

"How are they?"

"Not great." She looked down at her glass, moving the ice cube around with her finger. "My mom went into another depressive cycle. But she hasn't really emerged from it this time. They've tried different medicines, even ketamine—nothing's worked."

"I'm so sorry. Your dad?"

"Well, you know how he enjoyed drinking. Especially after . . . what happened." She cleared her throat nervously. "So my mom's depressed and my dad is angry and drunk."

"Fuck. Sorry. I didn't know it had gotten that bad."

"How would you? You weren't there."

A knife twisted in my gut. "I'm sorry about that."

She made a show of brushing my apology off, as if it didn't matter. As if me not being there hadn't been an issue, but I could see now that it had. For the first time ever, the real and very raw consequences of me leaving were apparent. And I wasn't sure I could ever forgive myself for abandoning her to deal with all of that alone.

I looked down at her arm. "Sunflower tattoo," I whispered softly. She nodded and ran her fingers over it.

"Do you still put a sunflower on her grave every year?" I asked. When we were together, I'd gone with her to her sister's grave to do it. "It's the seventeenth of August, right?" I asked, and she nodded. But I already knew the answer to that question. Because the seventeenth of August was the one day a year that I willingly let my mind drift to her. I always thought about what she was doing, and hoped she was okay.

"If I can," she said. "I'm not always around, so thought I would get this." She held her arm out for me and I admired the intricate work.

"It's beautiful," I said, remembering that photo of her sister dressed in a yellow and white sunflower dress.

She shook her head suddenly, as if shaking off a memory and then quickly changed her demeanor. "Top us up." She thrust her glass at me. I could see she no longer wanted to talk about this, and I obliged her.

"Bottoms up," she said, and we both threw the liquid back. Again, our eyes met.

"Thirteen years," I mused out loud. "It's crazy how fast time goes."

"As you get older, it seems to go faster."

"In the blink of an eye," I said.

"It's been so long that it's hard to imagine a time when we ever actually existed."

"We did exist," I insisted. "And for most of that, we were really good." I topped up our glasses again. The alcohol was definitely making me buzz now.

She paused and took a long, slow sip. "Yes. We were good." She licked the corner of her mouth with her tongue and the action was so fucking sexy that I had to cross my legs, because I could feel something stirring in my pants.

"We *were* really good together, weren't we," she continued, her words slightly lubricated with alcohol now.

"We were." I refilled our glasses. "We were good on email too, before we knew who we were speaking to."

She nodded at me thoughtfully. "Do you think if you weren't Logan, and I was just Leigh Smith, not Ash, and we met at a film shoot, we would hook up?"

"Do I think that our emailing would have led to a date and then probably led to us having hot sex in a tent like this?" I asked, locking eyes with her with as much intensity as I could.

She nodded and bit her lip at the same time. The gesture did not escape me.

"Yes. I do," I said.

"So then why do you think we weren't able to have hot sex all those years ago?"

"We were so young and totally inexperienced."

"And we're not young and inexperienced now?" she said. Her tongue came out to lick the corner of her lips again and now it was more than just a stirring. I was hard. And if she continued licking her lips like that while she talked about how "experienced" we both possibly were now, I was not going to be able to get rid of it.

"No, we're not," I repeated slowly.

"Do you think if we'd tried again, it would have gotten better, or do you think we're just fundamentally not sexually compatible?"

This was the ultimate question, wasn't it? And it had been the main reason that I'd made a very conscious decision to become good at sex. No, not just good, *the best*. And right now, looking at her like this, licking her lips, cute unruly hair that seemed untamable, just begging to be pulled at, tight tank top that showed the outline of her nipples and loose-fitting sleeping shorts that you could slip a hand into so easily, I had an overwhelming desire to show her just how fucking good I'd gotten—again and again and again—and just how sexually compatible I *knew* we would be!

"I can't answer that," I said instead.

"It's weird, because before we tried to have actual sex, things were hot between us. It's not like we hadn't done things, and the things we had done were . . ." She took another sip of her drink. As she talked, her face was getting more and more flushed. I didn't know if it was from the alcohol or from this conversation. "They were *really* good. And I think you're so sexy."

"Think? Present tense?" I shuffled a little closer to her.

"I meant *thought*! I thought you were sexy. Past tense. You know, when we were dating. Thought!"

"So you don't think I'm sexy now?" My dick felt as if it was going to burst through my pants.

"I'm not drunk enough to answer that," she said with a smile that was definitely flirtatious. In fact, it felt as if we were right back to being two people flirting with each other over email.

"Well then, have some more." I topped her glass up almost to the brim and did the same for myself. We locked eyes while we drank. I wanted to get fucking naked and swim in her eyes if I could.

"Do you think I'm sexy?" she said in a slightly small voice, as if I was almost not meant to hear it. But I did hear it and I was going to let her know in as many uncertain terms as possible, just how sexy I thought she was. I put the glass down on the floor and crawled towards her. Her chest expanded as she sucked in a quick gulp of air. I leaned in, bringing my mouth close to her ear. She let out the tiniest sound that was not lost on me. Sexiest sound I'd heard in thirteen years. I gently grazed her ear with the side of my face, but not too much, just a little. But enough to illicit another tiny sound from her.

"You're even sexier today than you were then."

Her breath quickened. More color rushed to her cheeks and I could feel warmth radiating off her. I brought my lips all the way up to her ear now, letting them drag against it. She used to like being touched there. "In fact, I think you're the sexiest woman alive, Ash." I kept my lips there and she began to turn slowly. Her head moved towards mine until we were centimeters apart, looking at each other.

"You say that like I should believe you," she whispered into the tiny space between us.

"You should."

"You say that like you didn't walk away from me once and don't have photos of gorgeous models on your phone."

I pulled away from her a little. I knew how that photo must have looked. And she would have been right about it, but she would also have been very, very wrong. They hadn't meant anything. They were a one-night distraction. Something to take my mind off the one thing that it just kept coming back to . . . *her*. She'd always been there, and maybe I hadn't been fully conscious of it, but now that she'd come back into my life, it had become crystal clear to me. All those years, those women and meaningless nights, what I'd really wanted—needed—had been Ash. And the more time I spent with her now, the more all the memories of us and the feelings I'd had for her, were flooding back. Nearly everything I'd done for the last thirteen years had been to try and cope with the pain of losing her. To try and escape it and forget her. But she was unforgettable.

"You're way sexier than they could ever be."

She poked a finger in my chest and looked at me very seriously. "Number one, I don't believe a word you just said, because I also have eyes, and two, more important than number one, even if I did believe you—"

"You should," I interrupted.

"Even if I did believe you, don't interrupt me, it means nothing to me. Absolutely nothing. Because I am officially on a dating detox. So you can be as flirty and hot as you want, I am not moved!" She downed her glass and I watched her closely, noticing a slight wobble in her hand. I took the glass from her gently.

"Let me make you a cup of coffee, Ash." I walked the glasses away and she let out a loud sigh and flopped onto her back.

"You okay?" I asked, but clearly she wasn't.

"I'm on a full-on dating detox!" she mumbled, her words slurring together.

Fuck! I should have noticed how much we'd drunk, but I'd been so swept up in the moment we were having, which had felt just like old times, that the entire bottle was almost finished. I turned the bottle around in my hand. *Shit*, that was a much higher than expected alcohol content. I pulled a bottle of water out the fridge and walked it over to her. I looked down at her lying on the carpet and she smiled up at me.

"Max, Max, Max. No matter how sexy you are, and how flirty you are on email and in person, and no matter how many orgasms you give, 'apparently' give, 'allegedly' give, women, maybe even more than one at a time," she laughed as she did dramatic air quotes in the air above her head. "I remain unmoved by you and your overtures." She suddenly grabbed my ankle and squeezed it. "God, your ankles are big. How the hell did you get so sexy? Seriously? Max? Maximillian Adam?"

I knelt down, pulled her into a sitting position and then held the open bottle of water to her lips. *I really shouldn't have kept pouring her drinks!*

"And you have facial hair now too." She laid her hand on the side of my face and I closed my eyes momentarily and breathed in the feel of it. I knew this wasn't the right time to be enjoying a moment like this, but I couldn't help it. I put my hand over hers and she brought her face closer to mine as if she was inspecting me now.

"Your eyes are the same, except for these . . ." she traced her finger around my eye and then stopped at the side. "Cute little wrinkles."

"Cute?" I smiled at her.

"So small and little." She was clearly drunker than I'd initially thought she was.

"You also have muscles now." She let go of my face and her hand traveled down my arm, squeezing as she went. And I swear, if she didn't stop doing that, I would have her naked and pinned to this pole in about five seconds. But I also didn't want her to stop either. Feeling her hand on my body after all these years must be akin to what a man who'd just crawled through the desert feels like when he drinks water for the first time. She ran her hand up to my hair and laced her fingers through it and I think I died ten times in a row.

"You have hair now too." She moved even closer to me, I could feel her breath on my lips now.

"I've always had hair," I whispered in some kind of strange daze. *She fucking had me now!* Had me under her spell. I was putty in her hands and she could do anything she wanted to do with me. And there was nothing I wouldn't do for her either. Do to her. She tightened her grip on my hair and pulled me so close that our noses touched. Sexual tension, like hot thick magma rose up between us. I felt it, and I knew she felt it too as she tightened her grip on my hair and her eyes moved down to my lips.

"Ash," I whispered her name against her lips. It was a plea and a promise.

"I think you should kiss me now," she said, and I registered the overwhelming smell of alcohol on her breath. I put my hand over hers and unlaced her fingers from my hair. I immediately sat back, creating the distance I needed between us. Her face fell and I watched a journey of emotions wash across it. Shock, embarrassment, anger.

"Come, let's get you up, hydrated and into bed." I didn't wait for her response, instead I pulled her to her feet.

She scoffed and tried to pull away. "So much for your so-called honesty earlier," she said. "*You're so hot, Ash. You're so sexy, Ash.*"

"You are hot and sexy. Trust me—that is not the issue here."

"What's the issue?" she asked as I put my hands on her waist and guided her towards the bed.

"The issue is that you and I have had too much to drink and you also made it quite clear you were on a dating detox, and I don't want you to do anything you'll regret in the morning."

"Detox shmetox."

"Here we go. Have a seat." I lowered her onto the bed, knelt down on the floor in front of her and started unlacing her shoes.

"What are you doing?" she asked, trying to wiggle free from my grip.

"Taking your shoes off."

"My shoes like being on!" She tried to kick me off defiantly, but it was too late, her shoes were off.

"Drink some more water." I passed her the bottle again and she gulped some more. I could see she was going to be unconscious very soon. I maneuvered her onto the bed in a lying position and tried to make her as comfortable as possible. She grabbed one of the pillows and clutched it. I smiled. She used to sleep like that, clutching a pillow as if she was hugging it. She put her face on the pillow and her heavy eyes started to close.

"I'm tired," she said through a yawn.

"Then sleep." I pushed away the strands of hair that had fallen into her face and she let out a happy, contented-sounding sigh.

"Sleep tight," I said.

"Okay, angel," she replied.

My chest tightened at the sound of my old pet name, and that was it. *The moment.*

If I was in any doubt about how I felt about her, it was all confirmed in those two words. I was no longer slipping. I had slipped and she had me completely. Maybe she'd always had me, maybe I'd been able to push that away just enough to convince myself I was over her. I wasn't.

I leaned down and pressed a small kiss to her forehead. I closed my eyes and let my lips linger there for ages.

"Good night, baby," I whispered as softly as I could.

I stood up and walked over to the chair in the corner of the room. The storm was still raging outside. Kicking my shoes off, I pulled a blanket over my lap and lay my head back. Resisting Ash tonight had probably been one of the hardest things I'd ever done, but it had also been the right thing. I didn't want her waking up with any regrets tomorrow. I didn't want there to be any more regrets between us. I already knew she was going to feel terrible about this tomorrow as it was.

CHAPTER 23

Ash

The first thing I noticed was the dry mouth and the pounding headache. I moaned and tried to sit up. The second thing I noticed was Max sitting in the chair in my tent looking at me.

"Morning," he said.

"Mor—" I stopped. The talking just made my head pound even harder, as if it was going to explode.

"Water on your side table, two aspirin, multivitamin and your phone is charging."

She nodded and reached for the water. She ripped the lid off and downed half the bottle with gusto. She chucked down the pills next and then looked at her phone.

"Crap! It's already nine. I have so much work to do."

"Best hangover cure is something to eat. There's breakfast waiting for us in the dining area," he said. "I'll leave you to get dressed and meet you there?" He strode out of the tent and I watched him curiously. Why had he been in my tent this morning anyway and why was I fully clothed and in bed and why was . . . *Oh. My. God!*

It all rushed back to me when I saw the empty bottle of African Dreams and the two glasses. I buried my face in my hands as one memory after the other rushed in like scenes from a horror movie. I had thrown myself at him last night. I had been drunk, and shamelessly thrown myself at him, despite my dating detox. I was mortified!

Shit, I had actually grabbed him by the hair and asked him to kiss me and he'd said no! Thank God he'd said no, because I had not been in my right mind. But still the rejection kind of felt a little bruising to my ego. My face burned and I touched my cheeks to try to cool them down. Well, that was it. I was never going to be able to look at him again. Not to mention be in the same room as him. I paced the tent a few times, feeling sicker and sicker by the second. And it wasn't a physical sickness—this was the kind of sickness you feel when you have made a total and utter fool of yourself.

You have muscles.

Sexy ankles.

How did you get so sexy, Max?

"Oh my God, oh my God," I continued, pacing frantically, but was forced to stop when my phone beeped. I rushed over to it and Sebastian's name lit up the screen.

> **Sebastian:** Loving everything so far. Feeling it. Seeing it. Can almost touch it. Vibing it. Agency says it now wants the pack shot on location, not studio. They want to feel Africa in the shot. You know how I feel about pack shots 👻 that's your department, I don't want to know about that shit.
>
> **Ash:** They want the perfect glossy slow-motion alcohol pouring into icy fucking tumbler shot on location? Not in studio where we have control over everything and it will be much, much, much easier?
>
> **Sebastian:** They love complicating their lives and ours.
>
> **Ash:** That they do. Okay, will look for a location.

I groaned. I really, really needed to get to work despite the pounding head and dry mouth. But I was *not* going to go for breakfast and sitting across the table from Max while eating eggs and bacon! My phone beeped again.

Sebastian.

Sebastian: Question. Don't freak the fuck out.

I didn't like the sound of that.

Sebastian: I just looked at this place's website again and they have a photo of sunset drinks by a watering hole. You know the cheesy vibe, blah, blah, at the end of the game drive they watch the animals by the watering hole, sipping on drinks, soaking in the African vibes cue Toto song or Lion King theme.

Ash: Yeeees.

Sebastian: I know it's not on the storyboard, but not me thinking we should throw in an African safari shot.

Ash: NOT you thinking, or you ARE thinking?

Sebastian had a Gen Z daughter and he'd made it part of his personality that he'd claimed their slang and was using it deliberately in his own unique way for shits and giggles.

Sebastian: I WANT an African safari watering hole shot vibe ASAP.

Ash: Not you changing plans last minute, not like the client also not wanting a studio pack shot.

Sebastian: Not you "notting" me.

I rubbed my aching temples. It did make sense, though. That shot would work really well for the ad. But it was going to take a whole lot of extra time, and I would need to arrange a game drive and find this watering hole.

Ash: Let me get through our existing storyboard and if there's time I'll go on a game drive. Couldn't work yesterday when we arrived due to massive storm.

Sebastian: Slay queen.

Ash: Please don't ever say that to me again.

Ash: And please, please never say it to a client.

Sebastian: Too late for that. I've been trying it out all week.

Ash: Not me cringing.

Sebastian: Got to go. Your Russ is not getting what I'm saying about this edit.

Ash: Perhaps that's because you talk like a teenager?

Sebastian: I don't know what on earth you mean.

I then dragged myself through the day like I was walking through thick mud. Every now and then I saw Max and the manager, either sitting and talking, or walking around the place. I'd discovered the most amazing pool too, also under a tented roof to stop the direct sunlight, but open on all sides so you could gaze at your surroundings while submerged in the water. But everywhere I went, Bongani the game ranger was hot on my heels, standing there with his gun. He'd warned me that this was an unfenced game reserve, so animals roamed freely and I was not to go anywhere by myself, especially at night. While I was working, a majestic herd of elephant had wandered past, followed by a rather large and hungry-looking hippo. But by late afternoon, I was feeling sick and faint from lack of food, the hangover and the relentless heat. I had not joined Max for breakfast, and I had also declined to join him for lunch. Apparently, it had not gone unnoticed.

"Hey." Max walked up to me as I was weighing up a potential shot of the swimming pool, also not on the storyboard, but a shot that I knew would totally work for the ad.

"Hey," I replied, but avoided looking in his direction.

"You haven't eaten today?"

"Not hungry," I said quickly, kneeling down lower.

"I put a plate of food together for you and left it in the dining area . . . I've finished eating now, so you can go if you want." The "I'm finished eating" statement lingered in the air between us with a whole chunk of subtext dangling off it. The subtext being he'd clearly noticed I did *not* want to be near him today, let alone look at him, because last night I had gotten way too drunk and had sexually tossed myself at him like croutons into a salad. And the worst part was that after tossing myself like a little sexual crouton, he'd batted me away as if playing pickle ball. *(Oh, God, I really was soooo hungry!)*

"Thanks," I said curtly, and then waited for him to leave. I watched him out the corner of my eye and as soon as he was far enough away, I ran and threw myself into the dining area to inhale the plate of food. Sitting in a post-food glow, I realized I'd forgotten to arrange a game drive. I looked at my watch. The day was almost over, and I'd gone through everything I'd had to, so I went looking for the ranger.

"Hey, sorry, it totally slipped my mind earlier, but I was wondering if there was any possibility you could take me on a game drive this evening. I'd like to look at a potential shot of a watering hole?"

"No need to arrange anything. We're leaving on a game drive in an hour," Bongani said.

"You are?"

"Your partner wanted to go on one," he replied.

"He's not my partner . . . absolutely NOT, at all." I laughed awkwardly and quickly cut myself off when something dawned on me. "Wait, he's going on *this* drive—the one in an hour?"

Bongani looked at me curiously and nodded.

"So, then, no time to organize another one, I suppose? Without Max, who is definitely *not* my partner?"

He gave me another strange look and shook his head. "Sorry, not with you leaving tomorrow."

"Of course. Thank you. I'll see you in an hour, then."

I walked off towards my room, weighing it up. Seeing Max again, spending time with him in a game vehicle, or *not* getting the best possible shots for the client. In the end, my professionalism won.

CHAPTER 24

Max

The last place in the world Ash wanted to be was sitting next to me in a game vehicle and she was making this very clear with her body language. Leaning as far away as possible, she was practically hanging over the edge of the vehicle. But here we were. I could tell how embarrassed she was about last night; she hadn't looked at me all day. It was written across her face, not to mention present in that tight, unnecessary throat-clearing she did from time to time, along with her constant fiddling with a loose piece of thread sticking up from her shorts.

I'd opened my mouth about ten times to say something, but closed it each time, since I had no idea what to actually say to her, or what to say about what had happened—or hadn't happened—last night. I think the "*hadn't happened*" was at the root of all this awkwardness if I knew Ash like I thought I did. But I couldn't exactly tell her that pulling away from her had been one of the hardest things I'd ever done, and if circumstances had been different, if there had been no African Dreams, that I would *not* have pulled away and she would *not* have stood a chance. Her clothes would've been lying on the floor and I would have buried my face between her legs and made her come so hard she would have seen stars. But I wasn't sure that level of detail would be helpful at this moment.

"Is this the watering hole you were talking about?" Bongani turned and asked Ash, pointing at the small dam in the distance. She checked a picture on her phone and then looked back up.

"Yes, that's it. The one with the baobab tree." The sun was setting and it was obvious why she wanted to see this place—it would make an amazing shot. Then she waved her phone around in the air and looked at it from various angles.

"I don't have signal either," I said, holding my phone up at her to confirm.

"The storm took out the cell-phone towers and also knocked out radio comms," Bongani added.

Ash grabbed her camera and then jumped off the vehicle.

"Can we go closer?" she asked. "It would be better for the shot."

Bongani nodded and started driving again, while Ash walked alongside the moving vehicle. Bongani drove slowly. The rain had turned the terrain into a thick, quicksand-like sludge.

"Oh my God!" Ash screamed through a wet, squelching sound, and I turned to see her leg sinking into a puddle of mud. She waved her arms around frantically, and without thinking, I jumped off the back of the vehicle and fought my way through the thick mud to reach her.

"Shit." I grabbed on to a handful of grass to stop myself from going in any deeper. I'd watched too many TV shows as a child where people had been sucked to their deaths in quicksand.

"Grab my arm," I instructed, using the tuft of grass to pull myself out of the knee-high sludge.

She gave my arm the filthiest look, as if it stank. "I'm perfectly fine. I can get myself out of here, thanks."

"I know, I just thought I would help."

"You've helped enough, Max." She rolled her eyes at me. "I am perfectly fine. There is no need to be jumping off vehicles to rescue me and running to my tent in the rain—I can rescue myself."

She seemed very determined, so I turned round and pulled myself out of the muddy puddle and back onto hard soil using the tuft of grass as an anchor. My legs were covered in mud from my knees down and it was pointless trying to wipe them. This was the kind of dirt that needed to be hosed off.

I stood back and watched Ash as she tried to pull her leg out of the mud and take a step. But each time she tried to pull it out, she seemed to topple to the left and had to put it down again.

"For fuck's sake!" she moaned loudly, and tried again. "And no, I still don't want your help!"

"I wasn't going to offer again," I called as she struggled in a particularly soft bit.

"Good, because I am not some bloody damsel in distress you can run around rescuing, Max!"

"I've never thought of you as a damsel," I said.

"I also could have gotten that thorn out of my foot myself, just saying."

"I'm sure you could have," I agreed, even though I knew there was no way she would have been able to yank that massive thorn out herself—God, no one would've been able to do that. But I knew what she was doing right now, so I let her. She'd made herself vulnerable last night and I had "rejected" her, and now she was simply trying to take back some of her power, so I'd let her. I'd stand here all night and wait for her to climb out of the mud if it made her feel a little better about what had happened last night. Anything to make sure she was okay.

I looked over my shoulder and vaguely registered that the vehicle looked as if it had also gotten stuck in the mud. But that wasn't my focus right now, my focus was watching Ash as she struggled through the thigh-high mud until she eventually managed to climb onto solid ground. She collapsed, out of breath and totally covered in mud. I turned my attention back to the vehicle now and finally registered the seriousness of the situation as I watched Bongani walking around the vehicle thoughtfully.

"I don't think we're going to be able to get out of this ourselves. I'm going to have to call for help," he said as I walked towards him. He began trying to radio out, but like he'd said before, the storm had knocked out the communication and a bad feeling sank into the pit of my stomach. I pulled out my phone and looked at the screen—still no bars.

"Do you have any reception yet?" I asked Ash, who was now bent over at the waist. She looked at her phone and shook her head.

"I also don't have cell reception," Bongani said, and a strange group silence descended in which we all took stock of our current predicament.

"We need some sticks to put under the wheels for traction—only way we'll stand a chance of getting out of this mud," Bongani announced.

"We need sticks," I called over to Ash. We all looked around. Where the hell were we going to get sticks from? We were in the middle of the bloody Kalahari Desert, on a salt pan, no trees except for that distant baobab. But baobab trees are protected so breaking any branches was out of the question. Our only hope lay in the possibility that maybe it had shed some branches that were now conveniently on the ground.

Bongani pulled his rifle onto his shoulder and called for us to start walking towards the tree. The sun was setting quickly now and I could make out the shape of a herd of wildebeest walking towards the watering hole.

Bongani declared the obvious. "Animals are coming out."

"I have a bad feeling about this," Ash said, catching up to me with her ridiculous brown legs and face. It was the most she'd said to me all day, so I tried to set her mind at ease.

"This guy is a pro. He knows what he's doing," I reassured her.

"I don't know. This feels like we're kind of . . . stranded." I could hear a quiver of panic in her voice. I turned, stopping her abruptly. Our eyes met for a second, before she very deliberately looked away.

"Why don't you get out your camera and do your work while we're doing this, but stay close to us. That should distract you."

She nodded. "Good idea." I almost melted at that, the first vaguely friendly words she'd given me all day. And I was also filled with the satisfaction I was able to help her, even if it was in a small way.

CHAPTER 25

Ash

"*T*hat's a fucking lion," I whispered, pointing at the animal slowly walking up to the watering hole now only meters away from us. It was a little past sunset, that time when the light was at its softest. It would be dark soon and there was a fucking lion drinking at the watering hole, and, *oh*, another lion, yes, here comes another one . . . An entire pride of lions was now having a sunset drink at their favorite drinking hole. Don't get me wrong: I like lions. I like watching them from the comfort of a game vehicle, though.

"Okay, let's head back to the vehicle." Bongani turned and started walking back. He didn't need to ask me twice; I was more than happy to climb back into the vehicle and get away from this watering hole where we were not at the top of the food chain.

I slapped my arm as a mosquito bit me. Another one got my neck and then another one. "Great," I moaned, briefly looking up at Max, who was smiling at me. I looked away as fast as I could. Mosquitoes had always come for me. If there was a group of us, I was the one that they gravitated towards. Max used to joke that it was because I had the sweetest blood. It had been cute at the time he'd said it, but that was not in the middle of Botswana, near a watering hole, at night when the sheer number of mosquitoes was such that I was sure I could be well and truly exsanguinated by the end of this ordeal. I slapped myself on the cheek this time as another one got me.

"Crap!" I jumped up and down and flapped my shirt frantically.

"They're in my shirt!" But the more I flapped it, the more the vampirical opportunists saw it as a free invitation to go inside. "Oh my God!" I slapped my thigh next and then my ass as the little bastards somehow wiggled their way inside my shirt.

When we were finally back at the vehicle, Bongani passed me a blanket and I wrapped my entire body in it and sat on the floor, huddled in a corner. But even then, I could hear them circling like mini bloodsucking vultures.

"So, what's the plan?" I asked through a little gap in the blanket I'd made for my mouth. "Or are we going to end up sleeping here tonight?"

"We are due back from this drive in an hour, so when we don't arrive another vehicle will come for us, because each car has a satellite tracker, which will not have been affected by the storm."

"An hour," I moaned, and then yelped as a mosquito bit my lip. Bastards!

"I'm sure it will only take them forty minutes to get here, so we'll be on our way soon."

I screwed my face up, marveling at this man's concept of "soon." Mind you, these trackers did sit in the bush for days on end watching animals. This was probably his version of the blink of an eye. I closed all the gaps in the blanket and hunkered down for the next hour and a bit, determined not to be bitten again, and determined not to have to talk to Max again either. It worked for a while, until my bladder began objecting to this situation.

"I need the toilet." I was relieved when Max said it first. "Anyone else?"

"Me too," I quickly said, sticking my head out from under the blanket like a tortoise.

"No, I've trained myself not to need it for long periods of time," Bongani said, and I smiled to myself. Of course he had.

"You'll have to go behind the vehicle, no other place," he added.

"Behind the . . . That's all well and good for you guys, men, but it's a little different when you're a woman, if you get my drift." In fact, it was very different. The difficulty of peeing as a woman on a game drive was an age-old dilemma that had given rise to some rather odd inventions, like the "ShePee", a device women could use to pee standing up, or so the inventors claimed. I'd tried it once and had only managed to pee down my entire leg.

"There's a small rock over there that could give you some privacy, but we would have to all go with you, with the gun."

"Both of you?"

"Can't leave anyone here in the vehicle alone."

"So this is a group activity," I said to myself, and sighed. "I'll just go behind the vehicle, then." There would be no privacy behind the small rock, in fact, there was probably more privacy behind the car.

"Do you want to go first?" Max asked.

"No, feel free," I said, and slunk my head back under the blanket again.

"Jump over the wet mud onto the dry part," Bongani pointed out, "or you'll get stuck again."

I heard Max jump, and there was a squelch as he hit the ground, which was probably unavoidable at this stage. I tried not to focus on what came next, though, but that was also unavoidable. I heard a zipper and then the inevitable pee sound. I shook my head. This so embarrassing! Sharing our pee sounds with each other felt so weirdly intimate and I didn't like it one little bit. I hadn't seen my ex-boyfriend in thirteen years, and now we were basically going to the toilet together. I cringed.

I jumped up when Max had climbed back in. "My turn." Bongani passed me some tissues and an antibacterial wipe for my hands. I climbed up onto the edge of the vehicle and tried to figure out where to jump, hoping my legs wouldn't plunge into the mud. They did, but luckily it was only to ankle depth. I walked round to the back of the vehicle, still wrapped in the blanket.

"Eyes to the front," I said to Max warningly.

"I would never dream of looking," he said.

"And make some noises, so you don't listen to the sounds of me peeing."

He laughed. "What kind of noises?"

"Have a conversation or something," I insisted as I worked my shorts down to my ankles and tried to get into a "comfortable" squatting position. This was ridiculous—almost farcical—and if I wasn't concentrating so hard on balancing, I might have laughed at this situation.

"What would you like me to talk about?" Max asked, and my bladder felt as if it was going to pop like a balloon, but I refused to pee until there was at least a conversation drowning out *some* of the inevitable noise.

"Something. Anything. Just talk," I said desperately.

"Uh, okay . . ." He paused for the longest time and I felt as if I might explode. "It's hard."

"God, don't talk to me about hard right now."

"Sorry, um . . . Okay . . ."

"Talk! For heaven's sake, say something." I was clenching my entire body and the second the first syllable came out of his mouth, I finally let go.

"Do you know that Ash and I used to date? Well, it was more than date, actually. We used to—"

"What the hell, Max?" I stopped peeing as fast as I could. "I said talk, not *that*."

I heard a laugh now, an unfamiliar one. It was Bongani.

"What?" I asked, peeing just a little.

"That makes so much sense now."

"What makes sense?"

"You two."

"What about us?" I wasn't enjoying this line of questioning, but at least it was giving me a chance to empty my bladder, a few words at a time.

"The way you act weirdly around each other. I get it now."

"Oh my God, that's ridiculous. We don't act weirdly around each oth—" I stopped talking when both Bongani and Max chuckled.

"Maybe Max acts weirdly around me, but I'm totally fine with all of this. Why wouldn't I be fine with having my ex-boyfriend join me for work, not to mention mutual toileting, when I haven't seen him in thirteen—Crap!" A mosquito had made a beeline for my ass and had bitten me.

"You okay?" Max asked.

"Mosquitoes in places I would rather they not be!" I said, pulling up my pants as quickly as I could. "Stranded with lions, having conversations I really would rather not be having, practically being eaten alive—this evening could not be going better if—Shit. Shit! Oh my God!" I winced a few more times as another three or four little assholes managed to sink their evil claws into me.

This was an actual nightmare. I was living in my own African nightmare. Screw African dreams, because this was not that!

CHAPTER 26

Max

By the time we were rescued and had made it back to the lodge, I was exhausted and all I could think about was climbing into bed.

"Stop scratching," I said to Ash as we walked to our rooms.

"Can't help it. I'm dying here." She continued to scratch at her arm wildly.

I stopped in front of her. "Give me your arm."

"No, I am not giving you my arm," she objected obstinately. Fucking hell, it was cute. In fact, that red bite on the tip of her nose was also cute.

"Just give me your arm, Ash."

"No, I'm fine." She was scratching so badly, and still not making eye contact with me. It was time to deal with this.

"I think we should talk about what happened last night," I said suddenly, and she immediately bristled.

"Nothing to talk about," she replied.

"Ash, you can't keep *not* looking at me, *not* talking to me and *not* eating food around me for the rest of the trip because you're feeling awkward about what happened last night."

"And what exactly did happen last night?" she asked, finally looking at me. I could see it had taken all her courage and resolve to do that.

"We had too much to drink, things got a bit flirty—very flirty, actually—you tried to kiss me and I—"

"Oh my God, stop!" She put her hands over her face and shook her head wildly. "Let's never speak about this again. Thanks." She rushed off down the path, scratching as she went.

"You have no idea how badly I wanted to kiss you," I called after her, which stopped her dead in her tracks. "It took all my willpower last night not to, Ash."

She turned slowly and faced me again. "Then why didn't you?"

"Call me old-fashioned, but I think after a certain amount of alcohol, consent no longer exists." I stepped closer to her.

She scratched her arm viciously once more and then nodded at me. "You did the right thing."

"I know I did. But clearly you're still feeling awkward."

"How can I not feel awkward when I . . . I basically manhandled your ankle, Max. God, this is so embarrassing. I don't know what came over me. It was *soooooo* not what I wanted to do—trust me."

"Not what you wanted to do? I think I feel offended by that."

"Well, do you think I wanted to be trying to kiss you?"

"It kind of looked like you did, to be honest."

"I didn't. I blame it on the African Dreams, otherwise I would never, I mean never . . . It would *never* have happened."

I took a step back. "That was an awful lot of nevers."

"It was. And I mean it," she said, but her eyes came to rest on my lips. They lingered there for a very long time, in total contradiction to what she was saying. But then very abruptly and dramatically, she flicked her eyes away and seemed to focus on something above my head.

I turned and looked. There was nothing there.

"I thought I saw a . . ." she started, and then just petered out, scratching her arm again.

I sighed loudly. "Just bring me your arm, Ash."

She sighed too, matching mine in intensity. I watched her

resolve finally slip away and she walked towards me, holding out her arm.

"Old bite remedy," I said, and then pressed my thumbnail through the bite mark twice, making a cross through the bump.

"My mom used to do this to me when I was bitten." She said this softly.

"Clever woman—it works." I carefully pressed some of the other bites on her arms and she didn't object. In fact, she made a few little happy moaning sounds as the itches began to disappear. "You can do the rest," I said, stopping at her arms. "But maybe you should take an antihistamine too. You know how allergic you can get."

"Thank you. I will." She turned and started walking away again. But then stopped.

"And, hypothetically, if we hadn't been drinking?" she asked, turning back to me with a tentative look that made my heart thump.

"If we hadn't been drinking, would I have hypothetically kissed you back?" I smiled and started walking towards her, my eyes trailing up and down her body as I went, from her lips, to her breasts, to that place between her legs and back up to her lips and eyes. I stopped right in front of her.

"Well, then I would have kissed you . . ." I moved even closer, until I was towering over her and she was craning her neck to look at me. I leaned down and put my mouth to her ear. "Every single inch of your body." Her entire body reacted with a shiver. I pulled away slowly, looking deep into her eyes. Her cheeks were flushed, and her chest was rising and falling quicker.

"Right! Okay!" she said awkwardly, jumping backwards. "Interesting information. Not that it matters or anything, but, uh . . . but . . ." She turned round and began beating a speedy retreat. I watched her with a smile as she looked back a few times at me, still scratching the backs of her thighs as she walked. But then she did something that was my absolute undoing. She stuck her hand down the back of her shorts to scratch and it was just enough time for me to see the shape and outline of her ass.

"Shit," I hissed under my breath, because now all I could think about was gripping her ass in my hand. Between last night, her hand tangled in my hair asking me to kiss her, and today, seeing that perfect curve of her ass . . . I wasn't sure how I was going to cope not touching her. I might have to take matters into my own hands.

CHAPTER 27

Ash

*E*very inch?

As soon as I was in my tent, I pulled all the sides closed as if I was hiding from someone. I was. *Him.* Him and all his whispered inches that were right now making me feel so hot that I felt I needed to peel my clothes off and climb into an icy shower. Did he mean . . .

Alllll the inches?

I got a chilled bottle of water out of the bar fridge and half downed it in one sip. I scratched my ear. It itched from the feel of his breath against it. I had never been more turned on in my entire life!

"Oooh dear," I mumbled out loud. A hot, sticky feeling of pure raw lust started building inside me, which was so inconvenient because I was on a detox—albeit a seriously tenuous one that seemed to waver every other moment—and because it was my ex, Max.

"Oooh dear!" I mumbled again, and physically fanned myself.

That inch too?

No one had gone near that inch in thirteen years. Not since the unfortunate blowing incident, of which, it is important to acknowledge, he was the very cause. Every single time a man had tried to do that, I'd grabbed him by the hair on his head, except the bald guy, and pulled them right back up. That inch had remained unexplored territory for so long. I furiously scratched my legs. I had bites all over my bloody body, but Max's trick was working. I started pressing crosses into the bites on my legs and the itching began dissipating somewhat. The itching on my back, however, was another story. I ran to the center pole in the room after trying all manner of pretzel-like yoga moves to scratch it, and started rubbing my back against it. I let out a very long, satisfied moan as the itch was momentarily scratched.

The mosquito bites were making me itch, but there was something else that was making me itch too—Max. And I wasn't sure which was worse as I continued frantically rubbing my back against the pole. I couldn't even work out what itch was Max and what itch was the mosquitoes anymore. The itches had combined and now my entire being felt itchy.

I kept rubbing, hoping to scratch both itches at once. Rid myself of the itchy mosquito feeling, but also rid myself of the itchy Max feeling. But truth was, Max had been making me itch long before tonight, before I even knew who he was. Those emails we'd exchanged had started it, and then seeing him, having him lock eyes with me, tend to my bleeding foot, whisper words in my ear . . . all that had only exacerbated the itch, which seemed to be growing and gathering momentum constantly. I pulled my phone out while still rubbing my back against the pole. Just because I was itchy all over, in more ways than one, did not mean I was about to ignore all my work responsibilities. But when I looked down at my phone, the phone that was picking up zero internet, I tossed it across to my bed. I would have to send Sebastian my watering-hole pictures later.

The itch on my back was just not going—the pole was not quite reaching. I looked around the room and saw the umbrella by the door. I raced over to it, and tried to use it to scratch, but the sharp top of the umbrella felt as if it was scratching through my skin. I threw it down on the floor.

Every. Single. Inch.

I couldn't get his words out of my head. Last time he'd been near that inch, it had been a disaster, but now I was in no doubt of his apparent sexual mastery. You couldn't look at Max and not feel on some primitive, instinctive level, that this man was going to give you mind-blowing orgasms. He oozed sex. Even when he wasn't trying to be sexy, he gave off this sexy-as-fuck, big-dick energy that was enough to turn any woman wild.

Any woman . . . and probably many, *many* if the rumors were to be believed. I didn't know how I felt about that, though. He'd probably kissed so many inches that if you lined them up, he'd already run a 10K marathon.

This Max, sexy, broody, whispery, hairy Max, was certainly not the young man I'd once known. Who'd waited to have sex with me, who'd said that I was it, I would be the first and last person he'd ever sleep with. I'd also thought that at the time. In fact, I'd never been surer about anything in my life, until I wasn't and realized what a naïve, stupid dream that had been.

He'd destroyed me. He'd been the one person that I'd been able to talk to and confide in, maybe even more so than Sarah at the time. He was the one person I'd told everything to, all the details of my sister's death that I've hardly shared with anyone. How I'd felt so powerless standing in the doorway and not knowing what to do. How I'd never felt more panicked and terrified in my life and how still today I get that same panicked feeling if something feels out of my control. I'd told him all about my mom's recuring depressive spells. She would be okay for a while, a year, two years, and then she would collapse into a pit of darkness and vanish while my dad disappeared into a bottle.

Everyone went away, even when they were sitting right there on the couch next to me. He'd also gone away. But now he was back and I had so many complicated feelings about him.

"Fuuuck!" I hurried back to the pole in the middle of the room and rubbed my back against it furiously. The itch was killing me and there was no way I was going to be able to relax, let alone sleep, tonight. I stopped scratching and realized that there was only one person here who could attend to that itch. He could probably attend to *all* the itches, but I certainly wasn't going to let him scratch that one . . .

Was I?

"Detox. I am on a detox!" I said out loud as I raced for the door.

CHAPTER 28

Max

I climbed into my shower and gripped my cock as the water ran over me. I gripped it as tightly as I could. I wanted her so badly it physically hurt. So badly that the more I stroked myself up and down, the worse it all became. Maybe the answer was not to do this at all, but rather turn the cold tap on full blast instead. But I couldn't stop, because with each stroke I was imagining sinking into her over and over again. And each time I imagined it, the closer I got to my release and the faster I went.

"MAX!"

"Shit!" I slipped on the shower floor and almost fell on my face when I heard her voice at the door. I grabbed the closest towel and wrapped it round me, trying to flatten my erection. Not working. Not working at all. I took another towel and draped it over my shoulder, making sure it hung over the tent that my cock was now making. I pushed the wet hair out of my face and walked over to the door as nonchalantly as possible.

I opened it and she looked away quickly.

"Oh . . . you're . . . uh . . . Never mind. Never mind." She turned and started making an escape, but I reached out and touched her elbow, bringing her to a stop.

"What's up? It must be serious if you're at my tent at eleven at night."

"I kind of have a problem."

"What kind of problem?"

"It's a mosquito-related problem. But I really don't think now is the time. You're wet and—"

"Don't go. What's wrong?" I tightened my grip on her elbow, not exactly holding her in place, but making it very clear I wanted her to stay. My cock wanted her to stay too.

"There's a bite I can't reach and I'm not going to be able to sleep and I need someone to press it and I wouldn't ask if it wasn't an emergency, but it is. And for the record, this is not you coming to my rescue either."

"Of course not." I stepped back and pulled the curtain aside. "Come in."

She walked in, eyes on the floor, avoiding my naked chest.

"Sorry to disturb you. I'm sure seeing me here was the furthest thing from your mind."

Oh, how wrong she was. If she only knew how I'd just been thinking about her, cock in hand, I doubt she would have come to my room.

"Not a problem. Where's this bite you need help with?" I asked as she shielded her eyes with her hand. I laughed. "Do you want me to put a shirt on?"

"Please."

"Hang on." I walked over to my suitcase, pulled out the nearest shirt and slipped it over my still wet body. It clung to my chest, but at least, thankfully, my hard-on had ceased and desisted.

"Okay, where is it?" I asked again.

"Right in the middle of my back, between my shoulder blades." She pursed her lips and then raised her brows awkwardly.

"Well, you're going to have to turn round and take your shirt off if you want me to help you."

She shook her head. "I can't believe this," she muttered almost to herself, and then turned round. She pulled the back of her shirt up, but didn't pull it off.

"Jesus, your back is totally red. What have you done, Ash?"

"I may have tried to get at it with an umbrella, and then rubbed it against the tent pole."

"God. It's really bad. You're going to need some cream on that—your skin is so sensitive."

"You remember that too."

"I remember having to empty bottles of after-sun on you every time you went into the sun—you would burn at the drop of a hat."

"True."

"I can't see the bite, though," I said after scanning her back.

She sighed. "It's under my bra strap. Don't ask me how it got there, but it did."

I stepped closer to her naked back. Red, naked back, but still naked and still more of her than I'd seen in years.

"I'm going to have to undo it." The words had gotten stuck in my dry mouth and stumbled out with a small stutter.

She nodded and gave me a nervous, "Mmmm."

I reached for her bra strap and my cock immediately hardened again. Shit, this was so inconvenient. I took the clasp in one hand and unclipped it with total ease, the kind of ease that comes from unclipping many bra straps one-handed. But this wasn't any bra strap—this was hers. It fell open and her back was completely naked now.

"Can you see it?" she asked.

"I can." I reached for the bite, but not before taking a total liberty. I laid my fingertip on her back, just below the bite and trailed it up slowly. Her skin pebbled in response, and I saw her shoulders rise as she sucked in a quick breath. I pressed my nail into the bite slowly, running my eyes over her back as I did it. I didn't want this moment to end, and when it was done, I took another total liberty and trailed my thumb slowly down her spine until it reached her lower back.

"I have some moisturizing cream," I said, removing my hand from her back.

She remained quiet for the longest time, and then gave an almost imperceptible nod. But it was all I needed. Was I being a total asshole, taking advantage of this situation? Probably. But was it going to stop me? Probably not. I reached into my bag for the cream, but when I saw the label on it I froze. It was a luxury body cream that had been gifted to me by one of the last women I'd dated. She was a model for the brand and had bought me the men's range. Her almost completely naked body, glistening from the moisturizing cream in that magazine, flashed through my head and there was no way I was going to put this cream onto Ash's body now. It felt contaminated in some way by someone else.

"Sorry, I must have left it." I walked back to her and was about to do up her bra strap when she stopped me.

"It's still itchy. Can you do it one more time, harder and deeper this time?"

I tried to pretend that her saying "harder and deeper" to me had no effect, but my cock immediately disagreed.

"Sure." I lowered my finger to the bite and put my nail into it, pressed down hard and held it there. "Better?"

"Getting there," she said.

I did it again, making another deeper cross in the bite and held it there for as long as I could.

"And now?"

"Much better, thank you," she said, but didn't move off.

I didn't move either and waited for her to give me some sort of sign or signal as to what I could do next. And when she leaned back the tiniest bit, I moved in closer. So close that my cock was almost touching her. The tips of my fingers felt on fire. They longed to be tracing her back right now, but that would be taking it too far . . . *or would it?*

I brushed her back with my finger tentatively. It could have been perceived as an accidental brush, or more, depending on what she was thinking. And when I saw the way her skin responded, the way her shoulders jerked up at the sensation, and then the way her breath came out in one sharp burst, I knew what she was thinking.

"What are you doing?" she whispered.

"Do you want me to stop?" I asked.

"I don't . . ." Her voice was so breathy I could barely hear her. "I'm not supposed to be . . ." Her words said one thing, but her body said another. Still, I needed confirmation.

"Tell me to stop if you want me to," I said softly into her ear.

She inhaled sharply and said the only words that I wanted to hear. "I don't want you to stop."

I didn't need any more encouragement. I ran my fingertips all the way down her spine until they reached the arch in her lower back. Her body tensed, as if readying herself for something, so I gave her *something*. I slowly dipped just the tip of my thumb under the waistband of her shorts. This tiny move felt like the most erotic thing I'd ever done in my life. Nothing had ever turned me on more. Well, almost nothing, because when I dipped it in again and she moaned, I thought I was going to totally lose it.

I didn't waste any time doing what I did next. I ran my hand from her back, to her side and then ran it round to the front of her, placing it on her stomach. I smiled. Her stomach was a little rounder now. It had been almost indented thirteen years ago, but I liked it way better now. I pulled her towards me, until her back pressed into my chest, her ass pressed against my hard cock and held her in place like that. I lowered my face to her neck and traced my rough skin on it. She moaned and pressed into me, giving me all the invitation I needed. I rested my chin on her shoulder and simply breathed her in for a blissful moment. She smelled amazing, even though there was no trace of that mystery scent from all those years ago. If this was going to happen, I was going to take my time with her. It was eleven o'clock now, and when morning came, I still wouldn't be done with her. Not even vaguely.

I dragged my fingers around her belly button, fingertips barely touching her skin, but her reaction to it was powerful. She dropped her head back and moaned. My other hand went up to her T-shirt, and in one move I pulled it over her head and dropped it on the floor. And once I'd done that, I gripped her waist between both my hands.

It was so small and petite. I remembered that so well. And my hands had grown, and like this, it felt as if I could wrap my hands round her entire waist. I tested that theory, moving my hands to her hips, stretching my fingers round them and pulling her back into me even more. She reacted by arching her back.

There were a few things I could do right now: I could run both my hands up her body and slip them over her breasts. I could run one down between her legs, cup her there, while the other sought out her nipples, which I was sure were hard. I could slip both my hands into her shorts. Use one to push her legs apart and the other to find the spot I wanted to start exploring for hours. But none of those felt right for this moment with her. Having her back to me wasn't right either. I wanted to see her. I wanted to stare into her eyes and convey to her every single thing I'd been feeling for the last thirteen years. But as I started to turn her, she pulled away.

"Jesus! Shit. Okay!" She pushed herself away from me and stepped back.

"What?" I asked.

"I'm not meant to be doing this." She gestured to the space between us. "We can't be doing this . . . *can we?*"

I was about to answer her, but she seemed to have started a conversation with herself.

"No, we can't. No, especially not . . . him . . . no!"

"I'm here!" I held my hand up and she looked at me. She was not wearing her T-shirt, a fact that I think she hadn't realized and, my God, her bra was completely see-through. The white mesh left little to the imagination, and her hard pink nipples pushed into the material, just screaming to be pulled into my mouth.

"What is wrong with you?" she suddenly asked in an accusatory tone.

"Sorry, what?"

"One minute you're pressing my mosquito bite and the next you're touching me and then we're . . . This should not be happening."

"I said you could tell me to stop whenever you wanted to."

"I know! And I have! But that's not the point, Max."

"What's the point?" I asked.

"The point is you're making it so, so hard to say no and that's not fair!"

I smiled at her, despite the fact that I could see she was currently battling some sort of internal war.

"Stop smiling at me like that!" she said.

"Like what?"

"Like this is all fun and games when it isn't, not after everything that happened between us. Not after thirteen years and a mountain of emotional shit."

I stopped smiling and started nodding. "Sorry, you're right. This isn't as simple as two people who are attracted to each other. It's complicated."

"Complicated is an understatement. And besides . . ." She started walking towards the door now, as if her internal battle was over and one side had won. She looked determined. "I am on a detox! And you are not healthy for me! You are cheesecake, Max, and I need celery juice."

CHAPTER 29

Ash

I rushed out into the night again. I should not be running back and forth between tents in the dark like this. This was dangerous! God, what was I thinking? This was all dangerous. *Max* was dangerous, and yet I kept flirting with the irresistible danger of him, despite my better judgement. I was waging a war between body and brain right now, and my body seemed to keep wanting to win.

"Wait!"

I stopped running and turned round at Max's voice.

"What?" I asked, out of breath.

"Your T-shirt, you forgot it." He was standing there in his towel, looking way too hot for his own good, dangling my T-shirt from his finger. It took my brain a moment to register.

"Shit." I gasped and tried to cover myself. How the hell had I not realized I'd run out half naked. I looked down and almost choked when I realized that the bra I was wearing was none other than my totally see-through white mesh one. I quickly cupped my breasts in my hands. God, why had I not chosen another bra for this? One that did not leave so little to the imagination.

"You can just toss it, thanks." I gripped my breasts tightly.

"Toss it?"

"Yes, just toss it there, onto the walkway. I'll get it."

"No, Ash, I am not tossing your clothes around. It feels totally disrespectful." He started walking towards me.

"No, stop. I'll come and get it then." I wanted to at least have some power and control over this moment, so I started walking towards him. He stood still, holding the T-shirt out for me. I locked eyes with him and started making my way down the walkway. He smiled. It was warm and . . . *Wait!* The way he was looking at me, the way a feeling was swelling inside as I walked, I'm sure this is what it felt like when you were walking down the aisle to meet your future husband or something equally, utterly ridiculous! This was ridiculous. It was all so . . .

"Ridiculous," I said when I found myself standing right in front of him again. Our eyes were still locked, even if I didn't want them to be.

"What is?" he asked, voice so soft I almost didn't catch it.

"All of this." I reached out for my T-shirt, but he didn't let go.

"You're still holding on to my shirt," I said.

"That's not what I'm holding on to," he replied.

"What are you holding on to then?"

"*You.*"

That one word cut through me like a scalpel. Everything inside me suddenly felt painfully frantic. As if it had all just been woken up from a long hibernation and had sprung back to life, desperate for something.

"I think you should let go," I managed.

"Should I?" he asked, the words *so, so loaded*.

I didn't manage to speak this time, simply nodded.

"Not good enough, Ash. I need to hear you say it out loud."

I straightened up, tightening my grip on my shirt. "I think you should let go of my shirt now, Max." I said it with as much self-assuredness as I could muster.

"Are you sure?" he asked, his eyes searching my face for something.

"I am," I said, and with that, he let go of the shirt and it fell into my hands.

"So, I guess this is goodnight, then?" His eyes left my face, and they momentarily grazed my breasts and stomach. My body physically ached for him, just as it had only moments ago when his hands had been all over it.

"It is. Goodnight, Max," I said, but was unable to bring myself to move off the spot my feet felt glued to. We looked at each other. One of us had to move, or this was *not* going to be the goodnight I intended it to be.

"Goodnight, then, Ash. Sleep tight." And then he moved. Off the spot, down the walkway, and into his tent. I stood and watched as he walked away, a part of me willing him to stop and look back, and another part of me wanting to run after him and let him have every single inch of my body in any way he liked. But I did none of that. Instead I headed back to my room and collapsed on the bed in utter exhaustion.

~

Max invaded my dreams that night. I tossed and turned, caught somewhere in an agitated state that I hardly knew what to do with. By 3 a.m. I simply gave up, and didn't even try to sleep. *Every single inch of your body.* That phrase ran through my mind over and over and over again.

Every inch?

All the inches?

That inch too?

No one had ever destroyed me like Max had done. Total emotional annihilation. But no one had ever made me feel this palpably, tangibly, sexually alive as he had these last few days either. But it would be a disaster. *Wouldn't it?* There was just too much between us, too much had happened, too many things said and done, or not done, in our case. It would be madness hooking up with him, wouldn't it? After all, he was probably the only person on earth capable of hurting me in a way that I never wanted to be hurt again.

But it would just be sex.

Nothing more.

Just sex.

My body was screaming "sex" and my mind was screaming "no," and I was finding it very disconcerting.

Do it. Just walk over there and have sex with him. Hot, wild, sweaty sex with the man who *does* own a llama and therefore *is* probably able to give a woman seventeen orgasms and make her come just by looking at her.

Do not do it. Remember all the pain and crying, and all the endless waiting and wanting and—

"Fuck it!"

I grabbed the gown hanging up behind the bathroom door and dashed out of my tent. My mind decided to berate and warn me one last time.

This is not a good idea. Not a good idea. At all.

But I ignored it and continued to run down the wooden planks as fast as I could in case I was going to chicken out. I was going to have sex with him! The thought made me giddy with a kind of effervescent euphoria. There were a few lights illuminating the path, not very well, but just enough for me to see where I was going. I jumped over a stick on the path and then felt a sharp, strange pain on my ankle. I stopped and looked at my ankle—it was bleeding—and then I looked at the stick and that's when my life started flashing before my eyes.

"HEEEEELP, HEEEEELP, HEEEELP!" I screamed until my vocal cords couldn't scream anymore. "SNAKE! SNAKE! HELP ME! I'VE BEEN BITTEN!"

The snake was clearly frightened too. It raised its head and looked at me with its black, beady eyes. It had a huge red smile on its face, as if it was mocking me while wearing red lipstick. I felt suddenly very sick, and then it slipped off the path and into the bush.

"What's going on?" Max was there in seconds.

"I'm dying!" I said, terror rising and exploding out of me. "A snake! It bit me! I'm going to fucking die!" I pointed to my ankle.

Max's eyes made a beeline for my ankle and then it looked like every last drop of blood he had rushed out of his body. I'd never seen anyone look so pale. It made me feel pale and dizzy too. A tingly feeling surged over my skin and my head started to buzz.

"I think I'm going to faint!" I grabbed for the banister but missed and started to tumble. Max caught me and lowered me carefully to the ground. "I don't feel good, Max. My heart, it's racing. I don't feel good. Help me."

"I've got you, Ash."

"I'm dying!" I whimpered at him as the second worst terror I'd ever felt in my life descended. "I'm too young to . . . Oh my God." I felt frantic now and tried to breathe, but couldn't. I started hyperventilating as I imagined all the venom surging through my body, attacking my lungs.

"What happened?" Bongani and the manager were there now with huge flashlights.

"She's been bitten by a snake!"

"Where did it go?" Bongani asked.

I pointed at the bush, and like some fearless gazelle, he jumped off the walkway into it.

"I'm going to call for an airlift ambulance!" the manager said, running off.

Max cradled my head in his hands and I could feel the poison working, feel the tingling in all my extremities and my vision went blurry.

"Max . . ." My voice was soft; it was taking all my energy just to talk. "I don't want to die. There are so many things I haven't done. So many things I regret. I mean, I want more time with my friends. I want more cats. I want to travel and I want to overcome my fear of roller coasters so I can go on one at least once before I die and I want to go to Bali and walk on the beach at sunset and I want to eat real curry in India and I want to swim in the Maldivian Sea and it would be great, just bloody great, to no longer be cursed and to have one, just one actual orgasm with a human being, and to have good sex at least once in my life before I die! Oh my God, I am going to die!!!" I started sobbing just as Bongani emerged from the bushes holding a snake.

"Is this the snake?" he asked.

My sobbing ceased as I looked at the evil thing. Clown-like, still mocking me with its red smile. "Yes! That's the one."

"Are you sure?" he asked.

"I've never been more sure about anything before in my life."

"Oh. Cool!" And with that, he released the snake back into the bush.

"What the hell are you doing?" Max shouted.

"It's a red-lipped herald, totally harmless. Very, very aggressive snake—not surprised it bit you—but totally harmless."

"Harmless!" I managed. "But I can feel it. My heart is racing. I'm sweaty, dizzy. I feel faint. I'm tingling all over. I'm struggling to breathe. I don't feel well at all."

The manager came running back down. "Helicopter will be here in fifteen minutes."

"No need, red-lipped herald."

"Oh, thank God!" The manager gripped his chest and exhaled loudly. "I'll go and cancel it." He sprinted away.

"You're in shock." Bongani walked over to me. "The sweat, racing heart, dizziness, tingling, it's indicative of shock and panic. I don't blame you, but you're going to be totally fine. Put the bite under running water for five minutes, and I'll go and get the first-aid kit. There's some antiseptic cream in there and a plaster."

"Are you sure?" Max asked. "Shouldn't she just go to the hospital, in case something happens?"

"I'll even give you some antibiotics to take if you're worried about infection," Bongani said to me. "But I promise the snake is totally harmless." He turned to Max. "Help her to the tent, get her some Coke for the shock and I'll be back soon."

Max threw his arms round me and I felt my body being lifted off the ground as he buried his head in my neck and squeezed me so hard I thought I was going to break.

"Thank God. I thought I was going to lose you again," he said, lips pressed into the side of my face. "And I can't lose you again, Ash."

CHAPTER 30

Max

I carried her to my tent while trying to fight back actual tears. I didn't want her to see them, though. They would only make her panic even more. But for a moment there I'd imagined losing her. I'd imagined her dying in my arms and never getting to say, or do, the things that I was so desperate to say and do to her.

"Let's get your ankle under some water." I carried her over to the bath and sat her down on the lip. She still looked ashen. "Hold on to the basin tightly. I'm going to get you some Coke." I rushed off and returned seconds later, helping her sip it. I pulled her slippers off and then angled her ankle so that the stream of water hit the bite perfectly. I watched the water run over the wound, taking a lot of blood with it and then held it in place like Bongani had said. I timed the five minutes, and just as I was turning off the water, he arrived with a first-aid bag.

"Antiseptic lotion, plasters, and antibiotics if you want to take them, just to be sure."

I thanked him and he left. But not before mentioning that this was the reason why guests should never walk around without him, and making me swear that neither of us would do it again.

"How are you feeling?" I asked Ash, now rubbing her back in gentle circles.

"I don't know," she said, her eyes tearing up. "I thought I was going to . . ." The first tear escaped her eye and I quickly wiped it away. She didn't have to say any more to me; I knew exactly what she was feeling. And I knew why.

"It's okay. You're alive and you're okay. Just in shock. I'll help you to the bed and we can put this cream on. You think you can walk?" I asked her, and she nodded.

But as soon as she stood up, the color started draining from her face again.

"Sorry, I still feel dizzy."

"That's okay." I put an arm round her and led her to the bed. "I've got you. You're going to be fine." I was trying to reassure her as much as I was trying to reassure myself. In fact, every time I said it to her, I needed to hear it just as much as she did. I put her on the bed and gently dried her ankle. I dabbed the cream onto two distinct puncture wounds in her skin. I quickly covered it with a plaster before she could see it. When I was finished, I looked up to find her watching me.

"Thanks," she said, perking up a little now after the Coke. "If it's not thorns, it's hordes of mosquitoes and storms and snake bites. Seriously, can anything else go wrong?"

"It has been a rather eventful trip. You forgot getting stuck in the mud and getting sick in a plane."

"How could I forget that?" She gave me the smallest smile. "It would be great to get through the rest of the trip without feeling like I'm dying all the time, or without something catastrophic happening." She tried to make light of it, but I knew this was not light to her at all.

"You okay now?" I asked, and wanted to take her hands in mine, or pull her into another hug.

"Much better, thanks. Are you okay?" she asked.

"Also much better. I got a fright there too."

"Do you need some Coke and a plaster?" she asked.

"Probably."

She patted the bed next to her. "Come here, then."

She sat up as I lowered myself onto the bed. She unwrapped a plaster and looked at me. "Where does it hurt?"

My eyes locked on to hers and I felt myself melting again. "Here."

I touched my hand to my chest and then laid my palm over my heart.
She looked down at my shirt questioningly and I pulled it over my
head and dropped it to the ground.

"There," I said.

Her eyes drifted over my chest and I could see a distinct flush of
pink working its way up from her neck into her face.

"Here we go." She stuck the plaster onto my skin and flattered it
with her hands, fingers grazing my skin and making me feel quite
euphoric. "How does that feel?"

"Better." I put my hand over hers, holding it to my chest. We
stayed like that for a while, her hand on my heart, my hand over
hers, looking at each other. But before I got totally lost in this
moment, I cleared my throat and stood up. Nothing was going to
happen with us tonight. She was in shock. She was rattled. She was
not thinking straight, and if something happened, would it be something she really wanted, or would it be a reaction to the moment and
needing some kind of comfort? Despite the endless sexual build-up
of the night, it had ended the second she'd been bitten by the snake.

"So, what were you doing outside anyway?" I asked, and she
looked panicked again.

"Reception! For my phone. I got it on the path earlier and I
thought I could get it again."

"You needed reception at three in the morning? I hope you
weren't working that late."

"What can I say? Bit of a workaholic."

I looked around the room. "Where is your phone? I didn't see one."

"Oh, shit. I must have dropped it. I'll go look for it tomorrow."
Her mouth was moving, words were coming out, but I did not
believe a single one of them. *What had she really been doing outside at
three in the morning?*

She started climbing off the bed. "I guess I better go back to my
room now that I'm—"

"You can't. Bongani gave us strict instructions not to walk around
at night. So you're kind of stuck here, with me."

"In your room."

"In my room," I repeated. "But don't worry. I'll sleep on the chair."

"It's fine. You can sleep here." She looked up at me and I was surprised to see her pull the covers back.

"You sure?"

"Yes," she said softly. I walked over to the bed, kicked off my shoes and climbed in. I was amazed how it didn't feel awkward or weird to be in bed with her. It felt right. In fact, I hadn't felt this comfortable and relaxed in a bed in years. I settled in, sighing with relief as I did.

"Thank you," she said, sounding sleepy now.

"It's a pleasure." I pulled the duvet up to my shoulders and although we were on opposite sides of the bed and were not even vaguely touching, I felt so close to her right now.

"This time I did need rescuing," she said.

"You did, did you?" I rolled over and looked at her. "So does that finally make me your knight in shining armor?"

She rolled over and faced me. I propped my head up on my hand and looked at her with a smile.

"*Only* in this instance." She smiled back at me and every part of me wanted to close the gap between us.

"But what if I save your life again?" I teased.

"Technically, you didn't save my life, because I was never actually dying."

"But we didn't know that at the time, so I don't think your logic works." We smiled at each other. Her smile felt as if it reached right inside me and physically tugged on my heart.

"You're not going to save my life again, because there aren't going to be any more situations to save me from. I mean, there can't be. It's too much, right?"

"Way too much," I confirmed. I took stock of the situation. I couldn't believe she was in my bed. She was very, very different from the last woman I'd had in my bed. In fact, this was different from all of them. I don't think I'd ever had such a long conversation with anyone who'd been in my bed in thirteen years. Ash opened her mouth and let out a huge yawn, and because it was contagious, I found myself yawning too. "Night, Ash," I said, and rolled over again.

"Night, Max."

I closed my eyes and as I started to relax, I remembered something.

"I want to have an orgasm and good sex at least once in my life."

I sat up in bed and looked over at her.

"What?" she asked.

"Have you really never had good sex?"

"What?" Ash sat up straight and looked at me. "How did you . . . Oh God!" she moaned, dropping her face into her hands.

"Have you seriously, seriously not had an orgasm?"

"Oh God, nooooo." Her moan was long and pained and she flopped back down on the bed, hands covering her face.

"Ash, you're joking, right?" I moved closer and looked down at her. "You've never had an orgasm?"

"Oh God, please stop saying that."

"This is crazy! I can't believe it. You've never had an or—"

"I have." She pulled her hands away from her face and glared at me. "Just not with . . . you know, a person who isn't made of silicone. And now I would appreciate it if we never spoke about it again. Like that other thing that I never want to speak of with you again either. I'm going to sleep now! And so are you!" She flipped over defiantly and pulled the duvet back up almost over her entire head. I stared at her back in total shock. She had never had good sex. Never had an orgasm with someone. My cock went hard, because, fucking hell, did I then want to be the man to change all that for her. But then another thought hit me: I had to make this up to her.

And there was only one way, and one way alone, to do that.

CHAPTER 31

Ash

I was having such pleasant dreams. Petal was rubbing up against my leg and I was stroking her. Her fur felt a little different in my dream though, coarser, not as smooth and silky, but it still felt good. I began to wake up, drifting from unconsciousness to semi-consciousness, to full consciousness, and when I did, I was still stroking Petal. I slowly raised my head. The pillow I was lying on was very uncomfortable, and my leg felt trapped between something heavy, yet weirdly familiar. But when I raised my head fully, the true gravity of my situation was revealed.

"Morning," Max said casually, staring up at the ceiling.

I had been using Max's chest as a pillow, not to mention stroking a little patch of his chest hair.

"Sorry." I pulled my hand away quickly and he smiled.

"Not a problem, I enjoy being called Petal."

"Seriously?" I asked.

"When did you start talking in your sleep?" He turned his head towards me.

"Don't know." I pulled the duvet back and looked down at my leg. It was threaded through Max's. He bent his knee and I pulled my leg out and apologized once more for having slipped it between his.

"We used to sleep like this," he said, sitting up and turning his back to me as he swung his legs off the edge.

"Like octopuses," I said, a memory coming back to me.

"Exactly."

That's what we'd called it. Going full octopus, when every single one of our legs and arms were tangled up in each other.

"So corny," I said, feeling slightly embarrassed by our childhood phrases that now sounded so naïve and ridiculous.

"Corny but cute," he said, standing up and raising his arms above his head in a stretch.

My jaw dropped on the floor. Exaggeration, it didn't drop on the floor, but when had he gotten so many muscles? They rippled as he stretched his arms, muscles that basically begged to have a hand run over them. I quickly sat up and climbed out of the bed.

"What time are we leaving for the next location?" I asked, trying to steer us away from being tangled up with each other and back to business. But it was hard to focus on work when he'd just turned to face me, shirtless, and was now stretching his chest.

"At ten." He hung down from the waist, put his hands on the floor and started bobbing up and down.

"What are you doing?"

"My morning stretches."

"You do morning stretches?" I asked, not hiding the amusement in my voice.

"I like to keep supple," he said, swinging from side to side. The word "supple" made my heart race a little, not in a comfortable way.

What was he keeping supple for, and why? And just how supple was he?

"And you?" he asked.

"And me what?"

"What new little things do you do now that I don't know about? Besides talking in your sleep."

"I try to meditate sometimes," I said.

"With that racing brain of yours?" He smiled at me.

"I went through a patch where I was struggling to sleep, on account of said racing brain, and my doctor told me to try meditating, so I went to some classes and sometimes I try and meditate."

His smile grew. "Ash, the meditator."

"Max, the stretcher." I pointed at him. His arms were up in the air again and he was swiveling his body from side to side, various muscles rippling.

"So many things have changed," he said, coming to the end of his stretches. We stood and looked at each other, the large bed dividing us. "But so many things have stayed the same too." He gazed at me meaningfully. The gaze was loaded, but it was way too early for loaded gazes and muscles.

"How's your snake bite?" He pointed and I looked down.

"Seems fine." I rubbed on the plaster to see if I could feel any pain. "Truthfully, I'm a little embarrassed about last night."

"You were bitten by a snake and thought you were dying!"

"But I was rather dramatic, wasn't I?"

He chuckled. "I would have probably acted the same way."

"You're just saying that to be nice, meanwhile Bongani is probably going to laugh with the other rangers over this, telling them how I rolled on the deck screaming that I didn't want to die and I wanted to swim in the Maldives and—" I cut myself off quickly. I should not have gone there, and I knew it the second I saw the look on Max's face.

"Have you really never had good sex?" he asked, walking round the bed towards me.

"No!" I held out my hand to block his approach. "I didn't mean it like that at all."

"Then how did you mean it?"

"Not in the way you think I meant it," I blasted back.

"I don't know, Ash. A statement like that doesn't exactly seem to have another meaning. It's a pretty clear, definitive statement."

"I meant lately. *Lately*. Recently. Not never. *Never* would be ridiculous." I forced a laugh. It sounded fake and stupid and—*why the hell had I done that?* I changed tactics.

"Max, I have a lot of work to do today. I'm already seriously behind, so I cannot talk about this now. In fact, I cannot talk about this ever, and especially not with you." He stopped walking, but didn't erase that smile from his face.

"I would never want to keep you from your work, Ash." His words totally contradicted the look in his eyes, just like my words had totally contradicted the feeling that was rising up inside me. This is exactly what I'd come here for at 3 a.m. But in the sober light of morning, after a dramatic snake bite or two, I was not so sure this was a good idea anymore. He continued his approach, walking slowly and deliberately. His walk said *man on a mission*. Shit, I knew exactly what mission he was on right now.

"You said *never* last night."

"Yes, well, people say strange things when they think they're dying."

"Like that they've never had an orgasm either?"

"I . . . I . . ." I couldn't get the words out, because Max had stopped his approach, and was now standing right in front of me. God, why did he have to be so good-looking? I blamed all of this on the fact that he looked the way he did. A man had no right to look this good, ever. It was unfair. Women stood no chance with a man like this, standing there with all those muscles and bare chest and eyes . . . eyes that ate you alive.

"You what?" he asked.

I shook my head, drowning in this cruel and unusual sexual spell he was casting over me. If I didn't swim to the surface now, I feared I would get sucked right under . . . *him*.

"I have to work, Max."

He took a step back, and I had this irrational urge to grab him by his hair and pull him back.

"Fine. But don't think this conversation is over, Ash." He took another step back, and with each step, the spell seemed to dissipate ever so slightly.

"Because this is something that we are . . ."

He paused, smiled, and then looked at me with the most sexy, filthy look I think I have ever been looked at with before. My entire body felt like it had been set on fire.

"*. . . coming* back to this."

Oh God!

"Uh . . . right." I scrambled for my slippers on the floor. "I need to find my . . ." I swung my head around, scanning the room, looking anywhere but at him, because if I did, I feared that my clothes might accidentally come off.

Fuck, too much coming.

"I have to go now," I declared loudly, and then didn't even bother with things like slippers, and made a run for it.

He gave me a small wave as I went and just as I was about to exit he called after me one last time.

"And that's a promise. I assure you."

I dashed out the door and ran as fast as I could back to my tent. One last look over my shoulder revealed to me that he was standing on the walkway watching me run, all naked-chested and sexy, smoldering eyes and hushed lusty tones.

He was definitely going to bring this up again. He was not going to let this go. Well, in that case, I would simply just have to avoid him for the rest of this journey, and for the rest of my life . . .

Or not. Because right now, my body seriously disagreed with that statement.

CHAPTER 32

Max

I loved watching her work. It had become my new favorite thing to do. The way she flitted around as if she'd been sped up. She also talked to herself as she went. At one stage I'd gotten close enough to make out her one-way conversation.

"Hang on, maybe if we do . . . . Nah! Where is the light coming fr—Aha! This, yup . . . we do this. Lens . . . Um . . . Maybe not. Shit, we need a crane . . . crane . . ."

I couldn't help smiling every time I heard her have one of these one-sided debates with herself as she climbed around, shooting things from different angles and taking light readings. She had a pencil behind her ear, her hair was messy and it was so hot that the neckline of her shirt was drenched with sweat.

The manager had shown me around the houseboat, our next location, when we'd arrived. The flight had been a short one from the tented camp to here. A quick transfer had taken us over to a small island on the Chobe River on the Namibian side where we'd boarded the houseboat. The houseboat was incredibly impressive, and I could immediately see what an asset this location would be. Not only would it make a great location for shoots, but also the perfect private holiday for a celebrity I had in mind, who loved fishing.

I did not love fishing, though, and the manager had already asked me at least three times when I would want to go tiger fishing. It was one of the main entertainment options offered on the boat. I declined several times and decided that if my client asked me what the fishing was like, I would simply lie and tell him a story about how it took me half an hour to wrangle the fish onto the boat, and how it was the size of my leg, or something like that.

The houseboat had five rooms, each one more luxurious than the next, each one with a small balcony that was accessed from large sliding doors. And with the doors open, the room felt as if it was simply hovering over the river. There were two decks, one with a lounge and dining area and the upper deck had a small plunge pool and a tasteful bar on it. And right now, I was standing on the upper deck by the pool, looking at some of the most beautiful scenery on earth. A herd of elephants had made their way down to the water's edge and I watched as two babies played in the shallow water, somersaulting and splashing like toddlers might do. I knew my friend Vincenzo was looking for a location for an upcoming stills shoot. He ran a very successful fashion-design company, and they were launching a new sunglasses range. He'd initially wanted me to find a beach location where they could shoot their models shirtless and in bikinis, while enjoying the sun. Sexy and aspirational. But I could see that whole thing playing out better here. I could see them here in this plunge pool, glasses on, champagne in hand, elephants in the distance, cruising down the river. This would make a much better location, I thought, not that I was their ad agency, but in my opinion, a luxurious houseboat cruising down a river in Africa felt far more interesting and unique than a bunch of models sitting on a beach.

I took my phone out and started taking photos, then sent them to him in a message. I'm sure the agency was going to be pissed I'd done this, but I didn't care. Sometimes agencies came up with such bland ideas, and I was often on locations that seemed better and more interesting than those the agencies had imagined. You couldn't blame them, really. Most of the people coming up with the ads sat behind desks. They didn't travel to some of the most remote and unique locations around the world and see what was on offer, like I did.

Vincenzo: Oh my God. It's like heaven. So sexy. I love it. I'll tell the agency. You're a genius, my friend.

Max: I think this will sell the concept of luxury far more than a beach.

Vincenzo: Sand is not sexy.

Max: Hahah! No.

Vincenzo: How is work going?

Vincenzo: Still in lust for your ex?

Max: Think it may be more than lust.

Vincenzo: Careful, my friend.

Vincenzo: Love is too much work. So inconvenient. Too much stress.

Max: Think it might be too late for that.

Vincenzo: Take her to the jacuzzi then.

Max: The idea had crossed my mind.

Vincenzo: I know you too well. I know that many things have crossed your mind.

Max: Too many.

Vincenzo: I change topic then.

Vincenzo: Maybe I don't ask the agency this time, because I can already see it in my mind.

Vincenzo: For our jewelry line. I want naked models, only wearing diamonds, but I don't want another studio shoot. I want them somewhere messy. Somewhere old and broken. Somewhere dark. Like construction site. Abandoned factory. But close to home.

Max: Balestrino. Ghost town in Italy. Some of it was destroyed by an earthquake, rubble everywhere. It will be perfect.

Vincenzo: Googling while we speak.

Vincenzo: YES! Perfect.

Vincenzo: Naked models, in diamonds, climbing over rubble in a ghostly town.

Max: My thoughts exactly. I'll figure out who to speak to and get back to you.

Vincenzo: Genius. Always a genius.

Max: Speak later.

I lowered my phone and Ash was standing on the deck tracking the sun with an app on her phone and taking some notes.

"Are you finished?" I asked, and she seemed to angle herself away from me.

"No, have to figure out a drone shot still."

"You look hot and thirsty. I was going to get myself a water. You want one?"

"No, thanks. I'm perfectly fine."

I smiled to myself as I walked away and grabbed two waters anyway.

"The weather app says it is thirty-eight degrees today. I hope you're wearing sun cream." I returned with the waters and walked straight up to her. She swung round as if she'd gotten a fright.

"Here." I held the water out and she stared down at it.

"It's just a bottle of water, Ash. Nothing else." I was amused by what had clearly been a very deliberate attempt to avoid me at all costs today. There had been a few moments when she'd seen me and then darted in the opposite direction.

"Thanks." She took the water, and within seconds had removed the lid and was gulping it down. As I'd suspected, she'd forgotten to drink while working. Probably forgotten to eat too. She always did this when she got caught up in something. When we were studying for exams, I used to make sure I brought her bags of snacks so she didn't fall over. I wondered who brought her snacks and water now. My stomach tightened. I shouldn't have gone away. I should have stayed to bring her snacks while she studied at film school and then ran around in the sun like this.

"The staff is setting up dinner for us tonight. And I have to warn you: it is going to have candles. It'll be under the stars, on a deck at one of their lodges."

"A lodge?"

"Yes, I wanted to see one of their sister lodges as well, so they suggested a dinner there, before we get back onto the boat. Is that okay?"

"That's actually perfect. I'm sure the lodge will have better WiFi than this boat and I need to send Sebastian a lot of footage today," she said, turning her head away from me.

"Great, but I do just want to remind you it will be romantic, because I know how allergic you are to anything romantic, especially with me and your detox." I couldn't help the small breathy chuckle as I said that.

She turned and looked at me. "Just what exactly are you trying to imply there, Max?"

"Nothing, just thinking that your detox is not going as well as you would have liked it to. Perhaps there are some things that are proving a little too hard to resist."

"Hardly," she said, rolling her eyes. *What a blatant lie!* She knew it and I knew it. She looked away again and started chugging back more water.

"You should have a dip in the plunge pool when you've finished working. You look pretty hot."

She gave me the side-eye as she drank.

"And I mean that in a purely weather-based sense, by the way, not the other hot, which you do too, also, by the way."

She lowered the bottle. "When did you become such a flirt?"

"A flirt?" I took a step closer to her and she stiffened immediately. "That was not flirting. I'm not flirting."

She scoffed and rolled her eyes again. "So what do you call all that stuff that happened earlier, if it's not flirting?"

I walked all the way up to her and stopped right in front of her. Her eyes widened and she swallowed so hard I could hear it.

"Trust me, Ash, you will know when I'm flirting with you." I fixed my eyes on her in that way that I knew made women take their panties off for me. I'd never met a woman that hadn't done that when I'd looked at them like this. I moved closer still, eyes locked on to hers, trying to convey the depths of my desire for her. Her and I both naked. Me driving into her over and over again.

She cleared her throat nervously and took a wobbly step back. "Right, I have a drone to, uh . . . uh . . ." She dashed off quickly, throwing me one last look over her shoulder as she went.

"Good luck," I called, and gave her the most innocent-looking smile and wave that I could. Even though my thoughts were very far from innocent.

CHAPTER 33

Ash

$\mathcal{M}$ax was asleep. I hadn't meant to see, but the drone had caught some footage of him through his huge window, passed out on the bed, as I'd done a low flyby just over the water. The second I was done with my drone shot, I rushed back to my room. I hadn't updated my friends in days, and so much had happened.

Ash: Max and I had a moment!!!! Well, several moments.

Sarah: What kind of moment?

Ash: A sexual kind.

Sarah: How sexual?

Ash: I've basically been having the best sex of my life and we haven't even had sex!

Yo: HAHAHA! I have no idea what the hell that means?

Ash: It means that the sexual tension between us is just soooo intense.

Yo: Are you saying you're going to have sex with him?

Ash: I sort of tried to last night but then I got bitten by a snake, so that kind of put an end to it.

Sarah: You WHAT?

Melusi: Hang on, is snake a euphemism for dick?

Ash: No! Like an actual fanged fucker.

Ash: Look.

I quickly sent through a photo of the bite marks on my ankle.

Sarah: You okay?

Charlie: WTF?

Melusi: OMG. Are you okay?

Ash: I'm fine. It wasn't poisonous.

Frank: Snakes are venomous, not poisonous.

Charlie: Seriously Frank. That's what you're choosing to contribute to the conversation right now?

Frank: It's a very common misconception though.

Charlie: 😊

Frank: I'm just trying to educate the group here.

Sarah: God, can you two not do this now.

Melusi: Agreed!

Charlie: Tell the self-appointed herpetologist here.

Frank: 😊

Sarah: Why don't you two take your snake argument elsewhere. We are trying to find out if Ash is going to have sex with Max?

Ash: I don't know. I think I just need to cool down. Dunk myself in cold water or something.

I turned and looked at my suitcase. My swimming suit was sticking out of it and Max was sleeping, so I could probably grab a cool moment alone in the plunge pool.

Ash: I've got to go, guys.

Charlie: Wait, you can't leave us hanging like that.

Melusi: Hanging. 🍆🍆🍆

Yo: No stop!

Charlie: You realize that was a teenage boy joke. I expect way more from you.

Sarah: Wait, has she seriously just left us on that cliffhanger

I slipped into my swimming costume and went back to the pool on the deck.

"Oh my Goooood," I moaned out loud as I lowered myself into the water. The sun was setting and this was actually bloody ridiculous. This was stupidly, insanely and unbelievably beautiful. To be submerged in a small plunge pool on the deck of a boat while huge herds of elephants, giraffes, buck, and baboons came down to drink on its shores. There's a magic to Africa. A feeling you get nowhere else on earth. It cannot be explained, or quantified. The air feels different here; it seems to vibrate with an energy that cannot be described. This moment was perfect, especially when the barman brought over a cool, icy drink for me. Just when I was convinced this was the most perfect moment of my life, a familiar voice greeted me.

"Seems like we had the same idea. Mind if I join you?" he asked.

Yes, I do mind, I wanted to say, even though I wasn't totally sure I believed that. I managed a feeble, "Sure," and shuffled up on the seat to give him room. There was not much space in this jacuzzi-sized plunge pool, though.

I tried not to look at his naked thigh as he stepped down beside me. Tried not to look at his naked stomach, as the movement made his six-pack tense, and then seriously tried not to look when he climbed into the water. I had wanted to avoid him today, and the inevitable, awkward conversation he was not letting go of. But it was impossible to avoid him now in this small pool, especially when he hadn't sat next to me, but rather opposite me, stretching his legs out so each one came up along my sides. He'd almost locked me into this position. In fact, if I moved and he didn't want me to, he could simply tighten his legs and clamp me in place. And I hated how much that idea thrilled me.

"The view is that way." I pointed over his head, ignoring the leg situation and not making eye contact.

"Depends on your definition of view."

I tutted loudly. "Trying to show me your flirting abilities again."

"Not at all. Like I said before, you will *know* when I'm flirting with you, Ash. And that was not flirting."

"When did you become like this?" I asked.

"Like what?"

"You're very confident, in this weird way I can't quite put my finger on. You never used to be."

"I was a boy back then. You're also more confident."

I didn't answer him, because I wasn't feeling all that confident right now. In fact, the opposite. Exposed, vulnerable. I sipped my drink and watched the river as hippo emerged and yawned.

"It's beautiful here," Max said. The setting sun had painted the world orange, and Max had put his head up and was looking at the sky, drenched in an orange glow himself.

"It's perfect here," he said, still looking up at the clouds, which were now pink.

"It's been kind of perfect everywhere, well, except for all the mishaps. Of which there have been many."

He laughed.

"No, seriously, I've never been on a recce where so many things have gone wrong. I'm all drama-ed out. I don't think I can take one more thing happening that spikes my heart and blood pressure. I'm done with all that eventful crap."

"It has certainly been eventful," he agreed, tilting his head back towards me again.

I sipped my drink. "Understatement. I don't think this trip could get more eventful if it tried."

"Are you sure about that, Ash?" he asked.

I swallowed. The way he'd just said "Ash," might have been the sexiest sound that anyone had ever made in the history of humankind and my body reacted to it on some base and primal level. My leg accidentally brushed his under the water and, without warning, he took my ankle and lifted it out the water. I gasped.

"What are you doing?"

"Checking your bite," he said, bringing my leg up to his face, turning it so my ankle was facing him. "It looks good—no infection or anything."

But he didn't put my leg down once he'd inspected it. In fact, he might have even pulled it towards him a little more. In this pose, I felt even more exposed, and was suddenly very aware that I hadn't shaved my legs in almost a week. I pulled my leg away quickly and put it back under the water. I mentally scolded myself for even caring that my legs were hairy in the first place. I mean, who was he that I should worry about whether my legs were hairy or not, but . . . *I did care.* And I didn't like that I cared so bloody much. My neck was in an awkward position now from the leg pull and when I slithered back up, I winced as a pain shot up it.

"What?" he asked quickly.

I rubbed my neck and tried to stretch it like the physio had taught me to. "I might have a mild case of whiplash."

"How did that happen?"

"Mmm, it was in an accident, of sorts."

"You want me to rub it?"

I looked up at him and shot him an "as if" look.

"What?"

"I'm not sure that would be a good idea. Last time you had access to my back, things happened."

"But you put an end to those things, which I totally respect, so no things would happen now, unless you wanted them to."

"See! This is what I mean! This weird sexual confidence you have." I pointed at him and winced again as I lifted my shoulder.

"Let me rub your neck. I've taken a massage class and I'm pretty good with my hands."

I rolled my eyes at him very deliberately. "I'm sure you have." I was sure he was good with his hands, but I was also sure it wasn't a Thai massage course he'd taken—it was possibly something a lot more erotic than Thai, but still beginning with a T.

"What is that supposed to mean?" he asked.

"Just . . . some things have been said about you—that's all."

"What kind of things?" he enquired, looking amused and smug. This was entertaining to him.

"They're not worth repeating—trust me," I said, and then tried to readjust my sitting position, so that my neck wasn't in so much discomfort. I pulled my knees up, and Max did the same, but with so little space in the pool our knees pressed into each other's, holding us both up and in position.

"I insist you tell me about these things you've heard," he said.

"Nope, not going to."

"Okay, then tell me more about not having good sex."

"Well done. At least you waited five minutes before bringing that up again. And I'm not telling you about that ei—" I gasped as Max opened his knees and my entire body slipped forwards. He slammed his legs closed round my legs and my body came to a stop.

"Sorry, accident." But the look on his face did not say accident at all.

"What are you doing?" I asked, out of breath from the very sudden and unexpected move that had now brought me at least ten centimeters closer to him.

But he didn't answer. Instead his finger was on my knee, rubbing a path across an old, faded scar.

"I remember that day so well," he said.

"Do you?" I asked, transfixed by the sight of his finger tracing the line on my knee.

"You fell out of that tree you were climbing because you were determined to save those baby birds from the nest after the neighbor's cat caught the mom. Do you remember what you said about the cat?"

"I called it a fucking evil bitch cat from hell and told you this was why I would never own a cat. I actually thought of that when I found Petal."

"You fractured your patella and had to have surgery. And then when you were coming round from the anesthesia, you told the doctor how gorgeous he was and asked if he would marry you."

I laughed at the memory. "I did. God, that was so funny."

"I was so jealous."

"He was hot, though," I said. Without warning, he opened his legs again and my body lurched forwards again. Another involuntary gasp escaped my parted lips. He closed his legs once more and this time, I was even closer to him.

"Hot?" he asked with a glint in his eye that was making all sorts of things fire away inside me. "When you came round, you told me it was just the anesthetic talking. That you didn't find him hot at all."

"Well, I guess I lied, then," I said, and a slow smile spread across his face.

"So you can either tell me what you heard about me or we can talk about sex—your choice." I was so close to him now that I could feel the heat radiating off his body. There was so much heat I was sure the water would start boiling at any moment.

"Well, funny you put it that way, because they are actually kind of one and the same thing."

"I see." He nodded at me, and then smiled that sexy, killer, panty-dropping, lopsided smile. His smile had never been this sexy before. His smile had been cute and dimpled, but there was nothing cute about his smile anymore. There was nothing cute about him either.

"What is it that you see exactly?" I asked, and as I did, he opened his legs all the way and I lurched forwards again. I reached out and grabbed on to the rim of the plunge pool. It was the only way to stop myself from totally falling into him. I stopped my body from crashing into his, but my face was now only one tiny movement from his. Like this, I could just kiss him. *What would happen if I kissed him?* Just one. A small one. All my inner resolve was crumbling. All previous detox thoughts faded away. Well, let's be honest, those might have faded away ages ago. Thoughts of what a terrible idea it would be to have sex with him were all but dissolving at a very speedy pace. One. Small. Kiss.

"Are you trying to decide whether you should kiss me?" he asked.

"What!" I was so startled that I pulled back from him and toppled over into the water, very ungracefully.

"I'll take that as a yes." He smiled while I spluttered and pushed water from my face. And then he laughed, languid and sexy and stretched his arms out, lacing his fingers together and putting them behind his head. I watched him curiously. I had never met someone so damn sexually confident and outspoken, and it was hard to reconcile it all with the boy I used to know.

"Are you ready for dinner at the lodge?" one of the staff members came up to us and asked. I started lifting myself up out of the pool, but Max leaned forwards, half blocking my exit. "We're *almost* done here," he said to the man, who immediately walked away.

"Almost?" I questioned him, sitting back down in the pool.

He stood up out of the water and then began leaning over me. A shadow fell across my face as his body blocked the sun. He reached out, put his hands behind me on the rim of the pool and brought his face all the way to mine.

Fuuuck! I looked up at him. In this position, him hovering over me, on top of me, he was in total control. He loomed above me, powerful and confident, and I felt small and vulnerable, as if he could do anything he wanted to me . . . *and I wanted him to.*

"W-what are you doing?" I managed to whisper, words sticking in my dry mouth.

"I just wanted to clarify something with you."

"Yeeees?" I whispered nervously as he leaned in even more.

"If you did decide you wanted to kiss me," he brought his lips close to mine. "Just know that there's no way in hell it would end at a kiss." And then he took my chin in his hand and tilted my face towards him. His lips touched mine. He didn't kiss me, though. Instead he dragged them over mine and let out a small, breathy groan as he did. "Let me know if you change your mind." And then he stood up and climbed out of the pool.

What the . . .

He walked away as if he'd not just said and done the sexiest, hottest thing anyone had ever said and done to me before. He walked away as if he had not just turned me on so much that I could feel my heart beating between my legs.

. . . *fuck.*

CHAPTER 34

Max

I didn't think I would be able to keep my hands off her for too much longer. Especially when she was sitting opposite me looking like *that*. God, she was gorgeous. The candlelight made her almost ethereal. The warmth of the light brought out the color of her eyes and bathed her skin in a golden glow. I wanted to reach out and trace that color across her collarbone, up her neck, and then lick it off her lips. We'd been sitting in silence for the past five minutes since she'd come back from sending off her work to Sebastian. She'd sipped her glass of wine, staring at me over the top of the rim, and I'd sat back in my chair, legs crossed, watching her as if this was the greatest show on earth and she was the star attraction. I was also waiting for her to deliver her verdict on the kissing proposal. I didn't know how much longer I could wait.

"You're staring at me," she said, breaking the silence. She put the glass down and slowly traced the rim of it with her fingers. Fuck, I wanted those fingers of hers to trace so many parts of my body.

"You look beautiful tonight—that's why I'm staring." She blushed instantly. "But you also look very fucking sexy too." The color in her cheeks intensified. "That's why I'm staring and finding something very, very hard to believe."

"What?" she asked.

I uncrossed my legs and moved closer to the table again. "I cannot believe that you're not having good sex."

She laughed unexpectedly. "You're just never going to let go of that one, are you?"

"Probably not," I said. Her laugh stopped and the smile that she'd had on her face suddenly disappeared. I leaned closer, sensing a very strange shift in the mood. As if the weather agreed with me, a cool breeze raced past, tossing one of our napkins onto the floor. Neither of us moved to pick it up.

"You know, it's so ironic that *you* are the one that keeps asking me that question, since you are the one that—" She stopped talking abruptly and pursed her lips together tightly.

"What?"

She shook her head. "I'm not going to say it."

"Say what?"

She took a large sip of her wine. Very large.

"Say what, Ash?" Things had turned from playful to serious in a matter of seconds and I didn't know why. "Ash?" I implored her to continue. I could tell we were on the verge of something big here. Something huge and unsaid. Something that clearly needed to be said. "I've told you everything. Every last awful embarrassing detail, but I get the sense there's something you're still not telling me."

She looked at me and let out a loud, long breath. My entire body tensed with anticipation.

"Okay, so . . ." she started, then stopped. Took another sip of wine and then her words flew out. "Okay, so you know that night we had sex—or tried to have sex, at least—well, as it bloody well turns out, that was also the night that—"

She was cut off by the appearance of a very harried-looking ranger at our table, clutching a gun. "A leopard's been spotted in the lodge, and as a precaution, we're asking guests to go inside while we deal with it."

"What?" Ash jerked her head at the guy.

"A leopard."

"No, you're joking." She sounded panicked.

"I'm not. I'm going to need you both to come with me now," the ranger said. I got up, but Ash seemed frozen to her chair.

"Come on, Ash. Let's go." I pulled her up by her arm and dragged her along as we followed behind the ranger. I'd been to lodges before when wild animals had walked through—it was always a risk when there was no fencing—that's why all the rangers had guns and you weren't allowed to walk around at night on your own. But I hadn't been in a lodge when a leopard had walked through it.

"Thorns, mud, storms, snakes, leopards," Ash mumbled softly to herself. "What the fuck?"

"This way," the ranger said, swinging his gun as he walked. Suddenly, the bush to our right screamed to life as a large troupe of baboons came hurtling out of it, running across the path, sending Ash flying backwards. I tried to catch her as she fell, but the ranger pushed me out of the way too as a massive male baboon jumped into the middle of the path, barking for his troop to hurry up.

"The leopard must be close." The ranger raised his gun and I tried to pull Ash towards me, without attracting the attention of the massive male baboon.

"Ow," she moaned, grabbing the back of her neck as I pulled her.

"In here, quick." The ranger opened a door I hadn't seen before and pushed us both into a dark room, and then I heard the click of a lock and the ranger ran off, shouting.

"You okay?" I asked, scrambling in the dark, trying to find Ash.

"Are you kidding me?" Ash exclaimed loudly. "A leopard?" She winced again. "And my neck is seriously killing me. Where's the light in this place?"

I felt around the walls, but couldn't find it anywhere.

"Just when I thought things couldn't get any more eventful, we are now locked in a dark room with a leopard prowling around outside."

"I can't find the lights," I said.

"Cell-phone torches," she said. I could hear her rummaging through her bag. I pulled mine from my pocket and flicked the torch light on. With both of our phones there was just enough light to see, and I could see that she was rubbing her neck as if in serious agony.

"You're going to have to let me sort that out for you," I said, glancing around. It looked like we were in some kind of cleaning closet, with cleaning products and mops and rags.

"We're in a broom closet!" Her eyes widened. "I really don't like this, at all."

"It's not ideal, I admit." I looked down at my feet and did not tell Ash that I'd just seen a rather large lizard scuttle past. Her hands were on her neck, and she was trying to stretch it, with little luck.

"Turn round. Let me at least look at your neck and see if I can help you," I said, putting my hands on her shoulders and turning her myself. I put my thumbs on her shoulders and started feeling around.

"There!" she screamed when I found the knot in her neck.

"God, that's huge. How did you get that?" I asked, starting to work it in small circles.

I hadn't expected her reaction: it started off small, a chuckle, but soon it escalated into almost full-blown hysteria.

I started laughing too, simply because it was contagious. "What are we laughing about?" I managed to ask. She was laughing so much it was hard to continue applying pressure to the knot.

"It's just . . ." She tried to talk, but her laughter cut her off. "It's just, you are . . ." It sounded as if tears were rolling down her face now.

"The suspense is killing me here," I said, still trying to work the knot as she threw her head back to let out an even louder laugh.

"It's . . . you . . . I . . ." She sucked in a large breath, gripping her sides as she did, trying to stop herself from laughing. "Okay, I'm okay now," she said. "I think I just needed to get that out—it's been building."

"Glad it's out now." I pushed her head forwards and then massaged up her neck and into her hairline.

"Oh God, that feels good," she said on a loud moan. "Even better than my physiotherapist."

"What did you do to it?" I asked again.

"Well, it's kind of a funny story, as you can tell." She started laughing again, but this time it was brief, and ended in a melancholic-sounding sigh. "It's the story of my life, really. And actually relates to what we were just talking about."

"We were just talking about why you don't have good sex." I pulled her head back slowly, and began manipulating her neck, left and right. There was more movement there now and the knot seemed to be releasing.

"Exactly. And it's *alllll* related. The reason my neck is like this is because when my last date tried to have sex with me, he dropped me on my head and I actually don't blame that on him——I blame that entirely on *you*." I let go of her head and turned her round to face me.

"A guy dropped you on the head during sex and that's my fault?"

"Yes, because you cursed me," she said softly.

"What? How?"

She giggled and slapped her hand over her mouth quickly. "Sorry, I'll stop laughing, because this is serious. Okay, here goes . . . That night when we tried to have sex, I think something happened, because I have been sexually cursed ever since. I've been living under some weird bloody sexual curse for thirteen years and I think you, *you*, are the one who caused it." She looked down at my pants. "With your cock! Your cock cursed me." She laughed again and I was lost. I shook my head at her and raised my brows.

"See, the reason I have a sore neck, is because last week my date dropped me on my head while trying to, you know . . . fuck me. And prior to that I broke my finger when the bed fell on my hand, and then there was the time that I got stuck in a sex swing and the guy had to cut me out with a pair of scissors. Oh, and worst of all, the leather was so hard to get through that he had to call a friend to help, and not forgetting the time a guy ate an olive out of my belly button, or the time I was rushed to ER after being attacked by fire ants, or the time I went to hospital because my labia swelled to the size of a——"

"Stop." I put my hand over her mouth. The last thing in the world I wanted to hear right now was coming out of her mouth. She pushed my fingers apart and continued.

"I have not had good sex, not once, or a good date that didn't end very badly because of terrible sex, or terrible *almost* sex, or having sex that was marginally better than other sex, only to have the guy cry on you because he is not over his ex, in thirteen years, Max. *Thirteen!*"

"What?" I removed my hand slowly from her mouth.

"Max, I have not had even vaguely mediocre sex since that night. In fact, I would welcome mediocre sex at this stage. I would probably welcome vaguely subpar sex, or sex that didn't end with me in an emergency room. And as for orgasms . . . *not one*! Not. One! Not even the start of one. In fact, I am very much convinced that orgasms during sex are a myth. Because I have tried very, very hard to have one. Believe me I have really, really, really—"

I cut her off. "Okay, I get it. You've tried."

"The only orgasms I've had are all by my lonely little self and that's because of you. *You.*" She poked me in the chest. "That sex we tried to have all those years ago has set in motion this sexual curse that I have been living under for thirteen years!"

"You think I cursed you?" My head was spinning. I was vacillating between taking this really seriously, getting turned on when she talked about giving herself orgasms, and then pissed off, so pissed off, when she spoke about other men, which I knew was totally hypocritical, but I couldn't help it anyway.

"Your penis fucking cursed me, Max! It's been all downhill since that . . ." She pointed at my pants and wiggled her finger about. "So while you've been running around having the time of your life and making Belinda, or Bianca, or Brice, Moon and Star or whatever her name is come ten times, not to mention making a vet pass out from screaming orgasms in the pool, I've been giving CPR to a man that had a heart attack while having sex with me and being secretly happy he did because the sex was so bad that I would have given anything for it to end. And now it seems like your penis might be cursing me all over again—well, the proximity of your penis at least! Ever since meeting your penis again on that plane, I have been literally out of my mind, and the weirdest things have been happening."

"How do you know about Star, the vet and Bianca?"

"I told you—I've heard the stories, Max. Everyone seems to know about Maximillian Adam and his amazing ability to make women squirt fountains and give them seventeen orgasms so they are not able to walk down the catwalk the next day!"

I laughed and she snapped her fingers at me.

"Hey, this is not funny!" she said seriously.

"Ash, you shouldn't believe everything that you hear."

"Well, obviously I know you can't make a woman come just by looking at her."

I paused for a moment and then couldn't help my smile. "No, that one is actually true."

"What?" She pushed me in the chest.

"What the hell was that for?"

"You made a woman come just by looking at her and I can't even come when I have a guy trying to *make* me come for, like, a full hour—it was so fucking awful I had to fake one just to make him stop! Are you serious?"

"He clearly didn't know what he was doing if he was at it for an hour," I said, and smiled at her, which was clearly the wrong thing to do.

"You think this is funny?" she asked, her face awash with anger now. I wiped the smile off my face.

"Sorry, I didn't mean to—"

"You should be sorry, Max. You should be!"

"Okay, I am. What can I do to fix it?" I asked.

"Well, it's not like we can flash back thirteen years and have mind-blowing sex with a million orgasms so that my sex life didn't start out on such a wrong foot that it is eternally cursed and doomed. Or

maybe it's just me. I don't know. Maybe I'm the one who's terrible at
sex and dating—"

"Stop it." I took her by the hands and pulled her towards me,
pressing her into my chest. "Don't say that. You're not. Trust me."

"Trust you?" she asked, her voice soft and apprehensive.

I stared down at her. I couldn't believe what I was hearing. I
walked us backwards. It only took two steps until I had pinned
her to the door. I pressed her back into it while I pressed myself to
her. Her eyes widened as she looked up at me. Her mouth fell
open, her chest began rising and falling as her breaths came out
shallow and fast.

"I can't go back and change what happened thirteen years ago." I
took her hands in mine, laced my fingers through them and then
pushed her arms above her head, pinning our hands to the door. She
gasped and gripped my fingers tighter.

"But I can do something else for you," I said.

"What?" she whispered.

I brought my lips to hers but didn't kiss her. "I can make you come
so many times that you'll beg me to stop."

CHAPTER 35

Max

$\mathcal{S}$he inhaled sharply, her breasts pushing into me.

"I . . . I don't believe you," she said. "Impossible, especially after our last time."

I dragged my lips against hers, and then moved them down to her neck. I kissed her there gently. Long, and slow, and then traced my tongue up to her ear. I took her earlobe in my mouth, bit it ever so softly and then whispered in her ear, "You'll find I've improved somewhat since then."

She threw her head back and moaned as I ran my tongue down her neck again. I let go of her hands and tangled my fingers in her hair. I pushed my body into hers, flattening her against the door. She gasped again. I made sure to push my cock against her so she knew how hard I was. I untangled my hands from her hair, cupped the sides of her face, and ran my thumbs over her lips, then dipped them into her mouth. She moaned again.

"Open your eyes, Ash." She did and I locked mine with hers, showing her every last drop of lust that had been bubbling under the surface for her. *Just for her.* I dragged my tongue across her lips and then pulled her bottom lip into my mouth. I sucked it while I ground into her. "And, Ash, *this* . . ." I stuck my knee between her legs and pushed them apart. "This is me flirting with you."

"Fuck!" she gasped, and I took the opportunity to claim her entire mouth, drove my tongue into it, lapped at hers until she was quivering and whimpering against my mouth. It was the hottest thing I had ever heard in my life.

"And don't worry—I'm not going to fuck you in a broom closet."

"Then how are you going to make me come?" she asked so innocently I actually thought she meant it, and I almost laughed.

"Are you saying you give me permission to try?" I took her top lip in my mouth, then grabbed her hands once more and thrust them above her head, pinning her to the door again.

She nodded at me.

"You have to do better than that, baby. You have to say the words. I never do anything with anyone unless they say the words. Say them."

Her eyes were as wide as saucers now. "I . . . I . . ." she stuttered as I covered her mouth with mine quickly, dragging my tongue over her lips once more. "I . . . Yes."

"Yes, what, baby?"

"Yes, I want you to."

"Want me to what?" I asked, keeping her in place, but ready to let go the second she said no.

"Make me come," she said, and that was all I needed, all I needed to grab her face between my hands and plunge into her mouth with an intensity that had been building for thirteen years. I kissed her like I'd never kissed anyone before. Deep, slow and sensual. My cock twitched against her and she responded exactly how I hoped she would, pushing herself into it as if she needed me inside her as much as I wanted to be inside her. But I wasn't going to do that. I was going to do something else. I pulled away and then dropped to my knees in front of her.

"Wait, wait, what are you doing?" She grabbed me by the hair and started pulling me back up.

"Well, I'm not doing anything yet, but I was planning on pulling your panties off and licking you until you come."

"I . . . don't let guys do that. I don't . . ." She looked panicked and I stood up immediately and took a small step back.

"Then I won't do it." I reached out and touched her face softly and slowly. "I won't do anything you don't want me to do. Ever."

She nodded. "Okay, do anything else but that," she whispered.

Without responding, I found the buttons on her dress. Her nipples were so hard they pushed against the soft material of her dress and I rubbed my thumbs over them. Her body thumped against the door. God, she was so responsive. If this was what she was like when I was just touching her nipples, then she would explode when I touched her clit like this. Which I was planning on doing shortly, but first I wanted to focus on these. I lowered my mouth to a nipple and sucked it through the fabric of the dress. She laced her fingers in my hair again and held me in place.

"You like this?" I asked her. I knew she did. It was clearly a rhetorical question, but I wanted to hear her say the words.

"Yes!" she moaned as I sucked on her nipple, making the material of her dress wet. She dragged my head over to the other one, and I chuckled against the nipple as she pushed my mouth over her breast. She wanted this so badly. So fucking badly, and so did I. I sucked hard on this one, so hard I thought she was going to explode right there and then as she ground against me. I didn't give a fuck about the buttons of her dress now either. She could borrow my jacket for the rest of the evening, because I needed access to her . . . NOW. I ripped her dress open, buttons flying across the floor. She gasped so loudly it was almost a scream.

"Don't worry, you'll be screaming soon, baby," I said, pulling her naked nipple into my mouth. I sucked, I licked, I lapped on them until she was writhing against me, until I was sure I needed to stop before I made them red and raw with my desire. She was panting, her chest rising and falling with each flick of the tongue, each nibble of teeth. Each pinch between my fingers, slight pain, followed by soft, gentle pleasure. She reached out for my shorts and tried to pull them off. I pulled her hands off me and pinned them to the door again.

"No. This is all about you." I managed to wrap both of her

wrists in one hand, leaving one hand free to do other things to her. I trailed my fingers down her arm, over her naked chest, all the way down to her leg, until I reversed and started making them climb up her skirt. I squeezed her inner thigh as I went, kneading it between my fingers, grabbing at her flesh. And each time I did, she quivered under me.

"I'm going to touch you now. I'm going to pull your panties aside and find your clit. You okay with that?" I asked. Even though I could feel wetness coating her thighs.

She nodded. "Yes," she said, and I smiled.

My hand crept higher and before I did anything to her, I cupped her in my hand and squeezed. Her entire pussy filled my hand—I was claiming it—and in this moment, it was mine. Even if it never would be again, it was mine now, and I was going to do things to her no one had ever done before. I squeezed a little harder and she gasped again. She was so close to coming, and I could see the shock in her wide eyes. I could see she had no clue what the hell was happening to her. So I squeezed a little more, feeling the moisture seeping. I rubbed my palm against her, focusing my attention on her clit, and her panting increased. She was going to come, and I wasn't even touching her properly.

"Oh, my, oh . . . fuck . . ." Her panting got louder and her hands started grabbing around for something to hold on to. She found it in the shelves on either side of the room and gripped them tightly, bracing herself for what she and I both knew was about to happen.

I cupped her again and moved her back and forth on my hand, making sure to grind the palm of my hand into that place I could feel throbbing through her panties.

"I'm going to . . . I'm . . ." She was writhing against my hand, pushing herself back and forth against it, almost bucking her hips. It was so fucking hot.

"So stop speaking and come," I said, and then gripped her tighter and pounded my palm into her as fast as this position would allow. I watched her face. Her eyes shut tight, creases forming on her forehead. Her mouth dropped open as she panted, hyperventilated and her fingers dug into the wooden shelves, making them shake before her entire body stiffened and then froze, as if she was suspended in a moment of pure pleasure. And then she let out a moan so loud, long and guttural I almost came in my pants. Her body twitched against me, and I dragged my palm up and down once more to prolong her orgasm for as long as I could, which it clearly did, her body giving a few more shudders before going limp.

CHAPTER 36

Ash

I stayed pressed up against the door in total shock. Shock was the main emotion I was feeling now, other than pleasure, wave after wave of pleasure until the waves had petered out and I was left trembling. *How the hell had he done that?* He hadn't even touched me, not really, anyway. He'd let me go now and was kissing my stomach, kissing further and further up my body. He planted soft kisses between my breasts, and then kissed around each one. He kissed my neck and then, finally, brought his mouth down to mine and kissed me slowly and gently. So slowly and gently that I felt dizzy, like I was falling. Falling into him and his kiss. He pulled away and looked me deep in the eyes and my chest felt as if it had cracked open.

"At least we've fixed that part of it," he said.

I was too stupefied to talk. My tongue did not work anymore. Nothing worked. And so I just nodded at him.

"Sorry about the dress." He tried to pull it closed, but all except one button was gone. "I'll buy you another one."

I shook my head. It was so not necessary to buy me another one. So not necessary at all.

"I just couldn't get to you fast enough," he said, drawing soft circles on my chest and then tracing his fingers over my collarbone. I nodded. My body was still trembling and I'd never, ever, experienced anything like that. Not even one of my many vibrators did that to me. That was better than any orgasm I could ever give myself. He was still touching my body—his hands had not left it—and with each brush of his fingertips, I was starting to get turned on all over again.

"Ready for the next one?" he asked me, and my body jerked at the thought.

I finally managed to speak. "You've already given me one."

"Only one kind of one." He smiled at me, hot and filthy and sexy. "One kind?"

"The next kind is going to feel very, very different. And as for these panties"—he pulled at them—"they're going to have to go."

I nodded at him stupidly. He could probably do anything to me right now—anything—and I would let him. Well, except *that*. He pulled my panties down and they fell onto the floor, then without warning, he put his hand under my left knee and pulled my leg up. I felt so naked and exposed now as I felt the cold air rush up my skirt and into me. What was he going to do? I waited with anticipation, but I didn't have to wait long. He slowly slipped a finger into me and my entire body shuddered.

"You're so wet," he whispered, and I clenched around his finger at those words, the hottest words that had ever been spoken to me. He slid his finger in and out a few times before stopping all movement and staying in. His finger was still, but applied a constant growing pressure to what was clearly my G-spot. The elusive g-spot that most men did not know how to find, had been found in one second by Max. Found almost entirely in the dark, in a broom closet. He applied more pressure and my internal muscles started clenching. I had no control over them at all. He increased the pressure until I felt so filled up by him. He was inside my body and it felt amazing. He lifted my leg up higher and pushed even more. Oh my God, I didn't think he could make me feel any better in this moment if he tried. But when he slipped another finger into me and then turned them around inside me and hooked them around that spot and started pulling and pushing his fingers back and forth, I thought I was going to die and then black out. The movements started out slowly, until they built up in speed. A hard, fast internal massage of a part I hadn't even known existed inside me. I ground into him, forcing him deeper. I had no inhibitions anymore. I reached down and wrapped my hands around his wrist pushing him in faster.

"You like it hard and fast?"

I nodded at him, panting now as I felt myself building to an orgasm that felt totally, entirely different to the last one. I felt myself slipping into some blissful, orgasm-induced semi-consciousness, until a loud knock on the door snapped me back to reality.

"Okay, you can come out now. The leopard has been scared off."

"Oh my God!" I tried to push Max out of me as another knock banged the door against my back. "Stop, stop! We can't . . . not now," I scream-whispered at Max.

But he didn't stop. In fact, he started slamming into me harder and harder, the sound of wetness growing with each thrust. The key turned in the door and then Max reached out and grabbed the door handle, slamming the door shut.

"We're busy in here," he said loudly, and I almost died of embarrassment.

"Uh . . . Okay! Yes. Fine!" the man said from outside, and then I heard footsteps as he ran away.

"Now, where were we?" Max asked, grabbing my leg and pulling it up even higher, until I was spread wide open for him. He continued to slam his fingers into me. He'd created a steady predictable rhythm, and with each move, I got closer and closer until finally, I broke inside. An earth-shattering feeling ripped me apart from the inside out. I reached down and held him in place and he chuckled.

"Don't worry. I'm not going anywhere." He pushed a slow steady pressure on me as I came. My head fell forwards, I squeezed my eyes closed tightly, and held my breath until the last of it rippled through my body and finally stopped. He began to pull his fingers out and I gasped. I felt so sensitive now it was almost painful. I winced in what was a mixture of pleasure and pain as he slipped out and dropped my leg back onto the floor.

"Oh my God, how did you get so good at that?" I finally managed to ask.

"Well, after you, and the disaster that it was, I was determined to get better, so I learned about tantric sex."

I burst out laughing. "Like Sting? So that part *is* true, then." I pulled my skirt down and looked at him. "Just how much tantric sex did you learn, exactly?" I asked, my skin feeling flushed. I felt like I had just run a marathon.

He smiled at me, the smile that made my bones turn to jelly and made my knees want to cave in. He leaned in close again, but this time there was nothing sexual about it. This time he ran his thumb across my cheek, pushed the wild strands of hair that were hanging in my face aside, tucking some behind my ears and trying to push some back into my ponytail which had definitely come asunder somewhat.

"I'm really sorry you've had such a bad time with sex and dating." He said it with such sincerity.

"Well, you know, what can you do?" I said sarcastically and flippantly, trying to make light of something that had not been light at all. He pushed the last strand of hair out of my face and then ran his finger over my lips. I closed my eyes and fell into the feeling of it, the slow, sensual feeling of him dragging his thumb across my bottom lip.

"You and I could practice a little more if you want?"

"Practice?"

He took my chin in his hands and tilted my face up to him. "Maybe we can break this curse together," he said with a smile.

"Don't joke—that's exactly what a psychic told me to do once. Have sex with you again to break the curse. And of course all my friends are telling me to do that too."

"I think I like your friends already. And I also think they're right, because there are still so many things I want to do to you, if you'll let me."

"Hahah," I laughed nervously. "A lot of things?"

"A lot."

"Like how many?"

He actually looked as if he was counting now.

"Only six or seven come to mind right this very second, but there will be more."

"Six or seven!" My words came out a little too loudly and he pulled back from me.

"Think about it. It's up to you. But I know what I want . . ." He moved backwards, eyes locked on to mine with an intensity that made me shiver and then he ran both his hands through his slightly damp hair, pushing it back out of his face, slowly, deliberately. "*You*." It was only one word, but I was sure there had never been a single word in existence that held as much meaning.

"I . . . um . . ." I tried to speak, but it was totally pointless. That one word had rendered my jaw too loose to move and my tongue too thick and swollen to form shapes around any words. So I just nodded at him. He nodded back and smiled at me.

"All right, then." He reached for the door. "I'll give you some privacy to message Sarah and your friends and discuss all of this in great detail, although this time, I'm pretty sure the messages are going to be a little different." He gave me the sexiest smile before walking out of the closet and leaving me all alone.

I didn't do dinner after that—my stomach was in too many knots. And, of course, as soon as he'd closed the broom-closet door, I messaged the group immediately. And, of course, there it was also apparently no longer up for debate: I was to have sex with him now. *All-the-way sex*.

And I don't think there was any part of me left that was still arguing over that.

CHAPTER 37

Max

I woke up late the next morning. I'd barely been able to sleep, as thoughts of Ash and what had happened in the broom cupboard last night kept me awake, and hard, for most of the night. I jumped out of bed and climbed into my clothes. I was almost running late for a meeting with one of the lodge's marketing team members, Beverly, to discuss all the elements of the boat and also the various lodges they'd partnered with, and to be honest, I was not looking forward to it. Before working here, Beverly had worked at an exclusive resort in Namibia, where some years back I'd booked it for a large energy-drink commercial, and one thing had led to another with her.

Technically, more than one thing. Several things might have led to several other things with her, several times. I'd only found out it was her a few days ago when we'd chatted on the phone, where she'd gotten somewhat flirty and suggestive. And had I not been consumed with thoughts of Ash, I can guarantee that I would have been equally flirty and suggestive, and would have probably been expecting one or two things to lead to one or two more when I saw her today. But that was certainly not going to happen now. In fact, since Ash, I had not thought of another woman at all.

I walked onto the deck. The sun felt particularly bright and hot today. The boat had stopped at a dock so Beverly could board. I ran a hand through my hair. I probably looked very disheveled this morning. Ash was running around working, and if I thought I'd liked watching her work yesterday, well, I really loved watching her work today. Especially now that I knew what she looked like when she came. She bent over to take something out of a bag and I couldn't help but stare. She must have sensed me looking, because she turned and looked straight at me too. My chest tightened, my cock tightened, and I looked down at her T-shirt to see her nipples had hardened too and she did not pull the gaping neckline of her T-shirt up either. In fact, she locked eyes with me and bit her bottom lip and, God, that was it. I grabbed the banister and squeezed hard, trying to remind myself I had a business meeting now and I could not run down there, pull those shorts of hers down and bend her over the side of the boat railing. Her eyes drifted down to my shorts and then widened. I tried to adjust the hard-on in my pants to make it look less obvious, while Ash watched me with a smile. Moments later, Beverly was onboard, though, and I could no longer stare at the object of all my desires.

"Hey," I said awkwardly to Beverly, who was already looking at me like a piece of meat she wanted to sink her teeth into.

"Hey, long time. You look great."

"Uh, thanks." She looked at me expectantly, clearly waiting for me to compliment her too. *Shit this was not good at all.* I was going to have to give off a very professional vibe today that would hopefully make it very clear to her that things were leading nowhere without having to actually say it to her face. The assumption most women made about me, because I was perpetually unattached, was that I was always game for anything. And that assumption would have been correct, right up until Ash had walked back into my life.

"You look . . ." I searched for the words. "Botswana suits you," I said, and had no idea what the hell that meant. It was a compliment, though. Wasn't it? She looked at me oddly.

"Insane heatwave we're having," I said, trying to steer the conversation away from physical appearances. But she did not give up that easily. The meeting took far longer than it should have: her eyes lingered on me when she spoke; her arm brushed mine a few times.

She kept me as long as she could, explaining the most unnecessary details. I kept trying to make her hurry up, which she clearly misinterpreted.

"Looks like you want this meeting to be over as quickly as possible," she'd said, twirling a strand of hair round her finger. "Have some other *plans* for when this is over?" She smiled coquettishly and I felt utterly stuck in something I did not want to be in, and knew that I was going to need to tell her soon. When the meeting was finally over and I walked her to the exit, I could feel an expectation boiling in the air around us.

She turned and looked at me, waiting. The question wasn't just in her eyes and her mouth, it was also in the clothes she'd worn today, not as corporate as they might have been, just a little too tight and a little bit too short. Beverly was beautiful and sexy, with an incredible body too, and yet . . . *I wasn't even vaguely attracted to her.* I didn't want her. Not one tiny part of me wanted this woman, who was making her intentions very clear by leaning seductively against the banister and pushing her chest out.

Beverly reached forwards and touched my elbow with her hand. She rested it there and I knew that this had gone way too far. I put my hand over hers and started pulling it off. Only, she read this move very, *very* wrong.

CHAPTER 38

Ash

Yes! Yes! And Yes!

I was going to have sex with him. And it wasn't from my friends urging me last night and this morning. I wanted to. *Fuck*, I wanted to so badly that all I had been able to think about last night was him. His hands, his mouth on my breasts and the pleasure I'd experienced last night. Best of my life. I had not even experienced that at the hands of a very expensive sex toy that promised to rotate, suck, vibrate and thrust all at once. It did. And the orgasm had been mind-blowing, but when compared to the ones I'd had last night, it might as well have been a small sneeze.

I had my leg up in the shower trying to shave myself. I was in a seriously awkward position, one leg perched on the taps, bending down at the waist, trying to shave my labia and surrounds without causing damage. *Yes!* I was going to do it. I was going to have sex with him and that was it. I shaved myself almost totally naked, which I hadn't planned on doing, but after slipping and accidentally shaving half the landing strip off, I had to commit to that look. I climbed out the shower and then smothered myself from head to toe in the very luxurious cream the boat had provided. It smelled divine and I slathered it on until I was shiny and moisturized. I brushed my hair and then dug through my bag to find the stuff that Sarah had insisted I pack *"just in case"*. I was glad she'd talked me into packing the *"just in case"* stuff now. I'd put it all in

a smaller bag that I'd put at the very bottom of the suitcase. I pulled
the bag out and unzipped it.

One red sexy lacy bra, *check*.

One red sexy skimpy pair of panties, *check*.

Wait, what the hell was this?

I felt something else in the bag and pulled it out. I laughed as soon
as I saw what it was and read the handwritten note attached to the
box.

In case it doesn't happen, and you get frustrated! Sarah x

A bright pink dolphin vibrator stared back at me. Only Sarah
could have packed me something like this. I put it back in, smiling to
myself. I was not going to be needing that this trip. Not at all. In fact,
if the old curse had been broken, which hopefully it had been, I
might never need a vibrator again for as long as I lived. I would
become "Orgasm Woman." My superpower would be sleeping with
men and *actually* having an orgasm! Maybe my days of vibrator
usage were finally over.

I climbed into the sexy underwear first and looked at myself.
Not bad, not bad. (Apart from the odd red mosquito bite, that is.) I
pulled a dress over it all, the only (non-ripped) dress I had, and then
looked at myself in the mirror again. I grabbed my make-up bag
and pulled out my foundation. I seldom wore foundation; I was
blessed with pretty good, even skin. But tonight called for me to at
least dab some over those two red unsightly bites I had on my face.
I put on some mascara, brushed some blush over my cheeks and
ran gloss over my lips. And then I left the room and went looking
for Max.

It took me a while to find him. He was not on any of the decks,
the dining area or the lounge. In fact, he was all the way at the back
end of the boat. And he wasn't alone. I froze and watched. A cold,
clammy feeling swept over my skin, despite the hot air. He was with
a woman. A particularly gorgeous one, who was leaning, and pushing her chest out, and swaying seductively from side to side as she
talked to him with a twinkle in her eye that was brighter than the

sun. There was something in the way she was looking at him too. It implied a certain familiarity, a knowing.

My stomach tightened. They knew each other. *They'd had sex, or something sexual had happened!* I could see it now as clear as daylight. You did not sway like that, deliberately making your skirt creep up your thighs if the man had not seen your thighs before. Or worse, been between them. You did not stare at his mouth so obviously biting your lower lip while you did. An image of her straddling Max, fucking him while she bit her lips filled my mind.

When the hell had they had sex? Last night after I'd gone back to the boat and left him at the lodge? Today while she was "showing" him around? Or were they building up to it? They'd shared a sneaky kiss or two, a grope, and now they were building up for the main course, and right bloody now it would seem, because she laid her hand on his elbow and he slipped his hand over hers.

I felt queasy, itchy even. My stupid red lingerie and shaved bloody everything felt uncomfortably unbearable now. Like it was mocking me for having done that. God, I felt so, so stupid. What had I thought? That I was special. That he was not seeing and sleeping with other women. Of course he bloody was. He'd tantric-sexed himself halfway round the planet and in the few months he'd been in Cape Town had garnered himself a sexual reputation that was almost godlike. But when he'd had me pinned against a door coming for the first time with an actual human, and he'd told me he wanted more, it had not even crossed my mind that I would have to contend with any others here, or now.

And then the worst thing happened. She leaned all the way in and kissed him. I didn't need to see any more. I turned away quickly as my ribs squeezed me and my stomach churned. I ran back to my room as silently and quickly as I could.

"Stupid!" I berated myself as I paced the room angrily. Max was out there, not even twenty-four hours after making me come in a broom closet, flirting with some ridiculously hot woman with huge breasts. Less than twenty-four hours ago, his hands had been all over my body, in my body, and now his hands were touching someone else entirely. I had to stop this! Enough was enough. My brain had been very right. Hooking up with Max was a mistake and now I needed to draw a very deep line in the sand when it came to him and never cross it again.

"No!" This was it! And not just for Max—if this wasn't a sign that I should not be dating and sexing with men, then what else could be? From now on it would be DETOX! I would live on celery juice and exercise. Self-improvement and sex toys. It was all just too painful, too exhausting, too embarrassing, and too soul-destroying. All the disaster dates I went on with various men that all let me down in some way or the other, and now dressing up like a clown, hoping to have sex with a man who was clearly about to have sex with someone else. *I was done!* I paced the room some more, thoughts ripping through my mind like bullets from a machine gun.

I didn't need men. I had Petal. I had the best friends anyone could ever want and I had Roger Rabbit, and now Mr. Dolphin too. And Roger had never let me down. He always gave me exactly what I wanted and needed and I didn't have to have weird, awkward conversations with him before, or after. Roger and I understood each other; we didn't need anyone else.

I stopped pacing as I remembered how I'd put Mr. Dolphin back into my bag. So sure I would never need anything like him again, so sure that the orgasms I'd had with Max were the best of my life and no toy could ever be as good as that. I hung my head and shook it.

No! Max could *not* be the best orgasm-giver of my life! He could not, because then he would have cursed me all over again, in a new, creative way. I refused to spend the next thirteen years of my life living under a new Max-induced curse. I had to break it, right here and right now, or else it was sure to follow me.

I raced over to my bag and in seconds ripped the packaging off my new vibrator. I was going to give myself seventeen orgasms with this thing to prove to myself that Max was not the be all and end all and I could be more than happy without him, without men and just my trusty vibrators. My little dolphin friend over here was going to knock all thoughts of Max out of my brain, permanently. Besides, who wanted to have sex with a man who'd probably slept with the population of an entire small country, and owned a smelly llama! *Not me!* As far as I was concerned, Max could kiss my ass goodbye, like he had done thirteen years ago.

I jumped onto my bed, put my knees up and tried to get comfortable and ready myself for the best multiple orgasms of my life. But it was boiling. The aircon had broken earlier today and someone was coming round to fix it later, but until then this room was hot enough to roast a chicken in. I jumped off the bed, opened the massive window for air and then closed the net curtain so no one could see in. Not that anyone could—we were on a boat in the middle of the river and we were about to start moving again. I jumped back onto my bed. I was going to prove to myself, come hell or high water, that Max was not the person who had given me the most intense, earth-shattering orgasms of my life. In fact, I was more than capable of doing that on my own . . . except right now I was feeling very, very, very *not* turned on. At all.

I grabbed my phone and opened my favorite female-friendly porn site and tried to watch some, but still . . . *nothing*. This could not be happening. I would be damned if Max was going to be the best orgasm of my fucking life.

"Hello, it's the handyman. I'm here to fix your aircon." The voice ripped through the room and—instant panic.

"Hang on!" I shouted, and threw myself off the bed while pressing the "off" button of the still-shaking vibrator. But the thing would not stop. No matter how hard I pressed the button, it was still vibrating.

"Give me a moment," I shouted, and looked around the room. Not very many options to hide a loud, shaking sex toy. I threw the dolphin into the bathroom and closed the door, but could still hear it shaking about. I put a gown on and then tried to shove it under the pillows in the hope that they would muffle the sound somewhat. They did not.

"Do you think you can come back in ten minutes?" I asked.

"Sorry, I'm from the lodge. I have to get back in ten minutes to fix something else, and the boat is going to be moving soon."

"Shit!" I hissed under my breath. I looked around frantically again. There was only one option. One thing left to do to get rid of this loud, shaking thing that would not turn off. I walked over to the large window and pulled the net curtain aside. The water was only a few meters away, and so I tossed it and watched, waiting for it to sink. Only, that did not happen.

"No! No!" I gripped the windowsill in horror as the vibrations acted like a bloody motor and the pink dolphin scooted over the water like a speedboat. "Shiiit!" I watched as the pink thing darted through the water, motoring past a group of crocs.

CHAPTER 39

Max

*T*hat had been awkward. Beverly had leaned in to kiss me, and I'd had to stop her right there and then and tell her I was seeing someone. She'd looked surprised, but had accepted it gracefully. Nodding and words of "she's a lucky girl" had followed. I didn't want to tell her that I was the lucky one—that would probably just make her feel worse. But then when the manager of the boat had leaned over and told me he'd just seen some tiger fish, I jumped at the opportunity to go fishing, even though I hated it. I hated touching fish; I hated looking at fish. They repulsed me, ever since I was a child and had fallen into my grandfather's koi pond. I was only three and at that age the fish had seemed so big and terrifying. I'd been so traumatized, especially when one had started nibbling on my toe.

But here I was, sitting on a little boat, some distance away from the luxurious, nice, fish-free houseboat, with my line in the water, while a man talked to me about how great the tiger fishing was if we went a little further down to the rapids.

"No, this is great here. I love this spot," I lied. Sure, it was beautiful here: the call of fish eagles above my head; the sound of the water lapping against the grasses which came all the way up to the banks; the vervet monkeys playing in the big tree branch that hung over the water. This was paradise on earth. What was not paradise on earth was the fact that the manager was now suddenly standing up and winding his fishing line in frantically.

"Caught something," he said, yanking the fishing rod backwards. "Feels like a barbel."

"Great," I said, trying to sound happy for him because he looked thrilled.

He wheeled in the line, fighting what was clearly a huge fish, and when it emerged from the water, I thought I was going to vomit.

"Grab the net!" he shouted at me as the fish flopped around, fighting the line to get back in the water.

"Me?"

"Quickly or the line will break."

I reluctantly picked up the net and angled it towards the fish, but looked away. The idea of seeing the entire slimy fish out of the water made bile rise in my throat. I felt the massive weight in the net and only turned again when I didn't. The manager had taken the fish out the net and was now asking me to take a photo of him and the fish before he released it. I took the photo, trying not to look directly at the fish itself, its big mouth opening and closing as if it were drinking air down in big gulps.

"It's strictly catch and release here," he said to me as he gave the slimy thing a quick kiss and tossed it back in the water. "But you still get a hell of a rush from catching it," he said, looking almost high on it.

I nodded and agreed, even though I felt sick to my stomach. I picked the net up again and was just about to put it away, when I heard something motorized behind me. I turned. Something pink was darting across the water, getting closer and closer to the boat.

"What the . . ." I leaned over the side of the small fishing boat and stared as a familiar-looking thing came straight for me. *But it couldn't be, could it?* Yet the closer it got, the more I recognized its shape, size and the noise it was making. I looked over my shoulder. The manager was rinsing his hands and rebaiting his line. The pink thing started to veer off to the left so I quickly scooped it up in my net before it motored away. I pulled it towards me and did a double take as I looked down and had my suspicions confirmed. I looked back at the houseboat and saw the net curtain in Ash's room billowing in and out in the breeze. I picked up the binoculars that had been given to me for birdwatching and quickly raised them to my eyes. And there, only revealed for a second at a time as the curtain billowed out, was Ash's very shocked-looking face staring at the door.

Oh, Ash! I smiled to myself and then quickly turned the vibrator off, slipping it into my pocket before the manager saw.

～

I knocked on Ash's door the second I returned from fishing. There was no answer, but I could hear shuffling inside.

"Ash," I called again.

"Go away," she fired back quickly.

"I've just come back from fishing," I said, trying to hide my amusement, not to mention the heat I was feeling at the thought of her playing with that toy alone in her room.

"And I caught something very interesting. Want to know what it was?"

"Not really." She sounded pissed off, and I wasn't quite sure why. The last time I'd seen her, she had been anything but pissed off, leaning over, letting me gaze down her top.

"I'm going to tell you anyway," I said, dildo safely tucked away in my pocket. "A very odd fish, actually. Unusual."

She didn't respond.

"Strange color – pink."

I heard something, as if she'd just gotten off the bed, or a chair.

"Such a strange species to find in a river too—a dolphin."

The lock in the door clicked loudly. "Dolphin?" she asked. I could hear she was right behind the door.

"I know, right? Strange. I was totally surprised, and what was even stranger was that it was motorized. Want to see it?"

The door flung open and she stood in front of me in a gown.

"Give it to me!" She stuck her hand out forcefully.

I took the dildo out my pocket, held it up and waved it about in the air. "This what you want?"

"STOP IT! What are you—" She grabbed me by the arm, pulled me into her room and slammed and locked the door behind her.

"It's, it's . . ." She stared at it open-mouthed and then snatched it away from me and threw it at her bag. It missed, hit the floor, and then turned on again. It vibrated so hard, it started to snake round the floor in circles.

"Shit!" She jumped for it and desperately tried to turn it off. "This thing won't go off!" She began hitting it against the wall, over and over again, but it persisted.

"Pass it here." I held out my hand.

"I'm not passing it to you." She bent down and started beating it on the floor now. I knelt, pulled it out of her hands, and turned it off.

"How did you do that?" she asked, a little sweaty from the exertion of bashing her dildo against the wall and floor.

"The button needs to be pushed in twice to turn it off."

She snatched it back from me and shoved it back into her bag.

"Well, not that I need to know that, since it's not mine and I'm certainly not using it."

"Then why was it on when I caught it in a fishing net?"

She glared at me, face going red for a moment, and then I saw something change in her eyes. She stood up straight and pushed her shoulders back.

"So what if it's mine!" She was clearly taking a different tack now and I smiled. "Nothing wrong with it being mine."

"I never said there was."

"I am not ashamed of the fact I pleasure myself!"

"And so you shouldn't be. You are a very, very sexy, sensual woman, and you should . . ." I stepped closer to her. "Pleasure yourself whenever and wherever you want to."

"Exactly!" She folded her arms across her chest and the gown pulled open a little, a sliver of red lace flashed at me and my crotch twitched. God, it was hot enough imagining her clenching around a dildo in here all alone, but in red lacy lingerie? My mind was officially blown. That image was almost too much to handle.

"How was it?" I asked.

"How was what?"

I looked down at her bag and then back up to her. "Better than me?"

Something flashed across her face. A strange wash of emotions that ended in something that I recognized as defiance. "Amazing!" she said too quickly.

"Amazing?"

"Waaaay, waaaay better than you."

I stepped closer and eyed her up and down. "I seriously doubt that."

"Stop it." She pushed me back. "Stop flirting with me. Just stop it!"

She seemed genuinely angry, not cute, flirty, playful angry that gave rise to sarcastic witty banter and hot as hell flirtatiousness. I stepped back immediately.

"What's wrong?"

"What's wrong, you ask?"

"Yes, what's wrong? I'm confused here. You're acting like I did something wrong?"

"Maybe you did," she said softly.

"Well, please tell me so I can make it right in some way."

"What was her name, by the way?" she asked.

I had no idea what she was talking about. "Who?"

"The woman I saw you kissing earlier?"

"Beverly," I stated factually.

"Oh my God, what's with you and women whose names begin with a B. Bianca, Beverly, who's next . . . Brigit?"

"I don't know any Brigits," I started. "And I was not kissing Beverly—she kissed me and I pulled away and asked her to stop. And then I went fishing to avoid her. And you know how much I hate fish!"

She looked at me as if she didn't believe me in the slightest.

"Nothing happened with her. I swear. I went fishing. She went back to the lodge. Nothing happened."

"Max, I'm not stupid. I could see something happened between you two. It was so obvious." She looked furious now. She took a step closer to me and I could almost feel the anger oozing off her.

"We hooked up about a year ago in Namibia. But nothing happened with her now. I promise you."

"Hooked up?"

"Past tense," I reiterated.

"I see."

"Why? Jealous?" I asked, and took a step forwards.

"NO! Not jealous, but—call me old-fashioned—I don't think I like the idea of the guy I was making out with last night, whom I'd decided to have sex with, who I'd even put red lacy underwear on for, kissing another woman while I had just shaved myself awkwardly in a shower that does not lend itself to shaving that part of yourself!"

"You shaved yourself for me?"

"That's all you took from that?"

"What kind of underwear?"

"This stupid underwear, Max!" She opened her gown and I gaped.

"Fuck!" was all I could manage. The sight of her stole all the words in the world.

She released the gown, but didn't close it. Instead, she covered her face with her hands and shook her head.

"I feel like such an idiot," she said through her fingers.

My heart suddenly ached. I walked up to her and pulled her hands away from her face, slowly.

"There's no need to feel like an idiot. Not with me. Ever!"

I leaned down so I was looking her directly in the eye. "Ash, nothing happened with her. Nothing ever could, not after what you and I did last night. There is no other woman in the world I want to be with, other than you."

CHAPTER 40

Ash

*B*ut I did feel like an idiot. I was standing in front of him wearing red underwear with shaved lady parts I knew would start itching in a few days' time.

"Nothing happened?" I asked.

He shook his head. "There's no way I could do anything with someone else, especially when you're standing there looking like that."

"Like what?"

He looked me up and down and despite the fact I think I hated him a little bit right now, I shivered.

"Like a goddess in red lace," he said.

"Aaargh!" I pulled my hands out of his grip and took a step back. "Why are you doing this to me? Why are *we* doing this? There has been this weird, constant, push-pull sexual vibe between us, even before we saw each other, via email even, and it's making my head spin and making me wear red lacy things. God, I let you . . . *that*, in a broom closet full of spiderwebs. You know I pulled spiderwebs out of my hair last night?"

"We clearly have some unfinished business," he said.

"Sex?"

"Sex." He repeated it like a fact. Some irrefutable fact. *Sex!* We were meant to have sex! *Fact!*

He walked away from me contemplatively, and then sat on my

bed. The image of him sitting on my bed made me want to sit down next to him, *or on top of him*. I fought that urge.

"Well, that's no longer an option. That is totally off the cards now."

He looked up at me and smiled, sexy and—

"Oh no!" I pointed at him. "You better stop all that."

"Stop what?" He acted innocent now.

"Oh, please. You drip sex. Sex oozes from your pores. Your entire DNA is sex and sexiness and steamy flirting. Your smiles, your whispers, your come-hither eyes."

"You think I have come-hither eyes?" He deliberately turned his gaze on me, and like laser beams of come-hitherness, they melted me.

"You are doing it now." I folded my arms. "But it is not going to work. I'm back on a detox."

"I've heard that before."

"I relapsed. Had a little cheat meal, and now I'm back on track."

He laughed. "I've never heard myself being referred to as a cheat meal. But fair enough." He stood up slowly and put his hands on his hips. "Far be it from me to keep you from your health goals. I would never want to derail that."

"You wouldn't?" Hang on. Was I a little disappointed by that?

"No. I respect your detox, Ash."

"Oh. Oh." I looked at him, surprised. "You're not going to try and talk me out of it?"

"No."

"Not like all the other times you've tried to talk me out of it?"

He straightened up and suddenly looked serious. "I haven't talked you out of anything this whole time. I would never do that. Never push you into anything you weren't sure you wanted. The ball has been in your court. It's always your choice."

"No, it's—" But as I said it, I realized it was true. I'd been the one that ran to his room, the one that had asked him to touch me, the one that had wanted to kiss him in the jacuzzi.

"So nothing happened?" I asked again.

"Absolutely nothing."

I stared at him. He was telling the truth. I knew him so well. I shook my head. "It doesn't matter now, since, detox."

"It's good that you are prioritizing your health, Ash," he said.

I fanned myself. It was hot in this room and in my body. "I just need a moment that's not all sexually charged and tense and full of things that are potentially dangerous and life-threatening." I felt like saying that he felt dangerous and life-threatening. Maybe more so than a snake, even. There was anti-venom for a bite, but I didn't think there was any anti-venom for Max's bite. Once he'd sunk his teeth into you, emotionally and physically—my nipple tingled at the thought of his teeth—you were done. Addicted. No cure. No anti-venom.

"You know what we need," he said, stepping towards me. "Dinner. A non-romantic dinner. Where we just eat food and talk about shit that has nothing to do with sex. A dinner without red lacy underwear, even though it really is very beautiful." He smiled, but it wasn't dripping with lust this time.

"Thanks." I looked down at my underwear and then closed my gown, I hadn't realized it was still open. "I spent way too much money on it."

"You probably make bucketloads of money anyway, what with you being the country's best cinematographer."

"Hardly," I said, but felt my cheeks blush.

"That's not what I read. And I've read just about every single article written about you. Quite an impressive list of awards too, I must say."

"Thank you," I said again, and then smiled to myself. "I like winning awards."

He laughed. "I don't doubt that. I still have some work to do today, so this evening let's have a casual and totally non-romantic dinner?"

I nodded at him. "Sure."

"And I'll just forget about the whole pink-fish thing."

"Please—that would be great."

"Done. Already forgotten. See you soon." He walked up to me

and kissed me on the forehead. My heart skipped a beat at the familiarity of it all. A familiarity that was still there after thirteen years.

He pulled away from the kiss quickly. "Sorry, that wasn't—I wasn't coming on to you. It just happened."

"You used to do that all the time."

"Must be muscle memory or something. Sorry."

I shook my head. "It's okay. It was . . . nice."

He smiled at me before exiting my room and leaving me all alone. I touched my forehead. The kiss had felt sweet and comforting. Just like it had felt all those years ago.

"See you this evening," he said.

I was back in my usual clothes. Shorts and T-shirt on, cotton briefs and a cotton trainer bra. The kind that was actually meant for teenage girls, but—given I was basically a teenage girl in that area—I wore them too. I walked up onto the deck, not the bottom one, but the very top one, the one that was entirely open to the sky. I found Max sitting on a lounger, looking relaxed and casual as well.

"Feeling more comfortable?" he asked.

"Much."

He pulled a lounger towards him and patted it. "Come sit here. You need to see this."

I walked over and climbed on.

"Lower it like mine and look up."

I did what he said. "Wow! I've never seen the moon look so big and close before."

"It's pretty cool."

"What's for dinner? I'm starved."

"I asked the chef to make something quick and easy, a burger, toasted sandwich and French fries. I've had enough of fancy gourmet food, anyway."

"Me too," I said, still looking at the moon.

We stayed like that for a while and then he spoke. "So, tell me, what have you been up to these last thirteen years. We sort of touched on it, but not really. And I want to know everything."

I turned on the lounger and faced him, resting my head on my hand, propped up by my elbow.

"Well, as you know, I was going to study accounting."

"I always thought that was way too normal and boring for you."

"You were right." I smiled at him, amazed by how the awkwardness and weirdness of before was gone. "I ditched it after a year and then one day walked into this film lecture by total accident, and that was it for me. Got my honors, four years specializing in cinematography. I was lucky enough to work under some really good DOPs early on, and then managed to work my way up pretty quickly."

"Did you meet all your friends at film school? The ones you seem to message all the time?"

"You noticed that?"

"Hard not to."

"A psychologist called us co-dependent once."

"No." He feigned shock. "Not at all."

"So what if we have a very active WhatsApp group and overshare every aspect of our lives with each other?"

He laughed. "I think it's great you have so many friends. And you and Sarah still seem as thick as thieves."

"Maybe even thicker than thieves."

"I'm glad you have a support system," he said meaningfully—the implication was that, of course, it was my only support system.

"Me too. And you?"

"I have a few friends, but because I travelled so much, they're scattered around the world, so I don't get to see them often."

"That sucks."

He shrugged. "I keep in touch with them, though."

"And why Greece?" I asked.

"Have you been there?"

I shook my head and he smiled at me. "You should. You would love it. It's obviously gorgeous, but the people and the vibe are what makes it so special. I felt at home there for some reason."

"Do you want to go back?"

An expression washed over his face with something that resembled sadness. "My mother needs me. And I don't know how much longer she'll be here, mentally."

"I'm really sorry about your mom, and the divorce. I would never have suspected that. They always seemed so happy."

"It was a total shock to all of us and she hasn't really been the same since that, and a part of me blames him for what's happening now. I mean, logically I know that divorce can't cause dementia, but stress and heartbreak certainly doesn't help."

"How bad is she?" I asked.

"She's in and out of reality, but the doctor has warned that at some point she will completely lose touch and will have no more lucid moments."

"That's awful. What do you do when she's not lucid?"

"The doctors told me to play along with whatever delusion she's having, so I do."

"Have you considered putting her into a place where—"

"No." He cut me off adamantly. "I don't want to put her in a home, so I'll be here for the foreseeable future."

"Sounds like you don't really like it here?"

"Not at all. I actually love where I live, I'm really enjoying work and I see a lot of other business opportunities I think I want to get involved in."

"Like what?"

"Well, as you know, tourism is booming here. I think I can create something very appealing for my exiting international market. I've seen a house in Camps Bay I'm thinking of buying, staffing up and then renting out to clients. I've also seen one in the winelands."

"Camps Bay and the winelands! You must have made some money over the years."

He smiled. "I've worked hard. You live in Camps Bay too, though."

"Not the part that only foreign money can afford. I'm further up the hill. A little way back from the mansions."

"So tell me more about cinematography. I only know a little. I know more about directing. Did you not want to do that?"

I smiled; this was one of my all-time favorite topics. "I sort of realized pretty quickly that being a director has less to do with actually shooting film, and more to do with managing actors and people. And I didn't want that—I just wanted to focus on the pictures. I'm the one who gets to really look at things and find the beauty in it all, and then figure out how to translate that to the film. That's much more rewarding and interesting to me than the actual performance, although you could say that the light is also a performer, and that's the one I like working with."

"And Sebastian, I've heard such weird stories about him. What's it like working with him?"

"It's actually great—I get him. And I wouldn't be where I am if it wasn't for him. He sort of discovered me when I was only twenty-five and saw something in me that I didn't even know was there. And he's 'latched on to me like a marsupial', as he says, and refuses to work with anyone else."

"Wise choice he made there."

"He lets me do what I want, too. Even this trip, usually a director would come to this, but he wants me to go out and 'find the magic' without him influencing me. He really trusts me. I'm lucky—it's basically a dream job."

"I'm sure he's lucky too."

"He is, and he does tell me that, in his own special way. He's a total genius, and I guess that comes with a little crazy too."

And so we carried on talking like this. Sharing stories from our lives with each other, things we had missed out on in the last thirteen years. I told him all about my life, my friends. And the more we talked, the more I relaxed into it. We laughed like old times, and the conversation flowed again. I was so glad we'd packed the weird sex thing away and were back to being, well, what we were: exes with a history who were catching up now like old friends.

But friends who also found each other incredibly attractive and who had a sexual chemistry that bubbled under the surface. Even now when there was nothing sexual about the moment, it was still there. Like a soft whisper in the distance that you could almost hear.

Chapter 41

Max

We landed at the Lilongwe Airport, ready to transfer to Lake Malawi, the last stop on the trip. I was excited to see the lake. I'd never been there before, but the pictures were incredible. Despite being a lake, it looked like a tropical beach. Clear blue waters, tropical fish, white sands and snorkeling. Since last night with Ash, we'd spent hours and hours talking as if no time had elapsed between us at all. The entire night three words had been bubbling up inside me. I'd felt them there on several occasions before that, when I'd kissed her goodnight, when I'd watched her sleeping on the jet, when I'd watched her come, but now they'd really come all the way up to the surface and it felt painful to hold them back.

I love you.

Plain and simple. I loved her. I was in love with her, and I think I always had been. It had become so clear to me last night, watching her talk animatedly about her life and adventures. I wanted so badly to be a part of her life and adventures moving forward. In fact, I couldn't imagine a life for myself anymore unless she was in it. I watched her as she walked in front of me in the airport. She had a bounce in her step, as if she felt lighter today, or happy about something. God, she was so sexy. Everything about her was sexy, even when she was bending down and scratching her ankle like she was doing now. I was so attracted to her, but I didn't just want to push her up against something and make her scream my name. I also wanted to hang out and chat with her about utter crap. Be with her, even if we only sat in silence together; and love her.

But then suddenly she was hugging someone.

"No way!" she exclaimed loudly and enthusiastically.

"Fancy running into you here," the person, a male person, replied, and I knew instantly by the tone of his voice that he liked her. In fact, now I thought about it, Ash's tone of voice implied something too. Implied a knowing of sorts. *How much knowing?*

"What are you doing here?" she asked the guy. I moved in closer to look at him, but hung back just enough so I was not obviously in sight. Smart executive type, the crisp expensive clothes told me. They were casual, but pricey. Good quality. He wore glasses, which made him look intelligent and gentlemanly, and then round his neck, a stethoscope. He looked like a young Denzel Washington or something equally irritating. What can I say—the guy was good-looking.

"I'm visiting some local rural hospitals. Doing some pro bono work."

"Oh my God, that's so amazing." She touched his arm. She *touched* it. I rolled my eyes. A good-looking doctor who did pro bono work in rural Africa. I stood up a little straighter when he reciprocated by touching her arm back.

"And you? What brings you here?"

"I'm doing some work for an upcoming shoot. We're off to Lake Malawi."

"It's beautiful there. Have you been?"

"First time."

"You're going to love it. I hope you don't have to work too hard, because you have to go swimming, and the canoeing is amazing."

"I'll do that," she said in a slightly breathy voice. Why was her voice breathy? I looked over at the hot doctor again. Maybe I would also be breathy if I was a heterosexual woman standing opposite him.

"Just be careful of mosquito bites."

"Mosquito bites are the least of my worries. I got bitten by a snake in Botswana. An actual snake!"

"*What?* Are you okay?" He looked genuinely concerned and I was irked. Very, very irked.

"Fine—it was nonvenomous."

"Where was it? May I look? For my own peace of mind?"

"Uh . . . sure." She hesitated for a moment, but it wasn't because she *didn't* want him to look. I could see that. It was because she *did* want him to look. Her hesitation had been a moment of silent anticipation.

"My left ankle," she said, and he bent down.

"May I?" he asked, holding her sock.

I rolled my eyes as she nodded at him. There was something in the way she was looking at him. *Something I didn't like.*

He rolled the sock down slowly and I watched her face as she took a little in-breath. He examined her ankle for a while, and when he smiled up at her and nodded that everything was okay, a part of me was relieved to hear that, but another part of me didn't like the fact that he had his hands on her ankle.

"Thanks," Ash said when he stood up again. He looked at her seriously now and tugged on his stethoscope nervously. I inched closer without being obvious.

"Last time, with us . . . I've been thinking about it a lot."

"That was over a year ago," Ash said.

"I guess you left quite an impression on me." He smiled at her, and I felt sick to the stomach.

"I wasn't in the best place back then, as you know. I'm in a totally different place now, a much better place."

"Yes," she said, a small flush coming over her cheeks.

"Thing is, I'd really like to take you out again. If you'd like to. No pressure, obviously. And I'll totally understand if you don't want to."

And there it was. I held my breath and waited for Ash to answer him. Surely she wouldn't say yes? Not after declaring she was on some detox. After getting so pissed off at the potential of me being with Beverly.

"I'll think about it," she said coyly, foot tracing half-moons on the floor.

Was she fucking serious?

"Sure, of course. No pressure, though, please. If you don't want to, it's also totally fine."

A doctor and a gentleman! I hated him. They exchanged a few more words. I wasn't sure what, because I'd had to turn now. Out of the corner of my eye, I did see them hug, though. Properly hug. A long, borderline inappropriate hug in which he ran his hand down to her lower back. It was the kind of hug that had a certain type of familiarity to it that only came from . . . *sex*! They'd had sex. But Ash had said all her sexual encounters had been bad, and this did not look bad. This looked like the after-effects of good sex.

"Who was that?" I tried to ask casually when we'd fetched our bags and were climbing into the transfer vehicle, but I could hear an edge in my voice.

"This guy I dated for a while. Actually, probably my longest relationship since you."

Dagger through my heart now! So painful I almost gripped my chest. I retaliated. I shouldn't have.

"Why did it end?" I asked.

She looked down at her phone and answered with an air of evasiveness. "Uh, it just didn't work out."

"Thought you were on a dating detox," I said.

"That's actually none of your business," she said firmly. "It's none of your business who I do, or don't choose to date."

"You seemed to make Beverly your business."

She stopped walking and swung round. "That was very different."

"How exactly was that different?" I asked.

"This was an invite to dinner, not what looked to be an invite to bed. Besides, after last night, we're over all that other stuff, right?"

She looked at me expectantly, and when I didn't answer, a look of mini-panic swept her face briefly.

"Aren't we?"

"Are you?" I threw it back at her, which clearly made her uncomfortable.

"There is sexual tension between us, okay. Obviously. But after last night, we don't have to act on it—that's what I'm saying."

"We don't have to act on it," I repeated, and she squirmed.

"No . . . we don't." She looked as if she was trying to convince herself now.

"And I'm sorry," I said quickly. "You're right. Who you date, or don't date, is absolutely none of my business."

"That's right?" She held my gaze and the statement felt more like a question. I matched her gaze.

"Unless you want it to be?" I answered the question I was sure she was asking me.

"Why would I?" She tore her eyes from mine. "That would be . . . ridiculous. Right?"

"Are you making statements here, Ash? Or are you asking questions that you want me to answer for you?"

"I'm not," she said quickly and defensively, holding my gaze again.

"Because I can't answer them for you. You have to answer them yourself."

I broke the eye contact with her and walked away.

"Exactly," she said, and then walked away too.

CHAPTER 42

Ash

Ash: Bumped into hot doc in the airport.

This was what we collectively referred to Sibu as.

Yo: As in the guy who cried during sex?

Ash: That's the one.

Melusi: That gorgeous young Denzel when he had all the muscles.

Ash: That one.

Sarah: You actually liked him.

Ash: I did. And the sex was going better than all the other sex I'd had, until he cried.

Melusi: Is he over his ex, yet?

Ash: Apparently so . . . And he wants to go on a date.

Sarah: I thought you were having hot sex with Max.

Ash: No, that's over.

Ash: So totally, totally over. And I'm feeling so relieved.

Ash: Like really relieved and happy.

After I typed the words, I lifted my gaze ever so slightly to Max. He was sitting in the row in front of me in the van. He was looking out the window and I ran my eyes over his profile. Oh God, why did he have to look like that? And smell like that? Because there was a particularly woody and intoxicating scent filling the van right now. I put my fingers back down to my phone and typed harder than I needed to.

Ash: Happy.

Ash: So happy it's over!!!!!!!!

Yo: Wait. I'm so lost.

Sarah: Me too.

Sarah: Last time we spoke you were going to have sex with him.

Ash: It kind of didn't work out that way.

Sarah: Your life is like a soap opera at the moment. I swear I can't keep up.

Charlie: Me neither.

Ash: I have to go, but I had to tell you all that.

Yo: I actually think a date with hot doc could be a good thing.

Yo: I liked the guy, besides it's always good to know a doctor, just in case.

Russ: I thought you were on a detox?

Frank: Me too.

Yo: Where have you been in this conversation, guys. She's not on it anymore.

Russ: No, I'm lost.

Melusi: It's simple. She was on it and then decided not to be on it after she and Max were flirting on email. And then after she knew it was him, she went back onto it. And then when they started flirting, she went off it again, and when they didn't have sex she went back on it, but now that hot doc is back, she might go back off it. Keep up!

I reread Melusi's message and it made my head spin. Had I really gone on and off a sex and man detox so manically and frequently?

Ash: Okay, just arrived at the Lake. Totally gorgeous by the way.

Ash: Have to run.

I climbed out the car and stared in awe at the massive lake in front of me. It was spectacular. In some places, the water was so clear it was transparent. Huge boulders rose up out of the water in parts, creating small natural islands where vegetation had grown wild. If I didn't know I was in a land-locked African country, I would have thought I was on a tropical island in the Indian Ocean.

I immediately got to work while we still had perfect light: tracking the movement of the sun so I knew what shots needed to be shot in which order, creating that shot list, and then coming up with a gear list too. I was busy contemplating an aerial shot when I started to notice that the sun was much lower in the sky. I looked at my watch. I had been working flat out for six hours. Enough for now. I walked towards the hotel we were staying in. It was absolutely gorgeous, built onto a rocky outcrop, almost perching on it, as if it defied gravity. The huge boulders had also been incorporated into the interior design, and the reception desk was actually made of one.

"Hi, I'm with the production company, checking in." The woman behind the counter suddenly looked a little panicked.

"Let me call my manager quickly."

I looked around for Max. This didn't sound good.

The manager arrived, looking worried as well. "Welcome," he said nervously. "Has your traveling companion told you yet?"

"Told me what?"

"There has been an issue with your rooms. A tap burst, and there was some unfortunate flooding. We're so sorry. We know you'd wanted to stay in those rooms specifically. But we are putting you up in another villa together."

"What? We're sharing a room?"

"Oh no, the villa has several rooms, but it does share common living areas."

I relaxed a bit. I'd thought he was going to tell me Max and I were going to be sharing a room. Luckily, we weren't.

"Not a problem," I said, and the man looked very relieved.

The villa was incredible, rustic chic, perched high up on the boulders with the most incredible view of the endless blue waters of the lake. We definitely needed an aerial shot! In my room too, a huge boulder protruded from the floor and the bed leaned up against it. I peeled off my clothes and went straight for the bathtub. If I'd thought the bath at Matobo Hills had been perfect, I was very, very wrong. This was undoubtedly the world's best bath. The bathroom was completely indoor/outdoor, and the tub had been carved out of one of the giant boulders. Green trees made a natural wall on the one side, but the front was completely open to the lake and view in front of me. And, what was better, a variety of bath salts and scented oils had been laid out on the Malawian rattan table next to the bath. I was going to make the most of this moment after what had been a rather long and hot day. The sun was setting over the lake and if perfection had a name, a place and a time, it would be the Takulandirani Villa, Lake Malawi, at exactly 5:39 p.m. I slipped into the floral-scented water and let out an audible moan of contentment.

God, this was amazing. I grabbed my phone and took a quick photo of my knees sticking out of the bath and the view behind it, and posted it on the group to a stream of jealous replies and photos of where they were. I put the phone down and muted it. I loved my friends, but I wanted some silence. Needed some silence. These last few days had been totally weird, to say the least. Things had been bizarre with Max, and I was just so happy to be free of all that. After last night's talk, it was apparent I could actually have a decent, normal conversation with the man without all the sexually loaded subtext that had been underpinning our reunion until now . . . *right*?

I closed my eyes and tilted my head back. I lay there in the water for so long that it started becoming cold as the sun set. Small fairy lights woven around the trees came on. This place could not get any more magical if it tried. I climbed out the bath and stood looking at the view for a while, the fat moon casting a silver glow over the water below. I reached for the towel, which was hanging from a tree branch that jutted from the foliage, making a natural towel rack. These people had put so much thought into every single detail of this place. I hoped Max would sign them on . . .

"MAX!" I screamed, and froze. He was standing in front of me. "What the hell are you doing here?" I whipped the towel off the branch, only for it to snap and fall to the floor.

"I didn't know your bathroom was here. Honestly, I was walking around to get some pictures of the villa at night."

I'd put my hands over my breasts, crossed my legs to try to hide my rather bald nakedness and was now trying to pick up the dropped towel with my toe. He was staring at me. "For God's sake! Stop staring. Stop—*Aaaah!*" My foot hit a wet patch on the floor and I lurched forwards. "Shit!" I lost control and toppled, wet and naked and totally mortified, right into Max's arms.

"You okay?" he asked.

"I'm fine!" I immediately and incorrectly said. "No. I'm clearly not fine, actually, because I'm naked. And you are . . . *here*."

"Sorry, it was a genuine mistake."

"Aaagggh," I moaned when the full picture of what exactly was happening right now came into crystal clear view, and as soon as it did, other things became crystal clear as well: the feelings surging through my naked body right now; Max's strong arms wrapped around me; my breasts pressing into his chest; his cock pressing into my stomach, growing harder by the second, which had not gone unnoticed by me, and it was driving me wild.

Knowing and feeling how hard his cock was sent a thrill

rocketing up my spine. The thrill rushed in both ways, to my face and lips and mouth, which tingled now, but also to the base of my spine. My hips, my thighs, between my legs. A warm throb deep inside made me swell for him, made my legs part ever so slightly. Of course, he didn't miss this tiny move, because his hands travelled down my back and settled around my waist. My heart raced a little quicker, my cheeks flushed and my breath quickened . . .

I was not over this.

No matter how much I tried to fight it with him, I was so far away from being over it that I might as well be under him right now. Legs wide open, inviting him to do whatever he wanted with me. And I wanted it too. I wanted it so badly and I did not think I had the energy, or the desire, to fight it any longer. I gasped when suddenly one of his hands left my lower back and came down on my ass, almost a spank, and then gripped it tightly. I looked up at him, wide-eyed, questioningly. He pulled me towards him and then ground me into his cock.

"Do you feel that?" he asked, and I nodded up at him in a stupefied state. "That's how much I want you, Ash."

I let out a moan when he did it one more time for good measure. In case I was in any doubt about how big and hard he was.

"Only question is, are you finally going to let me have you? I know you want me, but you're the one standing in your own way."

And then he let go of me, ran his eyes up and down my naked body—it felt on fire—and turned and walked away again.

Ash: We are like fire and gasoline.

Sarah: Hey, you're messaging privately. This must be serious.

Ash: It is. I just want to talk to you.

Ash: You were there at the start. I need advice. Proper advice.

Ash: Whenever we are near each other, everything feels combustible.

Ash: The sexual tension is insane.

Ash: What should I do?

Sarah: Are you asking me if I think you should have sex with him?

Ash: Yes.

Ash: No.

Ash: Yes.

Sarah: Do you just want to have sex with him, or do you want more?

Ash: Like a relationship more?

Sarah: Yes.

Ash: Absolutely NOT!

Ash: Not after everything that's happened. Remember how broken I was? How long it took me to get over it all?

Sarah: But you were in love with him back then. You're not in love with him now . . . are you?

Ash: WHAT?

Ash: No, absolutely not.

Sarah: Are you sure you're not having any feelings for him?

I put my phone down and bit my lip. Tapped my foot against the floor. Sure, there were feelings. Just not those ones. There had been moments with him that had been nice; he'd been nice, and it had felt familiar, but—

Ash: NO!

Ash: There are no feelings like that.

Sarah: And any chance of those kinds of feelings?

I tapped my foot faster this time.

Ash: Nope!

Sarah: And from his side?

I stopped tapping my foot and thought about the way he'd kissed me on the forehead. Tender, loving almost. Called me baby. Tended to my foot, ankle . . .

Ash: Definitely not.

Sarah: So then why don't you just have sex with him and get it over with and out of your system? You guys clearly have some seriously unfinished business and that's the problem. And I'm not saying this because of weird maybe curses, I'm saying this because you guys didn't have any closure, and maybe this is the thing that needs to happen so you can finally close the door on this. And . . . just in case, in case there is the tiniest possibility that curses do exist, have sex with him as well.

Ash: You think?

Sarah: As long as you're not lying to yourself about any possible feelings you might be having, then yes! Just have sex with him and get it out of the way.

I lowered my phone. My tapping foot was going ballistic on the floor; it felt out of my control. The chewing of my lip also felt out of my control. I wasn't lying about having those kinds of feelings for him. The only feelings I was having for him were of the very dirty, and lustful kind and Sarah was probably right!

I needed to have sex with him!

CHAPTER 43

Ash

I found him sitting outside by the pool. The sun had set and the moon was casting a silver glow across the water, the world, and him. He looked almost ethereal in this light. I walked up to him slowly, as quietly as possible. Taking these last few moments just to make sure this *was* what I wanted to do. But when I snapped a small twig underfoot, and he turned around and looked at me the way he did, I knew I was in no doubt of what I was going to say next.

"One time," I said, looking at him.

"One time what?" he asked.

"Just one time. Just once. And just tonight."

He turned his entire body towards me. "Wait . . . I just want to make sure I'm thinking what you're thinking—"

"Sex. You and I. One time."

"You're serious?" he asked.

"Dead serious. But just this once. And just tonight."

He stood up in all his hot fucking glory and took a stride towards me. "You sure that's what you want?"

"Yes."

"And you can do that?"

"Yes."

"And you can do that because . . ." He took another one of his big, hot-man strides towards me. "Because you don't have any feelings for me?"

"No feelings," I said quickly. "None."

"So just sex, then?" he asked again. What was he not getting about what I was saying?

I nodded. "Sex. And no . . . you know." I gestured below. "Nothing down there unless it's your hand, or cock. Just sex. And just tonight."

"Why now?" he asked.

"Because I've been thinking and I know why this keeps happening to us, why we have this constant sexual attraction. It's because we didn't get any closure all those years ago. It was all left up in the air and I think it's driving us both mad. So we need to have sex, right now, to get it out of our systems once and for all. Close that door."

"So you want to have sex with me for closure. That's it?"

I nodded, but my head wanted to shake instead.

"Just once. Just tonight and no feelings?" he asked again.

"Just once. Just tonight. And I *know* there'll be no feelings."

CHAPTER 44

Max

*B*ut she didn't know how wrong she was about that last part. There would be feelings, from me anyway.

"If this is what you really want, Ash?"

She nodded. "This is what I want. Is it what you want?"

"I want this more than anything I've wanted in a very, very long time," I said, and walked straight up to her. I took her by the hand and started walking her off the veranda.

"Where are we going?" she asked.

"Why, you want to go somewhere specific?" I asked, and stopped walking.

She shook her head. "I mean, I just thought we would probably do it right here, like over the chair or something. Last time was in a broom closet. Get it over with quickly."

I laid my hands on either side of her face. "Trust me, what I have planned for us does not take place with you bent over a chair or in a broom closet. And it will *not* be quick."

She swallowed hard and I knew I had her.

"Then where?" Her voice caught in her throat.

I pulled her face towards me and planted a kiss on her lips. The kind of kiss I'd wanted to plant on her lips since I'd seen her for the first time. Soft, gentle, loving. She quickly reciprocated, putting her hands on my face and pulling me closer like we used to do all those years ago because we loved each other more than two people could ever love each other. And right now, in this moment, I felt that love again. I wondered if she felt it too. I pulled away from the kiss and locked eyes with her.

"I'm taking you to my bed," I whispered against her lips, reluctant to pull away from them because they felt so good against mine. But I did, and took her by the hand again and walked her inside. Across the lounge area and then straight into my bedroom. I closed the door behind us and then locked it. I looked at her, and suddenly she looked nervous, as if second-guessing her decision. Her eyes were fixed on the lock on the door, so I reached out and unlocked it.

"You can leave any time you want. You can leave right now if you've changed your mind." I pulled the door wide open for her and she stared at it.

"No." She shook her head. "I haven't changed my mind." She walked up to me, put her hand over mine and closed the door again, and then I heard the lock turn.

"You can if you want," I said, pushing strands of hair behind her ear, relishing the feel of this simple touch.

"I know I can." She smiled and then untied her gown and let it fall open. She wasn't wearing the red underwear this time, just a simple sports bra and plain cotton panties, but she might as well have been wearing sexy, lace lingerie. Because she was fucking gorgeous. She walked over to my bed and sat down. My cock was so hard right now and there was just no hiding it. It pushed against my shorts, demanding to be let out.

"But you have to say the words too." I walked over to the bed and stood in front of her.

In response, she slowly opened her legs for me while holding my gaze. "I want you to fuck me, Max."

I didn't need any more than that. I reached up, pulled my T-shirt over my head, and dropped it to the floor. I undid the button on my shorts, then the zipper, letting them fall too. I stuck my hand into my underwear, gripping my cock. Her eyes followed me there and

I teased her for a moment, rubbing my cock up and down just out of her sight.

"You want me to take these off?" I asked.

She nodded immediately and I obliged, dropping them to the floor and kicking them across the room.

My hand found her bra strap and my other hand pulled her panties down as fast as I could. I wanted her totally naked, as naked as I'd seen her earlier tonight and as naked as she had been that night when I had fucked it all up all those years ago. But I wasn't going to mess this up. I was going to give her the best night of her life. If nothing further was going to happen with us, then I would give her something to remember me by forever.

"You don't need to ask me twice, baby."

"You used to call me that." She pulled away. "In fact, you called me that the other night too."

"Habit, I guess," I said quickly, trying to hide the fact that calling her that felt like the truest thing that had come out of my mouth in thirteen years.

"It better be—no feelings, remember?"

I pushed her onto the bed and climbed straight on top of her, pushing my hard cock into her stomach. "That's enough talking, Ash. No more talking, only moaning and screaming."

She suddenly laughed and I sat up on my haunches and looked down at her.

"Moaning sure, but no one actually screams during sex."

"You think so?" I grabbed her thigh, forcibly pushing her legs apart and then dropped back down onto her, dragging my now very hard cock across her. Her eyes widened as I rubbed against her, hard. But then she smiled again.

"I'm not going to scream, Max."

"Wanna bet?"

"Sure." She was teasing me now and, my God, it was turning me on so much.

"Okay, if I make you scream, then I get to do anything to you, and

I mean *anything*." I leaned down and slowly licked her lips. "Except these are not what I intend on licking." I stopped and looked down at her. Her eyes were wide and she was staring at my mouth as if considering it.

Consider it. Say yes.

"Maybe if you make me come seventeen times I might let you do that."

"Only seventeen?" I sat up on my haunches again, flipped her over onto her stomach so quickly she let out a small surprised scream. I smiled as I pushed her legs apart and rested myself between them, my cock on her ass now.

"You screamed," I said, flattening myself against her, bringing my mouth to her ear. I stuck my hand underneath her and went straight to her pussy. I ran my fingers over her clit and her entire body shuddered against mine.

"You're already so close to coming. Seventeen will be easy," I whispered in her ear as she moaned and writhed under me. I rubbed my cock on her ass and stroked her clit. I sat up on my knees and then took her by the hips and pulled her onto her knees, her back resting against my chest now. I reached round and slid one hand between her folds, and the other one to her breast. She moaned as I worked her in both places. She was so receptive; it was hard to believe someone this receptive would have not been able to come with anyone else. I'm not going to lie—the thought fucking thrilled me. She began to buck against my hand. Her hands reached round and she was trying to grab hold of something—my shoulders, my hair, anything—as she came so hard that her body shook. I waited for her to come down, waited for her breathing to return to normal before I lowered my mouth to her ear once more . . .

"One down."

CHAPTER 45

Ash

"*T*wo down," he whispered in my ear when he made me come again. He had skills; there was no denying the fact that Max knew his way around a woman's body. I was on my knees, back pressed into his chest while he played with my nipples with one hand and stoked my clit with the other, except now he was doing it all very, very slowly and softly. He'd timed all the movements. One slow stroke went with one slow pull of my nipple, went with a thrust into my back and a long, slow kiss on my neck. It felt as if he was touching me everywhere, all at once. The pleasure was so big, so vast, and it just kept building and building.

"Three," he whispered. "And I haven't even started yet."

Holy shit! I was going to have seventeen orgasms tonight. Because they just did not want to stop. It was as if they'd been building up inside me for thirteen years and now they were just exploding out of me. He turned me round to face him, and then he pulled me onto his lap. I gasped as his cock came into contact with me, but didn't penetrate. He gripped my ass and then slowly and rhythmically, started dragging me over his length. It rubbed right over all the best, most sensitive parts, and when he started sucking on my nipples while doing it, I felt it building again. I tried to make him go faster now, tried to buck against him, but he gripped me tighter and held me in place while he worked the slow, steady rhythm.

"No rushing. We have all night," he said, nipple between his teeth now.

I had to let go. I had no control over the speed or rhythm—that was all up to him; he was doing exactly what he wanted with me. I succumbed to it, and tried not to scream at him to go faster. Instead, I closed my eyes, took a deep, calming breath and let him continue without fighting his pace. He kissed my neck as he pulled and then pushed me up and down his length. I could hear how wet I was—he didn't need to tell me that—but when he did, it was so fucking hot. And then when I thought I'd managed to relax, he started going faster. My eyes flickered open and I looked down, watching myself sliding up and down him. It was the hottest thing I had ever seen, but soon he was doing it too fast to see what was happening anymore, not that I cared. I put my head down on his shoulder, dug my fingernails into his back and came once more. I bit his shoulder and clung to him for dear life. When it was over, I fell onto my back, gasping.

"Need a break?" He stood up and walked over to the bar fridge.

I nodded, unable to talk, and closed my eyes. My entire body jerked when I felt the ice-cold bottle of water on my nipple. I winced in pain and in pleasure as he ran the bottle over my nipples and then up and down my stomach. He stopped, opened the bottle and passed it to me. I sat up and took a sip.

"Wouldn't want you dehydrating," he said, and then lowered his lips to my neck and started kissing it.

"Wouldn't want that," I whispered, tilting my head back to give him more access. He took a sip of water, and then, with his mouth full, covered my nipple. My entire body jerked again. I didn't know if it was pleasure or pain, or both at the same time, and how was it possible to feel both at the same time anyway? Well, I hadn't thought it possible to ever come like this, but here I was. He swallowed and then started kissing me again. The kisses felt so at odds with the way he was touching the rest of me. Sometimes the kisses felt almost soft, sensual and filled with more than just lust. But then when he did things like flip me over, pull me onto his lap and stick his fingers inside me like in the broom closet, I knew that it really was only lust. The kiss slowed and deepened, though. He gripped the back of my head and held me in place as his tongue explored every inch of my mouth. His fingers traced my spine slowly, up and down, until I had goosebumps in places I didn't know were possible.

"So, Ash," he said, still kissing me.

"Yes."

"I think you're ready now."

I nodded at him stupidly as he got up and walked over to his bag. He bent down—God, what a view—and pulled out a condom. I wasn't going to wonder why he had condoms in his bag. Because when he turned round and held it up like a prize, I was so glad he did have it. Until I wasn't.

"Wait, is that a tingly, warming condom?"

He looked down at it and read, "Fire and Ice. Says it delivers a delicious warming and tingling sensation." He smiled at me. "Not my usual choice, but not a lot to choose from at a small spaza shop on the banks of the Chobe River."

"You bought that while we were on the houseboat? Presumptuous!"

"Well, it did seem to be going there."

"So, problem: I'm allergic to anything tingly and warming."

"Seriously?"

I rolled my eyes. "I landed up in the emergency room with a *rather* large problem."

He tossed it over his shoulder playfully, and then walked back up to me. He took my face in his hands and kissed me. It was tender and sweet and took me by surprise. He pulled away, looked at me and traced my lips with his fingers. "We wouldn't want that."

"No, we wouldn't," I repeated, somewhat transfixed by this moment. The softness, the genuine care with which he was looking at me. He kissed me again. Short and sweet. Then he lay back down on the bed next to me.

"So now what?" I asked.

"I could go out and buy some tomorrow, from that small village we drove through. Hope they have the good old-fashioned kind."

"And then have sex tomorrow night?" I asked. This deviated from the plan. "But I said one night: tonight and only tonight."

"I know, but . . ." He lowered his lips to my nipple again and my body reacted again, but with pure pleasure this time. "But sometimes deviations can be very fun."

"So you suggest that we stop what we're doing, and have sex tomorrow night," I asked.

"I never said we should stop what we're doing, but I do think we should have sex tomorrow night." His kisses trailed lower and lower down my stomach.

"That wasn't the plan," I gasped, as he licked the side of my stomach. It felt ticklish and sexy all at the same time.

"Plans change." He was kissing my leg now, down to my knee and it was so erotic.

Carry on like this, and only have sex tomorrow night? Truthfully, while I was coming for the third time there, I'd wished I'd said two nights. Because I didn't think I was ready to only have this for one. I smiled to myself as he reached my ankle and then started making his way back up.

I faked a slightly put-out sigh, even though I was now feeling very far from put out. "Okay, fine."

He laughed. "Well, don't sound so enthusiastic about it." He started crawling up my body.

What the hell was he doing? He was sitting on my chest now, his hard cock in his hand, almost in my face. And then he rubbed it over my nipple, and then the other one. God, this was a hot view. Him rubbing his dick over my nipples.

"Okay! Yes! Tomorrow night!" I said, but this time I didn't hide my smile. He crawled back down me, getting lower and lower and I started to imagine what it would be like to let him go even lower, to spread my legs for him and let him do what he was supposed to have done thirteen years ago.

I throbbed at the thought of it.

Maybe I would let him do that after all . . .

CHAPTER 46

Max

She was on her back and I pushed her legs apart again, slid my hand between them and cupped her once more. I lowered my face to hers and locked eyes with her. She stared back at me, as if she couldn't look away. I knew she couldn't. Because if she was feeling even half of what I was right now, it was impossible to look away. I lowered my mouth to hers and squeezed her a little harder in my hand. I held on to her eyes still and didn't let them go, even though hers were out of focus now.

"You know what I really want to do to you, Ash?" I slipped a finger between her wet folds and traced it over her clit.

"Yes, I do," she said rather boldly, which I had not expected.

"Well?" I asked. She didn't answer me with words, though. She answered me in the best way possible, by lacing her fingers in my hair and pushing my head down.

"Fuck," I growled as she spread her legs in open invitation.

"I'll go as slowly as you want me to. And I'll stop as soon as you want me to." I kissed her inner thigh. She rolled her hips and her fingers now gripped the bedspread.

"Okay," she whispered.

I lowered my face to her, but not before looking. Every part of her was beautiful, and this was no exception. I spread her legs a little wider to give me better access to all of her. I kissed her first. Softly. Her hips bucked against me and a startled gasp escaped her lips. I kissed her all the way around, once, twice, warming her up for when I was going to kiss her clit. And when she was writhing, grabbing more of the bedspread and begging me with those moans of hers, I did it.

"Oh my God." She let out a loud, long moan.

"That okay?" I asked, waiting for her to give me permission to continue, even if her body was telling me everything I needed to know.

"Yes, yes!" She raised her hips to me and this time dragged herself against my mouth.

I lowered my mouth and lapped at her in a way that was making her pant.

"Is this what it's supposed to feel like?" She spread her legs more and her muscles tightened.

"We've just gotten started," I said, putting my lips around her clit and sucking softly.

I did it all, every last thing I'd learned over the years. In fact, it felt like everything I'd learned and practiced was for this moment right here, with her. Everything that had come before was just preparation for this moment, when I was licking her, my fingers buried deep at the same time and she was thrusting and bucking against my face, coming over and over again. She came so many times I lost count and I carried on for as long as she would be able to handle it. I knew at some stage it would become too sensitive to bear. But while it wasn't, I drank her in, buried my face in her, breathed her, tasted her and ate her as if I was a starving man. I was. I had been starved of this, of her, for thirteen years and I was going to have my fill while I could. She grabbed at my hair and closed her legs.

"Stop, oh my God, I can't believe I'm saying this. Stop."

I bit her inner thigh quickly, making her jump and gasp and then climbed back over her.

"Enough?" I asked.

She nodded. I smiled at her and then wiped the sweat off her face. "More than enough."

"Good." I raised myself up on my arms and looked down at her. This would be my view tomorrow night when I drove into her.

She covered her face and giggled, kicking her legs under me. "Wow! Okay! So that's what that's all about."

"That's what it's about," I chuckled as she continued that cute, innocent giggle.

"Well, thank you, then, I guess."

I laughed and dropped off my arms, falling next to her on my back. "Pleasure, then, I guess."

She hoisted herself up. "And what about you? I've realized that I haven't even touched you yet."

I put my hands behind my head and smiled at her. "I'm more than happy, trust me."

"But . . ." She wrapped her hand round my cock and I jerked just like she had. "Don't you also need to come?"

I pushed a strand of hair behind her ear and traced my thumb across her jaw.

"Up to you. I wouldn't want you to do something just because you feel obliged to."

"I want to," she said, tightening her grip on me. I moaned and threw my head back. She started to jerk me off. I normally thought I could do this better than anyone else, but that was not the case with her at all.

"Ash," I moaned as she moved her hand faster and faster. "God, Ash, fuck!" I grabbed the bedspread just as she had and then my muscles started to tense. I was going to explode. Suddenly she let go, I opened my eyes, shocked by this sudden move until I felt an entirely new sensation. I melted back into the bed as she wrapped her mouth around me.

"Ash, baby, Ash." I put my hands in her hair gently, not guiding her to do anything, but just to be close to her mouth and her face. She licked me slowly and then put me all in her mouth. She alternated between running her tongue up and down my shaft and then plunging me into her mouth.

"Ash," I was panting now. "I'm going to come."

"So come."

I tried to push her head away. I wasn't sure if she wanted me to explode in her mouth, but she didn't move. Instead, she gripped the base of my cock tightly while her mouth delivered the final blow. My whole body tensed and I came. It felt as if it wasn't going to end, and it was, by far, the most intense orgasm of my life. When the last wave had subsided, I opened my eyes and found her looking down at me. I sat up and pulled her face towards me, and I kissed her as if this was the last time I was ever going to kiss her.

CHAPTER 47

Ash

I woke up once again tangled in Max's arms, something I hadn't planned on doing, but after our little session last night, we'd both collapsed on the bed and passed out. But this time I woke up before him, and took the chance to inspect him in his sleep. He was gorgeous. And when he was peaceful like this, I could definitely see elements of the boy I used to know, who I used to love.

Mind you, when he was awake, I still got those glimpses, like the other night when we'd talked for hours. It had taken me right back to thirteen years ago. But a lot had changed since then. He was this mash-up of the sweet boy I used to love, and the hot man I was going to have sex with tonight. Who'd made me come until I'd begged him to stop and who'd kissed me last night in the strangest way. I touched my lips. It had been so unexpected. Soft, slow, the kind of kiss we used to share when we'd stared into each other's eyes for hours and simply kissed, infusing all our feelings into it. For a moment there, that kiss had made me wonder if . . .

I shook my head, freeing my mind of that thought. He did *not* have feelings for me and certainly, certainly I did *not* have feelings for him. Okay, so for a moment there, maybe only a few seconds, that kiss had sparked all those intense feelings for him again. For a short moment when kissing him, I swear I'd loved him more than I'd ever loved him before. Loved him so much that I wanted to cry and melt into him and never emerge from his arms and lips again. But the feeling had been fleeting and definitely not indicative of how I *really* felt about him now.

How the hell did *I feel about him?* How does one feel about an ex-boyfriend who disappears for thirteen years? Who I'd spent months and months crying myself to sleep about, wondering where he was and why he hadn't said goodbye, and missing him so much it hurt. And then, of course, after the sadness, the anger had set in, which had caused Sarah to help me delete every single picture I had of him, well, except one. The one of us just before our farewell dance, dressed up to the nines, before everything went so wrong. I'd kept that single photo of us and had looked at it from time to time over the years. And after the anger, the acceptance had settled in and I started to learn to live life without him. And I'd done that pretty well—very well, in fact—but now he was back in my life and I was in his bed and we were probably doing what we should not be doing, but it felt so damn fucking good.

"Are you staring at me?" Max's sleepy voice asked as his eyes opened.

"No!"

"Mmmm, but I could sense it."

"Impossible." I sat up in bed and started putting on my clothes. "You do not have some sort of super magical powers."

He opened his eyes fully, then sat up in bed and looked straight at me. "That's not what you said to me last night."

"Ooooh! Okay. It's way too early for that! And I have work! I have work and you can't be"—I waved my finger at him—"trying to seduce me so early in the morning, and don't say something like"—I tried to put on his deep voice—"*that's not seduction. You would know when I was seducing you, Ash.*" I stepped back and realized I'd only put on my underwear and he was looking at me in a way I now recognized. "See! Stop looking at me like that. I'm going to be leaving and I'm going to be working and I forbid you to do that thing with your face and eyes and—do not flirt with me!"

He burst out laughing. "God, you're still as funny as ever, one of the reasons I love you so much."

Silence. Pin drop.

"Huh? You mean LOVED me, with a 'd', past tense, love*d* me?"

His smile disappeared and he got out of bed. "And what if I told you it didn't have a 'd'?"

"Uhhhh . . ." I looked around the room frantically—I don't know why. Maybe I was expecting some answer to pop out of the walls for me. "It has a 'd', Max. It definitely has a 'd', right?"

"But what if it didn't? What would you say to that? What would you say to you and I giving us another go?"

I was shocked into silence by his words. There had been that moment last night when for a second I'd imagined what it would be like to be with him again, then reality had crashed in. "That would be a very bad idea, Max. Things ended so badly with us. I don't think I would ever be able to take that risk again."

"Everything in life's a risk."

"I know, and that's why you have to try and control the aspects in which the risk can be mitigated."

"And you're choosing to try and control and mitigate risk in the love and dating aspect of your life? The one area that is the most impossible to control?" he asked.

"Well, I try! Okay?" I was frustrated. This conversation had caught me off guard and Max was now eyeing me with a look that bordered on pity and I had no idea why.

"Why are you looking at me like that?" I asked.

"Maybe that's why you have such bad luck dating," he said solemnly.

"What do you mean?" I asked.

"You've been trying to control something that is by its very nature totally uncontrollable." He moved closer to me. "I'm so sorry I've made you scared to love again."

"What are you talking about?" I rubbed my chest. This conversation was starting to make me feel physically uncomfortable.

"You always have to risk something when you go into a relationship. You always have to lose control when falling in love. You've stopped doing that, and it's because of me and what I did to you, and I'm so very, very sorry."

His words slammed into me with such intensity that I almost stumbled backwards. But the words also resonated with me, and for the first time ever, maybe, it felt as if I had an insight into a part of me that until now had been out of reach. *I was scared to love.* Scared to lose control. Maybe I'd always had a part to play in my relationships falling apart, just not the part I'd thought I had. I was holding back because I was afraid of love?

"Ash? You okay?"

I shook my head. But there was more to this too. I could feel it. There was something else bubbling inside. Another thought, just out of my reach. *What?* There was one other missing puzzle piece I was just not seeing yet.

Max picked my dress up off the floor. He folded it perfectly, then smelled it and smiled. "You still wear the same perfume," he said softly. He passed me the dress, and as I took it, he held my hand. "Of course it has a 'd,' Ash."

"It does?"

He nodded. "Yes. It's a 'd.'"

Instant relief flooded me. "Good, because if it wasn't with a 'd' then we would not have sex tonight!"

He smiled at me reassuringly. "So totally with a 'd.'"

"Good, good. Because mine are also with a 'd,'" I said quickly. "There is no present tense here at all. All past."

CHAPTER 48

Max

Only it wasn't with a "d." There was no "d" in sight. But she'd clearly needed to hear me say it, because for a moment there she'd looked as if she might have fainted. But I could see the truth, even if she couldn't right now. There were no "d"s, not for either of us anymore.

There had been a moment last night when I'd put every last drop of feeling into a kiss and called her "baby" and she had looked at me as if she was about to burst with love, just as much as I was bursting with love. I knew that look. I'd seen it every day for four years; it had been imprinted on me.

Or was I being naïve? Was I seeing what I wanted to see? My head was swimming. I was dizzy with these thoughts—I needed to get a grip and ground myself. I tackled some work emails, hoping to push her from my thoughts, and then since I had only been messaging the nurses while away to see how my mom was, I decided to call her directly. The nurse answered immediately and I was surprised to hear that my mom was having a semi-lucid moment. Well, she was at least able to talk and was asking to talk to me.

"Hi, Mom," I said.

"Son!" My heart thumped at that. It wasn't often she knew who I was, so when she did it always felt very special. A moment I would cherish when the other moments got too rough.

"Where are you?" she asked.

"I'm at Lake Malawi. I wish you could see it here. You would love it. Sun, blue waters and a beach."

"Sounds lovely. Maybe you can take me there?"

My heart snapped a little. I would not be bringing her here because she would forget about this conversation in hours. "Definitely! As soon as I get back, you and I should make plans to come here."

"Who are you there with?"

"I'm here with Ash. You remember her, Mom?"

"Of course I remember her! How can I forget my son's lovely girlfriend?"

I sat down on the bed and hung my head. She was back in this fantasy, and it was the absolute worst time for it. For me and my roller-coaster emotions anyway.

"How is Ash? And when you do think I'll be able to call her my future daughter-in-law?" she asked happily.

"She's good. And probably soon, Mom, soon," I said, and every fiber of my existence wanted this statement to be true. The phone went silent for a while.

"Mom?" She wasn't responding. "Hello?"

"Who's there?" Her voice came through faint and perturbed.

I sighed and my chest constricted. She was gone again.

"Just a friend," I said. "I have an idea. You should go and visit Lucy."

"Lucy! That's a good idea."

She dropped the phone and was gone, in more ways than one.

I straightened myself up for my day, despite the blow of emotion I'd just been delivered. The manager and I breezed through the discussions. We chatted about daily rental for shoots—one-day versus longer shoots; talked about prices for the entire hotel rental, for those clients of mine who valued privacy above all else; talked about what medical emergency and safety measures were in place, something that was always asked. I declined scuba diving, though, and the canoe ride. I'd seen enough photos of these activities to know what they were about and felt confident about adding them to my website.

I already had an idea in mind for this location. A production company with a smaller budget was looking for a place to shoot a film, somewhere tropical. I'd initially looked at what I had in Madagascar and Mauritius, but that had been too expensive. Now I was thinking that Lake Malawi, with its very tropical atmosphere, might definitely be a good substitute.

I took a few photos on my phone. I'd send my professional photographer here at a later stage to get better ones, and I sent the company an email with my idea. By the time I got back to my room, after popping to the nearby village to grab some normal condoms, I was hot and the cool water of the lake looked very, very appealing.

I found Ash stretched out across the couch, clutching her laptop as if she'd fallen asleep with it. I could hear something playing from it. Her laptop looked as if it was going to fall, so I crept round and tried to pull it out of her hands without waking her. I slid it out as gently as I could and then laid it on the table. It sounded like she was playing a video of herself. I could hear her talking about the light and location, probably something she'd sent to Sebastian, something she'd filmed earlier. I carefully opened the computer to pause it. An editing program was open. I made sure to save the file, then I minimized the program, and what she had up on the screen stole my breath.

It was the photo of us just before it had all fallen apart. God, I looked so different. I was tall and pale and somewhat good-looking, but in a bit of a nerdy way, as if I'd not quite come into my own yet, which I hadn't. I remember being that age, eighteen—you're on the cusp of being an adult, but so far away from really being one. It's an awkward phase you hover around, not quite an adult, not quite a child. But Ash on the other hand, she was gorgeous. Gorgeous then, and gorgeous now. I smiled to myself at her dress, which at the time had been the height of fashion. Red satin with about a million shiny diamantes on it. Shiny diamante straps that wrapped round her neck as if they hadn't decided whether they were a necklace, or dress straps.

I looked up from this picture to the sleeping vision in front of me.

Did this picture mean we did stand a chance? Did her having it still and looking at it today mean that maybe, just maybe, I wasn't being that naïve after all? And that maybe, just maybe, somewhere under her stubborn insistence that there were no feelings, there actually were?

I closed the computer quietly and slid it onto the table next to her. If there was even the slightest possibility that her having this photo meant that she still had feelings, and that there was still a chance for us, *a second chance*, then I was not about to let this day go to waste. I was going to make her see what we could be like now. And that we were still perfect for each other.

CHAPTER 49

Ash

"**D**id I fall asleep?" I asked, rolling over on the couch after hearing Max's voice.

"You did."

"Mmm, it was nice."

"You know what will be nicer, though?" he asked as I yawned and tried to sit up.

"Whaaat?" I said through a massive yawn.

"Swimming in those crystal-clear waters. Lying on that beach, relaxing, knowing we have both finished our work. Drinking a fancy cocktail with a twirly straw and an umbrella. Maybe even going out on the sunset boat cruise."

I stretched my hands above my head. "That does sound good."

He held his hand out for me, and without thinking, I slipped mine into his. I had a vague thought of how well our fingers fitted together before he pulled me onto my feet.

"Change into swimming costumes?" he asked.

"Meet you back here in five," I replied, and walked off to my room. I changed quickly, and when I got back to the lounge, Max was standing there in swim trunks and a T-shirt.

"Shall we?" he asked, opening the door for us. It was oddly formal, and I must say, cute. We walked outside and made our way down the path that led to the beach and the waters below.

"How is this a lake in the middle of Malawi?" I asked, walking onto the beach sand.

"Pretty spectacular." Max took his shirt off and dropped it onto one of the beach loungers.

My eyes were immediately drawn to that big, broad back, where I could just make out red nail marks criss-crossing his shoulder blades. My fingertips tingled at the reminder. He dug in his bag and produced a bottle.

"Sun cream?"

"Sure," I said, slipping out of my dress. A grass umbrella provided just the right amount of shade and I stood under it while I rubbed the lotion on myself. I managed everything but my back, and when I was done, Max was looking at me with a raised eyebrow.

"Fine! Do my back, but no hanky-panky. We're in public."

He smiled. That crazy, hot, sexy, filthy, devilish smile. God, I think I knew now why women came just by looking at him. There was a sexual intensity to him when he smiled like this that was enough to turn you inside out with wanton need.

I sat down on the lounger and he climbed on behind me. I heard him squeezing the cream onto his hands and then rubbing them together.

"So, are you saying that if we weren't in public, you'd let me do some hanky-panky?"

"Possibly," I teased. Well, it wasn't exactly a tease. Because the answer was a loud and resounding yes.

"How about we leave that for tonight?" He brought his hands down to my back and my entire body reacted. I tried not to let him know the effect that just his hands were having on me, but I was sure he already knew.

"Did you get . . . you know?"

He laughed. "You mean condoms?" He wrapped his arms round me rather suddenly, pulled me back towards him, and kissed the back of my neck.

"What was that for?" I asked.

"You make me laugh, and I just felt like doing that. I don't laugh that often. It's nice."

I looked at him over my shoulder. "You don't laugh that often?"

"Not really, but it's not like my life has been particularly humorous, not lately and maybe not for a while, either."

"Your mom?" I asked, feeling a knot in my stomach.

"My mom. My dad leaving, him cutting us out of his life, us ending too." We were silent for a while. The only sounds were the soft lapping of water on the shore, birds singing, and the flap of the umbrella in the breeze.

"Just because I was the idiot who walked away, doesn't mean I wasn't heartbroken over it," he said. "In fact, maybe I haven't quite accurately conveyed to you how much that messed me up. You may be under the impression that everything was fine for me, that I had this great time traipsing around Europe. I didn't. It was torture without you. Even though I was the one who walked away."

"Sorry," I said.

"I'm sorry too," he said, and continued to put cream on my back, although I was pretty sure he was done.

"What do you think would have happened to us if . . . *you know*?" He teased me with my choice of words.

"What, if we'd had earth-shattering sex that night and made each other come like we did last night?" I said defiantly in the face of the "*you know*."

"Exactly!"

"I don't know. What do you think would have happened?" I asked, feeling a shift in the mood between us, which also might have had something to do with the fact that the sun-cream application had begun to feel more like a massage.

"I think we'd still be together."

I spun round in shock. "Seriously?" My eyes connected with his icy-blue ones and I was immediately sucked in. They looked cooler and icier in this light.

"Seriously," he said firmly.

I turned back round and looked out over the water. He'd been so absent from my life these past thirteen years it was hard to imagine an alternate reality that he was a part of, but still, in moments like this, it also felt like he might have actually been with me all along. He continued to rub my neck, and for a second it felt like nothing bad had ever happened between us. This was what our future was supposed to be: us sitting together on a beach, talking, laughing and then being so in lust that we couldn't get enough of each other. I wanted to fight this feeling, because it also terrified me. But what terrified me more was that if I did fight it he would stop touching me. And being touched by him felt like coming home.

"How's your neck?" he asked.

"Feels a million times better when you do that."

He began to focus all his attention on my neck, his fingers rubbing up and down, kneading into my tense shoulders and back up again. He tilted my head forwards and ran his hands from the base of my neck all the way into my hair, squeezing my scalp as he went. I couldn't help my relaxed, blissful moan.

"You carry a lot of tension in your neck. You should probably go for regular massages," he said.

I moaned again as he began massaging my scalp. "You're setting the bar pretty high here—not sure I've ever had a massage that compares to this one."

"Well, then, why don't you keep me around and I'll do this regularly."

I shot him an eye roll over my shoulder. "And keep you from all your other ladies?"

"I don't have other ladies," he said firmly, working his hands around my shoulder blades, kneading knots away.

"You have ladies," I said nonchalantly. It was a fact, after all. He had them. Probably lots of them, probably multiple at the same time.

"It's all meaningless, Ash. And maybe I don't want them anymore." His voice was softer. "Maybe I don't want any of that anymore. Maybe I feel like making a change in my life."

"Maybe that's a good idea," I said, still feeling blissfully relaxed from the massage. "Can I be honest with you?" I asked, and he released his hands from me. But I didn't turn and look at him. "I kind of think you deserve more than that."

"More than meaningless sex?"

"Yes."

"I think you deserve more too." He said it with a smile in his voice.

"Oh, you mean like actual good sex. Or at least sex where I don't have to fake an orgasm just to get them to stop, or dodge a collapsing bed, or sex where I don't need to perform CPR, where I don't have olives put into my belly button—"

"I can't believe someone put an olive in your belly button!"

"The guy was Greek and we were eating olives, I guess. But the curse is strong I tell you!"

He pulled me back again, not playfully like before. He rested his head on my shoulder and wrapped his arms round me in a way that felt protective, not sexual. But that was very at odds with what he said next. He brought his lips up to my ear and his next words melted me into a puddle.

"Let's see if we can't break that curse once and for all tonight."

CHAPTER 50

Max

I raced her to the water and we both dove in. It was cool, crystal clear and refreshing after lying on those loungers for so long. We'd rested there with a cocktail and chatted about the people we used to know from school. Where they were now, what rumors we'd heard about them—divorces, love children, a stint in jail for white-collar crime—we reminisced and laughed about moments from school, and then almost fell on the floor laughing when we watched a video of an old classmate who'd become one of those seriously cheesy motivational speakers who used the word "transcend" over ten times in the three-minute video. It had felt just like old times, right up to us playing the silly word-association game we used to lie around playing for ages while screeching with laughter.

Malawi.

Lake.

Fish.

Pink Dolphin.

Not mine.

Liar.

"Have you seen how clear it is underwater? And you can open your eyes because it's not salty," Ash said. "Come down here." Her head disappeared and I took a deep breath and followed her. We found each other's faces and she started screaming something at me that I couldn't hear through the bubbles.

"What?" I yelled back. It was just as inaudible.

She screamed something back to me and then the words I'd wanted to say just came out.

"I love you!" I screamed, knowing that she wouldn't hear them.

We both popped up again.

"What were you saying?" she asked as her head emerged from the water.

"What were you saying?" I asked.

"I was saying, 'This is amazing.' You?"

I smiled at her. "I was saying something similar, but not quite the same."

She laughed. "So mysterious."

"Would you like to see it again?" I asked, and she nodded.

We both went back under the water together and this time I screamed something a little different. She smiled, and I knew she'd understood. We both popped up again.

"You said I was amazing?" she said, a questioning tone in her voice.

"You are. Amazing." I reached for her shoulders and pulled her towards me. She was as light as a feather in this water and came to me so easily. She rested her hands on my forearms as I swayed her from side to side in the water in front of me.

"I mean it, though, Ash. You are amazing. What you've achieved, who you've become, just *you*."

She looked away, immediately disengaging from this. I didn't know whether it was because she was uncomfortable with compliments, or uncomfortable that they were coming from me. She pointed to an island a little way away. It was made of big, grey boulders and had huge green trees growing out of them. "How's your swimming?" she asked.

"Good. Yours?"

"Then let's go." She started swimming and I followed behind her. After a few minutes, we reached the island and both dragged ourselves out of the water and onto the rock, breathing heavily.

"My swimming is not quite what it used to be," she said, lying back on a grey boulder.

"Mine too. We used to swim a lot in summer. God, we were always in the pool."

"Playing Marco Polo—I remember that. Although you broke the rules a lot, if I'm not mistaken." She turned her head to me. She looked magnificent lying on her back on the boulder, wet, red-cheeked from the exercise and looking more relaxed than I'd seen her in days.

"So I used to creep up and kiss you when your eyes were closed. So what?" I smiled at her, pushing my wet hair out of my face.

"It's a breach of the rules." She reached out and poked my knee playfully, but I grabbed her finger before she had time to pull it away.

"Since when did you become so obsessed with rules, little Miss Smuggling A Bottle Of Your Dad's Vodka To Carry's Party? Not to mention making out with me in the library at break behind the shelf of geography books." I pulled her finger towards me, forcing her to come with it.

"I liked reading about Papua New Guinea," she said quickly, and then laughed.

"Nope, I think you're lying, because you also let me get some under-shirt action behind the science section too."

"Under-shirt action." She laughed again. I loved seeing her like this. "God, I was a little naughty, wasn't I. Do you remember the time Sarah and I stole weed from her older brother's stash and we all smoked it in the woods behind your house?"

"How can I forget—we got so stoned that night!"

"I thought the trees were coming to life." She grinned. "I mean, I can laugh now, but at the time it was fucking terrifying."

"I remember. I carried you home and sat up with you all night, reassuring you that the trees would not be coming alive anytime soon."

She propped herself up and looked at me seriously. "You always took such good care of me."

"You took care of me too. Remember when I had to get my wisdom teeth out and you fed me jelly and soup with a spoon?"

"You were soooo cute. You went all puffy and swollen." She laughed and smiled and my heart exploded with love for her right there and then on a rock in the middle of Lake Malawi.

I brought her finger up to my lips and kissed it. Her smile faded. I put it between my lips and kissed it longer, then pulled it into my mouth and sucked it. Her smile was totally gone now. Her eyes had widened and her jaw slackened. I moved closer, pulled her off the boulder and brought her onto my lap.

"What are you doing?" she asked, looking straight at me.

"This." I took her face between my hands and kissed her softly. I kept my lips there, just dragging them back and forth, savoring the moment. Savoring the taste and smell and feel of her. I pulled her further onto my lap, not for any other reason than to have her as close to me as possible. I let her face go, wrapped my arms around her and deepened the kiss. She took my face between her hands and pulled me even deeper. I traced my hands up and down her back as I kissed her slowly, not ever wanting this moment to end. My cock was rock hard, but it almost didn't matter right now. He would have his chance later; right now it was just about her lips, and her tongue.

I stroked her face gently as I kissed her, slipped my thumb between her lips and traced them, and then ran it over her tongue, dipping it into her mouth and using it to pull her closer. She pulled my thumb into her mouth and sucked on it like she'd sucked on my cock last night.

"It's not even evening yet," she said. Her nipples were hard, her pupils dilated and she was just as turned on as I was. I ran the back of my hand over her nipple. One, then two. Her body gave two small jerks, the kind I loved.

"Is there a rule that says we only have to start when the sun goes down?" I put my hand under her ass and then stood up, hoisting her onto me. She wrapped her legs round my hips and her arms round my neck.

"Here?" She looked around.

I shook my head. "Definitely not here."

I walked us back towards the water's edge and climbed in, with her still round my waist.

"Race you back."

CHAPTER 51

Ash

As soon as we were back in the room, as if by sexual magic, I found myself naked and lying on the bed. He stood at the foot of the bed and pulled his shorts down. He reached into a bag on the floor, and took out a condom, all the while locking eyes with me.

"Regular." He put the foil between his teeth and ripped it in one swift move, spitting the corner onto the floor. He tossed the open packet onto the bed next to me and then slowly crawled up over my naked body. Something about the condom wrapper being tossed down on the bed next to me, ready to use, open, a promise of what was to come, made me instantly wet.

"Not yet," he said, smiling, looking down at my wetness, which had not escaped his notice. "There are still more things I want to do to you."

"How many more can there be?" I asked, climbing to my elbows.

His smile grew as he put a big hand on my chest and pushed me back down, pinning my body to the bed beneath him. "Baby, it would take me an entire lifetime to do all the things I want to do to you."

The word "baby" did not go unnoticed again, and this time, it had a different effect on me. This "baby" wasn't soft and gentle. Not with those eyes that penetrated me so deeply they rendered me transparent. Not with that breath against my face that smelled like a piña colada and tasted like salt, and not with that hand, holding me down underneath him so I had nowhere to go. This "baby" wasn't gentle at all; it was rough and dripped with the promise of sex.

"What are you doing?" I asked after he'd done nothing to me for what felt like an eternity of agonizing sexual frustration.

"Trying to decide how to take you."

"Take me however you like."

"Are you sure you know what you're saying to me?" His eyes were still consuming every single inch of my body.

"Yes." I nodded and bit my lip, and this seemed to be the thing that set him off. That set me in motion too. It was so quick, so sudden, that I felt dizzy and disorientated. He'd flipped us round entirely, him lying on his back and me straddling him. Before I had a chance to catch my breath from that gymnastic maneuver, he grabbed my ass and started working my body up his, until I was straddling his chest.

"What are you doing?" I asked nervously, unsure of where he wanted me.

"I want you to sit on my face," he said, holding me in place.

I looked down at him and gave a tentative nod.

"Is that a yes?" he asked, and I nodded again.

"You know what I'm going to ask you."

My nod grew more vigorous, but the words seemed stuck.

"I . . . I want you to," I finally managed.

He wasted no time. His head disappeared under me as I tensed my entire body, waiting for that first lick.

"Yes," I whispered as his tongue lapped at my inner thigh.

He licked my other thigh, licked it all the way to the crease, to the place where my leg ended and something else began.

"Fuck. Yes," I said again, and then gasped when he sank his teeth into my thigh. He bit my other thigh and I grabbed the headboard in front of me, using it to anchor myself. He tightened his grip on my hips. His hands were so big it felt like they enveloped my entire waist. And in that moment, it seemed as if he would never let me go.

I looked down at him. His mouth was under me, waiting, but he was looking straight at me.

"Say what I like to hear once more, baby."

"Yes," I whispered, and watched him as he licked me.

I threw my head back and gripped the headboard. "Shit!"

"Look at me," he said, and I instantly obeyed. We locked eyes and then he slowly licked me again. I slid my knees apart, opening my legs for him even more. Giving his tongue access to all of me. He licked me in long, slow moves, starting at the bottom and then working all the way to the top, to my clit, where he lingered only a second longer. But I needed more, and the next time he got to my clit, I ground into him, pressed down, and tried to hold his mouth in place for as long as possible. He laughed against me and, for a moment there, I worried that I might suffocate him.

"Just like that," he said.

I gripped the headboard tighter and bucked my hips against him, dragged myself over his open mouth, over his chin. More and more of his face disappeared under me as I rocked back and forth with a freedom that I'd never felt before. I'd never had so few inhibitions. Never done this. Never forced my legs as wide open as I possibly could and rode a man's face. The sounds of our wetness mingling together made me move even faster. He gripped my ass and began helping me, pushing me up and down, lapping at me messily, with no restraint at all. I began to pant. He let my ass go and grabbed my breasts, squeezed them and then plunged his tongue into me. I broke open for him. I threw my head back, gripped my thighs, dug my nails into them as I held myself in place so I could get every last moment out of my orgasm. When it was over, I fell backwards over his body and lay there, gasping for breath.

"So that's what I've been missing, again," I finally managed to say when my breathing had slowed enough for me to speak. I flinched at the feeling of his fingers stoking me and looked down. My legs were wide open, and he was looking straight into me. I almost closed them, but I didn't. For some reason I felt a surge of power when I watched him staring at me like that. Staring at me as if he was addicted to what he was seeing. As if there was nothing else in the world he wanted more. He slipped his thumbs between my lips, and then pulled them open. He pulled them wider, until I felt like he had totally opened me up.

"Now it's time," he said, and started climbing out from under me. I fell onto the bed, face-first and stayed like that. I heard him pull out the condom, heard the final snap of it as he rolled it down. I waited like that for him to take me from behind, drive into me hard and fast. That would be very in line with what was currently happening— only he didn't.

He rolled me over softly, placed his hands on either side of my head and then gently pushed my legs open with his knees. It was so smooth and slow it took me a moment to register his cock at my entrance, dipping in slowly and tentatively. He closed his eyes and groaned as he pushed it in just a little more. I watched his face, fascinated and exhilarated that I had this much power over him. I was giving him so much pleasure that he was moaning and trembling just by entering me ever so slightly. And then he finally slid into me. My muscles clenched around his length and width as he pushed his way in. He let out a long, loud moan, and for a moment there, I thought he'd come.

"Fuck, baby. You feel so good," he said, keeping himself deep inside me. He lowered himself onto his elbows, coming even closer. I held my breath, waiting for him to begin. For him to thrust into me hard, and fast, for him to bite and suck at my nipples while he hammered into me and made me scream, but again, he didn't. Instead, he kissed me, drawing himself in and out slowly and rhythmically as he did. He reached for my hands now, laced his fingers through mine and pushed them above my head, holding me in place as he made the smallest of moves inside me. He wasn't pulling in and out anymore. He was moving his hips in small circles, buried deep inside me. His cock was able to trace every angle of me in slow, steady circles. I felt it starting to build. My muscles began clenching and unclenching. I opened my legs wider, wrapped them around him and pulled him closer. He kept kissing me as he rolled his hips in slow, steady circles, building pleasurable pressure inside me. He let go of one of my hands, reached down for my thigh, and pushed it up until my knee was as flat to my chest as it could be. I had no idea it was possible, but he was even deeper inside me now. Filling me, stretching me, making me ride a wave of pleasure that was about to tip me over to the other side.

I arched my back and he held me like this as he thrust into me one more time and I came. He sped up as my orgasm began and drove into me harder and faster. The orgasm kept going with this new and intense pace. He gripped my hips suddenly and then pulled me onto his lap, holding me in place with his huge hands as he slammed into me hard and fast, the sound of him slapping against me just making my orgasm longer and longer until I felt like I might die from it.

He held me close as the last of it fizzled through me. I put my head on his shoulder and stayed there, our bodies slick and wet with sweat, the taste of salt in my mouth and the feel of him still hard inside me. He pulled my head off his shoulder, held me in front of him and started moving inside me again. We rocked together slowly, looking at each other, studying each other's faces as our bodies moved as one. I had no idea anymore where I ended and he began. I wrapped my legs round his back, sitting on his lap as he rocked me back and forth. He never sped up, never stopped looking at me, and I couldn't have torn my eyes from his if I'd tried. It was as if he'd locked them in place and thrown away the key. His breathing became louder and faster, but still the pace never sped up—in fact, it slowed. He rocked me gently and slowly on his lap, holding my face still, but kissing me now. I kissed back. Deeply. Our tongues finding each other's and moving together to the rhythm of our bodies. His grip on my face tightened, mine on his. We pulled our mouths apart when we were no longer able to kiss anymore, our breathing coming out fast and ragged and we moved together until we both came. I watched him closely as he came. His eyes tightened, every single muscle in his body bunched and froze in place as he held on to me as if he would never let me go, and I didn't want him to let me go. And we didn't.

When it was over, we wrapped our arms round each other and stayed like that. And this moment felt more intimate than any moment we'd shared before . . .

And it felt so, so good.

Too good.

And it felt like this was exactly where I was supposed to be.

And it absolutely terrified me.

I inhaled and buried my face in his neck. My face fitted there perfectly. My body fitted perfectly. His cock fitted.

Too perfectly.

Uncontrollable tears fell from my eyes. Thankfully, he didn't notice them because of all the sweat coating our bodies. They were not tears of sadness or happiness. They were tears of terror.

I kept coming back to that statement he'd made earlier about me being afraid to love. And then I sensed that other element that was out of my reach. Something else needed to be added to that equation. *What was it?* What was the final puzzle piece?

I felt it was becoming clearer to me. It was almost within my grasp. And I also felt that I was *not* going to like it when I finally knew what it was.

CHAPTER 52

Max

"Morning. I'm *soooo* hungry!" Ash said, flopping down at the table on the veranda. The lodge had brought our breakfast to the villa today, as I'd asked them to. I didn't think she would look so perky this morning. In fact, I was sure she would probably be tired and not want to walk to the dining area. But she looked like she was more than ready to walk. She grabbed two yogurts, tipped them over a big bowl of fruit, then drenched the whole thing with honey and granola and began demolishing the food with a big spoon.

"Sex will do that to you," I teased, sipping my coffee.

"Mmmm, hmmm," she mumbled, shoveling the food into her mouth enthusiastically. She put the bowl down and reached for the baked goods, grabbing two pains au chocolat. I watched her. There was something about the eating that seemed to be less to do with starvation, and more to do with avoidance.

"You okay this morning?" I asked, growing more concerned as she viciously beheaded the pastries and threw some granola into her mouth next.

"Can I get you a bowl?" I asked, looking at the granola she was clutching in her fingers. She quickly shook her head and then made a beeline for the orange juice.

"I get the feeling something's wrong?" I asked. She stopped eating and drinking and looked down at the table. I didn't want to tell her

she had a smudge of chocolate on her cheek either, because then she
might have wiped it away, and I didn't want that.

I was so in love with her.

And I didn't want this to end. I wanted her like this every morning for the rest of my life, shoveling strange combinations of food
into her mouth with smudges of chocolate on her face. I put my
coffee down, my hand shaking slightly. We were leaving soon, and if
I was going to tell her how I felt, it had to be now.

"There's something I need to tell you," I said as she poured herself
a cup of coffee.

"There's something I need to tell you too," she said, not looking
at me.

"Ladies first."

"Okay!" She inhaled deeply, as if readying herself to dive into
something. "So, last night was really, really good." She looked up at
me for confirmation, as if she needed it.

"Last night was fucking amazing," I said.

"Exactly. And I think you were right about the unfinished business we had, and getting it out of our systems so we can get over it."

I sighed. This was not where I was hoping the conversation was
going to go.

"So, obviously, we're not going to do that again." The words came
out so quickly I almost didn't catch them.

"Was that a question? Or a statement?"

"Uh . . . both. No. It's a statement. Because it's out of our systems
now."

"Is it?" I put my coffee down and leaned across the table, scrutin-
izing her face, because currently there was something very strange
happening on it. Like drama masks, or a clown that changes expression and emotion quickly, hers seemed to be jumping from one
emotion to the other.

"One night. That's what we agreed."

"It kind of wasn't one night, though, if you think about it. It's been
several."

"But the sex, that was one night! And that's what we said. What we agreed."

"Ash, what's really going on here?"

"Nothing is going on." Her tone was defensive. "I'm just clarifying and reiterating that what happened, happened, past tense, and now it's not happening, present tense."

"God, when did you become the grammar police? And why does it all have to be past tense? What if we both want it again, present tense? Because I know we both do."

"Jesus, you can't just say things like that. This was a one-time thing, to get it out of our systems. Nothing else. It's out now and now we can just be"—she waved her hand in the air, trying to grab on to the word that she was looking for in her head—"colleagues. Business associates."

"Friends?" I asked.

She gave me a deadpan look. "Max, after what happened between us last night, do you really think we can be friends?"

"Well, if it was such a meaningless thing, something just to 'get out of our systems,' and to 'get over,' then yes, why not?" I locked eyes with her, searching her for the answer I knew she was struggling to give me. "Unless it wasn't meaningless. Unless it wasn't just to 'get over things.' To break some imaginary curse, see how many times you could come, or scream, or whatever. And maybe that's the thing that is clearly terrifying you this morning."

"I'm not terrified." She looked panicked.

"So it was, then?" I pushed. "Just totally meaningless? Meaningless sex. That moment, when we were kissing, when we were looking into each other's eyes, that was meaningless?"

She stood up quickly. "Well, that kind of doesn't really matter now, anyway. I'm going on a date with Sibu, so . . ."

"Who's Sibu?" I asked, prickles up my spine.

"The doctor. I saw him at the airport."

"You already organized a date with him? Was this before or after last night?"

"What does that matter?" she asked, wringing her hands together.

I stood up too. "It matters. Believe me. It fucking matters."

She folded her arms and looked at me defiantly, clearly well aware of the impact her words were about to have on me. God, I knew her so well. I saw everything. And I saw through her too. Still, I braced myself for what I knew would still hurt like hell, even though there was a part of me that didn't believe her. Something had happened last night between us. And maybe she was just not ready to admit that. Maybe that's why she looked like a scared baby bird today that just wanted to fly away.

"After. This morning," she said.

It hurt more than I thought it would, even though I'd known it was coming. And I didn't really have anything to say back to her. It felt like something in my throat was broken. I walked all the way up to her. Her body stiffened in response to my presence. Then I took her face between my hands and lowered my lips to hers.

"Max, we shouldn't . . ."

"For the record, I think you're wrong. Nothing about last night was meaningless and you know it." I kissed her. No lust, no hunger, no desperation . . . *just love*. Pure, unadulterated, love. Thirteen years' worth. And she kissed me back. She leaned into me, laced her fingers through my hair. I cupped her face and kept pouring myself and my feelings into her until she was full to the brim and was left in no question of my intentions.

I pulled away and planted a small kiss on her forehead. She looked so unsure of herself. But she was going to need to work all that out herself. I didn't want to feel like I was forcing her into something she was unsure about, no matter how sure I was.

"We should start packing. There's someone coming to fetch our bags in about thirty minutes," I said.

She touched her lips, looked at me, and nodded. And then, despite how hard it felt, I walked away from her. A part of me thought she might come after me, say fuck it, and we'd kiss again. Another part of me wasn't sure if she ever would. But I really, really hoped she would.

CHAPTER 53

Ash

We caught a commercial plane back to Cape Town and the best part was that at least we weren't seated together. This distance gave me a moment to try and sort through my feelings. I hadn't messaged Sibu that morning. We hadn't organized a date, but it had felt like the only hand I'd had in that moment, and I'd needed a break.

I'd needed him to stop asking me if it had been meaningless, because I was not ready to answer that question out loud. Out loud would make it more real. In my head, I could still convince myself that . . .

"No, no, no." I picked up the inflight magazine angrily and flipped through it. A stupid advert for home insurance stared back at me: a cute, happy couple who'd just moved into their first house together, sharing a candlelit dinner of pizza on the floor, full of hopes and dreams and expectations. I flipped to the next page, a perfume commercial featuring a gorgeous couple on the beach, staring into each other's eyes: *Amour, the scent of love.* Next page a bloody article about star signs and whether or not you were compatible with your partner. I huffed angrily as I found myself running my finger over the page and finding the Aries/Leo paragraph: *the perfect match.* As if! I flipped to the next page and was now convinced this magazine was mocking me when I found a full-page advert featuring the most gorgeous, luxurious villa in Clifton, Cape Town: *For info and bookings, call Maximillian Adam.*

"Nooope!"

I closed the magazine and shoved it back into the seat pocket, the lady sitting next to me shooting me a sideways glance. I didn't blame her. I was talking to myself and being very dramatic with an inflight magazine. But I was feeling so much internal drama right now that it was spilling out of me.

I didn't want it to be meaningful with Max.

I could *not* let it be meaningful with him.

Because meaningful with him was too loaded. It meant loving someone so hard it felt like you could actually explode from the love you felt. It meant then missing someone so badly it felt like you were going to explode from the grief and pain. I looked up when I sensed him looking at me. I hated that I could sense him. I hated that I could tell what he was thinking and feeling, and I absolutely hated the fact that a few hours ago, standing next to the breakfast table overlooking a lake, I knew exactly what he was telling me, and asking me in that kiss.

Our eyes met for a moment and I tried to look unperturbed, chilled, relaxed, not like my inner world was collapsing in on itself because my heart and brain were waging the biggest war of their lives on each other. I contemplated smiling casually, but I knew he would see right through me. Could he see right through me now? Luckily, we were landing soon, and the second we did, I grabbed my bag off the floor and pulled my phone out. The plane hadn't even come to a stop and I was already messaging him.

> **Ash:** It was so great bumping into you and I'm really craving sushi. Do you happen to be available this week?

I hadn't been expecting a reply so soon, but one came through almost immediately.

> **Hot Doc:** You basically read my mind. Friday? At seven?

I really should change his name!

Ash: Perfect! See you then.

Hot Doc: Great! My brother-in-law has actually opened a sushi restaurant. It's an African take on sushi. It's called Geisha. Are you keen to try it? The food is amazing and I like supporting him.

My stomach dropped. What were the chances.

Ash: Yes, totally good.

Although I wasn't sure it was good, knowing I would be in such proximity to Max.

Hot Doc: Can't wait to see you.
Ash: Me too.

That was a lie.

CHAPTER 54

Max

We stepped off the plane and didn't talk to each other. She didn't even acknowledge me once by glancing in my direction. This lasted all the way from the plane to the baggage section. My bag arrived quickly, hers did not. But when she saw me there, still waiting for her, she told me not to wait. So I left her and walked out of the gates.

My eyes were immediately drawn to four people holding a sign.

Welcome home from prison, Ash.

I looked back at the people holding the sign and recognition and a smile flooded my face.

"Sarah!" I walked straight up to her. I was thrilled to see her. We'd spent almost as much time together as Ash and I had spent together in high school, and I'd honestly missed her.

She looked at me for a moment blankly, and then her mouth opened and she began shaking her head.

"*Nooooo!*" she said, looking shell-shocked. "I mean, Ash said you looked different, but you can't look this different. Surely not."

I held my arms open. "It's me," I said, and she walked straight into the hug I was offering.

"I can't believe it." She held on to me and we rocked from side to side for a while.

"It's so good to see you," I said, letting her go. She made a huge show of walking around me, examining me.

"You have hair! In lots of places. And, God"—she squeezed my arms—"where the hell did these come from?"

I shrugged.

"Come! Come meet the others." She pulled me towards the other people who were holding the ridiculous sign that I had to have a chuckle about.

"This is Melusi, this is Yo, and Charlie," she said, and I reached out to shake their hands.

"Um . . . world-famous agent." I pointed at Charlie. "I think, and . . . wait, best production designer Ash has ever worked with." I pointed at Melusi this time. "And amazing good musician! Did I get that right?"

"That was basically perfect," Melusi said, looking at the other two.

"Although I don't know about the world-famous bit, but whatever. I'll take it. I have to take something—my job is such a shit show," Charlie said.

"Her job is always a shit show," Sarah said. "But yours apparently is not. Congratulations! You've done so well for yourself. That's amazing."

"Thank you. I do love what I do."

"Mmmm, always a good thing," Charlie said. "I hate what I do. Can we swap jobs? How are you with handling models and actresses . . ." She suddenly slapped her hands over her mouth and her eyes widened. "Shit, I didn't mean it like that—"

"Oh my God," Melusi gasped, and burst out laughing.

Sarah and Yo followed suit and then Sarah gave me a slap on the arm. "Sorry, it's just that, well . . ."

"Let's just say there are many, many stories about you *handling* models and actresses," Melusi quickly added.

"So I've heard," I said, not sure whether I thought this was funny, or not.

"Sorry, ignore us. We've clearly spent *waaay* too much time talking about you these last few days and now you're just on our minds, in every way possible," Sarah said.

"No worries. I'm glad Ash has friends like you she can talk to."

"Speaking of, where is Ash?" Yo asked.

"She's still at the baggage claim, I think."

"You think?" Melusi asked.

"*Ja*, she's not exactly talking to me right now. She told me to leave her, so I did. In fact, I should probably get going before she comes out. I wouldn't want to ruin your surprise by being here," I said, and picked up my bag.

"Why aren't you guys talking?" Yo asked.

"I think that's her story to tell, not mine. But so nice to see you again, Sarah. I'm really glad that you and Ash are still so close. I like knowing she has someone like you in her corner." I looked at the others now. "And you guys too. Thanks for being such good friends to her." I gave them all one last look and then walked away before Ash came out and saw me standing here. It would ruin the happy surprise that this was clearly meant to be, and she needed some cheering up. I didn't want to spoil that for her.

Dear Ash,

How's work? Hope everything is going well and the shoot is on track. I'm sure it is with you as the DOP. It took me a while to get going, so exhausted from the trip . . .

I deleted the email message for the tenth time that morning. I had been trying to write emails to her all week, ever since being back.

Dear Ash,

I fucking love you. I am in love with you. I've been in love with you for thirteen years. Tell me you're prepared to give us another chance. I know we're meant to be together. I

*know, without a doubt, that it is you. It's
always been you.*

I deleted it. Obviously. But it had felt good to write. I had not been able to stop thinking about her, from the second we'd walked off that plane together, until now. Sitting here in my office after hours, writing emails to her that I knew I would never send. To make the whole thing worse, when I'd arrived back home, my mother had decided to have another semi-lucid moment, where she'd asked me if I'd proposed to Ash yet. I'd played along and told her I was planning on asking her to marry me after the dance that night. She'd said she couldn't wait for the wedding, and had then drifted off again.

I needed a distraction. I needed to get my mind off Ash in some way, any way, or I felt like I was going to die just thinking about her. If I carried on like this, I was scared of self-combusting, blowing myself to little pieces, and then never being able to put myself back together again. The problem was I could no longer turn to the distractions I'd used in the past. Work, yes. Traveling, yes. Sex, *no*.

Bianca had messaged me yesterday. She knew I was back, and she wanted to know if she could come round. And she made it clear it was *not* for coffee. I hadn't even thought about it. Some months back, fucking a gorgeous woman might have filled the void a little bit. Now it felt like there was only one thing in the world that could fill it, and that one thing was her.

CHAPTER 55

Ash

I stood in front of the mirror getting ready for my date tonight, Frank and Charlie were there, lying on my bed with Petal climbing all over them. They'd come over to babysit, in case I was going to stay out all night, because Anushka and Aayan were away at a cousin's wedding. After much back and forth, we'd all decided I should wear the light blue dress and that I should paint my nails the same color and wear the coral-colored lip-gloss that I'd stolen from Sarah.

"Your enthusiasm for this date is really radiating off you," Charlie said as I stood fiddling with my hair for a disproportionately long time.

"I'm kind of questioning why you're even going at this stage," Frank said, holding Petal up above his head.

"I do want to go, it's just that . . . *No!* I want to go. I want to."

"Clearly no psychologist here, but sounds like you're trying to convince yourself of that." Frank was swinging Petal back and forth now and Petal was attacking the air with her paws—adorable.

"I wouldn't blame you if you were. Max was really fucking hot, and nice," Charlie said.

"Christ, if I have to hear how good-looking this guy is one more time, I think I might get sick. We get it, Charlie—he's hot," snapped Frank.

"Why do you get so irritated every time I say that, but it's okay for everyone else to say it?" she asked angrily.

I turned round and watched them as they began bickering again.

"Guys, stop," Sarah said, coming into the room with a giant bag of chips.

"But he is," Charlie insisted. "He's hot as hell, and on top of that, he was so sweet and considerate, the way he put your feelings first like that, even though you could see how hurt he felt. Max gets my vote. I vote against this date with Hot Doc, and vote for a date with Max."

"For heaven's sake." Frank got up off the bed and walked out of the room with Petal.

Charlie flopped back down on the bed. "What's his problem again?" she asked, but honestly, I didn't quite know. These two had been at each other's throats much more than usual lately.

"Just because he's hot and nice, doesn't mean I should be dating him instead of Sibu."

"Then what other attributes does a guy have to have for you to date him?" Charlie asked, sitting up on my bed, glancing into the next room, presumably to see where Frank had gone.

"He's got to *not* be my ex-boyfriend." I turned back to the mirror and fiddled with my hair one last time.

"I hate to point out the giant, gaping hole in that statement, but technically Sibu is an ex-boyfriend too," Sarah said.

"But Sibu wasn't a boyfriend that totally broke me. With Max it's too dangerous. There's too much of a chance that it'll end badly again and then I'll find myself living under some new Max-induced curse for the next thirteen years."

Sarah eyed me suspiciously for a moment and then looked across at Charlie who nodded at her.

"You've got feelings for him!" Sarah started walking over to me and Charlie followed close behind.

"The only feeling I have for him is fear of having feelings for him. Not actual feelings."

"You fear having feelings for him, but you don't have feelings for him?" Charlie asked.

"Exactly," I replied.

"Or you're afraid, because you *do* have feelings for him," she said.

I blinked at Charlie, and then looked at Sarah, who gave me a small knowing nod. I didn't like or want small knowing nods right now.

"You have feelings for him!" Sarah reiterated. "And then you went and had sex with him."

"How could she not have had sex with him, though?" Charlie said, just as Frank came back into the room.

"Are you still talking about him?" He looked Charlie up and down and then walked out the room again.

"What the hell is going on with you guys?" Sarah asked, and Charlie shrugged.

"Guys, I've got to go on a date now with a really, really nice, sexy, hot guy. Who's kind and thoughtful and cared enough to check my snake bite in the airport. Who's family orientated and supports his brother-in-law's restaurant and does fucking charity work! He saves sick children's lives. In Africa. He's the guy I want to have feelings for! And right now, I'm almost running late for my date. I love you guys. Bye!"

I walked out of my bedroom and found Frank on the couch, still with Petal.

"Thanks for coming round and babysitting," I said to him. "And by the way, you and Charlie need to stop fighting, you should go in there right now and hug it out or something."

"I second that," Sarah said, walking past. "Hug it out!"

"Who's hugging?" Charlie asked, walking out of my room now too.

"You guys are hugging. You and Frank. You guys need to hug it the fuck out!" Sarah announced loudly. "Come on. Come, come. No more fighting. Make love not war and all that."

I was about to exit the front door when something about Sarah's statement made me turn round and watch the scene playing out in my living room.

"I'm not hugging him until he apologizes to me," Charlie said.

"Apologize for what?" Frank was on his feet now, walking towards her.

"Enough! You're friends. You've been friends for twelve years. Stop this stupid bickering and hug. I insist. Come . . ." Sarah started pushing them towards each other, and as she did, something in the room changed.

"Go on—don't be shy." She practically smashed them into each other, giving them no other choice but to hug each other, but the second they did, something invisible punched me in the gut and my mouth fell open. Sarah whipped round and looked at me, her mouth as wide open as mine. She raised her eyebrows at me and I nodded back. We both turned our attention back to Charlie and Frank. They were still hugging. And there was a seriously non-friendly energy emanating from it.

Sarah turned back to me, her mouth still gaping in shock. "We'll talk about this later," she mouthed, and I nodded at her vigorously before leaving my apartment with a massive smile on my face.

When I arrived, Sibu was already sitting waiting for me. He hadn't seen me, so I took a moment to look at him. He really was gorgeous and I really wanted to like him as much as I knew I should like him. He finally saw me, stood up and waved.

"You look beautiful," he said.

"Thanks, had my hair done." I touched my new hair, which I'd put some highlights in this week because I'd needed a distraction from thinking about Max one afternoon, and doing something with my hair had seemed like a good idea.

"It suits you, the lighter color. Brings out your eyes. And I love the cut."

"Not even a minute into the date and so many compliments already," I teased, and then was surprised to see him pull the chair out for me.

"Thank you." I sat down and watched him walk to the other side of the table and sit. "You're not looking too bad yourself," I said.

"Thank you. I'm feeling better too. Last time we were . . . Well, I wasn't in a great place. But I've been going to therapy, really working through some things, and can honestly say I've never felt better."

"Wow, that's amazing. I'm happy for you."

"I hope you don't mind—I'm not on call today and actually don't have work tomorrow either, which is a miracle, so I took the liberty of ordering champagne. I couldn't remember if you liked it."

"Fancy," I said. "I do love some champagne. But what's the special occasion?"

He sat back in his chair and looked at me solemnly. "You. You are the special occasion."

I felt my cheeks redden. And it was real excitement. Suddenly, I didn't feel like I was pretending so much anymore. "I'm flattered."

"So, I have a confession," he said, resting his elbows on the table and his chin on his hands.

"And what might that be?"

"I may have gone onto your company website from time to time to catch up on what work you were doing. I may have also watched the ads you shot, and I have to tell you that the one you did for that men's fragrance—"

I laughed. "The one with the unpronounceable French name."

"That one. You sold me." He stuck his wrist out and looked down at it.

"You did not!" I leaned down and smelled it. "Oh my God, you did."

"You got me! I was sold in seconds."

I laughed again. Hang on, had he always been this funny, and playful? Or perhaps this was a new development, along with his new state of mind.

"That shot when the bottle of perfume fell out of the air and into the water in black and white slow motion, those droplets flying out, you almost had me there. But you seriously got me when that shirtless guy was standing in the rain with the lightning behind him and then fell to the ground and crawled like a panther over the marble floor."

I laughed again and put my face in my hands. "I want to state for the record that I have no control over what those creative directors come up with. I only try and make it look good."

"You made it look good. Very good."

"Thank you, that's nice to hear. And how was Malawi?"

He shook his head and his smile was gone. "If you could see what terrible conditions those doctors are having to operate under. Sometimes with no electricity and barely any medication. Their dedication is astounding. They're saving lives with so few resources."

"It's awful. I must confess, I also did some research on you before I came. I didn't realize it was actually *your* charity foundation— that's amazing. I saw some of the photos on your website . . . I'm sure they're very glad to have someone like you helping them."

"We did manage to get a lot of supplies to them, but it really made me realize how lucky I am to practice medicine where I do."

"Well, it's amazing you were able to do that."

"I'm thinking of doing it more regularly."

"That would be great."

"Maybe one day you could come with me and do some filming for us? We've been looking at doing something like that for ages. Hopefully a video could get us some attention and bring in more funding, which we are always in desperate need of."

I sat up straighter in my chair. "It would be my absolute honor and pleasure. I'd love to do something like that." As I said it, our eyes locked and a small flitter of something made itself known in my stomach. The flitter was spontaneous and totally unforced. I smiled. The flitter had given me hope, hope that maybe this could actually work this time. The champagne arrived and we toasted together and the conversation flowed so easily. This was good. Very good. It was actually better than I expected. I was not pretending anymore at all.

Max . . . *who*?

CHAPTER 56

Max

I watched them, feeling sick to my stomach, and it took every last drop of restraint not to walk up there and throw him out. Christ, the way they were laughing and sipping expensive champagne together was enough to make me want to blow up the entire restaurant. I stood there feeling like I was a part of her life in some way, but also *not* a part of it. She had her own life and it did not involve me. Her own friends whom she laughed with, a cat, neighbors who she hung out with, a job, a car, and an apartment. And now she had her own doctor date, and all I could do was sit on the sidelines and watch.

No. Fuck this. I was going to march up to that table and put an end to this wrist-smelling and laughing and everything else that was happening right under my nose. I was going to be an asshole! And I would probably hate myself for it tomorrow, but I wasn't sure if I would hate myself more if I let her fall for this guy, and lose her. I straightened up and walked over.

"Hey," I said as soon as I reached the table. I could tell Ash was shocked and her champagne shook in her hands. I turned my attention to Dr McHottie and stuck my hand out.

"It's you!" Ash gasped, and spluttered.

"Max," I stated, looking at the guy.

"Hey, Max, nice to meet you. I'm Sibu." And then the guy stood up to shake my hand. He stood up. All respectfully, like a bloody gentleman.

"I saw you at the airport, didn't I?" he asked.

I nodded. "Briefly."

"Sorry, I was in a hurry or I would have introduced myself."

"Uh . . . sure." I was so taken aback by this man—it was hard to describe. He exuded this energy that was so likeable, and yet I was quite determined *not* to like him.

"How was the trip? I assume you have something to do with production as well?"

"I manage locations, and scout them."

"So you get to travel for work—sounds like the dream job."

"I get to go to some really interesting places." For some reason, I felt myself responding. He had this way about him that was engaging, it made you want to talk with him.

"What's the most interesting place you've ever been to?" he asked, turning his body to me now, as if he was fully engaged in this conversation.

"Socotra Island. Off the Yemeni coast," I said without thinking.

"How do you spell that?" he asked, taking out his phone. "I want to google it."

I spelled it for him and he typed it up and then put his phone away. "Thanks, I'm going to check it out later. So how do you guys know each other?" he asked, sitting back down all demurely.

"Funny story that—we used to date," I said.

"Back in high school," Ash quickly added.

And then the guy chuckled. "I bumped into my high school girlfriend a few months back and we had such a good laugh over some of the questionable fashion choices we made back in the old class of 2009."

"Class of 2009?" I asked. "How old are you? You look younger than that."

"I get that a lot. Can only put it down to good genes. Too lazy for a skin-care routine and too shit-scared of Botox. I stick needles into people all day, but I'm too scared to have needles stuck into me." He smiled at me. "I'm actually thirty-four. But I went through this huge denim-from-head-to-toe stage back in the day. And I even tried to bleach my hair."

Why did I suddenly like this guy? Why was I suddenly smiling at him?

"Ash wore this dress to prom that had so many shiny things on it, it was a literal disco ball. She could blind people with it."

"I bet she still looked good, though." He smiled over at her with . . . *fuck* . . . something totally genuine in his eyes. My stomach twitched. I looked over at Ash. This was the kind of guy that would not cause her distress, not like me. He seemed like the kind of guy who would be easy to fall in love with, and it would be uncomplicated and good.

"Yeah, she did. Prettiest girl there that night," I said, looking at her. She was still the prettiest girl here tonight too.

Ash forced a small smile and quickly looked away.

"Do you want to join us for a drink? I won't invite you for the entire date, if you don't mind. I would like some time alone with the prettiest girl in the restaurant over here. But I did order a large bottle of champagne and I'm sure we could both do with it having one less glass in it."

Damn. I liked this guy.

I looked over at Ash again and then took a step back from the table. My heart felt like it was cracking.

"Nah, I don't want to interrupt, just wanted to come over and say hi. You guys have a good time, and make sure she gets home safely."

And then he stood up again and took my hand. "Not to worry, I will. Nice meeting you, Max. And I'm going to check out that island."

I shook his hand and looked at him. "Yeah, nice meeting you too." I meant it, and I hated that I meant it. And then I walked away. I walked upstairs to my office and collapsed on the sofa there.

I loved her too much to see her unhappy. And if this guy was going to make her happy, then I needed to step away. And he seemed like the perfect guy for her. Not like me. This guy was a smooth ride in a luxury SUV. We had been like a rally car, tearing around, turning sharp corners, making our heads spin.

I put my hands over my face and felt like squeezing my head off. I needed to get her out of my mind. At least I didn't have to worry about her tonight. That guy was too much of a gentleman to let anything happen to her.

Handsome, nice Dr McNiceguy.

You need to let her go. You need to let her go. The thought repeated over and over again.

What I really needed was a fucking distraction. I needed to get her off my mind in some way. Any way. If I carried on thinking about her and Dr McNiceguy downstairs, or her and what was probably going to happen later tonight with Dr McNiceguy, I was going to drive myself insane. If I carried on like this, I was afraid of self-combusting, blowing myself to little pieces and then never being able to put myself back together again. So I turned to the only distraction I could think of, the only one that I'd used in the last thirteen years. I picked my phone up and sent a message.

Max: Hey, what you doing tonight?
Bianca: So weird, I was just thinking about you.
Max: What a coincidence, I was thinking about you too.
Bianca: And what exactly where you thinking about?

I was about to type something filthy about our naked bodies when—
"Fuck!" I dropped my phone on my desk and walked away from it. *What the hell was I doing?* I turned and looked back at the glowing screen and folded my arms in defiance of it. I couldn't do this. Not anymore. Not since Ash. Being with her had changed everything, had changed me, and there was no way I would ever be able to go back to the way I was, even if she and I were never together again. I walked back to the phone and started typing again.

Max: I have a confession to make . . .

Bianca: What? 🐱

She clearly thought this was still part of the flirtation.

Max: I've fallen in love with someone.

Bianca: What?

Max: Well, I've actually realized that it's more like I've always been in love with them.

Bianca: I'm kind of confused here???

Max: What I'm trying to say is that I'm not going to sleep with you tonight. Or any night. And I'm sorry that I messaged you like this. It was wrong of me.

Bianca: WTF, Max!

Max: Bianca, you're gorgeous and funny and smart and a serious catch.

Bianca: Are you drunk or something?

Max: No. I'm sober. More sober than I think I've ever been.

Bianca: I'm seriously still confused here.

Max: Let me unconfuse you. I'm no good for you. You deserve to find someone that will love you the way you deserve to be loved and then love them back as hard as you can! It's taken me thirteen years to figure this out, and this is going to sound cheesy as hell, but it's about love, Bianca. It's all about love. That's the thing that really matters. It might be the only thing that matters.

Bianca: I can't figure out if that is the weirdest thing anyone has ever said to me, or the nicest thing?

Max: Well, I was going for the latter.

Bianca: Well then, I guess, thanks . . . ?

Max: Take care, Bianca.

I put my phone back down on my desk. It felt very final. It was. I was putting that part of my life away as well.

CHAPTER 57

Ash

I banged on his door as hard as I could with both my fists, I was so angry. "MAX! MAX!" I screamed.

"What's wrong?" I heard his panicked voice from inside, and then fast-approaching footsteps. The door flew open.

"What's wrong? Are you okay?"

I pushed past him and walked into the middle of his office. "What's wrong? . . . *Everything.* And no, I am not okay . . . *thanks to you.*"

"Ash, slow down. What are you talking about?"

"I'm talking about you coming up to our table during my date with a man I could potentially be really good with, and being all nice and looking like that." I waved my hand up and down. "God, why do you have to look like that? And then why do you have to tell me I was the prettiest girl at the dance?"

"Ash, I'm sorry. I'm lost here."

"You came up to our table!" I felt like banging my hand on something or stamping my foot.

"Honestly, I'm actually glad I did. I like the guy. He seems very genuine. I'm happy for you."

"Well, I am not happy."

"Why?"

"Sibu is so good-looking, and sexy, and smart, and he made me laugh. And he smells amazing. He is one of the nicest guys I have ever met—he even does pro bono work with little babies in Malawi, for fuck's sake. He's thoughtful, he's genuinely interested in what I do, and the conversation just flowed. He's basically perfect."

"So what's the problem, then?"

"The problem was that he kissed me goodnight and then hugged me and told me what an amazing night he'd had and how he would like to do it again soon."

"I'm still not seeing the issue, Ash."

"The issue is I felt nothing! Not a bloody thing. This gorgeous, perfect man kissed me and had his hand on my lower back and smelled great and I felt absolutely nothing for him. Because all I could think about was you! How sexy you'd looked when you came up to the table, and how when you'd walked away all I had wanted to do was run after you and rip your clothes off. I don't want to rip his clothes off, and I'm so angry with you, and even angrier with myself, because now I think you've cursed me, but in a whole other way!"

He blinked at me rapidly and I didn't know why, but he looked so good. So good in that shirt of his that it needed to be on the floor . . . *now*.

I lunged at him, and in one move my lips were on his and my hands were working their way up his shirt. For a moment there, a brief tiny millisecond, he didn't reciprocate, but then he gripped my ass and started pulling me into him. He helped me pull his shirt off and I tossed it across the room. I pushed him back onto his desk. Things crashed on the floor, but I didn't care. I climbed on top of him, pulled my dress off and wasted no time in going straight for his zipper. I could already feel him straining against his pants, and I knew the second they were down, his cock would be freed and it would be mine to do with as I wanted. I unzipped him and his cock bulged against his underwear. I could see its outline perfectly through the white cotton briefs. I slid down, lowered my mouth to it and sucked it through the fabric while gripping his balls in my hand. He moaned and laced his fingers in my hair, tugging at it in a way that made me feel wild.

"I love your new hair, by the way," he said on a loud moan as I slipped my hand beneath his underwear and gripped him tightly, before fisting him hard and fast. He responded by lifting his hips, giving me more access. I pulled the tip of his cock from behind the material and with my tongue ran circles round it. This elicited more moans from him, but I wanted more. More, more, more . . . *now*!

"Condoms," I commanded.

His hand flew back and he started pulling out a desk drawer.

"Of course you have condoms in your desk," I muttered under my breath. He passed one to me and I ripped it open, working his underwear down. I rolled the condom on and then didn't even take my underwear off; I simply pulled my panties aside and climbed straight on top of him. I cried out immediately at the feeling of him sinking inside me from this angle. I was so turned on, and having my need met like this almost made me come at once. I put my hands on his broad naked chest, closed my eyes and rode him as fast as I could. Grinding into him, wanting him deeper inside me. I wanted him to fill me until I was overflowing with him. I lost myself somewhere there, somewhere in that moment with him on his desk, me riding his cock as if my life depended on it. I felt my orgasm build and I drove him into me even harder and faster.

"Fuck, Ash, I'm going to come."

"Come," I commanded as I sat fully upright on him, threw my head back, and started coming myself. He gripped my hips and bucked against me in a way that told me he'd started coming too.

"Ash, I love you."

"WHAT!" I looked down and screamed at him while I was coming. "You what?" He was gripping my hips, slamming into me as my orgasm rolled into another one. "What? What the hell? Aaaah! WHAT?" I panted, and shouted and moaned at the same time.

"I said"—he thrust deeper and harder now—"that I . . ."—he raised my hips off him and slammed me back down on his cock with a loud thump that felt as if it echoed around the room—"I love you!"

He threw his head back and came with such force that he lifted his hips and my entire body off the desk. I was shocked, but I was still coming, because he was not letting me stop as he kept on thrusting.

"I love you," he said one last time, and dropped his hips back down to the desk. I stared down at him in utter shock as my orgasm finally faded. He opened his eyes and looked up at me. We were both covered in sweat.

"You don't love me," I said, still shaking from the pleasure and panting from the exertion. "It's with a 'd', Max. A 'd'."

"There is no 'd', Ash. I love you. I'm in love with you. I've always been in love with you. You are all I've ever wanted. It's always *only* been you."

"Only been me . . ." I scoffed, and tried to climb off him, but he held me in place. "That's a lie and we both know it." He pulled me back down towards him, and despite wanting to fight it, I didn't. I let him pull my face towards his, let him put his lips to my ear and whisper.

"Everything I've done for the last thirteen years has been to try and get over you. But I never did. And now I can never go back to any of that again, because you've changed me. Loving you again has changed me. And I know what I want."

I pulled away and started to climb off him again. "No, that is not what we agreed to, Max. We said *no* feelings."

"*You* said no feelings." He sat up on the table.

"You *agreed* to no feelings." I pointed an accusatory finger at him.

"Well, then, I lied."

"Oh my God." I walked round in a small circle. "You are not allowed to love me, Max. That was not part of the deal."

"It was a crappy deal, Ash. And let's face it, it wasn't exactly a deal either of us could stick to."

"I could stick to it!" I said.

He looked me up and down. "If you could stick to it, you would not be standing in my office late at night, your dress on the floor because we just made love on my desk!"

"Made lo—" I choked on the words. His use of that phrase had me stumbling backwards. "We didn't . . . That's not—" I shook my head quickly. He stood up, his perfect cock and muscular chest on full display. He was gorgeous and sweaty and the king of dishing orgasms out and we could *not* have "made love".

I stepped away from him, scared that if I didn't, I might just fall towards him. "You can't do this. You can't come into my life like this after so many years, have endless sex with me and then tell me you love me."

"Why not?"

"Because . . . because . . ." I glared at him angrily, but when he smiled softly at me, my entire body softened, and worst of all, my heart softened too. "Because I think I love you and I totally hate that I think I love you," I said. My shoulders slumped. I felt absolutely defeated by this realization. I'd been fighting it since I'd seen him in the restaurant and I was now officially exhausted. I hated that I had said it out loud too, because saying it out loud had just made it very real, and there was no taking it back. I turned and started walking towards the door.

"Ash, wait. Please don't go." He walked up to me, put his hand over mine and stopped me from opening the door. "We love each other," he said with a smile that was too easy to want back in my life. He looked at me with his huge puppy-dog eyes, full of love and care, and again, they were way too easy to want back in my life. But I had gone down this road with him before, and it had ended, and it had nearly broken me. I had loved him so hard it had hurt, and I could feel myself on the brink of that all-consuming love once again and it terrified me.

"Ash, let's do this."

"No," I said softly.

"Let's give this another chance. We're meant to be together."

"How do you even know that?"

"It's obvious, Ash. I never stopped loving you and it's clear that you never stopped loving me too."

"I did stop loving you!" But the second I said it, I knew it was a lie. And I also knew that this was the final puzzle piece I'd been looking for. The thought that had been just out of reach. I'd never stopped loving him; that's why nothing had ever worked with anyone else.

The curse was never about the sex. The *real* curse was that I loved him too damn much, and always had. That's why all the dates and the sex had been so terrible. *Because it wasn't him.* Max was what I had wanted the entire time—I just hadn't realized it until now. He had cursed me, but it wasn't in the way I thought he had.

"We never stopped loving each other," he said with so much self-assuredness that it pissed me off. I hated the fact that he was right. And I hated him for making me love him so much. "It's meant to be us, Ash."

"Max, you and I are never getting back together!" It flew out of my mouth.

He chuckled. "Isn't that a Taylor Swift song?"

"This isn't a joke," I insisted.

"I know."

"So why are you trying to turn it into one, then?" I asked, frustration building.

"Because if I don't try and laugh about this, I think I might cry."

His words sounded jagged and wounded. His eyes ached with visible pain and all I wanted to do was take that pain away, but I also knew what a potentially dangerous thought that was too.

"Ash, give us another chance, please. This love we have is rare. Not everyone gets to experience this kind of love and that's why we have to give it another chance."

I shook my head at him. "That's exactly why we *shouldn't* give it another chance. I don't want to love you, Max. And I'm going to do whatever it takes *not* to love you again. Because if we didn't work out again, I would not survive it. I barely survived it the first time, I cannot risk my heart with you again." I turned and ran out into the night, tears falling from my eyes as I went.

CHAPTER 58

Ash

Dear Maximillian,

Sebastian has had a change of mind on the bar location. Initially he wanted a commercial bar, as you know, but now he feels that a more intimate home bar would be better. It will establish the group of friends well and more intimately before they all go on their adventure together. Can you please send through some references for a more intimate home-bar setting urgently? Sebastian would also like it to have a view.

Regards,
Leigh Smith
Director of Photography, DP
Moving Pixel Films
Kalk Bay
Cape Town

————

Dear Leigh,

Please find the link to one location I think could work, and also some photos of a second location that I think is also in line with Sebastian's vision. I actually agree with him— it would be much nicer to see the friends together in a more intimate setting. The first one is an hour out of town, great home bar, overlooking the sea. It is very modern and minimalist and has won several architectural-design awards. The second one has a more casual, homely feel, but has a great view too. They both have good, spacious home bars, but the houses have very, very different feels. Please let me know if any of these work. If not, I will have a look at what else I have and what else I could find.

Maximillian Adam
CEO
The Film Place
5 Longstreet Lofts
Cape Town

———

Dear Maximillian,

Sebastian does not like the first location at all. He says it looks too impersonal, like a "rich people's morgue." He loves the second location. He says, "At least it looks like dead people don't live there." He would like me to go through and do a tech recce of the place and see if it works for us. Please can you

arrange that asap. Preferably today or tomorrow. Sebastian would like to shoot the location
at sunset, so arrange for this time, please.

Regards,
Leigh Smith
Director of Photography
Moving Pixel Films
Kalk Bay
Cape Town

————

Dear Leigh,

I can arrange it for this afternoon? I will
send the location to your phone, the owner is
very flexible, and says you can go through
anytime to see the place.

Maximillian Adam
CEO
The Film Place
5 Longstreet Lofts
Cape Town

————

Dear Maximillian

Fine.

Regards,
Leigh Smith
Director of Photography
Moving Pixel Films
Kalk Bay
Cape Town

CHAPTER 59

Ash

I'd planned on never seeing or speaking to Maximillian Adam for the rest of my life, but unfortunately, Sebastian had other plans. And his plans included deciding last minute, days before shooting, that he no longer liked one of the locations. But this was a very Sebastian thing to do. I'd worked with him for seven years now, and in those seven years, this happened at least three times a year, where he made some last-minute call or change that threw the entire shoot into chaos, but in the end made the film so much better. So when he did this now, I no longer worried that it was going to end in disaster.

I drove along Chapman's Peak Drive, which was undoubtedly the most beautiful road in the world. It wound along the side of the mountain, with views over the endless sea. My new car handled the road beautifully, and I loved driving it. It had been that photo of my happy mother with her Mini that had made me get this one. I'd hardly ever seen her happy, and driving this car felt like the closest I'd ever be to her happiness again.

But my hands trembled the entire time I drove. I had not told any of my friends how I was feeling. I wasn't ready to say it out loud again. *Fuck, I should not have said it to him.* I had this strange tight feeling in my chest and everything just felt weird. My body felt weird. As if it didn't belong to me today.

I pulled my car onto one of the many look-out spots on the drive and climbed out. I needed fresh air. There was a flat rock about a meter up and I went to sit on it. It felt like I was on the edge of the world now. The sea was a turquoise color on days like this, when the sun was shining brightly, and the wind had decided to die down. Mountains rose up behind me and I felt sandwiched between these two great things, the mountain and the sea. There were only a few clouds in the sky today, and the sky was almost the same color as the sea. I took a deep breath, the cool breeze and salty sea smell filling my lungs. I was due at this home bar in about half an hour, but the owner was flexible, so I was sure I could arrive a little later. I just needed a moment. A moment in nature to clear my brain and try to make sense of all these weird feelings I was having. Terribly weird and strange and all-consuming. I also knew I needed to do two things. I pulled my phone out and typed a message on the friend group.

Ash: I'm in love with Max. And I don't want to be. I need you all to tell me why it's a terrible idea to be in love with this man, and how the hell to stop loving him.

If Max and I got together and gave things another go, and it didn't work out once again, I would be devastated once more and also, did that mean another thirteen years of not being able to love again? I couldn't take that risk.

What if we worked out, though?

I muted that thought too, as well as muted the group after my confession. The messages had come in quickly. I didn't want to know the answers right now, because I was afraid that if I read them all, I might cry. And I needed to work. And then I typed a second message to Sibu. It wasn't fair to him that I continued dating him if I was still in love with Max. It broke my heart to send him the message, and of course he accepted it like the gentleman he was. This broke my heart even more. I told him I would still love to shoot something for him in Malawi, though, and not out of guilt but because I really wanted to. He was a great guy, and he deserved all the happiness and greatness in the world, and maybe I could at least contribute to that in some small way.

The house was gorgeous. This whole area though was gorgeous. Noordhoek was a very laid-back coastal suburb. The houses were all on massive properties, so it had a farm feel to it. A distant sea view, set up in mountains, made the environment perfect. Most of the residents kept horses and chickens, and apparently some kept llamas too. I was very aware that Max lived in the area, and I was hoping very much not to bump into him. For a second, I'd wondered if it was his house, but when I'd been greeted at the door by someone who was not Max, I relaxed somewhat. The house was massive, you could fit ten of my apartments in here, easily, and that was just the ground floor. Huge folding doors opened onto a wrap-around patio and rolling lawns beyond.

I was led to the bar area, which, again, was perfect. Set on the patio, with a view over the garden and distant sea, it was casual, laid back, classy and you could see a group of friends sitting here enjoying African Dreams as the sun set.

African Dreams, I scoffed. Actually, that's what had caused it all. That had been the start of all the bloody chaos. That storm in that tent drinking African Dreams with Max. I decided I hated African Dreams, and would make sure I shot the best commercial possible to feature it, but I would secretly hate it while I lit it and zoomed in on it and tracked out for the stupid thing. I started taking light readings and filming the various shots from different angles. I got swept up in things for a while, but every now and then I looked up and took in the setting sun and the view of the home. I couldn't help but wonder who lived here. The place had an old-school feel to it; the house was traditional and farm-housey. Nothing in it was modern or minimalist. It felt cozy, even though it was clearly large. I imagined it was owned by a happy couple with kids. Kids who ran around the lawn and played all day without a care in the world. It was that kind of home, a happy home. A home I'd had for a while, until I hadn't. A home I'd always wanted to have. And for a moment there, all those years ago, I was sure that Max and I were going to build that kind of home together. A home just like this that screamed of nights by the fireplace in winter, and family dinners eaten outside on warm evenings.

"Ash, I wasn't expecting you back so soon from the dance."

I swung round at the strange voice speaking my name. "Sorry, what did you say . . . ?" I took in the face. It was lined and creased and the body was frail and thin, but there was no mistaking those eyes, those icy blue eyes. And was that a parrot on her arm?

"Mrs McAdamson!" I said, then looked around frantically for Max.

"Ash, I wasn't expecting you home so soon after the dance?"

"The dance?"

"Was it lovely? Your dress was so pretty. Red is the perfect color for you."

"The farewell dance?" I asked, and she nodded.

"Sexy girl, sexy girl," the parrot shouted, which only added to the utter bizarreness of the moment.

"Well, let me see." She moved closer to me, on very shaky legs.

"See what?"

"Your ring, silly." She walked over to my hand and looked down at it.

"Oh dear, has he not asked you to marry him yet? Have I messed it all up? Oh dear, he will be so upset. It was a surprise and now I messed it all up." She started getting very agitated and I began to panic, and the bloody parrot started telling me I had a nice ass. *What the hell was going on?*

But then I remembered something that Max had said. I quickly placed my hand on her shoulder.

"He did do it," I said, and smiled at her. Her agitation disappeared immediately.

"Was it very romantic?"

I nodded. "So romantic."

"Oh good, good. Where's the ring?"

I looked at my hand quickly and tried to think. "It's . . . at the jeweler. It's just a little bit too big for me, so it's being resized."

"Oh, lovely, lovely. You know, he saved up for that ring for a whole year. And I said to him that I thought you two were too young, but when he told me with such conviction that you were the person he wanted to spend the rest of his life with and he would never meet anyone like you even if he traveled the world ten times, I knew how serious he was. How much he loved you. Besides, you hear stories about high-school sweethearts all the time. So I'm really happy for you two."

I nodded. I felt tears in my eyes and my throat constricted. "I'm really happy too."

"Mrs. McAdamson, you escaped again." A nurse ran up to her and looked at me apologetically.

"I wanted to see Lucy!"

"Sexy Lucy. Sexy Lucy," the parrot shouted.

"Oh, shush your beak, you naughty boy," Max's mom said, and started stroking her parrot's head with a smile on her face.

"You should have told me you wanted to see her and I would have taken you." The nurse put her hands on Max's mom's shoulders and gently turned her round.

"Nice ass!" the parrot said. God, this was like the twilight zone. Nothing made sense.

"Do you want me to get your wheelchair, or should we try and get some exercise?" asked the nurse.

"I want to walk," she said.

"Good, I tell you what, let me message Grayson and ask him to bring the wheelchair just in case."

"I want to see Lucy," she repeated, as if she'd forgotten the entire conversation that had just taken place.

"Yes, let's go and see her. Come on, this way."

I turned and watched as she walked away from us and that's when

I saw Max standing there. His face was pale and I knew he'd heard everything.

We stood and looked at each other in total silence. He looked different. Nothing like the man I'd gotten to know these last few days. He looked more like the boy I used to know. Vulnerable. Soft. I started walking up to him. He didn't move, though. And I only stopped when I was standing right in front of him.

"You were going to ask me to marry you that night?"

He nodded.

"You had a ring?"

"In my pocket the entire night."

"You had a ring," I stated thoughtfully. And now that I thought about it, he'd had his hand buried in his pocket a lot that night, and I'd asked him what he was doing several times.

"But despite all the saving, I don't even think they were real diamonds," he said, trying to force a smile, trying to make light of a situation that was just not light at all. Max suddenly looked very uncomfortable and unsure of himself. He looked like the boy I used to know all over again. He had a different name now, he looked different, but he was the exact same person that I'd loved so much.

"Do you still have it?" I asked.

"I threw it into the woods behind my house the next day."

"Wow!" I shook my head. This was all so much to take in.

"I think that's partly why I was so nervous and why it all just fell apart. I kept waiting for the perfect moment to ask you, and it never came. In my head I'd imagined that we'd make love and we'd lie in bed together and then I would ask you. But that, you know . . ."

I finally knew it all. The full story. It had been more than just sex. It had been a proposal, a yes, a happy-ever-after. The sex had been wrapped up in the biggest question you could probably ask anyone in your life.

"You look totally shocked, like you had no idea at all," he said.

"We'd spoken about it, a lot. I knew I wanted to, and I knew that we probably would, but I had no idea that you'd already planned it for that night."

"What would you have said if I'd asked you that night?"

"I would have said yes." The words rushed out of my mouth without having to think about them. I didn't need to think about them. I knew the answer now, and I had definitely known the answer then too.

"Funny how things turned out. Our lives could have been totally different," he said softly.

I thought about the house and the cozy fires and the al fresco dining with the kids.

I nodded and felt a tear escape my eye. I hated crying. I hated people seeing me cry and I quickly wiped it away. As soon as I had, though, the other eye betrayed me with a massive tear too.

"Fuck it!" I put my head back to try and stop the tears.

"Ash, I don't want to make you cry, not now, not ever." He put his hands on my shoulders.

"Too late for that," I said through the start of little breathy sobs, which I hated. "You've made me cry."

"Please don't cry, baby."

"How can I not cry when I hear that you were going to ask me to marry you? And that if things had gone differently we could possibly be——" I cut myself off, but I'd said enough.

"Together? That we might be together."

I nodded, the tears spilling from my eyes.

"We can still be together." He lifted his hands to my face and gently started wiping my tears away. I closed my eyes and wanted to fall into this feeling and fall into him.

"Mr. McAdamson, sorry to interrupt, but your mom is calling for you."

"Of course." He pulled away, stopped and turned back to me.

"Do you want to meet Lucy?" he asked, smiling now, despite the heaviness and awkwardness of the discussion.

I wiped the tears off my face and nodded, giving him a small smile. "Yes."

I followed him outside, and when we rounded the corner, I gasped out loud. "Oh my God, it's a llama! An actual, living llama." I looked at Max and laughed. "You own an actual living bloody llama. I have to take a picture of this to show my friends." I took a photo of the llama and then posted it to the group with the words, "Don't ask the questions now. I'll tell you all later." I briefly noted that I had over a hundred unread messages. That was a lot of reasons *not* to love Max. And *not* to be in a relationship with him.

I stood back and watched Max interact with his mother, helping her stand and feed the llama. I smiled. In moments like this, I was taken right back, and reminded why I'd loved him so much, and why I'd wanted to spend my whole life with him. Mind you, over the last few weeks, there had been so many moments like this when I think I might have felt that exact same thing.

My phone started ringing and I initially thought it was one of my friends ignoring the "no question" thing. But when I pulled it out and saw Sebastian's name, a bad feeling crept in.

"Fuck. Shit, and fuck!" Sebastian said as soon as I answered the phone.

"What's wrong?"

"Lame asshole so-called creative directors who don't have a creative bone in their little pale bodies!"

"What, Sebastian?"

"Oh, so apparently tents are too Bedouin now—they are giving 'middle-east vibes.' Apparently, tents are not African. They don't give enough African chic."

"What the hell does that mean?" I asked.

"They don't want to shoot at the tented camp."

"They agreed to shoot there."

"Now they don't like it. The producer is all 'find somewhere else and make it work'."

"WHAT? The shoot is literally next week. They agreed to the tents, they liked the tents, they saw the pictures of the fu—" I cut myself off. "Tents."

"Well, now they don't like the tents. Little noncreative ratbags."

"Oh my God." I crouched down on the floor because I thought I might fall over. "So what now? We're talking new location, new shot list, new gear list, possible new crew for new gear list, new everything? Have you tried to talk sense into them?"

"When last did you try to talk sense into someone with a twirly moustache, who posts get-ready-with-my-mongoose videos on TikTok every day?"

"He has a mongoose?"

"Exactly."

I looked over at the llama and felt like laughing with a mixture of hysteria and terror.

"So no tents but still a safari lodge?"

"They hate the tents. I feel like I could strangle them with one, though!"

"We would literally need to find another location now, and be at it tomorrow if we can make this . . ." I turned round and looked at Max, who was staring at me with great concern. "Sebastian, I'll call you back. I think there's a possibility I can figure something out. But don't pin your hopes on it—it's a long shot."

CHAPTER 60

Max

I'd planned on not being at the house when she was there, and had asked my house manager to show her to the bar area and help her with anything she needed. But as soon as I'd gotten the notification on my phone that someone had arrived at my house, and as soon as I'd logged into the live feed of my security camera and saw her ringing the intercom, I grabbed my car keys and ran out the office.

I'd wanted to be the big, mature man and respect her wishes and stay out of her life. I really wanted to do that, but the second I saw her at my house, I knew that no matter how much I wanted that, practicing it in reality was going to be impossible. And now she was here in my house, with Lucy and my mom, clearly having an emergency.

"What's wrong?" I asked the second she'd hung up.

When she explained what had happened, I was only too happy to help her; there was nothing in the world I wouldn't do to help her. I had gotten straight onto the phone with someone I knew that owned three very upmarket lodges at Sabi Sands, zero tents. I'd had a celebrity client book out one of his lodges for a birthday party, and he'd made a good deal of money from it, so I knew that if he was able to help, he would.

Ash was standing over me while I was on the phone, biting the skin on her finger, something she did when she was very, very nervous. She was hanging on my every word and waiting for me to end the call, and the second I did, she pounced.

"So?"

"The proposed shooting date doesn't work for either of the lodges. There's a wedding at one, a conference at the other, and the other one is being redecorated."

"Shit." She collapsed back on the sofa.

"He's proposed another date, but that's during the Zimbabwe shoot. I could call them, though, and see if they're able to change dates. Do you think production would be willing to change the schedule that has already been decided on, as well as a new schedule for the new location, if we get it?"

"I'll ask."

She called Sebastian immediately. "Ask the producer if they are able to change shooting dates for other locations. I may have a location, but the proposed shooting dates don't work."

She hung up and then stared at the phone in her hand, as if willing the call to come as quickly as possible. And when it did, she answered on the first ring.

"And what did they say?" Then she smiled and breathed a sigh of relief. "There are no tents. Cool, I'll send you a link to the location in the meantime, make them look at it ten times and make them sign off on it. I'll ask my friend Sarah to draw up a contract. We want a signature. They cannot get there and decide it's not giving whatever the hell they want it to give, otherwise I am going to be giving them a kick in the ass."

The second she'd hung up she said, "Okay, start shuffling. Production will figure it out."

I got back onto the phone with the manager at Matobo Hills, as well as the other lodges, and began moving the location dates around to make it all fit. And when it was all successfully done, which was a total miracle, I turned to Ash and smiled.

"Oh my God!" She ran up to me and threw herself into my arms. "You're amazing! You've saved our shoot."

I wrapped my arms around her and pulled her as close as I could. We hugged like that, swaying side to side slowly. It was one of those long, happy hugs, the kind you only give to people you truly love, people you've truly missed. Slowly, we disentangled ourselves and parted.

"There's a little catch, though," I said.

"What?"

"Two catches, really."

"Mmmm?" She looked panicked again.

"You can leave tomorrow morning, early, at six and will be there by seven thirty, but it's in the lodge's small plane and I know how much you hate tho——"

"That's fine! I can deal with that. What's number two?"

"So . . . the lodge is fully booked right now, so you would have to stay in the staff village. They have a room there. That's the best he can do at short notice. He says he might be able to move you into a room at one of the other lodges the following night."

"Are you not coming?"

"Nope. No need to. I know them. They're already with my agency, so I don't have any business discussions I need to have with them."

"So, okay . . . just me." She nodded and looked unsure. "So you won't be on the plane either?"

"Are you okay with that?"

She started bobbing her head up and down enthusiastically. "Fine! I'll be fine. There's no way that plane ride can be worse than the last one. I'm fine, really. Thank you so much for this. I'd better get going. I have a lot to pack."

She started gathering up her equipment. I could see her hands were shaking slightly.

"If you want," I said, "I could fly with you. I'll fly back later that day. I know they're coming back to fetch some guests—they do a few flights a day—and when you're done, I could do the same if it would, you know . . ."

She stood up straight and looked at me. "I couldn't ask you to do that. Besides, I need to get over this. I'm nearly thirty-two years old, maybe this is a good opportunity for me to . . ."

"I really don't mind, by the way."

"No. I can do this. I'm fine."

She started walking towards my front door, then stopped and turned. "But thanks for offering to do that for me. It's really sweet."

"There's nothing I wouldn't do for you, Ash. All you have to do is ask."

She nodded thoughtfully. "A lot of stuff was said today, between us."

"It was," I agreed.

"And we should really talk about it."

"We should."

"Maybe when my shoot is over? I'll be going into post-production, but it won't be as hectic as this, so maybe we should do a dinner or something like that?"

"I'd like that," I said.

She started for the door again and these words, these huge words, bubbled up inside me and I wasn't able to stop them.

"And now, Ash?"

"And now what?" She turned, leaning against the doorway. She looked so good in my house like this.

I put my hands in my pockets to anchor myself. "If I asked you now? Today? What would you say?" She knew exactly what I meant. I could see it on her face.

"I would have to think about it, Max," she said, and then turned and walked out the house, closing the door behind her. I smiled. She had not said no. Fucking hell, Ash had not said no.

"Where did Ash go?"

I turned to find my mom standing there. "She had to go back home."

"She doesn't live here?"

"No, she doesn't," I said, but she did look really good in my house. Like she belonged here.

"Is that because you never asked her to marry you that night?" my mom asked.

"How do you know that, Mom?" In every single one of her recollections, Ash and I were either married, or engaged. This was a new memory that seemed to be surfacing.

"Well, you threw that ring over the fence and then went to Europe."

"Mom!" I walked up to her, put my hands on her shoulders and looked her in the eyes. "You remember that?"

"Sure I do. Why wouldn't I?"

Salty tears gathered in the back of my throat. "Of course you would remember that, Mom."

"Such a pity too—you saved all year for that ring," she said.

"So true."

"All those terrible double shifts you did at that smelly diner."

I laughed. I'd forgotten about that.

"You used to come home and your clothes smelled like fish. No matter how much I washed them, I could never get that smell out."

A wall of emotion hit me when I realized she was here again. She was remembering things the way they had actually been. It was such a banal thing to remember too, but it was everything. I was unable to hold back the small tear that escaped my eye as I basked in one of my mother's very rare lucid moments. I smiled at her. "Flipping fishburgers was not one of my career highlights, that's for sure."

"You can give it to her now, though," she said.

"What do you mean?"

"Well, I have it in my jewelry box." She said it so casually that I wasn't sure I'd heard it at first.

"The ring?"

"Well, after you threw it out, I figured maybe there'd been a lovers' tiff, and I knew you two would get over it, so I went and fetched it and kept it, for when you needed it again. Do you need it now?"

Did I need it now?

That was the biggest question in my universe.

CHAPTER 61

Ash

I was exhausted. I'd spent most of the night on the phone with Sebastian looking at the lodge photos and discussing how to translate the previous shots from the storyboard to this location. So when I finally found myself standing on the runway the next morning, I was utterly finished and had no idea how I was going to keep my eyes open long enough to work.

I walked round the plane in front of me. How was it possible that it was smaller than the previous one? This thing looked like it was made from a tuna can that had been tossed away and rusting in the sun for ten years. This plane did not inspire me with confidence. It inspired me with thoughts of a fiery death and plummeting from the sky. Years shaved off my young life and a no doubt agonizing death. But I was left with no choice but to climb in. As soon as I did, I buckled up and tried to distract myself by messaging Sarah.

Ash: OK. This plane is tiny!
Sarah: You're messaging me in private?
Ash: Because what the hell is going on between Frank and Charlie?
Ash: Are you thinking what I'm thinking?
Sarah: I'm thinking it.
Ash: Do you think something's happened between them?

Sarah: I don't know.

Sarah: I don't even know if they've realized how they feel about each other yet.

Ash: They are totally into each other.

Ash: That hug was a dead giveaway. This is huge!

Sarah: Something else is huge too.

Ash: ?

Sarah: Oh, I don't know, you dropping the bomb yesterday that you're in love with Max.

Ash: Yes. That.

Ash: Do you think falling in love with him is the worst thing I could ever do?

Sarah: I don't think you just fell in love with him.

Sarah: I think you've loved him this entire time.

Ash: What should I do about it?

Sarah: What do you want to do about it?

"Ready to go?" The sound of his voice gave me a fright and when I swung around, Max was standing there looking into the plane.

"Is there space in there for one more?" he asked, but didn't wait for the answer. Instead, he started climbing in.

"What are you doing here?" I couldn't hold back my smile. This was possibly the nicest thing anyone had ever done for me. Made nicer by the fact that it was Max doing it.

"I just had this overwhelming desire to fly today. It had absolutely nothing to do with you, by the way, just in case you think I think you're some kind of damsel in distress who needs rescuing, which I don't," he teased.

"Well, far be it from me to keep you from your desires." I smiled at him and shifted over a little bit in the seat.

He stopped and looked down at me, his eyes sweeping over my body, lingering in my lap for a moment too long. "Yeah?"

"Not those desires, and stop that," I said firmly, but I don't think I actually meant it. In fact, I meant the complete opposite. I wanted him to flirt with me, I wanted him to touch me, to hold me, kiss me, to wrap me up in his arms when he slept and . . .

I looked down at my phone. Reread Sarah's last message to me. Max bent forward to put his bag by his feet and I brought my fingers down to the screen.

Ash: I know what I want to do about it
Ash: I'm just not sure it's the right thing to do

The flight wasn't as bad as I'd imagined; these things seldom were as bad as I built them up to be in my catastrophic imagination. And once we'd arrived, the lodge too was perfect. If these idiots didn't like this, then they wouldn't like anywhere.

I ran around taking photos of it first, sending them straight through to Sebastian. We'd managed to work out a very vague shot list last night, and while I worked, I had him on a constant videocall while we talked it all through. He would have probably come with me today if he wasn't busy wrapping up post on our other job and driving Russ crazy. The day was hot and it was rushed and by 3 p.m. I realized that I hadn't eaten or drunk anything at all.

I walked off to the dining area, a huge wooden deck that was open on all sides. A massive tree that had definitely been there first was growing through a specially made hole in the floor and providing the most amazing, and much-needed shade. I found Max sitting at one of the tables talking to the owner, I presumed. They were drinking ice cold beers and for some reason it looked so appealing, even though I hated beer. But in this African heat, the beer in the frosted glass screamed at me. I walked over to the table and Max immediately introduced me.

"Thank you so much for making this happen," I gushed. "You don't know how you've saved us from what could have been a terrible situation."

"Not a problem. Anyone who is important to Max is important to me."

I flashed Max a quick look out of the corner of my eye and found that he was smiling at me.

He pulled out a chair for me, and as soon as I'd sat down, I asked him for a sip of beer. But I was so wrong. The fantasy in my head did not match the reality of the flavor that I was now struggling to swallow down.

"You hate beer," Max stated.

"But it looked so good."

He laughed. "You should have had some water first anyway; you haven't drunk all day."

"How do you know?" I asked, making deliberate eye contact with him.

"When you get wrapped up and excited in something, you always forget to eat and drink. It was like that at school too. I used to bring you those electrolyte sachets and practically force them down your throat."

"Bleghh. Those things tasted awful, but they worked—I admit that." Something dawned on me now. It was something I knew already, but in that moment, it felt like it needed to be spoken out loud. "You always looked out for me. So well. Always."

"So did you. After track, when my feet were sore, you used to make me put them in that foot spa you had."

I laughed at the memory. His feet were so big that they'd barely fit.

"You used to pour arnica oil in and massage them." Our eyes met for a while and we only looked away when the owner of the lodge cleared his throat. He stood up suddenly. I'd forgotten he was even there.

"I . . . need to do something," he lied, and then scuttled off.

Max and I made eye contact again and this time, nothing stopped us from holding each other's gaze.

"I've missed your foot massages like I cannot even tell you."

"I haven't missed electrolyte sachets," I said, and he laughed.

He turned in his seat and then ran his hands through my hair suddenly. "No knots to brush out anymore. In some ways, that's a pity. Even though it looks really good."

"I could sleep badly, roll around on the pillow all night and tease it, if you want knots?"

"I want knots," he said, meeting my eyes again.

"I still have some knots in my neck," I said, remembering how good his massage had been.

"Can I kill that guy, please?"

I laughed and he grabbed my shorts and then pulled me closer to him, my bum sliding all the way to the edge of my seat. He kept his hands on my legs. I looked down at them and then laced my fingers through his.

"Can I be a total Neanderthal here and tell you that the idea of you being with any other man makes me want to walk around hitting them over the head with a stick?"

I gripped his fingers tighter. "Is it ridiculously jealous of me to say that when I think about all the women you've probably been with, it kind of makes me feel sick to my stomach?"

"It makes me feel sick to the stomach too," he said, bringing our hands up and holding them in the air between us. "That's over, Ash. After you, after what we experienced together . . ." He moved, closing the gap between us. I quickly looked around to see if anyone was watching us, but we were alone. He took my face between his hands and pulled my face to his, resting his forehead against mine. "If it makes you feel any better, I feel like I was a virgin before we made love the other night. Because sex has never been like that for me, ever. You are my first as far as I'm concerned, and if you'll let me, I would like to be your last."

"Max." His name fell from my lips onto his. I wanted to slip and fall into this moment with him, but my constantly beeping phone reminded me of the work I still needed to do. I pulled away gently.

"Work!" I stated.

"I love how passionate you are about it," he said, making me want to slip and fall even more.

"I think I'm a bit too obsessed with it, to be honest. I think I've had to be." I looked at him meaningfully.

"Me too." He echoed my statement. "Maybe one day, hopefully soon, both of us will no longer need to use our work as a distraction anymore?"

"Maybe." I smiled at him. "But that time is not now," I said as I answered a call from Sebastian. Max ordered me a burger while on the phone, as well as a glass of water and a Coke. He made me drink the water first before letting me have the Coke—he wagged his finger at me when I reached for it. I smashed the burger, speaking on the phone with my mouth full half the time, and every now and then, Max wiped my chin with a serviette when a dollop of something ran down it. When I hung up, though, Max stood up with a strange finality to it all.

"I have to get going now," he said.

"You do?" My stomach dropped and every fiber in my body screamed a silent "don't go."

"I'll see you tomorrow afternoon, though. That's enough time to finish your work, right?" he asked.

"I'm actually almost done. I'll probably finish later this afternoon, with only one shot to work out in the morning light. We've agreed to keep the shots here to an absolute minimum, so it's easier to plan."

"Well, then I will see you tomorrow morning and we can get out of here."

"You're flying all the way home, and then all the way back? Just for me?"

"No, actually. I'm staying here for the night."

"Wait, you're staying here? How did you manage that? I thought it was fully booked?"

He smiled. "No, there." He pointed out into the bush, past the river and the elephants that were drinking by it.

I looked, and in the distance I could just make out another lodge, further up one of the hills.

"The thought had also crossed my mind to swap rooms with you tonight, but I knew you would say no anyway. If I'd told you I'd been swapping rooms with you all trip, I knew you would have said no then too."

"You've been swapping rooms with me all trip?"

"Did you think you always got the bigger, nicer one by accident?"

"No, Max, you didn't," I protested. "I didn't ask for that."

"See, this is why I'm not offering to swap rooms with you tonight, even though mine's a gorgeous luxury suite."

"How luxurious?" I asked. Having seen the staff accommodation with the shared toilets and ablution facilities, I was not looking forward to my sleep tonight. Coupled with the fact that the bed was very small and uncomfortable.

"Lap of luxury," he teased.

"I have to share showers."

"Really?"

"And let me tell you, those shower curtains are not what they used to be. You can almost see right through them."

His face turned serious and solemn. "See through them?"

"You would probably have to put your face all the way up to the curtain, but it is flimsy enough that I plan on showering much later tonight after everyone has already gone to bed."

"Okay, let's swap rooms."

"Max, don't be ridiculous. You're not staying in my room because someone might see my boobs through a shower curtain."

"Maybe I don't want anyone to see them."

"Maybe they are mine to show to whomever I choose."

He smiled at me, then looked me up and down. "You are absolutely right, but I am kind of hoping that lands up being me."

"Stop flirting. I have work to do and it is very distracting."

"Can I at least see your room?"

"For what reason?"

He shrugged. "Who knows? There might be an emergency in the night and maybe I need to come and find you, or——"

"Lame excuse," I said back to him quickly. "But I do need to get mosquito repellent, so I suppose I cannot stop you from coming with me."

"Lead the way." He gestured for me to go and I began walking through the lodge. I needed my repellent. It was that time of day when the little fuckers would be waking up and no doubt coming after me. I had only one more thing to do, but I did not want to end up with ten thousand bites.

Max followed close behind me, and when I got to my door, I slipped the key in and pushed it open. He walked past me and into the room. He did one full circle in it and then shot me a very displeased look.

"You can't sleep here tonight," he said.

"Why not?"

"Uh . . . I wouldn't let my llama sleep here."

I laughed and started digging through my bag for the cream. "I think I'll live. I've slept in far worse. When you're studying and shooting cheap student films, you get used to places like these."

"Seriously, though. I don't like the idea of you sleeping here, and having to share showers and—"

I stood up and gave him a look. "I can take care of myself, remember? I don't need you inspecting my room and deciding I can't sleep here and then swapping rooms with me. I've been taking care of myself very well for the past thirteen years without you being all protective."

He looked at me, something like sadness crossing his face. "You do take care of yourself."

"I do."

"You take very good care of yourself." He held out his hand for my mosquito repellent cream and I gave it to him. "You shouldn't always have to take care of yourself, though. Sometimes it's nice to let someone else help you reach the difficult spots that you can't reach alone." His words were loaded. "Take off your top."

I locked eyes with him and then very unashamedly removed my T-shirt. His eyes immediately drifted down to my breasts, and he made zero attempt at hiding that fact. I smiled at him and turned around, giving him access to my back.

He started rubbing the cream on the back of my neck, and then down my back. The places that I would not have reached.

"My life panned out in a way that there was no one really there to reach the difficult spots. I had my friends, but I had to learn to reach those spots on my own. I couldn't sit around waiting for someone to be there to help me all the time. I've had to get on with things by myself."

"I know. I wish I could have been there, though."

"Well, you weren't," I said. "You were gone, my mom was, my sister was, my dad might as well have been. I had to do stuff on my own. I didn't have a family, or a boyfriend to fall back on all the time."

"I'll never leave you again, Ash. If you give me another chance, I promise you I'll be there for you whenever you want my help. Because I know you don't need it." He wrapped his arms round me and pulled me into him. I rested my back against his chest. It felt so good here. But was it safe to be here? Safe to be letting go so much that I was actually contemplating a life with him?

"What if I shared the room with you?" I whispered, wrapping my arms over his.

"One room? One bed?"

I nodded, the back of my head against his chest.

"You do know what will happen if we share a bed together?" he asked.

"I do."

"And do you know what that will mean, Ash, *really* mean?"

"What does it mean?" I asked. He turned me round so I was facing him.

"If we do this, and you stay the night, I don't think I can ever let you go again."

I took in a slow, deep breath, and in that moment it all became so very, very clear. I knew what I wanted to do about it, and I knew it was the right thing to do. Because nothing had felt this right for the last thirteen years. And I also knew that was worth risking my heart for, again. I met those icy blue eyes of his with mine. "So don't ever let me go again."

CHAPTER 62

Max

"You weren't kidding when you said lap of luxury," she said, standing in the middle of the room once she had finished all her work. It was a huge space that opened up completely to the wild, untouched African bush outside. The enormous bed was set up again the back wall, which was made from chunks of grey granite rocks that sparkled in the light. In front of the bed was a huge, free-standing granite bath, which had a view down to the watering hole. There was a patio beyond the bath, and beyond that a plunge pool. This was one of the oldest private game lodges in South Africa, steeped in history, and it had a nostalgic feel that swept you away. She looked down at the bath.

"You can take a bath, if you want."

"Will you bath with me?" she asked.

"You seriously thought you needed to ask me that?" I walked over to the enormous bath and turned on the taps.

"I see an ice bucket with champagne over there." She pointed with a smile and I walked up to it.

"So much better than African Dreams." I poured us two glasses and then walked them over to her.

"Bubbles?" I asked, looking at the array of bottles they had on the rim of the tub.

"Yes."

I opened one and poured the liquid in. The bubbles were instant.

"Lavender bath salts?" I picked up a bottle and read off the label.

She chuckled. "The last time I used lavender bath salts was that night."

"That night?"

"I've never used them again. They remind me too much of that."

"Lavender! That's what it was." I smiled at her, the thirteen-year mystery over. "You smelled of something I could never recognize that night. Lavender."

We both looked down at the bottle and there seemed to be only one thing left to do. I opened the lid and tipped the entire contents in. We smiled at each other once the last of the salts and dried lavender pieces was in the bath.

"There's still a bath oil." I pointed at the last bottle.

"Let's give that a miss, you always feel slimy after bath oil."

"Okay, baby," I said.

"Baby," she repeated, smiling contentedly. There was such a sense of peace and contentment in this moment, making a bath together. It was comfortable and easy, as if this was exactly as it should be, and exactly as it had been for the last thirteen years. We had fallen back into that ease that I'd loved about us.

We locked eyes while undressing. I didn't even look at her body. Her eyes were what I wanted to look into. We dropped the last of our clothes onto the floor and climbed in. The temperature of the water was perfect and we settled on opposite sides, our legs tangling up into each other's. I breathed in the smell of lavender while I watched her pick bubbles up in her hands and crush them, small bubble debris falling back into the bath.

"I want this to be us every single night, Ash." I sat up in the bath and moved closer to her.

"We would go through a lot of lavender bath salts." She smiled at me. That huge, massive smile that bowled me over every single time.

"This is how it always should've been." I took her hands in mine, and our fingers tangled in and out of each other's, a playful game. We both watched our hands as if they had a mind of their own.

"What did the ring look like?" she asked, while tracing my ring finger with hers.

"Small, probably wasn't even a real diamond."

"I bet I would have loved it."

My heart pounded in my throat. "Do you want to see it?" I asked, pulling my hands away.

"You threw it in the woods."

"Seems like my mother fished it out and kept it all these years," I said.

"And she's had it this entire time?" Ash asked.

I nodded. "She even remembered where she'd put it, a miracle in itself." I sat up and moved closer to her in the bath. "I took that as a clear sign."

"A sign of what?" Ash asked, matching my lean.

"A sign that perhaps I should do now what I should have done all those years ago."

Ash inhaled sharply and her eyes widened. I smiled at her and then she gave me the best gift she could have in that moment, that vulnerable moment where I'd totally exposed myself to her—she smiled back at me.

"I'd love to see it sometime," she said.

"What about right now?"

"You have it?"

"I do." I stood up out of the bath and carefully climbed out. I could feel her eyes on my naked body as I crossed the room and took the ring out of my bag, and then I slipped something out of her bag too. I walked back to the bath, hiding one of the items on the table next to the bath and climbed in.

"Here." She held her hand out, I opened my fist and the small ring tumbled into it. Her eyes were full of all the emotions that I should have seen all those years ago if I'd actually done this.

She looked down at it. "I love it," she whispered, a tear slipping down her cheek. "Can I put it on now?" The question was such a loaded one.

"Yes," I said.

She slipped it onto her finger slowly, and it slid down as if it was meant to be there, as if it was always meant to be there. And in that moment, I don't think it was possible to love her more.

"It fits."

"I secretly measured your finger one night while you were sleeping, and it seems that hasn't changed."

She looked up at me, and managed a small whisper. "There are a lot of things that haven't changed."

"Well, there's something that *has* changed, hopefully." I held out my closed fist. There was still one more thing I had in my hand.

"What's that?" Ash asked.

I climbed back into the warm bath and laid the small box on the lip of it. Ash looked at it curiously.

"What is it?" She reached for it and I stopped her, taking her hand in mine and then pulling her onto my lap. I took her face in my hands, locking eyes with her. Those eyes that I could fall into forever.

"Ash . . ." I started, and smiled at her. I wasn't that nervous boy anymore, and this time I was going to do it properly. "I think you should marry me."

Her face cracked into a smile. "You do, do you?"

"I seriously, seriously do. And . . ." I took her hand and looked down at the ring on it. "I want you to wear this forever, but with one change." I looked over at the box on the lip of the bath. She followed my gaze and then climbed off my lap and moved towards it. "Turns out those aren't real diamonds and I thought you deserved some."

She opened the box and then burst out laughing.

"What?" I asked, very taken aback by her sudden outburst.

"Cheese!" She laughed even louder, but then quickly tried to cut it off. "Sorry, sorry, I don't mean to laugh." She continued to laugh, though. "It's just . . . I had this thought a while ago that if ever anyone had to get me a personalized ring—" She burst out laughing again, unable to speak once more.

"This is not how I imagined this moment going."

"Sorry, sorry." She shook her head and took a deep breath. "I was thinking that I would want a yellow diamond cheese ring." She laughed again.

"That's not cheese. That's a sunflower," I said, and her laughter ground to an abrupt halt. She looked down at the diamonds that I'd bought. I hadn't had time to have them set yet; I thought she could choose her setting anyway.

"A sunflower?" Her eyes filled with tears and I pulled her onto my lap again, taking her face in my hands.

"It's always been you, Ash. Always. Will you marry me?" I asked the question that was thirteen years too late, but right on time.

A small tear escaped her eye and rolled down her cheek. I wiped it away quickly.

"It was always you too," she said.

I pulled her in for a kiss. Long and slow.

"Is that a yes, then?" I whispered against her lips.

"Yes," she said, and buried her face in my shoulder. We wrapped our arms round each other and held on, as if we had both just come home and were finally, after all these years, right in the place we were supposed to be.

"So . . ." I said into her neck, "shall I leave you for a moment so you can message your friends about this?"

She pulled away and looked at me indignantly. "What makes you think I want to message my friends?"

I rolled my eyes at her.

"I don't, for the record, want to message them."

"Really?" I raised my brows at her.

"No, I'm not thinking about messaging my friends with the news that I just got engaged at all. Not at all."

I laughed. "That sounded very, very unconvincing."

"I don't want to message them," she insisted, but her eyes drifted over to the bed, where her bag was. "I mean, what kind of person would want to message their friends right when she's getting proposed to, naked, in the bath. That would just be—"

"Just admit it, Ash. You want it soooo badly."

She shook her head and then pursed her lips together.

"You do."

She shook her head again, but a smile was working its way onto her lips. "Okay, okay! I want to fucking message them. Okay!"

I burst out laughing. "Go do it."

"Are you sure?"

"Here." I reached for her phone—I'd anticipated this—and placed it on the side table next to the bath.

"You brought my phone?"

"I had a feeling you were going to want it." She smiled at me as I climbed out the bath. "Tell you what, why don't you message them while I go and make myself ready."

"Ready for what?" she asked.

I reached down and gripped my cock in my hand, her eyes immediately going there. "Ready for you. I'll be lying on the bed, waiting." I turned and walked off towards the bed. I heard a splashing sound behind me and turned back.

"My friends can wait," Ash said, running up to me and pushing me down on the bed. She climbed on top of me and looked down at me.

I looked up at her, pushing the strands of wet hair out of her face. "Fuck, this sight is never going to get old."

Two problems.
One solution.
A crash landing into love.

Available now!

Two rivals.
One holiday.
A trip they will *never* forget.

OUT NOW!

*Don't miss Jo's
glorious standalone
office rom-coms!*

HEADLINE
ETERNAL

Don't miss Jo's hilarious and heartfelt Starting Over Trilogy!

Available now!

For laugh-out-loud,
swoon worthy hijinks,
don't miss Jo's
Destination Love series!

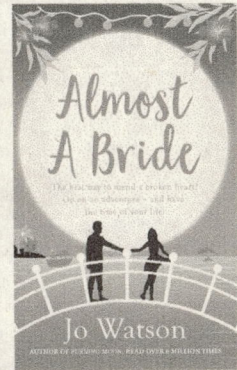

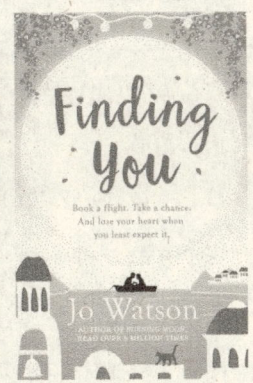

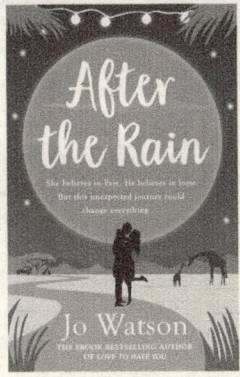

HEADLINE
ETERNAL

HEADLINE ETERNAL

FIND YOUR HEART'S DESIRE...

VISIT OUR WEBSITE: www.headlineeternal.com

FIND US ON FACEBOOK: facebook.com/eternalromance

CONNECT WITH US ON X: @eternal_books

FOLLOW US ON INSTAGRAM: @headlineeternal

EMAIL US: eternalromance@headline.co.uk